CW00435429

· FIRST PRINTING 36/50 ·

Goblins!

The Adventure of the Wise Wench

By Richard Pett

All rights reserved.
Copyright ©2018 Richard Pett
Cover design by Jeremy Zerfoss
Editing by Alistair Rigg
ISBN: 978-1-5272-3153-5
All characters and events in this book are fictional.
Any resemblance to persons living or dead is coincidental.
Contact the author at crookedplace@hotmail.co.uk

For
James Jacobs
who makes them better than anyone

Once upon a time, there were no goblins.

Most goblins agree this was an unacceptable state of affairs, but probably a much quieter, and less violent one. Definitely, in fact. Who would start all the fires and eat all the stuff that needed eating? Boring! And who would want to live somewhere boring?

Some goblins, however, fiercely disagree that it would be boring, arguing (as goblins do) that if there were no goblins to set fire to things—of course, goblins believe they invented fire in the first place—the world would be so full of unburnt things that it would collapse under all the weight. The ensuing apocalypse would kill everything, very noisily—something goblins agree would have been great fun to watch had they been there, which of course they wouldn't.

Most goblins share similar characteristics. They are small and weak and, because of that, are afraid of lots of things, depending upon where they come from: the sky falling on them, celery, brazen wild pigs, rudely-shaped fungi, escaped rams, captive rams, meat-mincers, the color yellow, things with pointy teeth, things without teeth, scissors, sheep, rain, hedgehogs, stringy fish, pigtails, things with too many legs, soap (uncleanliness is next to goblinishness), turbots, gangs of voles, and so on. Most things can be pretty scary to a goblin if it happens to be nearby and it tends to be met often.

A tall goblin stands about a foot high in their wooden-soled boots; something many of them wear, as goblins are clever at making things when they can be bothered. They are physically very weak, have appalling diets, and never do any exercise if they can avoid it, which they are masters at. Some might describe them as *extraordinarily puny*. The gob-girls (who grow into gob-wenches) tend to be fitter than the gob-boys (who generally do not grow up at all, and often remain gob-boys—in their own minds at least). This is because the ladies usually carry out the chores, something the gob-boys say isn't their job and flatly refuse to do. Often the females get so fed up with the males' laziness that they go on strike and refuse to work. This state of affairs lasts until everyone is almost dead of starvation or cold or a myriad of other reasons caused by the males' flat refusal to do anything—even if it kills them. A goblin's terrible diet makes developing muscles of any note virtually unheard of, although this, of course, is relative—some goblins are locally renowned for their physical prowess but, in any half-decent test, such a goblin would struggle to lift a thin, elderly mole above its head.

Goblins share a common belief that experiencing pain is very, very bad and to be avoided at all costs. They thus go to extraordinary lengths to avoid any kind of danger. So great is their fear of pain and personal danger that they often inadvertently put themselves in terribly dangerous situations just by trying to avoid trouble.

Goblins make up for their tiny size and encompassing fear by being sneaky and vicious. They love a good fire because fire is funny, and the bigger the thing being burnt is, the funnier it is. Goblins also like to sing. Songs remember things and are noisy (especially when tuneless, which is the celebrated goblin style), and noisy songs stop things being boring. Silence invites horrid things to appear out of the quiet and fill it with their hungry mouths. Goblins also love eating and they can and do eat practically anything. Sadly, most things they eat fill them up for only a short while and they soon get hungry again.

They also love to collect smells. Smells are good because smells tell a story, which they call their smell-story. Taking away smells is something bad. Again, soap is to be feared.

All goblins are also ugly. Even the very pretty ones, who are amazingly scarce, are really ugly. The ugly ones, well, they're properly horrible looking. The sad thing is that, even though all of them are ugly, the prettier ones still pick on the uglier ones about how ugly they are. Other creatures also find goblins ugly and make cruel jokes about them, often shouting them loudly within a goblin's earshot just to be extra nasty.

Goblins are, therefore, a menace to practically no one but themselves, and tend to hide away in corners unobserved until they starve or get stomped on, which is why you rarely meet one or hear of them. Very, very occasionally, however, a leader sprouts from the ground that changes things...

Our goblins have such a leader. They come from an incredibly long-lived clan and have stayed alive by avoiding any kind of danger by living deep, deep inside a forest—the *Great Forest* in fact, which was so named because it's, well, a forest that's really big. Goblins aren't very imaginative with names and generally focus on keeping them simple unless a particular goblin has a very long smell-story going back generations, in which case their name can be as long as their grandiose sense of self-importance. Goblins tend to be anxious about repeating long names to avoid possible pain meted out by other goblins with significant senses of pomposity when they are not pronounced properly.

Sometimes though, even the deepest forests aren't deep enough and eventually things from the outside come slithering or pounding in...but we're getting ahead of ourselves already. That's the trouble with knowing what's coming; it's very easy to get wrapped up in the when's and the why's as we'll see. Knowing everything isn't everything it is cracked up to be.

Our goblins aren't really that much different to the rest of their kin. They're unpleasant, nasty, sadistic, selfish, cowardly, and greedy. They're raised in a big pen far away from the grown-ups (who don't care for their squeaky noises) and life in the pen can be nasty, which makes for a nasty goblin, which all the grownups believe is a Very Good Thing.

How goblins all came about in the first place has been the subject of many violent arguments and conflagrations, but our goblins believe that one day the gods were wandering about bored, looking for things to squash or stretch into amusing shapes when they found the first pair of goblins hiding under a rock eating slugs and arguing about who should get the biggest one. The gods took pity on how small and ugly they were and gave them fire, which they argued over until one goblin set fire to the other, which was funny to watch but left only one goblin. Luckily, the gods made that goblin a girl—a gob-wench as goblins often call them—and she had lots of goblin babies.

Unfortunately, the babies irritated her so she cast them out and went off to look for something else to burn. The babies, having nothing to eat, ate whatever they could find—privet, spiders, very small rocks...most things actually...and soon grew fat and bored. So they made noise to fill the boredom, and that made them laugh, and they thought laughing was good, so they went out to find other things to amuse themselves and soon were setting fire to anything they could find. Before long they nearly ran out of things to burn and got scared of the silent dark, so they invented singing, because singing remembers things like really big fires and how much fun they are and might bring them back. Plus, singing is noisy, and noise is fun, so they kept doing it more and more.

Until one day...

CHAPTER 1

The devastation was considerable. And it had a name.

The goblins called the place Bliss, their home, the place they hid from the countless very bad things outside. It was one of a dozen scattered little shanties lurking within the deep depths of the deepest wood in the lands, the unimaginatively named Great Forest.

Burnt stumps of trees huddled forlornly at the edge of an unpleasant collection of collapsing hovels as if trying to keep away from them. A mob of ruin loitered atop a low hill surrounded by fallen sticks and piled stone that could—only very loosely mind you—be considered a fortification. The buildings didn't look so much ruinous as abused, and were arranged in a haphazard mob about a large central structure, although structure was too kind a word. This building was particularly repulsive and huge, a legend of collapses and fires and mistreatment, its presence threatening the space around it. The locals called it the Moot House, or sometimes the Boot House, because that's where they go to be booted and bullied into action by their chief, who lived upstairs with his fearsome wife who no goblin had ever seen.[1]

Beyond, the—let's call it a village—the nearby forest had been decimated. Not a single leaf grew on any tree, not that many trees were left standing there. Beyond the trees were mountains, but they were too far away to notice unless you really concentrated, and the locals didn't bother with concentrating as a rule because their heads might burst if they did.[2] The ground was just mud—and thick mud at

---

[1] Except the chief, of course. Being married to someone you never saw could cause all kinds of problems.

[2] Goblins have often been known to think so hard that their heads pop. This is something very bad for the goblin in question, but highly interesting and amusing for anyone stood nearby, providing they aren't too close. Indeed, goblins have a very unpredictable biology and strange events can occur to them at any time, such as overthinking making your head burst, working too hard making your arms fall off, or laughing so much that your mouth opens wide enough that you swallow yourself whole. Because such events are known to happen, and every goblin aches to have something interesting happen, they go out of their way to cause such events to

that—which extended about a quarter of a mile around the wasteland in which nothing grew. By a disgusting collection of fleapits squatted a teetering mound of moldering filth collapsed into a huge filthy mire; a flotsam apocalypse of gnawed bones, unidentified carcasses, and bits of goblin. They called this mire the Poo-Pit. It proudly held the smells of generations of goblins and kept a magnificent smell-story they were all rightly proud to inhale. Lucky flies buzzed contentedly, seemingly thriving in everything, making their palace in the mire. Further away was a wide pit surrounded by spiked timbers and filled with noise—the nursery. The spikes, it should be added, pointed inwards.

In the distance something was singing—singing being a charitable word for the screeching chaos of random noises and words that echoed across the blasted meadow where once birds sang, flowers grew, and a brook tumbled. In the strictest sense, what they were actually singing was something along the lines of '*There's no place like home*,' but unless you were trained in such things, its true meaning was lost amongst the trumping and shouting and belching and evil laughter.

Only one goblin in the whole Kingdom knew how many summers it had been since anything had grown in the destruction their voices molested, and she wasn't telling. It seemed that they had been here for all time. The goblins had—under strictest instruction, on pain of pain—cleared the trees
many summers ago to stop enemies sneaking up, but they soon got bored, forgot what they'd cleared the forest for, and started building a huge bonfire of the trees they'd felled.

Charging over the horizon came the words of the song, which extolled the virtues of pulling apart starlings and sitting on badgers until they were flat and crunchy and ready to crackle.

The squabble of ruins we are calling the village of Bliss, lay in the center of the clearing, bordered by a little dead stream over

---

occur. Sadly, lots of enemies (which is pretty much everything else alive that doesn't lurk under rocks) also know this fact, and try to capture goblins to see these things happen.

which ran an aged collapsed stone bridge, twisted on one side from the summer when a massive ewe had escaped and charged it. The debris huts and cottages cringed close together in the heart of this chaos, clustered around the great round Moot House, which was the king's meeting and working place, as well as his home. Noises came from those upper stories where the unseen queen lurked and seethed and shouted, but no one had ever dared go up to investigate, let alone tell her to shut up.

Crowds of bored gob-boys were sitting around the village, while gob-wenches were out searching for food and smells to collect in devotion to Lord Noc, their god of smells and smell-stories.

Inside the Moot House sat King Stormgrunties the many-many-and-lots-after-more-than-many-dead-king-Stormgrunties-after-the-first[3] King of Bliss and the surrounding lands. He was seated in his great high chair, fully one-more-than-one goblins in height. His royal, ample posterior shuffled within the confines of a silk cushion, while his hands were idly playing with the chair handles, which were carved in the likeness of goblin milkmaids cavorting with cattle. A large elaborate looking key swayed from his belt made of udders. He had a very round head split by an enormous grin of pointy teeth. Below swung a very fine collection of chins, which had, in truth, taken him his whole life to acquire. His stomach, while similarly considerable, had a tendency to praise Lord Noc without its owner's permission, and seemingly at the most inopportune moments. He wore his bright yellow and red-striped pants of high office, for he alone in the village had permission to wear stripes in a public place. His shirt was of a very ruffled silk type favored by the line of Stormgrunties. He had a broad, friendly face, which belied his broadly unfriendly nature. He was the king of the goblins of Bliss,

---

[3] Goblin chiefs, kings, sultans and head-bullies are often convinced of their own indestructability and thus tend to be short-lived. Goblins being pretty short-lived anyway, their rulers are expected to—and almost always do—perform acts of ridiculous bravery (and/or stupidity) to impress their subjects. Their descendants keep their father's names because names are powerful and the longer the name, the more power the goblin has, at least in theory. In truth, it's usually the girls who pull the strings anyway, but they don't let the men know that.

and as such, was not allowed to treat any of the scum beneath him with anything but contempt.

Except the Wise Wench.

The Wise Wench.

She knew everything, absolutely everything. No guilty secret was hidden from her gaze, no matter too trivial for her attention, no future happening was a mystery to her, and no known thing was unknown to her knowingness.

She was a gift from the gods. Or was she a curse?

The goblins were naturally terrified of her and wished she lived somewhere else where she could deliver divine messages to some other poor soul. But they tried not to think that, of course, because she knew what they were thinking all the time, which made life nervy to say the least.

The king rubbed his chin guiltily, milk still dribbling down from when he'd taken his traditional breakfast from his favorite heifer—the king was the only goblin allowed to hunt fresh milk from the royal herd. The goblins thought it was funny that he used the word *hunt* to make suckling milk from an udder sound grand, but no one ever told him.

'Ahem, Your Majesty!' said Kringe Notbrave. Kringe, the king's advisor, stood beneath him looking up expectantly, holding a battered glove puppet mole, and looking like he was about to cry. Kringe always looked like he was about to cry. The look came with the job. So did the mole, which was allegedly the brains of the outfit. In truth, it was more a dead mole than actual fabricated glove puppet. The mole stared up knowingly at the adviser.

'Yes, carry on, Kringe,' said the king, regally, and shuffled the royal posterior into a more comfortable position.

Kringe made a great show of consulting the glove puppet in considerable earnest, carefully nodding and noting what it was apparently telling him. 'The Great Mole,' he shouted, weakly, 'has spoken and reminded me of today's duties, Your Splendid Corpulentness! This morning, you are due to meet the Wise Wench, to discuss *the plan—*'

'—Ah yes, *the plan*,' said the king, and knitted his brows. 'What is your advice concerning this *plan* of hers?' he added, leaning forward as far as he could. The high chair groaned a little beneath him.

Kringe stepped back a little, cleared his throat loudly, and swiftly consulted The Great Mole before saying, thinly, 'my advice is, erm, Your Milky Splendidness, that you should take the Wise Wench's advice!' He grinned feebly.

The king scowled and thought for a moment before saying, 'but that's always your advice. What's the point of having an adviser if their advice is always to do what the Wise Wench says? I may as well make her my advisor.'

Kringe's face avalanched, and he began drumming a tune with his fingers, nervously, before squeaking, 'far be it for me, mere scum, to dare to, erm, disagree with Your Goblinsmellness, but that would never do. Always have a one-after-the-first-one opinion, as my father Sloppy Notbrave used to say.'

'Sloppy Notbrave, the adviser, advising that it's always worth having another opinion from an adviser.'

Kringe grimaced a little before agreeing. 'Yes, Your Dribbletude.'

'I see,' said the king, and made an odd little harrumph of self-gratitude for cleverness.

'Although I have found the Wise Wench's advice is, in most matters, correct,' Kringe added, professionally.

'Most?'

'Well, all.'

'I see.'

Kringe looked like he was losing the thread of his argument but struggled heroically on by debating the matter with The Great Mole on his hand. 'But,' he continued, 'Your Divine Vastitude, it always pays to have a one-after-the-first opinion. Remember your ancient history! Was it not the Very Wise Wench of your great, great grandfather King Trumpet Stormgrunties the lots-and-then-some-and-one, who advised him about what would happen if peasants saw more than one member of the royal family at once?'

'Nope.'

'Oh, well, who was it who—'

'—advised him about peasants seeing more than one member of the royal family at the same time?'

'Yes!'

'I don't remember. But it wasn't him.' The king looked pleased with himself.

'Oh, but what good advice it was, Your Plumpitude!'

'True.'

'For is it not true, that if a mere peasant sees more than one royal at a time—'

'—the peasant's head bursts.'

'Exactly!'

'Yes, an explosion!' said the king, and laughed, wondering if some sort of explosion might not brighten up the day. Then he remembered it was better not to disturb Her Majesty during daylight.

'Exactly,' smiled Kringe, and took a confident step forward, 'for our eyes are too feeble to behold a regal splenditude of royals in one place at one time. Such beauty—like that of the crooked medyusa—is too much to see at once, something has to give, resulting in the explosion you so rightly described. And don't forget, as it said in the old song:

The king stepped out with his wife so fey,
For walking around the village they did go,
And several goblins blew they up that day,
Burn, burn, burn it, oh.'

The king scowled, and wondered why every song seemed to have '*burn, burn, burn it, oh*' in it somewhere. Perhaps he should change it? He was king, after all, and he could change—or do—anything he pleased.

* * *

14

The Wise Wench checked her knitted list once more as she left her cottage. In truth, it wasn't so much a list as a daisy-chain of knitted reminders, figurines, scenarios, and divine aides-mémoires—in wool—which she kept beneath her bodice. Her house lay outside the village, mainly because she didn't like visitors. She was, however, fortunate on that score in that she always knew when someone was coming around unexpectedly, and made sure she was out at the time.

She crunched down the neat little gravel path and headed toward the village of Bliss, turning over the little woolen goblin figure in her hands. The figure's head was the wrong way on, but this was no knitting-calamity—this was deliberate. Just like everything else the Wise Wench did.

* * *

Not far away, a goblin with his head on upside down bounded through the forest, lovingly gripping a small furry animal. He was torn between hunger and love, gently caressing the creature in a mixture of choking and stroking. He was called Wrong Face, sometimes Upside Down Face, and sometimes other, less charitable, things, but he was mainly just called Urgh[4], or to those that knew him better, Urgh Tricksy, on account of his magic. The furry thing purred endearingly and Urgh put it on the ground, quietly saying, 'run away, little fellow, lurk in the deep woods and live a long happy life.'

But then a mallet suddenly squashed it. A mallet held by a triumphant goblin who somehow had no shoulders whatsoever. He wasn't, but his name was: Sorry.

'Got it!' shouted Sorry, heroically.

Urgh looked up angrily, words forming but then ending on his lips. He felt at his sides, gripping his magic fetishes—bits of flammable badger, stoats crammed with fire sprinkle, eggs bloated with itchy-scratch—hung from his belt of plucked and shaved

---

[4] Pronounced *ū-r-h.*

porcupine. His pockets bulged with other hedgerow spells. He stared at his slavering friend, thought long and hard about doing something to him, and decided that as he hadn't done anything to anyone before now, it might be a bad time to start. He was just hungry after all.

'Good to see you,' lied Sorry, adding, 'that was lucky. He'd almost escaped! Imagine what they'd say about you in the village if you let it get away. You weren't *letting* it get away were you?' he growled feebly. 'You know that wouldn't go down well with the lads in the village, would it? *"Goblin frees small, defenseless, furry animal."* How my very many, very tough mates would anger at the thought,' he added, untruthfully.

Urgh bit his tongue in his time-honored tradition of thinking tough and clever thoughts but never acting on them until later when he was alone. He changed the subject, saying, 'we'd better get back. There might be a big fire in the village and we wouldn't want to miss that.'

Sorry began to shake in excitement.

Urgh was a cheerful soul, despite his head alignment challenges. When he was born, the Wise Wench paraded him about the village. 'This fatherless child,' she said, sagely, 'has been born with a head that is upside down, and shall therefore be called Upside Down Face.' She went on to add that he was destined to become village hero, and that one day he would save the entire kingdom, as well as several other useful tidbits, but by that time everyone had stopped listening to her and were too busy gawking and saying, 'Urgh, 'orrible!' and other such uncomplimentary things. The really ugly goblins in the village[5] were delighted that a new lowest common denominator had been set and celebrated wildly by swinging puppies on strings about their heads until they all fell over dizzily. Sadly, Urgh had the unfortunate and lamentable habit of kindness and thoughtfulness, something every goblin naturally saw as weak and wicked. He didn't even have a dad to defend him, or at least pretend to defend him. Some rumours had it he was a foundling; others that

---

[5] Most of them, in truth.

his dad was still in the village but was hardly likely to admit to fathering something with a head that was on upside down.

The friends formed a bond united in a wish to avoid being hit, finding things to eat and setting fire to objects. Urgh was the brains, Sorry the sneak with the nasty streak, both were bottom of the pecking order in Bliss.

Sorry, who had been shaking with anticipation since Urgh had mentioned fire—for fire was Sorry's favorite thing, ever—feebly punched Urgh in the ribs (as was his custom on meeting him) and proceeded to attack him with all his strength, which was inconsiderable. Urgh was easily managing to fight off what he thought were his friend's playful grapples when suddenly a pair of sturdier, hairier hands grabbed him. Then another pair; and another. Sorry was dragged back by other hands and began to cry.

Urgh looked up.

His gaze met Durth. Durth Dimbits, son of Durth Horriblebits. The village Head Thug.

The terribly feared Head Thug.

'Watch him, Durth,' squeaked one thug from a safe distance. 'E's got magic.'

Durth grinned a grin that threatened to cut his face in half, and began violently checking Urgh over for magic. At that moment, Durth's hair—or rather what was left of his hair, which had been so carefully combed over his bald pate—fell at an alarming angle away from his head. It flapped in an oily, unruly way, as errant goblin hair can, exposing pale blotchy skin.

His helpers, village under-thugs who Urgh recognized but could never remember the names of, stood open-mouthed.

Time seemed to halt.

'So!' said Durth, reddening. 'Assaulting the Head Thug's good looks and extra-thick hair with your foul magic, eh? You'll pay for that!' he yelled, pointing to one of his thug assistants. 'The charge is assaulting the Head Thug's prettiness with necromancy! How does the prisoner plead?' He carefully combed his strands of greasy hair back over his bald acreage.

Urgh tried to open his mouth.

'Guilty,' shouted another thug, happily.

'Then it falls upon me to pass sentence,' said Durth, grinning and taking hold of Urgh to make sure he didn't cast any spells. 'I have to say,' he said, staring upwards and shaking his head, 'that this case appalls me. Having heard all the evidence, you have repeatedly shown no remorse, and it has pained me to listen to your tissue of lies. Have you no shame for your long years of horridness, I ask myself, again and again? Alas, no. I therefore have no regret in passing the heaviest sentence upon you.' Durth grinned evilly at his little band of thugs. 'Bring me the nasal siege pliers and the village hedgehog!' he hissed, venomously.

A few minutes later, after painful punishment which Head Thug Durth graciously bestowed upon both companions just in case the other was guilty, Sorry and Urgh found themselves so coiled up in rope that they were struggling to gain breath. A pair of thugs were carrying each prisoner along on a pole, while Durth marched ahead idly, kicking anything that caught his eye. When an opportunity presented itself, Sorry cleared his throat, tried to stop shaking in terror, and making sure Urgh couldn't hear, whispered weakly into Durth's bouncing passing ear. 'Sorry, great thug Durth. I can quite understand and, indeed, sympathize with why you've arrested this soft traitorous wizard here,' nodding at Urgh, 'but why arrest me? What have I done?' Sorry smiled winningly at his captor.

Durth stopped.

They all stopped.

The Head Thug took a rather pained step backwards from Sorry and winked at his companions. 'Let me state the charges!' said Durth, who smiled and cleared his throat before continuing, 'Sorry Moth-Ripper and Urgh Tricksy, you are charged with selling military secrets to another tribe, attempting to stop the forest being burnt down, consorting with gnomes, being wantonly boring, crop-planting, performing poetry in a public place, and juggling hedgehogs on a Thodsday without permission!' He grinned widely, the gaps in his teeth soon occupied by his lolling tongue.

18

'The penalty for which is death by sea, death by acorns, being hanged until death, death by frog, and imprisonment with the village crocodile for the summer.'

Durth smiled.

'Erm, excuse me, your Durthness,' croaked Urgh, 'but who says so?'

'The Wise Wench,' said Durth, and grinned broadly. The thugs began to laugh very, very loudly.

Both Urgh and Sorry realized they were guilty, even though they didn't remember the crimes they'd obviously committed. The Wise Wench was never wrong about anything.

* * *

Not far away, the Wise Wench stopped under the eaves of a great dead burnt sycamore, its remaining bough gently creaking arthritically in the wind. The tree reminded her of the Great Oak of the Gods, the place where she first heard *the plan* she would conceive and implement.

The plan that would save the village.

She tied her black woolen bonnet tight about her head and carried on.

The wind suddenly picked up.

* * *

'—and badger worrying goes unchecked,' said Kringe and scowled.

The king was making unconscious milking motions with his hands and mooing silently to himself.

'—and badger worrying goes unchecked,' said Kringe, patiently.

The king grinned broadly and dribbled. A minute passed before, realizing Kringe was watching, the king shook himself and said, 'so Master Whippet is still building it, is he? Well that's splendid news.' The king smiled and glanced over at the clock, which ticked quietly on the mantelpiece next to the Mop of the

Dreaded Magpie People. 'I thought you said she would be here by the-one-after-one of the clock?'

The clock began to chime.

The Wise Wench opened the door—which was known affectionately as the Great Mouth—and, marching straight past Kringe before he could announce her, she stood, arms folded theatrically, before the king. 'Well, have you thought about it?' she barked.

'It is as you say, oh Wise Wench,' said the king. He didn't really dare disagree to be honest. She was the Wise Wench after all. *THE* Wise Wench, but he was the king. King Stormgrunties the many-many-and-lots-after-more-than-many-dead-King-Stormgrunties-after-the-first, slayer of Lucy Carter and her puppy Snuffles. The dilemma made his head hot; thinking things always made his head hot. He worried that one day something really complicated would make it catch fire, which both amused and worried him at the same time.

He finally found that bit of uneaten woodlouse he'd been searching for in the corner of his mouth and was just about to say something when the Wise Wench interrupted. 'When you've finished going over your dinner, we have one or one-more-than-one important things to discuss.'

The king was scared of strong wenches, and this strong wench more than the others, but they were far too numerous in his view. In fact, most of the wenches in the village frightened him to one degree or another. He had once decreed that all women should be banished, but that hadn't worked out very well at all and, luckily, The Great Mole had rescinded his order, under his whispered instruction, just before everyone died of starvation.

'There's nothing wrong with being a strong woman,' she snapped, before adding, 'and in a moment you're going to start reminiscing about your youth. Don't.'

Her mentioning his youth took him back to when his uncle Rabrab, his beloved Great Uncle Rabrab, with his unrivalled collection of stuffed—

'—I told you NOT to reminisce about your youth, and now I'm forbidding it.' Her face stared at him again. It was quite a face, it looked like it should be climbed or have a flag sticking out of the top of it.

'Sorry, oh Wise Wench,' he meekly whispered before frowning and adding, bravely, 'but what do you mean YOU forbid it. I'll have YOU know that I am king, and you are merely a, well, a wench.'

'There is no such thing as 'merely a wench' as you know well. And remember, I am a wench that knows everything,' she reminded him, and looked knowingly, a tight little smile assaulting her face. 'Everything.'

He never liked it when she smiled. It always meant trouble. Or more usually trouble and a near-death experience.

'Now, *the plan!*' she said, and smiled again, broadly.

* * *

They had got bored of carrying Sorry and Urgh, who were too heavy, and had decided instead to pull them along by anything handy. Hair, feet, teeth, and such.

Sorry squawked as he was pulled over a small gorse bush. 'Where are you taking us?' he shouted, as politely as he could.

'To the village to kill you,' said Durth, and dragged him back over the gorse bush to teach him a lesson for asking too many questions.

* * *

'Explain *the plan* to me again, oh Wise Wench,' said the king. His brow was very furrowed; in fact, something seemed to have taken sudden root in there. He was confused, thirsty, and didn't want to be king anymore. Kringe shook in a corner nearby, whispering to The Great Mole.

'As I have told you many-and-many-after-one times now,' she said. 'The nearby village of Miffed-by-the-Mire will be attacked this

21

evening by giants.' She smiled for effect at the nervous looking king when she said *giants* loudly, and then said it again, rather unnecessarily, to add to the drama. 'The whole village will be wiped out except for Moaris[6] the Minor Apocalypse, son of BigBad Chief Runty Miffed the many-one-and-many-more after the first dead Chief Miffed the Miffed of Miffed village. Moaris will run into our village tomorrow evening at exactly quarter-past-the-one-after-many-not-many of the clock.'

'But Miffed is the nearest village to us. If Moaris will run in, as you say, what exactly will he say?' intoned the king.

'*Exactly*– hmmm, let me think. He will run in here and say, 'Your Majesty, I come from Miffed Tower, I have dreadful news. Your Majesty, your coat appears to be on fire.' You will then rush out to the village pond, but all that is irrelevant. All that matters is *the plan.*'

'Yes, *the plan*,' he said. 'On fire, you say—we'll just see about that, won't we?' He gave a smug look to himself in the Magic Mirror of the Vain Jackdaw, and decided that whatever happened, he certainly *wouldn't* be on fire tomorrow, oh no. And then she'd be wrong, wouldn't she? She'd be wrong then—wrongity wrongly wrong—and he'd be king, and she'd have to apologize; her, the Wise Wench, would have to say, 'sorry, Your Majesty. I made a mistake.' What a fine teatime by a bonfire of crispy puppies that would make.

The Wise Wench gave him a sharp stare and thought about saying something but instead continued. 'That is why *the plan* is so important, and why we need the one-more-than-one expendable villagers.'

Wrongity wrongly wrong, thought the king.

The Wise Wench looked smug and cleared her throat. 'Aha,' she muttered and stood to one side of the door.

The Great Mouth was flung open and Durth the Head Thug entered noisily, followed by his under-thugs, who had Sorry and Urgh in some sort of bizarre, vaguely perverse, looking grip.

---

[6] Pronounced *mor' is.*

'Well, put them both down, then,' said the Wise Wench, forcefully.

They were both put down.

'Thank you, Durth,' said the Wise Wench staring at the prisoner's injuries, and noting they were not, as she knew some time ago, life-threatening. 'Admirably professional, as always. You may go now. The king has urgent business to attend to.'

Pausing only briefly to deliver a kick to Urgh's feet, Durth escaped with the other thugs rapidly, his screaming commands echoing away as the Wise Wench surveyed the crumpled figures lying before her.

'Well, aren't you going to ask why you're here?' she said.

Wrongity wrongly wrong, thought the king, before noticing the vagrants in his throne room. One of them was dressed in a dirty brown smock and appeared to be considerably soot-stained. He was also ugly, had no visible shoulders, and was a strange shade of greenish brown. The other one had a head that was on the wrong way. 'Names, pointless scum,' he shouted, regally.

'Sorry Moth-Ripper at Your Majesty's service, and this is Urgh, so called because he—'

'—Yes, yes, I know all about that,' smiled the king, thinking he could soon get into this wisdom business. *Lord Wisdom* they would call him.

Sorry looked towards the Wise Wench. Up close, she was much shorter than he'd thought, and dressed in what appeared to be one large black knitted coverall. Then he noticed its constituent parts of bonnet, skirt, and bodice. Her face was as fearsome as ever, and looked cross.

'Now, then, I'll ask you this once more, and if you don't show some interest, I'll have you thrown into the Poo-Pit. Don't you want to know why you're here?'

They nodded.

She smiled. 'Well,' she said happily, 'you are the one-more-than-one villagers I, personally, have chosen to go on a great quest.'

Sorry bolted for the door, closely followed by his companion. They knew all about the Wise Wench's quests. The last local to go on one came back as a pound of turnips. Escape was the only option.

'Stay where you are!' bellowed the Wise Wench. The king jumped. Kringe began to shake and whistle *The Pig-Keeper and the Frisky Turbot,* a lullaby his auntie used to sing to him when he was a gob-boy to stop him crying after she'd set him on fire from time to time.

Sorry and Urgh stopped.

'You will go on this quest because I—sorry, because *the king—* commands it, and what he says happens. If it doesn't happen, which it will, I will summon the village crocodile to eat you. Not that I will have to. And, anyway, you might enjoy it. Well, not both of you, perhaps,' she added, glancing at Sorry sympathetically.

Sorry looked horrified. He'd heard of Petal the crocodile and certainly didn't want to meet him. Urgh didn't want to meet anything; he just wanted to curl up in the magical fluffy Prince of Beds, and not get up again, ever.

'That's better. Now, tonight the village of Miffed-by-the-Mire will be attacked by giants.'

'Giants!' they yelled in unison.

'Yes, giants,' she added. 'They will kill everyone in the village except Moaris the Minor Apocalypse, who will arrive here tomorrow and tell us all that his village has been destroyed by giants.' She paused and looked at Kringe. 'Well, actually he won't tell *ALL* of us that his village has been destroyed by giants,' she added, continuing to stare at him.

Kringe looked nervous.

'He will come in and tell those of us that are still *AROUND HERE* tomorrow,' she smiled at Kringe sympathetically before continuing, 'that he heard some giants saying our village will be next. You will then accompany Moaris on a journey to the giants' stronghold to deliver something that will bring peace to the forest forever. And that will save the village from horrible doom, terrible destruction, and her occupants from being properly and terminally squashed.'

Everyone looked incredulously at her.

Peace to the forest forever? How boring, thought the king, sanctimoniously.

Kringe looked up. 'P-p-p-pardon me, Wise Wench,' he said, nervously, 'but what did you mean when you said 'one of us, perhaps, won't be around tomorrow when Moaris arrives?''

'Well, actually, to be blunt, you'll be struck by lightning tomorrow morning, Kringe Notbrave. Very tragic and excruciatingly painful, but quick.' She patted him on the back and turned to her other victims, continuing, 'anyway, this is where you volunteers come in. You will deliver a message to the giants' stronghold which will solve all our problems and bring peace between us and the giants for ever more. Now, come with me,' she added, before heading for the door, taking hold of Urgh and Sorry by their ears.

Kringe Notbrave looked crestfallen as the group walked out. 'Farewell then, oh wisest of Wise Wenches,' he whimpered.

'Yes, cheerio,' she said and shut the door.

He looked up at the king. 'Farewell, oh Lord. It has been a pleasure to serve you all these years, and I trust I have given good service. I hasten to add that if—'

His Majesty leaned over in his chair, '—yes, well then, er—'

'—Kringe.'

'Yes, Kringe. Try to keep your pecker up, and while you're at it, better put the word out for a new adviser. Best do that now actually. And since you haven't got long left, be a good chap and get me some biscuits, the ones with slugs baked into them. Unless I'm *wrongity wrongly wrong*–heh, heh—I'm famished.'

CHAPTER 2

Not far away, and a bit later on, at the nearby repulsive little village of Miffed...

'And with that, he put the bagpipes to his lips, and every new born pig in the kingdom exploded!'

He may have been short and repulsive, but Bulby the Talecantell could tell a tale magnificently. The audience roared their approval. Members of the Gubb family were so entertained that they set fire to a small number of their relatives, much to everyone's amusement. The Meet Hall of Miffed was packed to the rotting rafters with baying, biting, pinching goblins having fun.

Bulby had a head like a bulbous sack of rotting beetroot poised to explode at any moment, and a nose at some perverse angle to the rest of his body. That wasn't what you first noticed about him, however. What really caught your eye was the hair coming out of that crooked nose. It was vast, bushy, magnificent. Bulby had won the Great Forest Inter-Village Nasal Hair contest for the past many-lots-many-lots-and-more-than-many summers in a row. No one could touch his nasal follicles with a barge-pole—not that goblins were familiar with barge-poles. If they were, they would have just burnt them anyway. His was the longest, strongest, most prodigious and shiniest of all conk-carpets ever beheld in the forest. He simply was *the master* at growing nose hair. Fully lots-a-few-and-lots feet in length when uncurled from his nostrils, it was now carefully rolled up for the nosetache-resting season. He'd been growing it for countless years—so long, in fact, that even the Wise Wench pretended not to be sure how long he'd been cultivating it.

How sad—and yet, at the same time, strangely fitting—that this was his final performance. In a few minutes, he'd be dead along with everyone else in Miffed, save one.

* * *

An owl took flight from the noise which was pushing its way through the forest, despite the noise-makers' best efforts to be sneaky—which is practically impossible when you're each over ten feet tall, horribly violent, and vast in number. Oh, yes, and you have two heads.[7]

The noisemakers carried no torches—they could see equally well in day or night, with either head.

Not far away, a particularly repulsive goblin guard stared out into the still air. From her vantage point in the high timber watchtower—which had a habit of swaying in the merest of winds—she could see the forest for miles around, when it wasn't dark, which sadly it was. It all seemed calm and peaceful save for the rustle of the wind through the boughs of the great trees in the vast expanse and the stomping of distant giant feet, which sadly sounded like very small feet, very close by, and nothing to be alarmed about. 'Yes, on a clear night you can almost see all the way to Smell,' she said to her companion, Young Tuppy the Sheepswain's many'th son. Tuppy was a promising thug, except for the scabs, and the sores, and those things that popped in the sunlight.

'Looks like we're in for a quiet night,' squeaked Tuppy with uncanny incorrectness, as he put on his orange nightcap.

His companion paused, shielding her eyes from the moon. 'Wait, I think I hear something.'

'Hear what?' mumbled Tuppy, sleepily.

'Yes, something's coming. Look, there, just beyond the clearing. It sounds like something with a great mouthful of big pointy teeth and wings and extra legs, lots and lots of legs in fact. Too many to count in truth.'

'I can't see or hear anything,' said Tuppy, rising and looking out.

'There, look, I'm sure. Lean further,' she answered, slyly.

Entirely missing the hint of deviousness in her tone, Tuppy leaned out, straining to see in the fickle moonlight. But then, he wasn't so much looking as plummeting, the sound of goblin laughter

---

[7] Not you, them. Unless you do have two heads, in which case my sincere apologies for being headist.

behind him growing more distant as the ground rapidly rose to meet him.

* * *

Fate is fickle. Take the Scorbington's Dimcuckoo[8] currently sitting atop the highest chimney of the Meet Hall, a hall topped by a vast crooked tower known affectionately as Miffed Tower. She is blissfully ignorant to the twist fate has in store for her and the doomed goblins below, and snuggles into her nest. For once, fate will be kind to the fat ugly bird, which is destined to survive the coming conflagration. By next Thodsday, however, fate will be wearing a different hat, the *large fanged fox steals upon you in the night little birdie flat cap of woe*, to be precise, which will transform the Scorbington's Dimcuckoo into supper.

But until then, the bird sat on her nest of reeds and sticks, oblivious of the future, her feathers ruffled by the passing wind as dark clouds roared overhead, her stolen eggs nestled below her. Only the screams, laughter, and distended singing from the great building below disturbed her slumber.

Miffed Tower had been built[9] by Lord Miffed the Miff of Miffed-the-many-and-one-cause-he-says-so nearly many-times-lots-many-and-many years ago. He had put his soul, best finger, and the tip of his nose into that building, that momentous tower of thatch, wattle, stone, chicken carcasses, a live swan, parts of a boat that wouldn't burn, and many angry pigs. Many-more-than-one-and-many summers and an autumn it took him to finish, and somehow it had stayed up.

The Meet Hall cackled with sparks, spit, and goblin laughter. 'Tell us another, oh great Bulby,' croaked a reedy gob-boy, who was immediately stung with a switch-reed for his impertinence—goblin children should be seen and not heard.

---

[8] So named because Maester Scorbington discovered it picks up other bird's eggs, takes them to its nest and incubates them instead of its own, which it eats.
[9] Piling things on top of each other and hoping they don't fall down.

'If you youngsters have quite finished playing games, yammering and interrupting us with your endless tuneless whistling?' said Bulby, calmly, and somewhat untruthfully. 'Now,' he said, purposefully, 'before I tell you the story of how good Prince PranceQuiff stole the Whisk of Oblivion from Ikky, Lord of the Wickedly Bad MenSheep from Beyond the Great Forest, I'd like the Not-at-all-Wise Wench to say a few words.' He coughed again as the wood smoke drifted around him in a thaumaturgical cloud, and turned to the Not-at-all-Wise Wench.

She was a runty little creature, and as far away from 'pretty' as a gob-girl could get without not being a gob-girl at all. This would be her first speech after Moaris decided she would be the new Wise Wench. He'd accidentally broken the last one when she'd disagreed with him over who was the toughest goblin in the Great Forest, so quite clearly she wasn't wise after all.

The wood smoke was thick, and clung spectrally in a strange band at about head height all the way across the chamber, which was full of goblins, all smiling. Nervously the Not-at-all-Wise Wench, a title Moaris had kindly given her as a start until she proved herself, walked toward the wicker stage and pulled her skirts about her. Trembling, she adjusted her lucky brooch depicting the day when Noc, Demigod of All Wind, laid low the Great Oak of the Gods with a particularly venomous silent one. She looked around cautiously to where Chief Miffed lay snoozing. Moaris the Minor Apocalypse, his eldest, scowled at her and mouthed for her to get on with it, while playing provocatively with his rolling pin.

Everyone was scared of Moaris. He was the most vicious thug in the kingdom. No cruel or heartless thing was beyond him. When he was not-many-months old, he'd killed a hedgehog with his rattle—although, to be fair, later it was indeed discovered the rattle was none other than Prickledoom, the Rattle of Hedgehog Slaying. By the time he was almost grown up, everyone in the village was scared of him, or were scared of him *and* had had their house burnt down by him. Or were scared of him, had had their house burnt down by him *and* had had at least more than one near death experience attributable to him. Now he was some summers old, and thoroughly annoyed with everyone about the fact.

The Not-at-all-Wise Wench gulped and tried to pretend Moaris was looking at the wall behind her and would be waiting for it after the feast and not her.

Oh, Lord Noc, she gulped, aware that his presence was all around her. 'My dear goblins,' she quaked, 'and my especially dear BigBad Chief Runty Miffed the many-one-and-many-more after the first dead Chief Miffed.' She smiled, but being toothless it was a little like attempting to whistle without any lips, and it invaded her face like a nervous grimace. Nearby, Chief Miffed continued snoring through his majestic walrus moustache. 'This year will be a great year,' she shouted, 'I foresee, hmm, lots of really, really good things for the village.'

The goblins cheered.

Gaining in confidence a little, she continued. 'And our chief will have a new son.'

Somewhere in the room, a chief's wife began sobbing.

'And,' she added, 'there won't be any more pigs born with too-many eyes, and the summer will go on all winter, and fires will break out everywhere, and food will walk into our village every morning. We shall all live long and happy lives with full tummies and no boredom!'

The goblins roared, chittered, and pinched their approval.

She was happy now, and stood proudly at the edge of the stage. She would be the Not-at-all-Wise Wench for the rest of her days and everyone would listen to her. This was easy.

Outside, the stillness in the air was suddenly pierced by a roar, which was met by another roar, which in turn was met by more roars, until the whole forest echoed with anger.

* * *

Sorry was staring about the Wise Wench's lair-cottage enviously. It was crowded with all manner of interesting looking objects, lots of them for luck, which always made him want to take them. He

30

reached out for one magnificent mummified lizard—sure protection from snakes when you were sleeping—but then saw the Wise Wench's head move and put his hands back in his pockets guiltily. Even the dusters had a particularly magik look about them, with mystic prunes sewn into them. But prune lore was beyond Sorry, and made him frightened. Magic of any form was scary, especially magik with a k, and sometimes even Urgh's magic scared him. Never before had he dared to venture into the Smellcopse, the darkest and vilest part of the Great Forest, home to the Wise Wench and where the gods lurked. He still shuddered and thanked the gods that he hadn't met Queen Quench lurking out there behind a bush, but then the forest was still just outside the door wanting to come in and do something bad to him. He shivered and moved closer to the fire; so close, in fact, that he almost became a part of it. From somewhere above, a raven wearing a cravat peered at him and then slipped back into the shadows.

The Wise Wench ladled the strange smelling stew she'd been laboring over since before dusk into brown bowls, and handed them out together with some particularly worn wooden spoons. She then fetched a bucket of water from beside the table and eyed Sorry purposefully while hefting it slightly. A smell of smoldering goblin wafted toward her.

The duo looked at the spoons like they were objects the gods might use: alien, unfathomable, ridiculous.

'Try to use the spoons,' said the Wise Wench. 'They won't bite,' she added, casually, and threw the bucket of water over Sorry. 'No, don't thank me, just get on with your stew.'

Sorry looked damp and dumbfounded. 'Thank you? For half drowning me? Why should I thank you?'

'Because,' murmured the Wise Wench impatiently, 'if I hadn't thrown the bucket of water over you, you would have started smoldering because you were sat too close to the fire in an effort to cringe away from the door for fear of the gods that lurk outside, and my assistant above you. After a couple of minutes smoldering you would have caught fire and begun dashing round the room screaming: 'Aaargh I'm on fire! Wise Wench, get some water!' At

31

which time, I would probably have gone to fetch some water. In the meantime, Urgh would have tried to put you out with his stew, bumped into you, and also caught fire, badly. The death of Urgh, the future village hero, would lead to the ruin of not just you, the king, and the whole village, but also lead to a significant diminishment in my reputation as a Wise Wench amongst other local, not quite so Wise Wenches as I. This would lead to the end of the Great Forest, which would be hacked down, leaving nowhere for the goblins to hide, and a great rain would fall upon the world ending all fires. We would all die hungry and cold. That's why you should thank me. Small stones lead to an avalanche.'

'All right, THANK YOU!' shouted Sorry, wringing out his smalls.

Urgh had a huge grin on his face, although—upside down as it was—you might have mistaken it for a frown if you didn't know him better. 'Hero,' he beamed to himself, contentedly. He didn't feel like a hero, he just felt scared a lot. Then he remembered that everyone bullied him and felt even less heroic.

After Sorry had dried himself off they slurped in silence[10] while the forest made its own cacophony outside—the screech of the screech owl, the jabber of the jabbering fox, and the QQuuQQuuHumfrey of the QQuuQQuuHumfrey grubs.

'Why do you live alone in the Great Forest, oh Wise Wench?' asked Urgh, who was having some difficulty eating his stew without spilling any down his nose.

'Well, child,' she replied, 'if it was easy to reach me, all the local goblins would be forever knocking on my door asking questions. Wise Wench, does he love me? Wise Wench, do you think this dress suits me? Wise Wench, is it wrong to be in love with a ferret? Whereas out here, with the bloaters and trunters[11] and the

---

[10] OK, maybe slurping silently isn't really the case. That is to say, they slurped and did not speak or make coherent noises at the same time.
[11] Obviously, there is no such thing as a trunter. The Wise Wench made it up to stay one step ahead of the crowd and enhance her aloof air of detached mystery.

floating luminous deadly land lampreys, I am safe. No one troubles me.'

Sorry thought back to their journey to the Wise Wench's cottage in the thickest part of the forest: the eyes staring through the dusk, the ancient gnarled trees which seemed to watch them, and the ever-present threat of treading on a ripe boomacorn[12]. 'What is it like, being so wise, oh Wise Wench?' he said almost as a thought, and then realized what he'd said and wished he hadn't. He was being familiar with the Wise Wench, and that could be dangerous. After snatching a quick glance at her narrowing eyebrows, he decided to keep quiet for a long time. Perhaps, days.

She smiled. That wasn't good. She was doing a lot of smiling, just now.

'It is no easy thing being a glove-puppet of the gods,' she said, and her eyes were lost in the rafters of her cottage, where she kept her most dangerous chutneys and where her special adviser lived. '*ALL* gods that is, gods great and small, from Dun the Mighty, Lord of Thunder, to Tarquin, the Nowhere Near As Mighty, Prince Demigod of Queasy Hedgehogs. I am a tool to them all, they speak and I must listen. I know all things. *All* things.' Her eyes fell to the fire and the log that burnt thereon. 'All things are mine to know: how quick the wood burns today, which way the wind blows tomorrow. What lives, what dies horribly in boiling jam. It is no easy task to know everything.' She looked up suddenly at Sorry, which made him jump and look over his shoulder.

Urgh, who had been staring at the fire, suddenly said, 'Wise Wench, will I—'

'Yes.'

'And will it—'

'Yes, once-more-than-once.'

'Will it be—'

'Yes.'

---

[12] As celebrated in the famous goblin song, 'Go fetch me a boomacorn, my son, a nice big fat one to show, make sure it doesn't go off in your hand for fun, burn, burn, burn it, oh.'

33

'And—'

'Yes, one-and-a-few.'

'So, will I—'

'No.'

Urgh looked suddenly disappointed, turned again to admire the flames, and become lost in goblin thoughts of how much fun it would be to feed them to a lovely dry pile of kindling bigger than a massive thing.

The Wise Wench cocked one ear to the door outside. 'It's beginning,' she said and added another log to the fire.

* * *

Back in the village of Miffed, the Not-at-all-Wise Wench was still talking. Well, shouting. The noise of enthusiastic goblins had reached a cheering, baying madness that had not been seen in Miffed for many-and-lots-many years. 'And everyone will have more children. Some will have many children, especially me. I shall marry a handsome prince with lips and teeth, and he'll wear a golden crown and be handsome. And all sheep in the kingdom shall be so white that they will glow at night, and goblins will say, 'These are the days of the extraordinarily luminescent sheep,' and all will be happy. And all the naughty things will be dead, and the sky will stay where it is always; a little bit further away, in fact!'

In all her enthusiasm she hadn't noticed the small, murderous group of Moaris and some under-thugs wearing under-thug muzzles, who had stolen onto the stage behind her carrying a large, gob-wench-sized sack.

Moaris grabbed her from behind and, with the help of the under-thugs, put her in the large sack. As his under-thugs carried her away, Moaris stood, legs wide apart, on the stage. 'NOW THEN!' he shouted. He loved shouting, and was a devout servant and worshipper of Aaaaaaargh the Mighty, Lord of Shouting. 'YOU WILL ALL LISTEN TO ME!' Chief Runty Miffed the many-one-and-many-more after the first dead Chief Miffed woke up with a start; a false start, as it happened as he fell instantly off his stool and

34

knocked himself out. 'That's enough talk about having babies that glow in the dark,' said Moaris, aggressively. 'It's time to talk about discipline. It has come to my attention that everyone in this village except me, is soft. You're all like big fluffy kittens puffed up on piles of soft feathers and kisses! Eurgh! From tomorrow morning, things are going to get a lot tougher; a *lot* tougher! For starters, you'll be woken an hour before dawn for a run while being chased by wild boars. I'll be using these meat skewers to—' Moaris halted midsentence; something he'd never done before.

An under-thug Moaris couldn't put a name to stood before him squealing through his muzzle. He was holding a goblin's severed head. Both looked worried. Well, actually, the muzzled thug looked worried for about a second—exactly the same amount of time it took a huge axe to smash through the wall and door and most of the center portion of his body, and then spark as it hit the stone floor. He abruptly ceased worrying. Permanently.

Outside, the remaining guard in the watchtower had seen the giants come toward the village but had suddenly forgotten, amongst other things, what the alarm was, when she was supposed to sound it, and how to talk. So, instead, she hid and watched as the giants marched into the village and pointed at what they were going to break and squash, which was everything.

The giants were a vile race: huge, ugly, and monstrous. They lived in the swamps around the forest but were always entering the woods to raid, squash things, shout Mnarrrrr![13], take timber, and—worst of all—sing. The goblins, who were, after all, only a tenth their height, a quarter their weight (at best), and scared of practically anything, feared them accordingly. Which was why the guard quaked in the tower as she watched the giants crash great axes and roll huge siege cheeses through the flimsy village walls. She saw them march purposefully toward the great tower of Miffed when suddenly a

---

[13] Mnar! is the universal cry of monsters—the standard (and infallible) rule of which is that the more 'r's,' the bigger the monster, of course. Giants, scoring 6 r's on the Mnar! Scale, being very large indeed, but nowhere near as large as the krayken, which with its Mnarrrrrrrrrrrrrrrrrrrrrr! is one of the largest and most fearsome monsters in creation, and almost as bad as a dragon.

group of brave goblin warriors, armed only with a sack containing what seemed to be a struggling gob-girl, came heroically out to meet them. Alas, the conflict lasted but the one blow before the goblins were forced, after many of the briefest of moments of considered debate and angst, to run back inside.

The giants then set upon the tower.

Inside, the goblins scattered in panic, heading for any available door, window, or orifice to run through or hide in. Moaris put down his rolling pin and reached for Spike, his heftiest pointy club among the many pointy weapons dangling from his battle-braces. 'To me, goblins!' he cried and charged for the door, pushing past the many flailing arms, legs, and crowded orifices until, confronted by a particularly impenetrable panicking barrier of fat goblin thighs and large heads, he was forced to seek other means to get at his opponents.

The side of the building shuddered, and a great chorus of giant roars came from outside. 'AGAIN!' a huge booming voice echoed from outside. The building shook again.

Moaris looked out through a window[14] to see a group of giants charging the tower side. He ran back and then charged, closing his eyes as he leapt through the window to get at them. 'Defend the village!' he shouted.

There was a tremendous crash and then a terrible pain down his left side. Moaris opened his eyes. He'd missed the window and hit the wall. With a groan he stepped back and climbed through the hole instead; less heroic but more practical. Once outside, Moaris looked around, but at that moment the giants hit the wall and there was another terrible crash, followed by a few seconds of awful silence. Then a groan came from the timber, and the tower began to topple.

Moaris ran into the darkness. It was the second time in the evening he'd done something for the first time, and remarkably it wasn't the last time he'd do it.

---

[14] Hole in the wall.

With tears of pain stinging his eyes, he rushed into the blackness for all he was worth, aware always of the increasing groan of timbers falling, he hoped, behind him. He'd never run away from anything before in his life.

The crash told him the tower had fallen, and he wasn't under it. He wiped the tears away and turned to see the ruin of Miffed Tower. A few dazed survivors were pulling themselves from the billowing ruins, but the giants were quickly setting upon them. One had an enormous cheese grater and was being very cruel indeed with it.

'Only softies cry!' he said to himself, defiantly wiping his eyes and punching himself in the stomach to teach himself a lesson for crying for the first time ever. Then, checking he had Spike with him, he thrust his pointy weapon to the sky. 'Miffed! Charge!' he yelled and ran back towards the giants.

'Do you think they've gone?' whispered the guard to herself as she crouched in the corner of the tower, wishing she was a bird of a very swift, great winged variety who lived in a huge high nest, very far away, and was just having a bad dream.

'Yes,' she answered, in a slightly deeper voice[15]. 'It's perfectly safe now. I just heard Moaris say it was safe and that you were to go down to see him and receive your medal for bravery.'

A chopping sound came from below her.

Suddenly, the stars began to circle above the brave warrior's head, swirling and pirouetting gracefully in the heavens. 'That's beautiful,' she said, absentmindedly, before the tower hit the ground.

Moaris saw the tower crash down. 'Fight me, damn you!' yelled Moaris, as he plunged his deadly pointed stick into the buttocks of a particularly hefty giant. The mightiest weapon in Miffed seemed to

---

[15] Goblins, like many people these days, tend to talk to themselves quite often. To make it seem normal, they put on different voices and, if discovered, pretend to be possessed by some benevolent fire-making demon, spectral mind-controlling squid, or some sort of fierce, beatific bear who physically lurks nearby ready to avenge any punishment to its goblin vessel, or at least that's what the goblin says.

37

have little effect upon the vile creature's posterior, which—he saw to his horror—was clad in armored pants. He decided upon another tactic. He strode purposefully toward the ruin of the tower and hefted out a large burning timber. Then, without pausing, he ran back towards the giant and plunged the scorched timber into the hideous creature's bottom.

There was a tremendous roar as the giant leapt forwards.

'NOW, fight me!' bellowed Moaris and stood, legs wide apart, staring at the giant. It bent its heads down to look at him and gave a large 'MNARRRRRR!' from under its extremely unpleasant breath; a potpourri of sheep bits, wood, linseed oil, gravel, decayed teeth, giant beer, and massive pickled onions. It struggled to make out what had bitten it and bent further forwards, saying 'ERE, ONE'S FIGHTING BACK. THE NEXT VILLAGE BETTER NOT HAVE ONES THAT FIGHT BACK!'

Moaris whacked the giant's head with his burning club and it roared angrily. For a moment, the giant was confused, so Moaris brought Spike heftily across its kneecap. There was a preternatural squelch, and the huge creature toppled like a massive sweaty tree to the ground with a satisfying crash and a vague waft of pickled vegetables.

Moaris stepped back and grinned. 'Next!' he roared, while failing to see the wall as it fell toward him after another reckless giant's strike.

Everything went dark.

* * *

The mist clung spectrally over the ruins of Miffed Tower as Moaris slowly stood up, disrobing himself of the huge pile of dust and timbers that had hidden him for the night. The morning sun groped its tentative way toward him, perhaps afraid to disturb someone so vicious.

Slowly, he regained his focus and then wished he hadn't.

Everyone was dead.

Even the poultry was dead. They'd all been killed by the giants. Squashed! Well, at least the lucky ones were squashed.

He had to admit it, giants were very good at destroying things.

The giants! He looked around and found what he sought: his beloved Spike. Drawing it up to the wan sunlight he yelled. 'Attack!' he screamed, and looked around, aggressively.

Then he marched around, aggressively.

Then he ran around swinging his mighty weapon and yelling 'kill!' at the top of his voice, aggressively, until it was obvious that he was the only living thing within some distance. He considered attacking himself for a while to show how tough and good at fighting he was, but then he realized he was so tough he might end up giving himself a good kicking, which would be unacceptable. 'Cowards!' he shouted. 'One-more-than-one headed smelly disgusting wretches! Come back and fight me, damn you!' But it was no good. They were gone.

Moaris sat down, aggressively, and wept angrily, pausing only to give himself a good pinching for being soft.

After a short while, he stood up and shook himself very violently. So violently, in fact, that his nose began to bleed. As the blood slowly trickled over his lips he came to a conclusion. Mounting the rubble of the village, he stood with his legs extremely far apart, ripped his shirt open, and roared. 'REVENGE!' he shouted, so loudly that he made himself cough.

He walked down from the rubble, pleased with his new found and undoubtedly extremely violent purpose in life. He began to march northward through the forest. The storm was now fierce and lightning was striking the forest near the home of King Stormgrunties, the finest udder-duelist in the Great Forest. More importantly, home to *the* Wise Wench. She would know what to do about REVENGE all right, and if she didn't know, Moaris would have to kill every goblin in the village of Bliss until she *did* know.

The boughs of the great oaks welcomed Moaris into their domain as he marched angrily on over a deep carpet of moss ever northward toward his destination.

CHAPTER 3

'You really are the most handsome, mightiest, handsomest goblin in the whole forest!' thought the king to his reflection in the mirror in the corner of the royal bedchamber. Then, just to ensure he'd heard himself the first time, he thought it again, but this time in more of a roaring, triumphant way. He smiled, then glanced around suddenly and nervously, staring at the mountain of smelly blankets that enveloped some sort of vaguely goblinesque shape in their sweaty embrace. He was always worried about his thoughts popping out of his head and announcing themselves. Things like that happened when you were king and everyone else wasn't—disturbing the mound would be dangerous, in a stick and ants' nest kind of way. So he quietly ruffled up his yellow scarves about his neck and silently adjusted his flowing green striped robe of office. Then he mutely tweaked his yellow daffodil-motif-covered underthings of office, and smiled heartily.

He tiptoed across the bedroom and gazed at the bloated pile of blankets, straw, snoozing pigs, and half-eaten—occasionally moving—objects that lay before him. *No, please don't wake up! Keep snoring. That's the way.* Her Majesty obliged by choking out a snore that caused a flock of starlings to flee a tree a quarter of a mile away, and turned over. A small hair-covered chin emerged, seductively.

His Majesty slunk out silently and creaked downstairs, put on his best stomping boots, and went outside. He headed purposefully toward the distant Childpit at the edge of the forest to check on Spoilt, his son and protégé.

The noise there, too, was considerable, consisting variously of crying, shouting, singing, belching, pretend barking, yelling, vomiting, ordering, threatening, injuring, and retching in a symphony of naughtiness. He approached one of the guards. She was dressed as a crocodile, a cloud of flies buzzing about her entire being. In one hand she held her halberd, in the other a megaphone. Naturally, the king had no idea what she was called.

'Good morning, scum!' said the king, cordially.

The guard curtsied and accidentally dropped her halberd.

His Majesty gazed out across the mass assault that was occurring below him in the pen, which was dug just too high for children to get out of unless they worked as a team, which had never happened. Just in case, spears had been arranged pointing downwards to make it harder. In the middle of the pit was a hairless, repulsive, fat little gob-brat who was giving out all the orders while pulling the legs off a fat spider that had the misfortune of dropping into the pit a few moments earlier. He paused to throw a rock at a young gob-girl who sat with something that might have been a gob-boy or a pile of muddy rocks. It was too dirty to be sure. 'Get me some breakfast or I'll splat you! And you, build me a harpsichord! Now!' shouted the hairless gob-brat menacingly. His victims scuttled off, one looking considerably more concerned and confused than the other. The gob-brat slapped another child that had come within reach, and then pulled the remaining legs off the spider before swallowing it.

'That's my lad!' said the king proudly, and grinned at the guard, who beamed back.

'Spoilt is the image of Your Majesty!' said the guard, simpering, while retrieving her halberd.

Somewhere in the distance, dogs began to fight.

His Majesty left happily and continued smiling as he wandered through his kingdom. How fine the pigs seemed today, how grand the Poo-Pit, how statuesque the quaint little rural idyll called Bliss was. Some distance away, something exploded, accompanied by the sounds of flying poultry. Nearer, all the gob-girls were off hunting, allowing the boys to sit around competing with each other in some idle, puerile way for the rest of the day. The gob-wenches waved and giggled at him as they left the village. *All is well with my world*, he thought, and smiled the biggest smile he had in many-lots-many-and-many days. He stared up at the sky; it was still there. Good. A storm was brewing. He marched off towards the Moot House singing a little song whose lyrics revolved around words that rhymed with *wrong*.

* * *

Exactly a mile away, down a rabbit-hole, crouched Kringe. He stared up at the sky through tear-filled petrified eyes and tried to dig himself further downwards.

* * *

'That's the worst kind of storm,' said the Wise Wench as she looked through her kitchen window. 'That's badger-bite-lightning or I'm no Wise Wench,' she added, turning her attention to breakfast. The guests sat at the kitchen table before the fire looking hungry, worried, and expectant. Neither had slept or managed to escape. Sorry wondered if the fire needed more fuel, perhaps lots more, but kept the thought to himself for now. He started shaking.

The Wise Wench marched around her kitchen like someone inspecting a regiment, checking that everything was in its allotted place, and making sure that certain naughty, strong-willed kitchen utensils—most notably the arcane egg-whisk, which had a mind of its own—hadn't moved about during the night[16]. Somewhere above came the noise of gently flapping wings followed by what sounded like someone knitting. The Wise Wench moved over to a great cupboard and, immediately, strange noises echoed, quaked, and yelped from within. She pulled out a huge cleaver, opened the cupboard wider, and stepped in. A cacophony of petrified sounds enveloped her. 'You have a big day ahead of you, so you'll need filling up,' she added, as she emerged holding a selection of ugly things by their necks.

'Pardon me, Wise Wench,' said Urgh, 'but why exactly is it called badger-bite lightning?'

'Because it's attracted to holes.'

---

[16] The almost divine presence of the Wise Wench tends to rub off on everything near her—regardless of how mundane it is—and some spontaneously become *aware*. This can be a terrible thing for something as boring as, say, a whisk, which quickly realises how pointless life as a whisk is, and promptly tries to escape or seek *vengeance* for the woeful cards fate has dealt it.

42

The Wise Wench spent some time with her back to them, using a selection of hammers, axes, and meat cleavers to kill breakfast, before finally the slaughter stopped and everything was tossed into her cauldron. She stood, soaked in gore, gently stirring the cauldron with an enormous, and entirely inappropriate, spoon almost as big as she was. She started to hum quietly to herself, pausing only to carefully straighten the painting of her favorite horse Roger, which brooded above the fire.

'Why is Urgh the hero, oh Wise Wench?' said Sorry, as he watched her suddenly strike something swimming in her cauldron. 'Why not me?'

'Because he is,' said the Wise Wench, rhetorically.

'So why am I here then?'

'You'll see.' She killed whatever it was with a pointed strike of her spoon.

'What's so heroic about him anyway?' muttered Sorry, jealously, under his breath while eyeing his companion up and down disapprovingly, but hoping he wouldn't notice.

'How would you feel if the village was burnt down, Urgh?' said the Wise Wench.

'Horrified!'

'Why?'

'Because it's my home. My friends—not that there are that many—my family, everything I like is here. It would be terrible.'

'And how would you feel, Sorry?'

'Could I watch the fire from a safe distance, sure of my personal safety?'

'Yes.'

'Great! What's not good about a massive big fire?' He bounced on the spot momentarily with anticipation, assuming it was about to start.

'That's why,' said the Wise Wench, closing the subject.

Sorry decided to let it drop for a little while and moved over to Urgh, who was amusing himself by looking through the Wise Wench's collection of mummified dead pets. There was a handsome chicken, a prancing pig, and a well-groomed goat wearing a top hat amongst many other preserved specimens.

'How come you get to be the flippin' hero?' growled Sorry under his breath. 'If it wasn't for you, I'd be sat staring at breedbound Luggy Lumplips right now.'

Urgh stared at him and smiled. 'Just think, Sorry—we'll both be heroes, everyone will want to be our friend, and not bully us anymore. You might even get your hands on Luggy's sister Troubled.'

'I hadn't thought of it that way,' said Sorry, and suddenly looked momentarily happier before adding, 'but I still don't like it. It's bound to involve being hurt at some stage.'

'There's bound to be lots of fires,' added Urgh, by way of encouragement.

Sorry wasn't sure but decided for now that escape was impossible, and he was hungry anyway—so hungry, in fact, he was sure he was about to faint. He did a little pretend faint but no one seemed to notice. At that precise moment, breakfast was served. The goblins attacked it.

A short while later, Urgh ladled another huge mouthful of meat porridge into himself. His stomach had visibly grown over the past few minutes and something inside it moved.

Can you tell us anything that will help us in our quest then?' said Sorry, bluntly.

'No,' said the Wise Wench. 'There are some things that the knowing of may prevent the doing of, so finish your porridge. I'm not saying it is, but it *might* be the best meal you'll get until you get back.' She smiled at Sorry sympathetically, which made him worried. 'But you'll need your magic, as much as you can both carry.'

'Sorry, but I haven't got any magic, oh Wise Wench,' lied Sorry.

She looked at him.

'Apart from the few bits I borrowed...' He looked guiltily at Urgh, who scowled back and carried on with his breakfast, a trotter sticking from his mouth.

'Once we've finished breakfast we'll need to pack—and pack quickly. It won't be long before the news from Miffed unexpectedly arrives.' The Wise Wench looked pleased with herself and went over a few things in her head. Pausing to stare for some time at the kettle, she finally opened the windows and looked outside. 'There certainly is a storm coming,' she said.

Outside, clouds were brewing down in Noxy Dale and heading towards Bliss. The morning sun was rising steadily but its face was worried by thick storm clouds. From somewhere very far away, a faint smell drifted inland from the distant sea. It was an unpleasant aroma of sweat caused by an enormous number of enormous armpits.

'One thing I *can* tell you, though, is about your companion for the journey.' The Wise Wench looked to the rafters. 'May I introduce my associate and familiar, Lady Prudence Sophronia Carline,' she said, with great respect.

There was a ruffle of feathers, a stirring of dust, and the raven reappeared, gazing disapprovingly at the goblins. There was something oddly cosmopolitan about the bird, her gaze was steely, her feathers neat, but perhaps, more than anything else, it was the monocle that confirmed her as a bird of some refinement. She looked down her beak. 'To whom am I being introduced?' she said, in a cultured voice. As she spoke, the smell of lavender and tea and mothballs bounced across the chamber.

'Pardon me, Lady Carline,' said the Wise Wench. 'This is Upside Down Face, the hero of our quest, and his friend, Sorry Moth-Ripper. They have volunteered to help in this little, troublesome issue.' Sorry raised an eyebrow at the use of the word 'volunteered.'

'Ah, yes,' said the raven, 'I have heard you mention the hero before. A pleasure to meet you, hero-to-be.' She bowed, gracefully. Urgh, not sure what to do, held out his hand to shake before realizing that, as a bird, she had no hands to shake his with. He reddened, bowed, and then went back to self-satisfaction at being referred to as 'the hero,' even if his subconscious couldn't work out

45

the when's and the why's of the coming event. Nor, indeed, why anyone as runty and terrified as he could become heroic.

'Lady Carline was once a familiar to a powerful wizard. She's a carrion bird of breeding,' said the Wise Wench, proudly. Lady Carline coughed disapprovingly at the word 'carrion.'

Urgh nodded, not quite sure what to say. The raven glided over to the fireplace and began preening her feathers.

'Excuse me, Wise Wench,' said Sorry, smugly, 'but how come she can talk? I mean she hasn't got any lips, has she? How does she form words then?'

The Wise Wench scowled at him and said, 'Stop asking awkward questions.'

* * *

'Good morning, pointless subject,' said the king, as he marched through the village and passed the assistant village goose-worrier.

The worrier nervously grinned at his ruler. 'Good morning, Your Roundedness,' he stuttered nervously as he doffed his worrying hat and caused a lightly-abused kipper to fall from it onto the floor. They stared at it for a curious moment, the worrier's face reddening before he scooped up the kipper. 'Ah, *that's* where she put it!' he said, with an obvious air of forced nonchalance. He quickly placed it back under his worrying hat and marched on, whistling guiltily.

'Good morning, Your Majesty!' cried Pilt the Poo-Pit Maester, captain of all things related to the collection and making of smells[17]. 'It is a very grand day today, and a fine one for inspecting the Poo-Pit, if Your Majesty wishes and has the time to do so.' Pilt bowed very low.

The king stared closely at him for a moment and then grinned. 'His Majesty most certainly does wish it, Pilt. Conduct me upon a tour this instant, and spare me no detail of your nidorous occupation.' They strolled down the hill towards the meadow,

---

[17] A position of great importance to goblins, of course.

squashing the few hairs of grass struggling to escape the mud beneath their feet. Beyond, at the edges of the wood, despite the goblin's best efforts, bluebells made skirts for the trees and formed a never-ending carpet of vivid color. 'That needs sorting[18],' said the king, making a mental note to have them burnt and/or eaten. Soon, they beheld the Poo-Pit—the vile mass of unpleasantness that squatted at the edge of the village.

'Tell me Pilt, you loathsome nobody,' said the king, thoughtfully. 'How does it work, exactly?'

Pilt gave a smile, dusted down his wax-coat and adjusted his cravat. 'Well, Your Stinkship, the Poo-Pit is the lowest point in the village, and so, by force of nature, everything flows downwards into it. This acts as a conduit for the tribes' collective odor, announcing, in a wide area, that this patch of the Great Forest is most definitely ours. Sorry, Yours,' he added, catching the king's stare. 'I might add, modestly, Your Highsmellness, that I have added—ahem—one-and-more-than-one modifications. Helped, of course, by my cousins Ferret and Whippet.'

'Yes, I see,' said the king, while nodding furiously and making encouraging noises.

'You see that small group of new cottages up yonder? The ones that belong to the Wotyoulookinat's?'

His Majesty did.

'Well, to enable their smells to become part of the whole village, I've dug a narrow trench, enabling all their odors to flow downwards into the Pit below—a distance of many-and-lots-many yards, I might add.' Pilt stopped and smiled humbly, legs parting slightly. 'I call them pong-trenches, Your Majesty,' he beamed, proudly.

'Aha, I see! Well, that really is fascinating,' said His Majesty. 'Tell me more about these pong-trenches you mentioned.' Putting a friendly arm around Pilt, they marched towards the Poo-Pit deep in smell-related conversation.

---

[18] Burning. The Goblin word for *sort* and *burn* are the same. In fact, lots of words mean the same as burn.

A little while later, the king marched through the Great Mouth and into the Moot Hall. 'Kringe!' he bellowed. 'Get out my festival braces, open up a bottle of finest whelks, put a cat on the fire, and commission me a portrait of Pilt the Poo-Pit man! I'm feeling particularly *right* today.'

He looked around.

No one.

But there was *never* no one.

Strange, he thought. *No fire lit, no ladder next to my high chair, and there aren't any dead magpies over the mantelpiece. But it's Thodsday, isn't it? I'm sure it is! What in the blazes is going on here?*

Something coughed in the corner of the room and stepped into the daylight. It was unpleasant, its head far too big for its body, its tongue too big for its head.

'Your Majestic Majesty,' it slavered. 'My cousin Kringe has taken the liberty of hiding down a rabbit hole all day so that the lightning can't get to him, Your Vastiness.'

'What lightning? Why does no one ever tell me these things?' grumbled the king, impatiently.

'The, er, lightning the Wise Wench prophesied would kill him today, Your Girthness,' added the goblin, his tongue struggling to let the words out of his mouth.

'Oh yes, *that* lightning,' he answered in a disinterested way.

'I am his cousin Tongue, Your Divine Considerateness. He's suggested I take over his duties on a purely temporary, one day in a lifetime, basis, Your Wiseness. I have the magpies,' he added, proffering a small group of dead, mangy birds. 'One for luck and more-than-one for bad, lots for suddenly finding auspicious whelks in a bag[19].' Tongue stopped, his swelling tongue momentarily blocking his mouth.

---

[19] There are, of course, many variations of the traditional lucky magpie song. Tongue is merely recanting the local version: 'One for luck and more-than-one for bad, lots for suddenly finding auspicious whelks in a bag. Many for a fortune stoat in dress, many-many and we'll be in a bad mess, burn, burn, burn it, oh.' Really clever goblins (who are few in number, to be honest) have argued that magpies

King Stormgrunties the many-many-and-lots-after-more-than-many-dead-King Stormgrunties-after-the-first scowled at him, peering up and down at this new, somewhat unwelcome, visitor.

Tongue crawled in front of the king. 'Your Majesty knows that today is bad-people day, does he not? Of course he does. I am fully versed in bad-person day proceedings, and have ironed the stoat bonnet.'

The king climbed onto Tongue's back and into his high chair. 'Of course I know! I'm the bloody king! I know everything. I'm the only one in the village who has never got anything wrong.' He began to chuckle to himself.

Tongue somehow got up without standing and joined in with the king's laughter, over-eagerly, causing himself a coughing fit. 'Is there anything else I can help you with, Your Wonderfulness?' he spluttered, and as he finished, a long line of dribble extended from Tongue's lower lip and slid, slowly, to the ground, watched by both himself and His Majesty.

'No,' said His Majesty, and struck him on the head with the large stick.

A little while later, Tongue awoke.

'Hang him over there in the corner,' said the king. Durth and his thugs swung Tongue round on the pole which was swaying dangerously over the fire-pit and balanced the pole in the corner. 'That's much better. I think I'll keep him there as an ornament.' The king looked around expectantly. 'Now then!' he shouted, and everyone in the room jumped. 'I want you to go out and find Kringe. He's hiding in a rabbit hole somewhere, so go and get him.' The little crowd began to move out, bowing, scraping, and giggling at Tongue. 'And if I hear one more squeak out of you, Tund or whatever your name is, I'll have you boiled in jam.'

The door slammed shut. His Majesty looked about his chamber, mouthing the word 'wrong' and laughing. There was a knock on the door. 'Yes, what do you want?' he said.

---

can't possibly be lucky, since every time goblins see them they try to catch and kill them for luck.

49

There was a lot of mumbling from outside, which went on for some time.

King Stormgrunties scratched his head and wondered why his subjects were so stupid. 'Come IN and tell me what you want!' he yelled. The door opened slowly and a small group of wretched-looking goblins marched in, all averting their eyes. This wasn't easy for Dome Eyes, the youngest goblin, who stood at the back averting his eyes unsuccessfully.

'You, at the back,' shouted the king. 'Yes, you,' he said, responding to Dome Eyes innocently pointing to himself. 'Just what are you then?' he said accusingly.

'I beg your pardon, Your Majesty?' it said.

His Majesty looked put out and sighed. He leaned forward in his great chair, paused, remembered what happened the day before yesterday when the whole thing toppled over, and leant back. 'I said 'what are you then?''

'Well, I'm called Dome Eyes, Your Magnificence. Sorry,' he added swiftly.

'Irrelevant. What do you want?'

The little group shuffled about from one foot to the other, nervously.

'You're dancers, I see.' said the king regally, and began clapping. 'Get on with it, then.'

'No, no, not at all, Your Massiveness. It's bad people day, Your Majesty,' piped one from near the back; an ugly, shifty-looking goblin with a yellow head and purple body.

'Of course, of course,' grinned the king. 'Well, get on with it then,' he added, and leant back.

The little group appeared confused. 'But Your Eminence,' croaked one of the goblins, 'it's you who are supposed to start things off. You know, the stoat and things?' They all looked disappointed. Some of them had never seen the Stoat Bonnet of Justice before and were looking forward to it.

'Kringe!' bellowed the king.

Odd thought Kringe far away, looking warily up at the circle of light above him. It had been steadily growing darker for the past hour or so. *I felt sure I heard my name.* 'Oh, Lord Noc!' he cried, 'it's coming! The lightning is looking for me!' He pulled himself further down the rabbit hole and became stuck fast.

* * *

The Wise Wench shut the door and turned her cloak collar up. 'Time to go to your destiny,' she said, and put on her best bonnet. Her companions looked at her nervously and wondered exactly what kind of destiny the Wise Wench was talking about. Was she, in fact, Urgh wondered, talking about a destiny prepared by Plentitude Fullcrop, Demigod of Good Fortune and Food that Squeals When You Crunch It, or was it fate prepared by Nargggruff the Terrible, Eater of Gob-boy pie and Doer of Foul Things Involving Knitting Needles and Other Pointed Spiky Things?

'Neither,' she added, and walked down her garden path.

'I meant to ask you last night, oh Wise Wench,' said Urgh in his kindest, friendliest voice. 'What exactly is that huge shed full of vast amounts of blacksmith equipment doing outside your back door, and what is that thing which appears to be some kind of huge, kettle-like device which is adorned with mystic prunes that lies in the room's center? And why is there a huge swathe cut through the forest in an almost perfectly straight line in the direction of the village? And would it be impertinent to ask what those hefty parallel lines of metal rods that stretch in a seemingly endless line down the center of that clearing are for?'

'Yes,' said the Wise Wench, and marched past them purposefully.

'*Yes* to *what?*' whispered Sorry to Urgh.

'All of it,' she said. 'No,' she added, as Sorry looked round.

They followed her through the forest, the storm churning nearby, the group carefully crossed the rails leading from the huge shed. They looked nervously at a huge kettle inside. As they stared, they could see a few gob-girls at work on the strange massive object

51

of metal. Urgh thought he also recognized Master Whippet inside. He liked Whippet. Whippet was clever at making things.[20]

'And when you meet Moaris, try not to upset him at all,' said the Wise Wench. 'It'll just make him cross.'

'Try not to upset him?!' cried Sorry. 'Upset Moaris Miffed, son of the Miffed of Miffed? Moaris Miffed who once set fire to several goblins for not saying his name aggressively or deeply enough? Moaris Miffed who pulled the ears off every gob-boy, gob-wench, and gob-brat who shared his birthday so only he could hear 'happy birthday' being sung? Moaris Miffed who, armed with a huge iron-bound courgette, got—'

'—Yes, that Moaris,' said the Wise Wench. 'Don't upset him.' The sky grew blacker and the Wise Wench picked up her pace, pausing only to put up an umbrella.

Seconds later, it began to rain.

They continued walking on along the iron rails, which seemed to be leading back to the village. Urgh wondered what part the rails played in the strange machinations of the Wise Wench. Sorry wondered if they would get pudding when they arrived.

A crack of lightning above brought them to their senses. 'One, one-and-one, more-than-one...' whispered the Wise Wench under her breath. 'Lots—'

Crack! Another bolt of lightning struck nearby.

'—lots-many-lots, lots-many-many-lots—' Suddenly, the Wise Wench pulled Sorry and Urgh toward her with surprising force as a bolt of lightning struck a tree very close by. The heat and sound was too much to bear, Urgh and Sorry rolled on the floor, covering their ears.

---

[20] Goblins have quite clever fingers and can fashion items of extraordinary complexity when they are scared enough or can be bothered. Such events of course are rare; goblins lack the focus or desire to make things properly and tend to get bored after a few minutes of really hard thinking and go off to torment a slug or something that can't fight back.

'—many-the-many MANY!' shouted the Wise Wench, as the tree split in half and the heavier, bough-laden section of the oak fell with a mighty crash before her, missing her by inches.

'Wha—' mumbled Urgh bravely between tears and shaking.

'Wait!' said the Wise Wench while peering purposefully at the tree, and more particularly at a nest which was built into the bough immediately before her. Inwardly, she seemed to reach some vital conclusion and very carefully put the nest upright again, being careful not to disturb the eggs inside. She checked her knitted list and found, right near the end, a figure of a young bird hatching from an egg and startling a giant. 'This is absolutely VITAL, so don't interrupt! If we didn't do this, Durth would die in the final battle,' she sneered while making her final adjustments to the nest. 'Now little chick, prepare to be in our story, when the time comes, fly before your foe and make him drop his club. Now, one more thing I think,' she added, and leant against a heavy bough for a few seconds, her eyes drawn to the middle distance while holding a figure being hit by a yellow bolt near the start of her knitted list.

Another bolt of lightning cracked somewhere in the distance, followed by a scream.

'Poor Kringe,' said the Wise Wench, momentarily removing her bonnet. 'Well, come on, COME ON, we haven't much time before Moaris arrives out of the blue, and we must make sure we are there at the allotted moment when he unexpectedly arrives or we will suffer his wrath.' Pausing only for a moment to check that the iron rails were undamaged, she marched on through the storm.

Sorry and Urgh plodded miserably behind her[21].

* * *

'I think it goes on your head, Your Spherity,' said Dome Eyes, apologetically.

---

[21] Rain makes goblins really miserable as it stops them burning things so much and scours their smell-stories away.

53

'I know where it goes,' said the king, trying to take his leg out of the dead stoat that had been fashioned, with considerable lack of cunning and talent, into a hat. *This really should be easy,* he thought. *If only Kringe were here.* Suddenly a violent crack of lightning made the room shake. Little piles of dust from the beams fell onto the king's head, giving him the appearance of an aged lore-master. He shook the grey dust grumpily from his head, and plonked the dead stoat there. It looked regal. The goblins in the room bowed and muttered in awe.

'Now, that's better,' said the king, as another crack of lightning struck the forest. 'Right, having carefully considered the evidence brought before me, it falls upon me to find all of you lot on the left guilty of cannibalism. The rest of you can go.'

There was a confused babble as the goblins on the right made a break for it.

'No! No! NO!' squawked Dome Eyes. '*They* are the ones accused of badness, not us.'

'—*Your Majesty,*' said the king.

'Sorry! *They* are the bad people, not us, *Your Majesty,*' he corrected himself and looked in different directions at the same time.

'That's nonsense!' said one goblin. 'This fool is implying that Your Majesty has made a *mistake,* and, as we all know, that is impossible.' He smiled smugly to himself and stepped back with his legs apart. Everyone paused.

'Good point,' said the king, and rubbed his chin thoughtfully. Then he rubbed his nose, shoulders, and brow thoughtfully. Everyone waited.

The king, having glanced at Tongue and adjusted the stoat hat, looked solemn. 'Having carefully considered all the evidence, it falls upon me to find everyone in the room guilty.' There was a collective gasp.

'What of, exactly?' said Dome Eyes, somewhat aggrieved.

'Being common.'

Everyone began running around the round house, arguing. *Odd things peasants,* thought the king, and wondered if he might not be better off just burning all of them. The little group of goblins were now chasing each other around his high chair, and the commotion was beginning to annoy him. Dome Eyes was the only goblin behaving reasonably; he was squatting next to the king's high chair, liberally stuffing tobacco into an enormous pipe.

Suddenly, the Great Mouth crashed open—almost taking the old faithful door off its hinges—and in walked the Wise Wench, closely followed by Sorry and Urgh, who both cringed nervously at her side.

'And about time too, oh Wise Wench!' shouted the king. Silence and stillness fell on the room. Goblins who had previously been accusing each other of all the heinous crimes ever devised suddenly found solace in hiding behind each other.

'I see you have everything under control,' said the Wise Wench smugly, casting her eyes about the room at the kindergarten scene that met them.

'SILENCE!' roared the king, and fell off his seat.

Sorry helped him back up as subserviently as possible, while taking great pains to avert his eyes. 'Take your hand out of my ear, scum!' said the king to Sorry. The king, regaining his composure, clumsily remounted his chair.

'Let me sort this little problem out for you,' said the Wise Wench, and proceeded to single out half of the goblins, gently pushing them away from the high chair. 'You, you, and you are guilty. Norty, you are guilty of stealing eggs from old Bentmind the village Madwench; the fine is and one-and-one starling eggs. You, Trumpily, are guilty of trying to eat the village smithy without the king's permission; you are banished from the village until the next full moon. And you, Wetly Baddoings, are guilty of whistling on a Dumsday; you'll go with Trumpily. Take them away!' She shouted to no one in particular. The other goblins, pleased at the relative ease of proving guilt, took hold of the villains and marched them out, slamming the door behind themselves.

Suddenly, Dome Eyes looked up from his pipe, and feeling that he was in precisely the wrong place at the very moment when it was worst to be so, found the safest place he could, hiding in the curious wicker folds of the king's high chair. It was nice and hairy, a repository for dust, feathers, and bits of straw, and so great for hiding in.

The king harrumphed disagreeably under his breath and mouthed the word 'wrong' to the Wise Wench's back. She smiled to herself and opened the door very purposefully before standing aside and crossing her arms. In the distance, Kringe's screams could be heard. He gave out one final yelp and was silent.

'Was that...?' inquired his lordship.

'Yes,' she said, noticing that Dome Eyes was hiding below the king, and still trying to light his pipe.

Dome-Eyes struggled heroically on with his fire-make-stick while the oblivious king eyed Sorry and Urgh suspiciously. 'Well?' he said, to the pair of them.

'Well, what, your grace?' said Sorry, subserviently.

'Well, what are you waiting for?' the king added, reproachfully.

The Wise Wench gave the king a scalding look and he fell silent. She looked outside again and frowned. 'He's late,' she said, and noticed that Dome Eyes had managed to light his pipe.

Dome Eyes smiled as he puffed on the clay object, enjoying the hot sensation of the smoke in his throat and feeling calmer immediately. He closed his eyes and sucked hard. A tiny ember danced from the pipe and slowly drifted toward the king. And onto his clothes.

The Wise Wench smiled and opened the door a little wider. Outside, the storm was passing and the clear air welcomed itself into the room—fanning the ember—which became a flame.

Suddenly, a figure appeared in the door; a huge, cross-looking goblin wearing a great red battle cloak, and holding a vast, pointy club in his hand. Countless other pointed, bladed, and barbed things dangled off his battle-braces, along with raindrops. He cut a fine, fearsome figure of a goblin, with the grey and alternate green braces that bespoke of high goblin rank. He marched past everyone in the room and knelt before the king. 'Your Majesty,' he shouted, 'I come from Miffed Tower. I have dreadful news!' He shot the king a disdainful glare as he watched the flames gathering around the royal posterior. 'Your Majesty, your coat appears to be on fire!' he added.

The king's smile wilted, to be replaced by, firstly, a look of horror, and then one of hatred towards the Wise Wench. He leapt from his chair and headed towards the pond at considerable pace, muttering under his breath about women.

'Fear not, brave Moaris,' said the Wise Wench. 'His Majesty will live. Now, you were about to tell us that last night poor Miffed-by-the-Sea was razed to the ground by giants, and that you were the only survivor. You were then going to elaborate about the battle, how fearsome the giants were, how many heads they had, and how they felled Miffed Tower. You were about to then add that you heard them mention attacking another village and think it might be this one. Let me save you the trouble. Come, meet your destiny!' She smiled smugly to herself, and pulled Sorry and Urgh before her. They both looked at their feet, afraid of catching Moaris's eye.

In the distance someone screamed as they leapt into the duck pond.

'Are you all right, Your Eminence?' cried Pilt the Poo-Pit Maester, as he dragged King Stormgrunties out of the pond and away from the eager eyes of the village pike. With some difficulty, His Majesty pulled himself up to his full not-many feet in height, and glowered at Pilt past the reeds sticking out of his braces. 'Guards!' he cried, hoarsely. 'Take this villain and enemy of the Great Forest away and let him play with Petal!'

A sweaty group of guards, led by Durth, soon appeared on the scene and led the sobbing Pong-Lore Maester away to meet with a terrible, crocodilian fate.

King Stormgrunties marched back up to the Moot House, squelching as he stepped, his royal posterior a dank, swollen, hanging, mass of singed, saggy, underthings, and sticky pond weed.

Moaris wasn't sure if he'd hit him hard enough. His opponent dropped, groaning and pleading for mercy. So, he was right—a softie. And not just a softie, a softie he had been saddled with for an adventure. 'Please don't hit me, Moaris. I'm very sorry,' pleaded Sorry, as he tried to pull himself away.

'It's no good being cross, Moaris,' said the Wise Wench. 'You can't escape your destiny—your whole destiny, that is.'

'But these wretches are total weeds! They're just rubbish! This one hasn't even got any shoulders, and this other one has a head on upside down,' protested Moaris, violently. The Wise Wench looked on impassively while Urgh quaked mightily in her shadow.

Moaris suddenly turned around and crossed his arms. 'No!' he said, simply.

'No, what?' said the Wise Wench, not used to having the word *no* said to her.

'No, I'm not taking them. He has no shoulders, is ugly, and could snap like a twig.' Sorry heard a twig crack somewhere nearby and began to cry a little. 'And his head is upside down. I'm not doing it. Being associated with them would be bad for my image.'

For a moment, Urgh thought she looked stumped, but then she smiled. 'Alright Moaris, have it your own way. Ignore the prophecy.'

'Prophecy?!' said Moaris, his eyes lighting up—prophecies almost always involved extreme violence and death for the majority of those involved. He glowered. 'What prophecy?'

'The ancient prophecy of Codly Darkarts, sorcerer of Noxxly Wood,' she lied.

'Never heard of him!' said Moaris. Sorry and Urgh nodded visibly in agreement, keen to become friends with Moaris in the hope that he wouldn't hit them quite so much.

'Then mark me well, child, for I shall repeat it to you now,' declared the Wise Wench.

'One-one-and-one stand and fall,
On the whim of a storm,
Many-many cockerels' call,
Burn, burn, burn it, oh!

And a lamprey shall smile on the west and be caught by him as a token,
That and many-one-less-than-many tearful cockerels,
One-and-one blue ewes made shall also be gathered by him,
Burn, burn, burn it, oh!

Only the one called Moaris can help solve the riddle,
When all things shall be killed horribly by him,
In the enormous, bloody apocalypse, but deliver a message first,
Burn, burn, burn it, oh!'

She stood, legs slightly apart, and smiled benevolently at Moaris, who caught the merest look of sympathy in her gaze, which he dismissed as trapped wind. 'Now, Moaris,' she said, earnestly, and moving to put a conspiratorial arm around his shoulder. 'Does any of that prophecy ring any bells? It's very ancient and tells of terrible, terrible violence...'

Moaris sat down and thought for a while. He looked cross. 'No, not really. I can't think any of it sounds familiar...' Then, very slowly, a grin came across his face and he said, 'Wait a minute— you said 'one-one-and-one stand and fall,' and—just a minute— there are one-one-and-one of us in here, oh Wise Wench,' while patting Urgh and Sorry on their heads. 'And those other words you said, I'm sure I passed some cockerels on the way here, or was it just one? And those other things, they seem almost to make sense somehow—wait, what was the last bit again?'

'Only the one of the *name of Moaris* can help solve the riddle when all things shall be killed horribly by him in the enormous bloody apocalypse, but deliver a message first,' she said with a furtive smile.

'Enormous bloody apocalypse!' smiled Moaris as he marched forward and picked Sorry up—who winced and cried and shook more violently, although only half as violently as Urgh did when Moaris put a friendly arm around his shoulders. 'Then, we must fulfil our destiny! Soft, ugly, pointless weeds as you are, it is in the

59

lap of the gods. We one-one-and-one against the coming apocalypse! REVENGE!' roared Moaris.

'Huzzah!' shouted the Wise Wench, staring encouragingly at Urgh and Sorry.

'Huzzah,' they answered, weakly.

His Majesty came in, dripping wet.

CHAPTER 4

'Moaris is giving them both weapons training,' said the Wise Wench, in answer to the king's stare. From somewhere outside came the sounds of crying and continual verbal abuse.

'I see. And you're absolutely sure that's right?' said the king, handing her back the bag he'd just spoken into.

'That's it,' answered the Wise Wench happily, taking the speakme bag back. 'When have I ever been wrong?'

The king thought about saying something and managed to stop himself just in time. 'So how, er, does it work?' he asked, diplomatically.

'Speakme bags? Well, it's quite straightforward, really. You take this special magic bag, and you just speak your words—'

'—*your* words, I think you'll find,' said the king as he crossed his arms and looked annoyed.

'Alright then—*my* words into this special bag, and when it's thrown on a fire, the words come out again, with a rather handsome image of your face speaking them.'

The king smiled at the last bit, then realized she was joking. 'It's a bit short, isn't it? The message, I mean.'

'Exactly. Short and to the point.'

'Oh well, you know best, I suppose,' said the king. 'If we've quite finished, I need to get out of my moist attire.' He squelched into the back room of the Moot House thinking *but if you ask me, that's the end of that lot,* before quickly moving on to think about turnips and other matters of more importance to a king than the lives of commoners.

It was later. The fire cast eerie shadows about the Moot House, and the food on the great roundtable seemed to dance in them; some of it, in truth, actually did dance a little before Moaris hit it with his dining mallet.

61

The meal had appeared very suddenly and promptly after Moaris had arrived back on the scene with his new trainees[22] and declared himself hungry. The king had changed into his substitute regal pants after sentencing Dome Eyes to quite-a-few-and-one-more-because-he's-ugly years' imprisonment with the village wolverine for the rarely heard goblin crime of lighting a fire that wasn't funny[23]. He had brightened up considerably when the first course of whippet squash had been brought out. The Wise Wench had kept mostly silent during the meal, a large sack by her side, as Moaris carried on a monologue about violence, setting fire to things, and dangerous adventure. He had, by this time, already decided tactically what he was going to do to the giants, and what sort of armor and pointed weaponry would be required to fulfil the rhyme of Codly Darkarts. Nearby, Sorry was trying to hide the fact that he looked pleased with himself, despite the bruises from training. He was also doing a lot of gazing about the Moot House, looking for things to steal and/or set fire to, and his eyes kept flicking back to the Great Mole which was stood regally on its molestand nearby.

Moaris was tearing up the last of his meat when the Wise Wench stood and raised a goblet. 'To adventure!' she said, and the others followed her toast with startlingly varied levels of enthusiasm. Moaris was so enthused that he set fire to several things, and, alas, it later transpired that this was how the Koppy, the Mop of Prophecy met its unforeseen end.

'And death,' added Moaris, helpfully.

'Would you like some more squash, Moaris?' asked the Wise Wench. 'Oh dear,' she added, apologetically. 'Sorry, I didn't mean to say *squash*,' she added, looking mischievously sad.

Sorry looked around at the others, built up his courage, and stood up, coughing loudly.

---

[22] Victims.

[23] The list of goblin crimes—not that they keep lists—is pretty endless, and generally only constrained by the imagination of the justice in question and the length of their memory. Some famous goblin songs, such as '*Guilty! Guilty! Bring out the pig!*' make lengthy references to countless things considered criminal, starting, of course, with putting a fire out for any reason.

Everyone carried on eating.

He coughed again, louder this time. 'Excuse me, I have something important to say,' he said, and smiled broadly to himself.

'Pass the potatoes,' said Moaris, angrily.

Sorry went red, and then stuck his hand in the air.

Some time passed.

'Yes,' said the king, testily.

'Well, erm, excuse me, Your Wondrous Wise Wenchnessness,' said Sorry, trying to suppress a grin, 'but what, exactly, does this adventure entail?'

'Death!' screamed Moaris. 'Death and burning!' he added, violently, and stood up on the table. 'Death, burning, beheading, death, and glory!' he roared, helpfully, and stood with his hands on his hips somewhat flamboyantly—not that anyone dared tell him.

The king looked frightened, then remembered he was a king and resumed looking down his considerable nose at his guest.

'Why?' said the Wise Wench, with a look suggesting she was already in possession of the answer.

'Well,' continued Sorry, beaming, 'this mission you speak of. Will it be a success?'

'Of course, dullard,' she snapped, her pride clearly hurt.

Sorry smiled very smugly, and squeaked, saying, 'well, if the gods have already deemed that it will be a success, then what's the point in going on it, eh? I mean, if *THEY'VE* decided it works, then it works and we can all save time by not bothering. I'd suggest that instead of going on the adventure, we all sit at home and organize a hunt to find some stoats to burn. Burn!' Sorry looked very pleased with himself.

His Majesty looked in wonder at Sorry. 'The repulsive, scrawny, cowardly, devious, pointless little wretch has a very good point there, hasn't he?' he asked the Wise Wench. All eyes turned to her.

She paused for effect. 'Wrong on every count,' she said. 'The mission, smarty-pants, can only succeed if you, the one-one-and-one—the *chosen* adventurers—take up the message and deliver it to the giants. Let us say, for the sake of the pointless argument, that Durth and his thugs went instead, very able though they are—'

Durth thrust his chest out and his thugs all colored up a little, sure that *no one*, ever, had received the praise of the Wise Wench for anything.

'—and stupid enough to do it—'

Their faces dropped.

'—it would fail, for Knowall, the Seer of the Gods, would be offended that I had chosen the wrong goblins to take on the quest. He would, I am very sure, unleash the Many-Headed Goose of Oblivion on all of us as punishment. So, you'd better start enthusing about this adventure and accept you're going.' She finished by leaning, thaumaturgically, against the wall near the fire-pit, staring upwards, her eyes blinking frequently.

Nearby, some hens began to fight.

Sorry sulked and sat down, stealing the Great Mole as he did so and stuffing it into his very dirty pocket.

'So, before we go to bed,' announced the Wise Wench, 'I shall tell you a cautionary and very pertinent tale: the story of Crookmouth Slopeyface, the great goblin hero! You young lads might find some details of the tale—many of them, perhaps—useful to remember, so pay attention.'

Urgh swallowed a boiled scronk and settled down, the creature momentarily lodging in his throat before being gulped down with a squeal and purr. Sorry secretively fondled his mole. Moaris looked cross, almost as cross as the king, who couldn't think of any instructions to give out.

'The Great Forest was young,' said the Wise Wench, gently, 'when Crookmouth Slopeyface, the great goblin hero, walked in it.' She paused to toss another log on the already roaring fire. 'For he was the father of all goblins who, having taken his breed-bound Prikkli from the clutches of the Dog That is Chained at the Gate of Doom, made the Great Forest his own.

'Once upon a time, Crookmouth,' she stared towards Urgh, pointedly, 'was charged with a great task by his adviser, the dazzling beautiful WenchWise.' She walked around the table and stood behind Sorry and Moaris. Moaris was pulling the legs off a big spider. 'With Crookmouth went Violent and Useless, his companions. They had been charged by the WenchWise to deliver a message to some naughty fearsome giants that lived over the other side of the forest.'

'Kill the giants!' yelled Moaris, before crunching what was left of the spider.

'The one-one-and-one friends had many adventures on the way to fulfilling a prophecy that guided them. This prophecy demanded that to be fulfilled as a prophecy, the adventurers follow the prophecy. This prophecy told them to deliver a message to their foe and failing to do so would anger the prophecy, and so no more prophecies would ever appear again, and the whole forest would be buried in boring forever. Prophecy.'

The goblins looked worried when the word 'boring' was used.

'So, although they had many adventures—Useless fled, Violence attacked, and Crookmouth thought—they all made sure that the prophecy was fulfilled. They used their cunning and the prophecy to enter the giants' stronghold by, say, entering a chimney, sneaking into the upper tower, and delivering the message to the giants' chief. Thus, fulfilling the prophecy, and thereby bringing days of great abundance. They all learnt one lesson—even though for one of them it was his final lesson,' she patted Moaris on the back, 'that by fulfilling the prophecy they all guaranteed themselves a place at the Table of the Gods where boring never starts and everywhere are piles of interesting things to burn throughout all eternity.'

As she finished her tale, she threw her skirts theatrically about herself and leaned, deep in thought, against the mantle. Her knickers were showing. Sorry grimaced, averted his eyes, and uttered a prayer to make them go away. He thought about asking the Great Mole what to do, but felt it was the wrong sort of question for a mole of such importance.

'Try to remember that lesson, Moaris. Which brings me to the task at hand,' she scowled, and viewed each of them in turn. 'For some time now, I have been aware that the giants have been preparing to destroy us!'

'Destroy us?!' quizzed the king. 'You never mentioned this! You started talking about building kettles and—'

'—SILENCE!' she screamed. Sorry started coughing again.

Silence indeed thought the king, silently.

'Destroy us,' she continued, 'and it is up to us, as the rightful heirs of the forest, to take care of it and defend it, so that we can burn it down when we choose to, or just burn selected parts as and when we wish.'

They all cheered. Moaris stared at the king's mace collection, and began to formulate a back-up battle-plan. The king put his hand up.

'Yes?' she asked.

'Can we burn the forest down now, please?' he asked, mightily. Everyone nodded in agreement. Moaris hefted one of the maces down off the wall and stared at the back of Sorry's head.

'No. If you'll just let me finish my monologue,' she croaked, 'I was about to say, 'which is why I have a plan." She opened the sack and whipped out an ancient leather bag sealed at either end with wax and covered with many, many mystic prunes, the meaning of which was doubtless a powerful warding spell.

'Hey that's the ba—' started the king.

'—You, Moaris, together with your companions, will head out for the giants' kingdom and deliver this speakme bag, tossing it into the fire before their chief in his dreadful blood-soaked great hall high in his terrible tower. The contents of this message will be so witheringly soul-destroying to the giants that they will leave the forest forever, and then we can think about burning it all down.'

'Hurray!' shouted almost everybody present.

Sorry unwisely decided now was the perfect moment to make a break for it. For the record, it was the phrase *dreadful blood-soaked great hall high in his terrible tower* that had broken him. He dashed for the window, screaming. Finding it bolted, its panes too small to squeeze through, he made for the door, past Moaris, who was standing with a huge mace and smiling. The door was suddenly blocked by Durth, who had a siege ladle full of battle sprouts in his hands and looked very, very cross. Durth looked over at the Wise Wench and smiled.

'Well done Durth, disciplined as ever, Noc smile upon you!'

Durth pushed Sorry back into the room and went out, shutting door after his thugs had followed him.

Sorry began to cry.

'Tomorrow,' continued the Wise Wench, grumpily, 'you will all set off for the giants' kingdom, enter their stronghold, meet their chief, and deliver the message. The forest will then be secure for all of us—well, most of us,' she said, patting Moaris on the back, 'to decide what to burn next. You, Moaris, must take care of the note until you, erm, until you find need to pass it on to someone else should any *accident* befall you, say, and you need to ensure its delivery. Any questions?'

'What's in the sack?' said Urgh.

'Magic. Your magic from your hovel. I took the liberty of gathering a few things together that will—sorry, might—prove useful.' She handed the sack over to Urgh, who gazed inside.

'What's that rolled up canvas for? It looks like a picture of a giant fox.'

The Wise Wench snatched it from the sack and scowled. 'How did that get in there? That's not for now. That's for later,' she said, and placed it behind her, carefully. 'I have one final...*condition*,' she added. 'This little troupe needs a feminine hand, a touch of grace, wisdom in case things go awry, so I would like my beloved familiar Lady Carline to accompany you as my—representative[24] in the field, so to speak.'

The monocled raven suddenly peered out of the rafters and bowed to the king.

Sorry started rolling around the floor, pounding his fists on his legs, using the logic that, if he was too injured to go, they wouldn't make him.

'We've had this conversation before,' whispered the king to the Wise Wench and glancing harshly at her. 'I'm not speaking to a

---

[24] Spy.

bird, and how did she get into my Moot House, anyway? I didn't invite her.' He paused. A moment of little noise but great import passed between them, eyebrows danced, something was decided. 'A pleasure to meet you again, Lady Carline. We are graced by your presence,' said the king and then scowled hatefully at the Wise Wench.

'I am ready whenever you wish, mistress. I'm all packed,' said Lady Carline. *There she goes again, talking without lips,* thought Sorry while bending his foot back until it almost began to hurt.

'Packed?' whispered Urgh dubiously under his breath.

'But isn't the Great Forest around the giants' land full of terrifying monsters, things with heads in their stomachs, deranged cattle, Wonkty Beasts that breathe syrupy fire, naughty woodwose, things so foul to behold that a goblin would eat his own feet rather than see them close up?!' asked Moaris.

'Yes,' said the Wise Wench, smiling. 'It is the haven of the Bogan, home of the Appalling Tog, and lair of the Terrible Dun Cow of Spot, as well as copious amounts of giants.'

'Great!' added Moaris and picked Sorry up. 'We have nothing to worry about, weedy fellow adventurer without shoulders. Tomorrow we shall march to glory!'

'Right then, time for me to talk,' said the king, regally. 'Now, since you're going to represent the village in an adventure, I'd like to know a bit more about you, you more-than-one in particular,' he said, staring at Sorry and Urgh. 'As far as I can make out, you are about the least qualified in the whole forest to go on an adventure and I don't doubt that I'll never see you again. You haven't even got any shoulders and quite clearly find everything petrifying. And you are very ugly. Well, what have you got to say for yourselves?' The king reddened as he spoke, what he was saying was so important he forgot to inhale and ended his speech out of breath, bright red, and staring at the still hanging Tongue, who smiled weakly back at him from the corner.

'You lads had better get some sleep now,' said the Wise Wench, ignoring him. 'You've got a good few days march ahead of you. Oh, and Moaris, if there's anything you want, you know any little thing that you would like to achieve in life and say, haven't done yet, then I should just go ahead and do it now, because you never know, do you? I mean, accidents do happen. But don't worry. Why worry, eh!' She put a consoling arm around him which he shrugged off.

Moaris continued to heft the mace in his hand and smiled blankly but aggressively, which isn't easy.

'Come on, king. Let's let these lads sleep,' she said to Stormgrunties, who wore a surprised look on his face as she led him out. 'Good night, Lady Carline,' she added as she left.

'If they start to snore, I'm off,' said a refined voice from the rafters. 'How I'll cope living with them for days I don't even want to begin to think about. Goblins have some horrible habits,' added the voice to no one in particular.

'But, Wise Wench,' stammered the king, 'what about the kettle? You didn't mention anything about that at all—'

Playfully, she put her hand over his mouth and led him away. 'Now you lads can lie flat out over by the—oh dear, I am sorry, Moaris. Come on, my lord.' They went out.

'Well, time for bed!' said Moaris, and fell on the floor, snoring aggressively.

The light from the fire was dying down, and Sorry and Urgh threw a few of the king's cushions on the floor before deciding it would be more fun to watch them burn, and tossed them into the flames instead. Then they felt lumpy and uncomfortable and wished they had some cushions to lie on. From somewhere above came tutting. Urgh seemed to be taking the business better than Sorry who was still sniffling but both sat uncomfortably in the gloom.

'I—' began Sorry.

'—BE QUIET AND SLEEP NOW!' shouted Moaris before falling asleep again.

The fire had almost died, its weak flames twisting feebly when Sorry woke Urgh. Nearby, Moaris lay as still as the grave in his deathly slumber, more resembling a huge bundle of blankets than a living creature. Quietly Sorry put a hand across his friend's mouth. 'It's me,' whispered Sorry.

'I know it's you,' whispered Urgh.

'Listen...he's asleep, now's our chance to escape.'

'Escape?'

'Yes, escape.'

'But what about the Wise Wench, the prophecy of Codly Darkarts, the giants...?' Urgh looked alarmed and leaned closer to his friend, who pinched him as hard as he could, which in truth was not much.

'Let someone else go to giant land and get disemboweled. Anyway, Moaris would still go by himself—in fact he'd prefer it that way because it's much more dangerous, so we'd be doing him a favor really.'

'But the Wise Wench said we should go—one-one-and-one stand and fall, remember?'

'How can I forget? I've thought of nothing but the 'and fall' bit since she told us. Now come on and let's go. We can be in Mumps by dawn.'

'I'm not going,' said Urgh.

'But we'll die,' whispered Sorry, heroically.

'She hasn't mentioned anything about dying. The Wise Wench has spoken, and that's all there is to it. The village needs saving. Besides, I want to be the hero. I'm fed up of being the joke.'

'I'll escape without you,' warned Sorry unconvincingly.

'I can't stop you going, but if you do, she's bound to have laid a trap for you and will just catch you again when you walk into it. If you come with us we'll share an adventure and come back heroes.'

Sorry took a step back. 'Not going to happen, I'm afraid. I'm too scared,' he said. He crept to the door, holding his breath as he turned the great handle. It gave and soon the door was open. A cool breeze greeted him as he ran out into the night air.

Not far away in the moonlight, the Wise Wench paced back and forth. The king stared anxiously. 'But it was totally different when you said it first,' he said, anxious to get the matter done and dusted, but nervous that things seemed to be amiss. 'Wasn't it?'

'You do try my patience,' she said, scowling at him. 'I'm scowling at you,' she added to be sure he'd noticed in the dark. 'I had to tell them something for the plan to work, and as I've explained many-many-and-lots-many times now, the plan is the same, more or less, as I told you earlier, and—' she paused and looked northwards '—he should just about be running into Moaris now,' she added and smiled. 'Now I'm smiling,' she said, by way of an explanation to the king.

Sorry was at a full pelt when he ran into the shape which he mistook for a tree.

'Running away is a very cowardly thing to do!' said the tree.

Odd that the tree sounds just like Moaris thought Sorry.

'And cowardly things must be punished, and punished very swiftly and very, very painfully!' said the tree again, doing an uncanny Moaris impression. 'Members of the court!' it said into thin air, 'the charge is treason, the penalty is death!'

'Death?' said Sorry to the Moaris-impersonating tree.

'However!' added the tree, 'in this case, owing to the timely warning and personal intervention of the Wise Wench, who told me you would try to escape tonight, I am advised, against my better judgement, to be lenient...' The tree stepped into the light and further enhanced its impression of Moaris by turning into an exact likeness of him. From nowhere, it produced the only barbed loofa Sorry had ever seen.

Screams echoed from the distance. 'Ah good, he's caught him then,' said the Wise Wench. 'Time for bed I feel,' she said and marched into the darkness.

'I'm still not happy with this whole thing,' mumbled the king, mightily.

The darkness sighed.

'I mean, the plan keeps changing and getting more confusing, at least to me. And those heroes you've chosen—they're just rubbish.

One's afraid of his own ghost and the other is just ridiculously ugly. What I really don't understand is why you keep fetching the weedy one without shoulders back into the affair. Just let me sentence him to a month with Petal the village crocodile and let's get on with it.'

'No, he has his own important part to play,' she said, and carried on walking away into the darkness.

'I could order it,' said the king into the dark, and then realized he was on his own.

In the cold morning light, Sorry could see the guards coming and going with bundles and boxes; they'd been at it for hours now, with Moaris barking orders at them. Sorry was still pretending to be asleep. It was safer that way, even though he was still sore. Urgh was nearby checking his potions and magic and bundles happily. *Git*, thought Sorry, unkindly, and whispered it to the Great Mole. The mole nodded in agreement. 'Ugly git,' it said, conspiratorially. They both giggled.

'Attention!' shouted Moaris into Urgh's ear. 'Ready for action, funny features?!' he asked him. Urgh nodded, nervously.

The door opened and the Wise Wench came in, looking oddly at the assembled military hardware before her. 'What is all this?' she said to Moaris.

'Weapons! That, for example,' he said, waving a finger vaguely in the direction of a barrel, 'is a barrel of caltrops. Very useful against galloping sheep!'

'But there aren't any galloping sheep in the adventure, Moaris,' sighed the Wise Wench.

'Yes, but if there *were* any, it would be handy to have them, and that is called military planning, my friend. So we'll take a barrel or more-than-one, just in case!' He walked on, pointing and smiling. 'That is a box of siege crossbows—you know, the ones with the barbed heads. I have cunningly added to their devastation by adding pink paint to the barbs so that they don't just kill and mutilate but also humiliate their victims with sissy color, heh, heh. There's many spears, lots-many-and-many swords, many-more-and-lots-many battle axes and I've even managed to get hold of a trebuchet, but the lads are having a job fixing it together! To be honest, they keep setting fire to it. I may have to leave it. Shame, really, as I'm sure it would come in handy.' Finally, Moaris moved to a particularly huge box and said, 'And THIS is the thing I *really* need!' He opened the box to reveal a gigantic cheese grater with papier-mâché' wings and painted with a grinning evil face. 'This,' he said, proudly, 'is my demonic siege grater. One look at this and the giants will start crying!' He stood back, legs slightly apart, and tore his shirt front open.

'Didn't your mother ever complain about the amount of sewing she had to do?' snapped the Wise Wench, irritably. 'Moaris, dear Moaris, you won't need all these weapons. This is supposed to be a peaceful mission, where we appeal to the giant's good nature.'

"Peaceful?!' grumbled Moaris.

'Good nature?' mumbled everyone else nearby.

'Well, quite peaceful, Moaris. Very peaceful for one of you— well, a little bit violent possibly, at one stage.'

'Which stage?!' shouted Moaris, angrily.

'Well, the violent stage, I can't elaborate any more lest the many-faced gods of fate are hiding in bushes nearby.'

'Or up the chimney?' added Urgh, helpfully.

'Very good, Urgh,' said the Wise Wench, 'you have been paying attention.'

Everyone looked around nervously, except Moaris.

There was a distant scream and an explosion.

The king walked in, resplendent in his alternate yellow and green stripy pants of royalty which dazzled his dull subjects. He also wore an orange tunic decorated with squirrel feet. He smiled as he took in the chaos. 'Well done, Moaris lad! Good to see you're going well prepared. Ah, I see you have my demonic siege grater. That should come in very handy, my lad.' The king smiled.

'No it won't,' said the Wise Wench.

'But surely he needs to take a few essentials—'

'No he doesn't,' added the Wise Wench curtly, and gave Sorry a tap in the ribs. 'You can stop pretending to be asleep now, Sorry. It's time to depart, so stop pretending you're superfluous.'

Moaris marched over to Sorry and picked him up by his nose hairs. Sorry gave a little squeak. 'Now, super flowery one, the Wise Wench wants us to get going, so let's get ready, and the next time I hear any cowardly talk about going home and baking I shall be forced to burn the village to the ground!' He finished with a roar and everyone except the Wise Wench winced. She just stood shaking her head. In the rafters, Lady Carline did exactly the same.

An hour later, Moaris had whittled his selection of weaponry down to a-few swords, an axe, a spear, a military rolling pin, more-than-one crossbows, some-and-many caltrops, one-lots-and-one knives, a net, some spiked clubs, one-and-one halberds, a barrel of tar, something spiky wrapped in a leather sack and a lifelike picture of the siege grater, courtesy of the Wise Wench. The little band of adventurers stood before her.

'Well, goodbye Moaris,' she said, tearfully. 'It was a pleasure knowing you. Take care of Urgh for me.' She scowled at Sorry. 'And don't forget, the message you deliver will bring peace at last between us and the giants. In time. Don't forget the prophecy.' She smiled and patted Urgh on the shoulder, 'Not that you will,' she added under her breath.

'Yes, good luck, scum,' said the king, leaning down from his high chair, 'and don't forget, you carry the honor and smells of the whole kingdom on your shoulders, even those of you who don't have shoulders at all. Bear it well, act with dignity, and make sure you bring back any dairy-related paraphernalia you may find in the dreadful tower where the giants dwell.'

Lady Carline suddenly swooped from the rafters with some sort of leathery sack tied about her midriff. She flew onto the Wise Wench's shoulders and they exchanged whispers. They both nodded and looked around at Urgh. 'Absolutely,' said the raven, earnestly.

'And send my regards to the LadyFloppsy,' added the Wise Wench, handing Urgh a much-reduced sack of magic. He took it merrily.

Everyone wondered who the LadyFloppsy was but didn't dare ask.

Durth opened the door for them with a smile, and as he did so a cheer rose from outside. The whole village was waiting to say farewell. The one-one-and-one heroes wandered into the happy crowd, all eager to say good riddance and wish them luck and happy uncontrollable bonfires. It was the first time Urgh had ever felt popular.

Eventually they passed through the smelly crowd and reached the edge of the village. Moaris drew Spike. Everyone ducked, a few slipped and twisted their ankles. One of them died as a result. Not because of the ankle, but because he later fell into the Poo-Pit and drowned. Moaris stood with his legs slightly apart and ripped his shirt slightly. 'We one-one-and-one,' he shouted, 'against all giants in the Great Forest!' To cheers from the villagers, Moaris roared. 'To death, glory, burning, bonfires made of small furry animals, and death!' The crowd cheered him some more. Lady Carline swooped by, shaking her head.

'He's a nutter and no mistake,' whispered the village sheep charmer. Everyone within whispering distance nodded in agreement.

With a final heroic and aggressive wave, Moaris led the little group away and into the forest. 'Well, that's the last we'll see of them,' added the sheep charmer as the villagers went back to work[25].

The king and the Wise Wench walked back towards the Moot House. 'Now,' said the Wise Wench leading the king away, 'back to the real plan.'

---

[25] That is to say, the gob-girls and wenches went back to work, the gob-boys went back to idle time-wasting, puerile games, and setting fire to things that didn't require too much effort to get to easily.

CHAPTER 5

The Wise Wench stood back as the tree fell with a mighty crash, Durth walked past with his axe. 'Well done, Durth,' she said. 'Now, get the stump out and lay that rail over there, you lot,' she shouted to the crowd of work goblins nearby. His Majesty appeared, being carried in his favorite palanquin, a huge bright red affair with lanterns on each corner and a gob-boy lashed to the top. 'King! Make way!' he shouted repeatedly.

'How goes construction of the rails, oh Wise Wench?' asked the king over the noise of digging, grunting, swearing, and warnings.

'Adequately, oh king,' she said, side-stepping suddenly and unexpectedly.

The king looked at her oddly for a moment and then, suddenly, a shower of shoveled earth shot over where she'd just been standing and directly into his seated lap. The workers carried on digging.

'I've been giving thought to an adviser to replace Kringe now he's, er, well, dead,' he said. 'I'm thinking of asking—'

The Wise Wench raised a hand, reached into her nether garments, and pulled out a very battered speakme bag. 'I'm far too busy to talk, right now,' she said, 'so I prepared this earlier to address Kringe's unexpected death by lightning.' She handed it to him.

He eyed it suspiciously, conscious of the fact that it might explode. It was battered and dirty. 'It's pretty old, isn't it?' he said to her back, noticing she was walking away. 'Boy,' shouted the king regally to the roof. 'Fire, immediately!'

The gob-boy scuttled down the palanquin like a monkey, while the sweaty regal bearers lay the palanquin down carefully and began to assemble a small pile of pinecones and twigs. 'You may proceed,' he added, as he noticed all was prepared. The gob-boy was lit and led towards the fire, where the embers soon crackled. The king tossed the bag onto him, aware of the Wise Wench's distant voice giving out instructions to the workers behind while the burning gob-boy dived into a puddle nearby.

A shadowy figure rippled into existence in the flames, slowly forming into a picture of the Wise Wench, her hair wrapped in rollers made from corn cobs. She grimaced at the king and said, 'you will find your new adviser in the hut with the yellow windows by the leaning beech furthest away from the Poo-Pit. Her name is Looti Lovelilips. She will be a very good adviser.'

The king laughed very heartily. 'Oh, very amusing, oh Wise Wench, quite droll, very funny. Now, who is to be my *real* new adviser? Do you have any real opinions?'

The vision scowled at him, pointedly.

'I was being serious,' she said, 'and watch out for the soil. Oh, sorry, that just happened didn't it. Now, don't forget to ask me for the speakme bag to be given to Urgh when I have been kidnapped by the Winged Ones when we go to the All-Goblin-Chief's Moot.'

'When will that happen?'

The image checked a knitted line of figures and noticed it had somehow got wrapped into another line. 'Oh, never mind,' she said, 'just forget I ever said that. That's another adventure. Not to worry.' She crossed her arms mysteriously and smiled. 'Oh, look, take the bag now, anyway. It'll help.'

The real Wise Wench suddenly appeared at the king's shoulder and handed him another bag from beneath her skirts. Below there, the king saw too-many-to-count similar bags. 'Thanks for the reminder,' said the Wise Wench to her image.

'You're welcome,' said the image.

Oh this is just ridiculous. I can't even bear one of them, certainly not one-more-than-one, thought the king.

'One-more-than-one heads are better than one,' said the Wise Wenches in unison.

No they aren't thought the king, silently. 'Looti who? This really is going too far,' said the king. 'I can't have some gob-wench advising me what to do, day in day out. Good burning heavens, can you imagine what the kingdom would be like if I let some old maid tell me what I should do and when I should do it? It needs a firm

77

ruler's touch. The place would be in chaos and Queen Quench would drown us all in boring, I'd wager!'

He suddenly stopped and realized what he was saying. 'I'll just go and meet her,' he added meekly and lashed his whip. His bearers resumed their positions, bit hard on their bridles, and made a highly unrealistic pretend neighing noise before rushing off in the direction of the village. The smoldering gob-boy climbed back on top. 'King! Make way!' he yelled in between whimpers.

'And don't disturb us for the next few days. We'll be too busy,' both Wise Wenches shouted after him and began laughing at some secret joke. The Wise Wench saluted the fading burning image of herself, which saluted back as it vanished. Then the real one turned to the task at hand.

The king, having heroically crossed the village, was lowered down by his bearers who stood respectfully back, wheezing. The cottage he found himself outside of was small and had yellow windows, fitting the description the Wise Wench had given. Coughing, he marched up to the door and gave it a solid 'king about to enter the cottage' knock.

There was a faint gurgled response from within which the king couldn't decipher, so, adjusting his trousers as regally as possible, he stepped in. Pigs, the room was full of pigs, and not just any old pigs; they were big pigs, most of which made towards Stormgrunties as soon as the door opened.

'I told you not to open the door until I'd put them in their harnesses!' yelled an extremely repellent looking gob-wench in the corner.

The king looked at her a bit closer, while being careful not to be stepped on by any of the escaping pigs[26]. She was, to put it plainly, very repulsive. The king thought that at first it was the extra eyes that made him think that, but later, after careful consideration, and quite a few unflattering and rather talentless drawings he did of her,

---

[26] And thus risk the wrath of Barneyes, Demigod of Escaping Pigs and Freedom-Pursuant Poultry.

decided it wasn't just that, it was the warts—there were a lot of them, and some of them had hairs.

Those and the hump.

And the beard. It most definitely had a beard.

And the horn.

In fact, taking into account the eyes, the warts, hump, beard, and horn, the fact that she had huge, huge ears was almost a flattering bonus. They were so big that they detracted from all the other things.

'Hello, gorgeous!' she said and winked at him.

His Majesty located a chair and sat down, frowned, and looked up again. She was still there. 'You're not Looti Lovelilips by any chance, are you?' he said, and bit his lip, which began to bleed profusely. His Majesty had always been quite a bleeder. He once bled for many's-the-many-and-one-more days when a really vicious ferret had cornered him in a barn. He'd banned anyone from keeping ferrets after that, although he did privately suspect Jed the Secret Ferret-Keeper of having one on the sly.

'Goodness no, Your Luscious Majesticness. I'm Mummy Lovelilips. My daughter's out worrying and oiling the hog at the moment.'

'Well, thank Noc, Bagflaps the Mighty, and the Not-Quite-So-Terrible Tantle for that!' exclaimed the king, who sighed in relief. 'No offence,' he added. The last of the pigs got out and the sound of frightened excitement came from somewhere beyond.

Mummy Lovelilips took a few steps closer and looked seductively at the king who was very, very concerned that she was somehow making a slurping sound and that he couldn't quite determine how. 'Will I do instead?' she said and smiled. Well, she probably smiled—the king wasn't quite sure as her tusks covered the corners of her mouth.

'Oh goodness me, no!' he said rather tetchily and saw that he'd offended her. 'Please put down the pitchfork and let me explain,' he added, hastily. She did so, and then slurped her way across to a very old and gnarled rocking chair, the slurping noise reaching a crescendo before suddenly halting.

The king stood. 'You see, Mummy, I'm in need of a new adviser.' From somewhere outside a scream wrenched the air followed by cheers and the sound of flapping.

'Now,' he continued, importantly, 'as all you pathetic underlings know, I am a goblin who likes to move with the times, a goblin of vision who thinks nothing of taking bold steps into new directions. I am a great leader, fearless in all matters. One who delights in rewarding great insight and knowledge in whoever or whatever I behold, whether they be a mighty warrior or a not so mighty fruit herder. Some might say a massive visionary, a king whose legend will live on beyond the funeral fondue. 'What a great and mighty lord he was,' they will still be saying in many-many-and-one-more-many gob summers' time, and they will wonder what things I said and did. Indeed they will *long* to know it. And that is why, Mummy, I am here; here in your pig-bereft hovel with its crude drawings of lusty farm hands aggressively shaving sheep, to take one of those bold steps I mentioned, bold steps I take all the time. I am here, in short, Mummy, to offer your daughter the position of adviser!'

'Oh yes, the Wise Wench said you'd be along this morning.'

The king seethed quietly while Mummy Lovelilips continued. 'But she's had to go out. The hog's been being an absolute swine lately. He needs a very, very thorough worrying. She could be a good one-more-than-one hours. Would you like to wait?' She stood up again and there, from somewhere, was that slurp.

His Majesty backed towards the door. 'Oh no, no hurry. Tell her to come along when she's finished. Bye now,' he added and turned, fell under a monstrous pig and crawled away into the sunlight.

The Wise Wench inspected Durth's handiwork. It seemed to be in order, but then *seemed* wasn't enough; it had to be perfect. Everything had to be perfect for *the plan* to succeed. She kicked the rail as hard as she could. It gave a metallic clang and everyone applauded. Durth stood back and smiled. 'We'll soon be able to see the village, oh Wise Wench,' he said, and, sheep-like, everyone followed his stare south, beyond the trees towards the distant smoke of the village fires.

A sheep ran by.

The Wise Wench scowled and pulled out her daisy chain of knitted figures, counting them off one by more-than-one. 'Captured, yes; struck by lightning, yes; meets Mummy Lovelilips, yes; attacked by the— hmmmm, not yet; squashed to a pancake, no; head off for the Atrocious Meadows, no.' She frowned, looked confused for a moment and then after seeing a worm struggling about on the ground seemed to regain her composure. She held up a knitted worm with a goblin with a bald head falling over it. 'See worm on ground that trips Durth up and knocks him out,' she said, 'so that makes us about quite-a-bit of the way through. Okay Durth, start building your tracks this way now. I'll go back to the kettle hut and make sure the iron is good and ready.' She indicated the direction for Durth to carry on and marched very purposefully back towards her cottage.

Durth tried to forget that the knitted goblin was bald, looked down at the worm and across at his fellow thugs. 'Knocked out by a worm, eh?' he said and laughed. Turning suddenly to grin broadly at his thugs, he then tripped, fell over, and knocked himself out.

The Wise Wench smiled as she heard the crash and laughter, and secretly congratulated herself on the way the plan was going. She began to hum a little rhyme about ferret-folk as she strode off into the wood.

Many-but-not-too-many minutes later, she arrived back at the Kettle Hut, a huge timber structure which was a mass of noise, activity, goblin-sweat and swearing. She marched past the gob-girls and in between the huge braziers and forges which had so recently been built under her baleful stare.

Master Whippet was bare to the waist and sweating profusely. It was hard work, and even though the future of the whole forest rested on his expertise (subject to instruction from the Wise Wench, of course) this did not make the work any easier. That and the fact that the average goblin knew as much about metal as it did about juggling ferrets. Indeed, they often knew more about juggling ferrets and had the scars to prove it. Plus there was the need to motivate goblins to work—the reason why gob-girls and wenches had been chosen. Whippet was a fine figure of a goblin considering his age, which was nearly many-many gobsummers now. His arms were thick and hairy, and his grinning mouth, being a good foot across, would have been enough to trap the prettiest of young gob-girls in summers gone by.

'Ah, Master Whippet!' shouted the Wise Wench over the throng, and walked next to him. She was smiling, and that usually meant bad news for the village smithy, or indeed anyone. He'd learnt over the past few months that seeing any of her teeth (not that there were that many left) always indicated trouble for him.

'The plan is progressing nicely,' she said. 'Once Durth regains consciousness, he'll start turning the tracks for the final leg of the journey to the village. In fact, his annoyance at being knocked out by a worm will make him demand more work than ever. The tracks will enable our dragon to build up enough speed to roll into the village when the time comes. But,' she smiled a little broader, 'I need you to build me one of these!' She unfurled a huge drawing of what appeared to be an enormous hamster made of metal. 'And I need it now!'

Whippet stared at it, sucked his teeth, then stared at it a little more.

'Can't be done,' he said.

'Can.'

'Can't.'

'Can.'

'Can't.'

'Can.'

'Can't.'

'Can.'

'Can't.'

'Can.'

'Can't.'

'Can.'

'Can't.'

'Can.'

'Can't.'

'Can.'

'Can't.'

'If I said *please* would it help?' the Wise Wench grinned at Whippet.

'We can't do everything at once.' He stared at her smile and added, 'hang on a minute. You know this gets done anyway, don't you?'

She smiled enigmatically at him.

He sighed. 'Alright. If I'm bound to do it anyway, I'll do it. You can't fight destiny.'

'You're right, which is why I like you, Master Whippet, and why the gods preordained exactly the right person to inevitably do the task and complete it successfully exactly when you need to, and fate commands and ensures that you do.'

'Hang on. What happens if I have an accident?' Whippet wiped sweat from his considerable brow.

'You don't,' she said.

Whippet picked up a gnarly stick ending in a metal point and held it to his hand, 'And what happens if I plunge this into my hand and can't work anymore.'

'It'll hurt.'

'Well, I wish you'd said about the hamster before. You said you just wanted the rails and the great dragon kettle—which is enough of a job in itself, particularly with your exacting deadlines. Where does the hamster come into it?'

'Bluff,' she said and took him by the hand, leading him towards the huge metal kettle which dominated the room.

The kettle was enormous; a great iron beast fully more-than-one-and-some goblins high, it had the skeleton of a huge head that had a few scaly plates hammered to it. A gob-girl poked her head out of its mighty spout and gave it a loving rub. Other gob-girls and wenches were hard at work on the mean and higher platforms, carefully following the Wise Wench's intricate drawings she had spent the last year perfecting with, she said, the aid of Tullula,

Mistress of All Things Related to Kettles and Teapots[27]. She mounted the ladder and came up to the lower platform, a bramble of glistening pipes and strange dials none of the other goblins could comprehend, winding their way in and out according to design. Carefully, she moved a dial and noted down something that seemed important. She opened the kettle's stomach and gazed into the huge blackened space where a few gob-girls worked away, playing echo games whenever they were alone. Then she pulled a lever and the mouth clanged open and shut, giving a kind of wheeze as though something was missing.

'You are doing a good job, Master Whippet,' she said. 'The gods chose you well. No other goblin within too-many-too-count miles could have done it.'

'The gods chose ME, oh Wise Wench!' shouted Whippet above the clatter of iron and the noise of hammering. He stood back looking amazed.

'Yes, personally chosen by someone VERY HIGH UP,' she said and looked upwards suitably reverently. 'In fact, between you and me, you couldn't have been recommended much more highly,' she whispered and winked at him.

Whippet took his flat cap off. 'Noc?' he said, with a look of awe on his face.

'Higher even than he,' she added and left it at that.

They proceeded up to the one-after-one level, a level so high[28] that only the bravest of goblin workers, or those lucky enough to have wings, would toil at. Here, the whole hut stretched out, the goblins toiling away below like lots of slightly smaller goblins a short but terrible distance below, toiling away at something very important. Whippet breathlessly joined her. 'If it wasn't for you and how important this is, I doubt I'd have the courage to work at this dizzy eyrie!' he shouted, clinging onto the kettle and staring down at the

---

[27] Another fabrication by the Wise Wench. There is no god of kettles and teapots. That would be silly.

[28] Amongst many other fears, heights are something many goblins fear. Well, not so much heights as falling them.

84

dizzy depths below, nearly half the height of a young sapling it seemed, maybe more. Perhaps one, maybe even more-than-one cows' high.

'Don't worry, you won't fall,' she said. 'I have it on the highest authority,' and she winked again. He began laughing.

There was just the one control here, a huge red button. She looked at him mysteriously. 'No, I won't tell you, but it's far from finished yet; grand though it is. Just don't press the button until I say so. We need some milk to go with our tea for this dragon kettle!'

'It is grand and no mistake. The greatest kettle ever made as you so rightly said to me at the start,' said Whippet as he admired the machine. 'Let's just hope it works, whatever it is for—'

'Oh it works,' she added and gave it a loving rub. 'But keep up! We have many days' work ahead and time is short!' The Wise Wench headed down and out, a gappy smile on her face. Then she went dizzy and everything suddenly changed.

She was in familiar territory now, she knew these woods well, for this was the Old Bit, deepest and most ancient part of the Great Forest. She had been here many, many times before to receive the instructions of the gods. Slowly, the Wise Wench picked her way through the barbed briars that were so profuse here in the divine realm. She walked as quietly as she could, for here, in this ancient land, dwelt not only the great and good, but also the vicious and the bad; beasts so foul that even she feared to meet them. Beasts such as the terrible Bean-Nighie[29] and the appalling washer-woman of the Great Forest, whose washboard was misery and whose scouring brush was doom.

The tangled roots looming before her were immense. She had to clamber up and through their snarled vastness. She smiled as she finally came into the clearing beneath the Great Oak. Here, sunlight filtered endlessly through the canopy and illuminated the clearing before the mighty tree, greatest in the forest, and home of the gods.

---

[29] As opposed to the bean-nightie, a rarely used wedding-night garment aimed at goblins who entered wedded bliss with an appetite.

The Great Oak was an awesome sight, a tree that passed beyond mortal vision in height and breadth, its boughs as vast and ancient as a huge, ancient gnarly tree celebrated in legends should be. She bowed, reverently.

'Who calls me from my mortal, if slightly predictable, domain?' she shouted up into the branches. Her words echoed and returned, only in a slightly different language; the words teased into strange and obtuse references.

'I DO!' said a commanding voice from high, high above.

The Wise Wench stared upwards but could see only ancient boughs, gnarled through the eternity of growth and carved occasionally with the names of certain naughty gods, and gods who loved each other very much and wished everyone else to know about it.

'And who are you, my lord?' she answered.

'Tis I, Lord Noc!' came the reply, and, slowly, the Wise Wench became aware of a rather unpleasant—yet friendly—smell, the odor of the Prince of Pongs himself. He came scurrying down the tree, a rather blackened creature with wild hair, which blew about him ceaselessly. From some angles, he appeared as a goblin, yet from others, his twisty turny form was impossible to determine. The air was never still near him; always some faint little eddying breeze or some tiny unexpected nidorous gust shrouded him. He wore a huge cloak of many colors, which always curled and flapped about as if it had a mind of its own.[30] His boots were enormous and black, and gave forth a strange squeak and powerful leathery smell, while his staff, which he relied upon to give him balance within his ever-present cloak of wind, was of gnarled, ancient wood, and feral smelling.

'Why have you called me here?' she said, ensuring to take a good few paces back lest Noc was in a wrathful mood.

'Fear not,' he said in his rasping voice, 'for I have brought you here to warn you. My children have unexpectedly escaped and will menace your brave adventurers!'

---

[30] This was because he wore Flappy, the Cloak Which Has a Mind of Its Own.

86

'But you said there wouldn't be any trouble until the giants' keep, apart from the meeting with rabbits and ferrets!' she shouted, very much offended by this unrehearsed change of plan. 'How am I supposed to gain their respect if you go about changing the plan halfway through? We agreed that they would get to the keep safely, deliver the message and escape—well, most of them would. Can it be that times are so dark that the gods themselves cheat and change plans? I can hardly believe that Lord Noc, who once laid low the very oak we are standing by with a particularly venomous silent one, would stoop so low as to pettifogging, diddling, and flimflamming! Shall we change your name to Lord Flimflam Man?' The Wise Wench stepped back and wrung her hands furiously.

'Durst thou dare to call I, Flimflam Man, mortal?!' roared Lord Noc, windily.

'Aye, I durst say it! And, more, I call thee yarner, prevaricator, and perjurer!' She was furious now, and determined to speak her mind, no matter what the cost.

Noc stood back and laughed. 'Perjurer?' he said dubiously.

'So, now you mock me!' she shouted. 'I am but the plaything of the gods and ever do they deceive me. They have barely metaphorically unwrapped me and yet already they tire of their game and seek other diversions. Am I to be the broken rocking-horse of the gods? Is my saddle disdain and my mane mockery? Do the gods see my bridle and call it folly? Do they observe my poorly-painted eyes and say that they are blind?'

'Stay yourself from your obtuse self-pity, oh Wise Wench,' said Noc, benevolently. 'The gods chose you well and do not seek to deceive. If you will calm yourself and have a cup of cocoa with me, I shall explain.'

The Wise Wench looked angry but realized that, to anger Noc unnecessarily, would risk smell-related danger. And anyway she did like the Cocoa of the Gods.

Soon she was sat amongst the roots of the Great Oak sipping cocoa with the Lord of Smells. The Cocoa of the Gods was a heady chocolatey brew and one for which, as Lord Noc knew, she had a weak spot.

That and beetle cake.

'It's like this,' said Noc, producing a huge cake brimming with juicy beetles from nowhere and offering the Wise Wench a very generous slice with godlike benevolence. 'The gods have had a bit of a problem with Queen Quench.'

'Ah, Queen Quench, the Moist One. Queen of Boring, the Extinguisher of Bonfires, Bringer of Black, Lady Funless, Madam Dull-and-Damp, Mistress Tedium, the Insipid Crown Princess of Dreary, the Bore,' said the Wise Wench, slowly beginning to understand.

'The same. As you know, she is the naughtiest of the gods, and oftentimes comes to the mortal forest to do bad things in the land of mortals. Her aim is to end all fun and fire! I'm afraid she's been naughty again. It seems that she has had something to do with your young friend Urgh. What she's done, exactly, we are still trying to find out, but we suspect that it could be very mischievous indeed.' Noc raised an eyebrow. There was a noise. 'And on my return from tiffin with the gods yesterday evening, I went to my mystic, godly farmyard to inspect my little pets and found that the pigs had gone. Someone—or some*thing*—had left the gate open!'

'Not the hogs!' said the Wise Wench, nervously.

'The same! But do not worry, I have a smell-related plan to rescue them,' he said, pressing a tiny phial into her hands.

'She just looked up, smiled, and fainted,' said Master Whippet, as he cradled the Wise Wench in his arms.

All the other workers looked on with concern on their faces; the death of the Wise Wench would be a grievous loss and might even—gods forbid—cause them some personal pain or trouble.

'Is she dead?' said a bright orange gob-wench, her hammer drooping in her sweaty palm.

'I'm not sure,' said Whippet, mirthlessly.

Durth Dimbits marched in, rubbed his head and scowled at the crowd around the Wise Wench. 'OK, stand back now, nothing to see here!' He pushed the workers back and, peering at the Wise Wench, he smiled. 'Oh, I see. Well, don't worry, she's just having one of her visions. By the smell of her, its Lord Noc she's visiting. Just wrap her up warm and put her in the corner so no one trips over her, and, while you're at it, GET BACK TO WORK OR I'LL HAVE YOU ALL KILLED! WORKWORKWORK! He roared and began throwing hammers, nails, and wire brushes at everyone who didn't seem to be doing enough fast enough for his liking.

The goblins began to get back to work on the great kettle, and soon the hall was a din of hammering, grating, singing, and cursing.

'Hold it up higher!' shouted the king.

His bearers lifted the mirror up higher.

'That's better. Now I can see behind me more clearly. I tell you all that that is positively the last time ever that she gets one over on me. Hiring her minions to set fire to me to make me look an idiot, ensuring her predictions come true by means of subjugation, deceit, and tartuffery?' He looked down at the little group of goblins that were normally his bearers and whom he had temporarily promoted to the positions of assistant mirror holder (one-after-the-first class) for which, he had assured them, they would be handsomely rewarded, then promptly forgotten about. The king continued to stare at himself regally, sure that, with no one to disagree to his thoughts, he was the most handsome goblin in the forest. His eyes halted on Tongue, who smiled limply from his hanging place nearby. The little goblin's tongue flashed out and swallowed a daddy-long-legs that had danced its way too close.

There was a stifled knock at the door.

'Open the door, come in, and tell me what you want,' said the king, royally, as he adjusted his red neckerchief of office, regally adorned with heraldic pictures of bantams rampant.

In walked the most beautiful gob-wench the king had ever set eyes on. She was lovely. Her hair was thick and bristly and cascaded around her perfectly circular face. Her double chins created a frame of exquisiteness about her smiling mouth with its impossible number of pointed fangs. And slender tusks. She had tusks—and neatly polished too. Her nose was barely visible beyond two small snotty slits. And her warts, her warts were attraction personified, clustered as they were about her wide, ample eyes. She wore a pond-weed green dress, into which were sewn the claws of many dead chickens, to protect her from the unwanted attentions of Barnvelder—the Cockerel That Preferred the Company of Women.

She curtsied, her blotchy skin glistening perfectly in the light. Her eyes glanced at the king and rested on his key. Then she smiled up at him.

'Wwwwwwww—' said King Stormgrunties, powerfully.

She glanced up at him, questioningly.

'Gruufffhdggg?' he added, by way of regal extrapolation.

'Looti Lovelilips, Your Majesty,' she said, and curtsied again.

'Llllllllooo—'

'—Yes, please my Lord.'

'Wwwwhhhlll?' he added, leaning forward, dangerously.

'Oh yes, Your Clarity!' she said and smiled, backing away rather swiftly, her smile turning to horror as the king pitched forward too far in his chair and began to descend.

'His Majesty is falling!' shouted one of the temporarily promoted assistant mirror holders (one-after-the-first class). 'Fetch the catchers immediately!' he added at a shout. They all looked at each other.

There was a crash and all went black for the king.

'Are you feeling better, my lord?' asked Looti. It was a little later, or was it? The king eyed the room suspiciously but regally.

She was still there, now mopping his brow while around him anxious figures wrung their hands nervously. 'Yes, thank you,' said the king, majestically. He stood up and looked around. The temporarily promoted mirror holders held the mirror up so he could inspect his royal head for any regal damage.

'No harm done, I trust, Your Plummetness?' inquired one of the bearers as he helped the king back up into his somewhat damaged high chair. The king carefully placed his royal bottom on his royal cushion. What a fine figure of a goblin, they all thought. How broad and flat his nose is, how numerous his regal chins, and how warty his royal warts. He smiled at everyone.

'Now!' he said, and took the moment to adjust his regal nether wear. 'I first make a royal decree this day, that Looti Lovelilips shall be my new advisor, and that from this day she shall be known as My Lady Looti the Advisor, keeper of the Stoat Hat, and mistress of the Great Mole.' He smiled and his hands fell to idly caressing the handles on his high chair. Everyone stared in awe at their king. 'Assuming you have no objections, my lady,' he finished with a smile and a rather un-regal giggle.

'No, Your Vastness!' she said, and smiled back.

'And for my one-after-the-first proclamation,' he said, regally, 'all the royal catchers are dismissed. See to it that they are set to expanding the Poo-Pit day and night.' He dusted himself down and smiled at Looti. 'Right,' he said, 'well, now that's settled, you had best go and meet the Wise Wench so that she can tell you what I'm doing this week.'

The collection of goblins wandered about for a while uncertain of what to do, then began arresting each other.

'No need, Your Hugeness,' she said happily, 'I met the Wise Wench more-than-one weeks ago last Thodsday, and she took me through all the important items. Now, let me see,' she slowly ran a finger, a very long, very pointy finger, across her thin lips. 'Ah yes, now. Firstly, we should give Kringe a regal burial.'

The goblins below began fighting.

'*Regal* burial?'

'Yes, Your Effectiveness. A regal burial.'

'No, don't like that. Regal burials are for regal folk, like me. He was just scum.'

'Well, that's a shame, Your Correctness. He was, after all, your adviser, and as such he was in your company at all times. Of course, Your Grace is so handsome and regal that a small amount of your own vast royalty must, in time, have rubbed off on him. As such, he does deserve a royal burial, in my opinion. However, if you think Your Massive Mightiness didn't rub off on him...?'

'—Well, yes now, since you put it that way, and since, as my advisor, you advise me to do it, and, of course, as a—what did you say?'

'Which bit?'

'The mightiness thing.'

'Oh, Your Massive Mightiness.'

'Yes, Massive Mightiness. I like that, and I'd like it added to my titles. See to it.'

'I've already taken the liberty of doing so, Your Toweringness.' She smiled very delightfully and cleared her throat. 'The King Stormgrunties' she said, very clearly, 'the many-many-and-lots-after-more-than-many-dead-King Stormgrunties-after-the-first; king of the Great Forest; be-keeper and guardian of the Great Mole; holder of Gwordoomdoomdoomdoomdoom, the Mop of the Dreaded Magpie People; ruler absolute of the Kingdom of Mudge, Spray, and Tottle-by-the-Mire; keeper of the Stoat Hat of Justice; Arch-magicmaster supreme; His Cunningtude Grace, the Honor of Tunt, slayer of Lucy Carter and her puppy Snuffles, *and His Massive Mightiness.*'

The king sat back and smiled. Then his smile turned to a frown. 'Hang on,' he said, 'wasn't there a bit about the Wise Wench having to obey me in the old title?'

'Well, yes lord, but the Wise Wench said it would be dangerous for it to stay in.'

'Dangerous, why?'

'She didn't say, but she did say it would be very dangerous.' Looti looked convinced she was right.

'Well, we'll see about that. Send for her,' he said, aggressively.

'Yes?' said the Wise Wench as she marched into the room.

It was a bit later. The king had a headache. He sighed; they were both still talking away. Different though they were, they were too similar for his liking, even if Looti was lovely in her loveliness. The fighting below had concluded with a draw and the goblins patted and bound their wounds. *Good, they've finally stopped,* he thought, and stared about the Moot House, bored. *Maybe I should organize a hunt? I wonder if we can get a hold of any kittens? They're pretty easy to catch.*

'Well?' said the Wise Wench.

'Well, what?' said the king, absentmindedly.

'Do you accept my advice, and that of your lovely new adviser, or are you still a fathead?'

'*King* Fathead,' rebuked the king, royally.

'Good. So that's an end to it,' said the Wise Wench.

'But.'

'No.'

'B—' said the king.

'—no, and that's it! No more arguments!' The Wise Wench moved over to the fire, threw a large log on it, and raised her skirts to let the warmth seep into her posterior. Sparks flew. The king seethed quietly and wondered if he could get away with making a special royal decree that exempted the advice of the Wise Wench and made her subject to his direct rule. *And* made her wear a big hat with a gob-boy strapped atop who shouted the word 'wrong' all night and day. He harrumphed.

The Wise Wench smiled. 'No. And besides, great king,' she said, 'there are much more important things to think about than hats.'

'More important than me, the king of the forest?!' snapped the king, kingishly.

'Yes.'

'Oh.' The king looked flummoxed.

'Even more important than you.' She continued. 'I've been talking to *them* this morning.' The Wise Wench stood back away from the fireplace where she could be sure she looked her most shadowy and sinister.

'Oh,' gulped the king, and his hand fell to caressing his brow.

'Excuse me, but who do you mean when you refer to *them*?' asked Looti in her quietest voice.

'Pardon?' shouted the king.

'Er, who are *THEM*?' she repeated, louder this time.

'The gods! The gods themselves!' said the Wise Wench, and stepped forward. 'It seems we have a problem.'

'We?' said the king, skeptically.

'Well, you,' she added, by way of clarification.

'Me?'

'Well, not you specifically, Your Weightiness—'

Weightiness! I like that. Or does she mean...

'—more specifically, *them.*'

'Them?'

'The one-more-than-one returning heroes.'

'*One-more-than-one* returning heroes? You haven't mentioned that before. So, one dies then?'

The Wise Wench bit her lip, looked slightly sheepish and gave a giggle. Everyone stood back alarmed and gazed at the ceiling, confident that the sky was about to crash through it at any moment. For the Wise Wench to trip herself up, however slightly, must mean a grave situation indeed. The king looked ruffled and began fiercely rubbing his chair arms while muttering the old goblin lullaby,

'little baby eat your many worms one-and-one-more-than-many,

and go then quickly to your bed,

or the sky will tumble down upon your head.

Burn, burn, burn it, oh!'

'Yes, alright then. One-more-than-one returning heroes. But I'm not going to tell you *which* one doesn't come back to lend their return an air of suspense. In any case, it seems that they may return to the village with an unexpected retinue. Well, being very closely chased, actually. Being chased by *our problem.*'

'Ah, I see,' said the king, calming himself somewhat by finishing his lullaby and ignoring everything she said.

'Our problem. Yes, quite,' said another goblin nearby, indicative of the lack of deep-thinking in most goblins.

'Our problem,' said the gathered goblins, smiling blankly and nodding.

The Wise Wench waited for it all to sink in and took one-one-and-one very precise steps back. She signaled for Looti to do the same. Everyone else looked on vacantly.

94

Problem, what problem. Oh problem, being chased, chased by our problem, I see. The king's thought danced about inside his head with the imaginary milkmaids that always danced there. *What problem? The lack of a good bonfire? The difficulty in getting a juicy slug? We don't have any flippin' problem.* Then the magic happened and the thoughts coalesced inside his head and into a conclusion. Suddenly the king stood up in his chair. 'YOU'RE TALKING ABOUT THEM COMING HERE BEING CHASED BY GIANTS!' he screamed. 'You're talking about *GIANTS!* GIANTS coming to the village! We shall all be KILLED! Call out the funeral masters! Make me my fondue pyre! Call the mourners! We are all going to die!' And he rode his chair as if it were a deranged bullock intent on escape through the nearest door.

There was a moment of calm as he realized that he was falling again.

'GIANTS! We're all going to DIE!' wailed the other goblins, as they ran for the exits.

'And you need to hire some more royal catchers,' said the Wise Wench, as the king crashed down right where they had been standing a few moments before.

CHAPTER 6

They travelled all day through the forest, which became ever denser as they headed on. Not far from the village, the devastation[31] caused by the goblins petered out and the Great Forest's undisturbed and unburnt undergrowth began to pull at them—brambles tearing at their skin, roots tripping them, branches slapping them. Sorry got tired of getting scratched and began to suspect that Moaris was deliberately bending branches back as he moved past them so they would thwack him. He didn't dare complain to anyone except the Great Mole in private, however. Urgh kept his thoughts to himself, while Moaris gave vent to all of his plans for military supremacy over the giants, schemes to enslave the giant race once peace had been established by killing them all, his messiest killings, and how he was going to rebuild Miffed Tower in the shape of a giant barbed tortoise.

They halted in the bowl of a great sycamore tree which looked to be many years old. From somewhere up in the branches came the sound of refined flapping. Moaris carefully laid out his weapons in areas where they could be reached in case of ambush, while Sorry and Urgh lit a fire for no reason whatsoever, and began to kill some snacks.

'Er, hello up there!' shouted Urgh to the branches. 'Would you like something to eat? I've got a few juicy worms.'

'I do not eat worms,' said Lady Carline, haughtily from somewhere up above. 'But thank you anyway. Does he never shut up?'

'Who?'

'This life suits me!' said Moaris, while casually removing a ring of bark from the sycamore. 'The outdoors, adventure, being heroic and amazingly tough; that sort of thing! That should kill it!' he added smiling, and admiring his handiwork on the venerable old tree

---

[31] Fun.

before sitting by the fire. 'Now, to stories. You, ugly, what's the biggest thing you've ever killed?'

They both looked at Moaris until it was obvious he was referring to Urgh. 'I once blew up a badger,' said Urgh, hopefully.

'How?' said Moaris, sharpening a stick.

'By using magic. Look, here,' he said, trying to get Moaris's attention while rummaging some of his magic totems from his pockets and sack. 'This is a magic egg that makes smells that can drive enemies away, and this is a vanishing bag made from a cow's udder—once tossed into the air, it'll make you disappear. Ow!'

Moaris smiled as he pulled the point from Urgh's leg. 'Yes, very interesting, I'm sure. You! What about you?' Moaris stared at Sorry, angrily.

Sorry hadn't really killed anything of note and so began to blubber a little, afraid of what Moaris would do to him. 'He's killed a storm-hedgehog,' said Urgh, helpfully, 'and a pair of Thrunkers,' he added, before averting his eyes so that Moaris couldn't tell he was lying.

Sorry wondered what a storm-hedgehog was.

'Has he, by Thruppnin?! Not bad, not bad at all, especially for someone who—were I to be king—would be compelled to stay tied up in a bag all the time. Now, let me tell you what I've killed!' Moaris began his list with gusto.

Somewhere in the branches above, a bird took wing.

Urgh became lost in thought. What had the Wise Wench meant about 'his destiny?' Why did she keep apologizing to Moaris all the time? She never apologized to anyone.

'—one-one-and-one slay-squirrels, many-lots-and-one fell-goats, lots-lots-and-lots-again pilklys, more-than-one old woe-pilchards—' Moaris seemed to be able to carry on talking without taking a breath.

It was a complex web that the Wise Wench had crocheted, and no mistake, but Urgh couldn't help wondering about that huge kettle-like object which seemed to run on those rails. What was that all about?

'—the Legendary Sheep of Dung Sprightily, oh, many-lots-the-many hooded crap-starlings, lots-and-one bulls, many-lots-and-many-lots—'

It didn't make sense, but whatever the Wise Wench said was true, so it must be right. Urgh eyed the speakme bag dangling from Moaris's belt, just between Spike, the bag of caltrops, and his battle rolling-pin. What mighty speech must it say to make the giants wish for peace? What subtle machinations must she have intoned to get them to change so wholeheartedly?

'—Now, the vegetable kingdom. Too-many-to-count tulips, many's-the-many sprouts, some oaks, many-more-than-lots—'

Urgh couldn't work it out; he would just have to trust the Wise Wench. After all, she said he was a hero—or at least was going to be. When would that happen? He'd never been a hero. His magic was useful; it stopped others wanting to hit him, certainly. Perhaps that was it? In the background, Moaris seemed to be running out of breath. He was finding he quite admired Moaris, even though he was horribly violent. He was brave and—

Moaris momentarily stunned him with a strike from the flat of his axe. 'You will pay attention when I'm educating you, wrong-features!' he shouted, and began kicking burning brands from the fire at Urgh and Sorry. They rolled into tight balls and pleaded for mercy. 'Sissies!' he screamed into the night. 'I've got sissies for company. Right, I thought I'd have this kind of trouble and luckily I'm very prepared for it!'

His companions looked very worried.

He marched off to his heavy pack and began to rummage aggressively. 'Now get these on!' shouted Moaris, flinging a pair of brightly colored smocks at his companions. 'I just knew I was being too reasonable with the pair of you! Well, I've been soft up to now, but from this moment on, things are going to get TOUGH! Now get those on and I don't want to hear another squeak out of either of you for the rest of the adventure. You will speak when spoken to, or you may raise your hand and I may speak to you if I have time and inclination. You will not answer back, however. If you do answer back, I will be quite unpleasant. Do you understand?'

They looked at the floor and began putting on their new clothes, noticing one was decorated with tulips and the other daisies.

'Tulip!' said Moaris, from ahead of Sorry and Urgh. It was later, and they had been marching for a very long time without rest. They were covered in scratches and bites, mostly from Moaris.

'Am I Tulip or are you?' whispered Sorry, nervously.

'TULIP!' shouted Moaris, impatiently.

Urgh trotted off towards the knoll that their leader was stood on. He had laid his weapons out in a neat line in case of imminent attack. As Urgh reached the hilltop, gasping, he realized why Moaris had stopped. Here, there was a break in the forest and the land ahead could be seen. A broad river cut a swathe through the trees and made a majestic curve ahead. Moaris had unfurled a great big map covered in strange pictures—mostly of things lurking in the area ahead that had lots of heads and teeth. 'Now!' he said, noisily. 'According to the map, that is the Gashy River. We must avoid crossing it at all costs, so I intend to cut through Tulgy Wood here, to the east!'

'Tttttulgy Wood?' whimpered Urgh.

'Yes, Tulip, Tulgy Wood! Home to the dreaded Magenta Death of Tulgy Wood, pointy-toothed eater of goblins, swallower of pigs, and devourer of fire. Now, go and get Daisy, and set up camp. I've decided we'll spend the night here and push on through the wood tomorrow. If we're lucky and shout enough, we will have met, killed, cooked, and eaten the Magenta Death by this time tomorrow. Now, get the fire going, and make it a big one!'

Urgh miserably signaled Sorry to get a move on and began gathering sticks for the fire. Sorry came up, puffing and panting. 'Ah yes, Daisy!' said Moaris. 'I've just told Tulip that we're heading through Tulgy Wood tomorrow!'

Urgh looked on with a frown, which sadly resembled a smile

'That's the spirit, Tulip,' smiled Moaris, fortunately mistaking his expression. 'Now, I know the Wise Wench said to avoid it at all costs, but she is, after all, not battle-hardened like me, so what does she know? The best thing to do, is bring your enemy into your space

99

where you hold all the cards. So, at first light, I intend to march through the forest shouting taunts until this so-called Magenta Death appears. We'll then butcher it into too-many-to-count pieces and be feasting on Magenta pie tomorrow night! Any questions?' Moaris smiled and sat down contentedly.

'What about the giants, Moaris?' said Urgh. 'Shouldn't we be heading to them?'

'Are you suggesting I'm wrong?' growled Moaris.

'Not at all, Moaris,' said Urgh, who then wandered off to collect a lot of wood and look about for the raven. She appeared, suddenly, flying onto his shoulder.

'Yes?' she said, testily.

'Ah, Lady Carline. How, er, delightful to see you.'

'You do realize you smell quite considerably, do you not?' said the bird. 'Perching on you is odious, but my hearing is not too great these days, being so old. When I was a chick in the city, I could hear everything.'

'City? I don't know what that is.'

'A very, very big village with lots of people in and lots of nice things to buy.'

'Buy?'

'Purchase. When you spend your money to get things you like.'

'Money?'

'Never mind. But you still smell, even to my nostrils.'

'Well, er, yes, I have a long smell-story, you see.'

'Yes, smell-story—interesting concept. In point of fact, what you're actually saying to me is, the *more* you smell, the bigger your smell-story, and the happier you are. Is that correct?'

Urgh nodded, somehow feeling slightly awkward. 'Er, Lady Carline? Moaris intends to go through Tulgy Wood.'

'We know.'

'We?'

'Yes, we.'

'But the Wise Wench expressly told him not to go that way; she said it was very dangerous.'

'That's precisely why she told him not to go to the place she wanted him to go to in the first place.'

'I see,' said Urgh, confused.

'Trust in the Wise Wench my odorous travelling companion, and best get some wood. Moaris will be cross if you don't, and I wouldn't think making such a bigoted, annoying, self-important bully as Moaris cross would be good for your skin.'

Urgh nodded and dashed off, looking for kindling.

Their morale was raised by setting fire to something, and soon they watched the dancing flames of a large bonfire, which seemed, in Moaris's eyes, to be depicting in flames the way he would disembowel the Magenta Death the day after.

Suddenly, he shot up, armed with a particularly vicious barb-headed axe he'd kept close by for just such an emergency.

'What?' whispered Sorry in terror, already eyeing up escape routes.

'Did you hear that?' whispered Moaris, loudly, squinting into the darkness of the surrounding forest for opponents.

The pair looked vacantly at their leader, thinking he was having one of his funny turns, when they all heard something very close by— a sort of snuffling noise. Moaris cunningly ran into the night, screaming 'Kill!' at the top of his lungs. He soon disappeared, his voice trailing away in a series of taunts and threats, leaving the frightened goblins clinging to each other. Urgh looked fruitlessly about for Lady Carline.

They made a very odd sight to the other creature watching them—frail, little goblins wearing flower-decorated smocks, clutching each other, and shaking.

The figure moved closer.

'What do you think it is?' mumbled Sorry on the verge of hysteria, his eyes darting into the inky darkness.

'I don't know, and I don't want to guess,' replied Urgh.

'You mean it could be HER!' answered Sorry. 'Queen Quench?'

'No! I hadn't thought of *that* possibility at all,' croaked Urgh, growing ever more afraid as the seconds wore on. 'I thought it could be the Magenta Death, out on a night's hunting. Keep close and don't worry, I have a magical vanish-me udder at hand.' Urgh pulled a withered, paper-thin udder crammed with magic out of his pocket. The goblins huddled closer when, suddenly, something moved into the edges of their fire light.

The figure was difficult to make out with its hood. Short and plump, certainly, but no goblin—it was far too unattractive for that; it didn't have a mouth dominating its face, for starters. As the old goblin song ran:

> 'She was a hag, for sure, for sure,
> For her nose was long and bent,
> And her mouth was small and tiny,
> Burn, burn, burn it, oh!'[32]

'Hhhhhhhello,' said Urgh, heroically, and took a step back in case the creature replied and he needed to make a dash for it. Sorry was trying to make out as much as he could about the creature's appearance while putting a sack over his head and pretending to be, simply, a very large non-threatening appendage of his companion. 'Dddddo you speak?' added Urgh, apprentice-heroically.

In the background, the cries of 'kill, maim, deform, remove!' were getting closer. The strange figure looked up alarmed, and, in that moment, the firelight caught a pair of huge protruding teeth beneath the hood. Not barbed teeth, or spiked canine teeth, but great, big, long rabbit teeth. The figure pulled its hood about itself, and put its hand on a pointed stick by its side.

'Beware Tulgy Wood!' said the figure in a whisper, and then was gone into the night.

---

[32] The song continues with a description of the rules of gob-wench loveliness, namely: width of mouth; pointedness, number, and variation in hues of teeth; narrowness of eyes; and blotchiness of skin.

The cries came closer, and became more aggressive. 'Death to all! Cleave and hack! Avenge Miffed! The Magenta Death has a hat with flowers in! Let Big Ears the Demon Cat fear me and yowl in horror! Slay the wicked barbed ones! The giants shall fall!' Moaris stumbled into the firelight. 'Damn! I think I scared it off!' he said, and swung his axe above Sorry's head, laughing. 'Nearly got you there, matey!' he cried. Sorry hated it when Moaris said, 'matey;' it always meant that some near-death experience was at hand.

Urgh began pointing into the forest, in the direction the hooded figure with the rabbit teeth and sword had gone. Sorry stood behind, sack on head. Both looked scared; well, in truth, it was impossible to tell if Sorry looked scared beyond all the shaking but it was quite easy to make a reasonable assumption he was petrified.

Moaris immediately took in the situation and came to an instantaneous conclusion. 'Now!' he said, quietly and firmly. 'I'm going to count to one-one-and-one. If, by the end of that time, you haven't both calmed down and told me what's going on, I'm going to make you both eat each-others' ears—wax and all. One—! One-more-than-one—!'

'It was a stranger!' blurted Urgh, pointing to where the figure went.

'With horrific rabbit teeth,' added Sorry.

'*Rabbit* teeth?!' said Moaris, incredulously. 'Rabbit teeth? What's so horrific about rabbit's teeth?!' He stood above the companions and made a fist. 'I'm waiting to know what's so horrific about rabbit teeth?!'

'Well, they were so terrifyingly blunt,' said Sorry, and wished he hadn't.

'Blunt?' said Moaris, impatiently.

'And,' added Urgh, 'it said something. It said 'beware of Tulgy Wood."

Moaris grinned, saying, 'It wasn't purple-ish looking, was it?'

'No, not at all, Moaris,' answered Urgh quickly.

'In that case, you imagined it,' said Moaris, gleefully rummaging through his pack, and flinging knives, caltrops, huge mousetraps, and various pointed objects about as he got ready to sleep. 'Everything else would be far too scared to approach, wouldn't it?' he added, more pointedly than the point on his pointed sticks.

Urgh and Sorry looked at each other, nodded. 'You're right, Moaris,' said Urgh, 'we imagined it. That's woods for you; full of imaginings!'

Moaris was already snoring.

'What do you think it was?' whispered Sorry from behind his sack.

'I may be wrong, but I think it was a friend. Best get some sleep now,' Urgh said, staring at Moaris's snoring form, before adding, 'if we can?'

It seemed only a matter of moments before Urgh was disturbed. 'Sleeping will stop now,' grumbled Moaris, relatively quietly. In fact *very* quietly considering who he was, and how he shouted everything, even whispers. Urgh woke up and looked around. Sorry woke up and looked depressed. From somewhere above came the sounds of refined flapping. Moaris walked around the edge of the camp where the...*thing*, the terrible, rabbit-toothed monstrosity had appeared from the night before. He paid careful attention to the ground, searching carefully for tracks. Having satisfied himself that, even though he couldn't track, there weren't any, he made his way back to the fire. The huge and obvious iron shod bootprints remained firmly in the mud nearby.

Urgh pulled a bag of whelks from his bag and began sucking them. 'Will we cross Tulgy Wood today, Moaris?' he asked.

Moaris frowned. 'Will we cross Tulgy Wood today, *LORD* Moaris, *slayer of the Magenta Death apparent*,' he added. Again, despite the content, Moaris was almost calm in his words.

Urgh put his hand up. Moaris smiled. 'Yes, you may speak, Tulip.'

'Why are you being so quiet, m'lord Moaris, slayer of the Magenta Death apparent,' asked Urgh, quickly adding, 'even though it's quite clearly great that you are?'

Moaris smiled, broadly. 'Well spotted, Tulip. I am, in fact, using subterfuge,' he said, took the whelks from Urgh's mouth and began chewing them. 'That Magenta Death will have been up all night scared of me, and now it'll be sleeping. But in a few moments, I shall destroy its peace, as well as destroying its person. I suspect it is nearby—even as we suck these delicious whelks—slumbering. And the moment I commence shouting, it will scream in terror, showing me where it hides. So, the plan for today is this: we will shortly head through the forest making as much noise as possible, shouting taunts with a magenta-derogatory tone. Anyone not shouting anything derogatory enough in my view will be burnt. Is that understood?'

Sorry and Urgh nodded, miserably.

'Right, let's pack up, head out, and kill us some purple-hued beastie!'

A few minutes later, they were walking into the edges of the deeper wood and Moaris looked at the trees, angrily. Then, he pointedly put his hands to his mouth and began shouting. 'All monsters of a vaguely purple nature are sissies! They like to crochet, enjoy making pots and admire the beauty of sunsets!' He stood back, legs slightly apart, and tore his shirt open. Then he noticed it was already torn and smiled.

The forest stayed the same. Pine trees swayed gently in the breeze, birds circled and hid high above, the ground remained slightly moist from the recent storm.

'AND,' added Moaris, crossly, 'the same monsters are not really monsters at all! They are SISSIES!' He roared the word 'sissies' so hard he began coughing and fell on his knees, gasping for breath. 'What are you looking at?' he choked to his companions, 'get taunting!'

'All purple monsters are not scary at all!' said Urgh, loudly and confidently. 'And not only that, no one likes them either! They haven't got any friends and everyone thinks they're really stupid!'

'Not so loud,' whispered Sorry.

'Don't worry, I know for a fact that nothing bad is going to happen,' said Urgh, quietly, as he winked at Sorry. 'We are not afraid of anything purple!' he shouted at the top of his voice.

'Good work, Tulip! Very heroic,' shouted Moaris. 'And you, no shoulders! What about you? I'm not hearing any taunts.'

105

'We aren't frightened of you much at all, Magenta Death!' said Sorry, quietly.

'Louder!' shouted Moaris

'We aren't scared of you at all, Magenta Death' said Sorry, slightly louder. Then he looked at Urgh smiling. 'We aren't scared of you, Magenta Death,' he shouted, and began laughing and nodding his head gleefully at being brave.

'See?' said Urgh, quietly. 'Nothing to worry about. Being a hero is easy.'

Suddenly there was a noise.

A crashing, whistling noise, followed by a definite, distant grunting. As they listened, it grew very loud, very quickly.

The noise came suddenly thick and fast: a terrible whistling and grunting; a frightful oinking and trumping; a fearful flapping and furious beating of comically small wings.

'Ayeee!' yelled Moaris and plunged into his pack, swiftly emerging with a pair of crossbows which he loaded and held, one in each hand. 'Manic guff-hogs[33]!' he roared, and peered into the forest, joyfully.

'What?' added Sorry and Urgh incredulously, as they peered in the same direction.

'Manic guff-hogs! Don't you know anything? They have no will to live, and all they want to do is bang into some living thing as hard as they can, to put themselves out of their misery! Everything fears them!' said Moaris, as urgently as he stood. 'Except me,' he added, hefting his crossbows.

'Why does it have to be living?' asked Urgh, disbelievingly.

'It just does,' snapped Moaris, testily, as he skewered huge slugs onto each bolt and aimed, wildly.

'Why don't they burst when they hit each other then? Or why can't it just be a tree that they...never mind,' said Urgh, abandoning his question as he saw Moaris's increasingly angry look.

---

[33] Also known as cheerless wind-pigs, forlorn chuff-porkers, and Chubley's moribund squall-swine.

'And how do they put themselves out of their misery?' whispered Sorry, knowing he didn't want to know the answer.

Moaris stood up alert and suddenly something huge flapped and oinked its improbable way out from high behind a pine tree. It was like a vast bloated balloon with a pig's face and tiny flapping wings. Moaris fired a crossbow and the creature exploded in a huge fireball which felled the tree next to it. Sorry and Urgh were thrown many feet backwards through the air. Moaris stood firm and, dropping the first crossbow, tore his shirt off. 'They explode!' he said, and turned to smile at Sorry and Urgh. 'This could get serious!' he said, before cocking a considerable ear to one side.

There was a hush for a few moments, even the birds seemingly anxious to know the outcome. Moaris stepped forward and snarled. Urgh reached into his sack and pulled out a pale and rubbery bloated cow's udder tightly tied at one teat.

'What's that?' asked Sorry, nervously, glancing ahead while occasionally looking incredulously at the object.

'It's magic,' said Urgh.

Sorry smiled and waited for the sparks to begin. Then his joy at a possible magic show was burned to the ground by reality.

'I think..!' said Moaris, as he heard a distant oink. 'I think..!' he added, as the trumping, flapping, and oinking began to rise again, building steadily into a crescendo of improbable pig-related noises. 'I think...that just made them happier!' he added, and turned as the air began to fill with the ominous approaching flap of countless manic guff-hogs.

Moaris threw down his remaining crossbow and ran away.

Sorry had never seen Moaris run away from anything. In fact, Moaris told him that he only didn't get killed by the giants because something big fell on him and knocked him unconscious. He decided that whatever Moaris was scared of, he was very, very scared of, and so ran after him; the magic show would have to wait, even if it involved a truly massive bonfire.

Urgh turned to follow them, tripped over a root, and crashed to the ground. His magic udder bounced just out of reach, his cries for help echoing and then being drowned in oinks. He tried to stand, but the pain in his ankle felled him instantly. He glanced up, suddenly aware of movement in the canopy. He gave once last cry for help and then saw the hogs flapping towards him, a mass of smells, noise, and misery.

For a nanosecond, not far away, Sorry thought he should turn and help his friend. It could have been a moment of awakening. But alas, he was a goblin, and the admirable thought was quickly abandoned, smothered beneath fear and self-protection, and glad the noise was getting further behind him.

The hogs hurtled towards him, a mass of stink and desperation. Urgh could see their miserable tear-brimmed eyes, their hunger as they craved to burst, their almost joyful oinks as salvation stood, quaking and tiny, before them. Urgh rolled backwards, his arms cradling his head as he waited to explode.

Then his hand brushed something rubbery. His fingers groped and found a sickly teat, which he pulled, a smile growing across his miserable features.

The udder burst, erupting into a sparkling, billowing mass of silver leaves and popping glitter stars which surrounded Urgh in its caress. Beyond his starry vision, Urgh could hear the frustrated oinking of the hogs, desperately coming to the conclusion that life was even worse than they thought it was by teasing them with potential escape only to snatch it away. A few braved the stars and flew close by through them, miserable masses of flesh which Urgh easily ducked away from. He crawled along the ground and into a tiny hole in the roots of a tree.

When the glitter finally drifted to the ground, Urgh had vanished. Mortified, the hogs flittered off into the forest, chasing the sounds of distant redemption from the other fleeing goblins.

The cow jumped over the moon thought Urgh as he stared at the spent udder and glitter on the forest floor. The last of the hogs spurted off, wretchedly, leaving the little goblin alone. Urgh sighed with relief and slowly crawled out of the hole. The sound of oinking and flapping was fading, and birdsong began to nervously return to the air. The outrageously noisy devotions to Lord Noc, which helped power these strange creatures, was now all but a windy whisper in the distance. Urgh smiled to himself, collected up his belongings, and studied Moaris's collection of weaponry. His empty crossbow lay in a patch of brown bracken where he had hurled it, and nearby lay several axes and knives, as well as something huge and pointy with barbs all over it which Urgh had not even seen Moaris carrying. As he looked at it closer, he couldn't even see anywhere where it could be picked up and decided that he would fetch it later, after his friends had escaped.

If they escape. Urgh dismissed the unpalatable thought swiftly, deciding that nothing, but nothing, could possibly kill Moaris Miffed and live. With a smile, he picked up what he could of both his own and his friends' baggage, and began to quietly and carefully walk after them.

He had taken barely a step when a huge explosion ripped the air, followed by a definite goblin scream. Urgh's bottom lip began to wobble and he hardly noticed as the strange hooded figure, which had been hiding nearby all night, slowly staggered out behind him, grinding its teeth.

'Are you injured?' said a curious voice.

Urgh stepped back and yelped as he put his foot on Moaris's completely barbed weapon. He yelped a little more as he took another step back and stood on the edge of an axe, then tripped over another weapon and ended up on the floor surrounded by crossbow bolts.

The sinister, hooded figure stepped forward and held its hand out. 'Fear not, mighty warrior,' it said, in a somewhat comical lisping voice. It was like a goblin and yet not—its skin was furry, it had one-more-than-one hands and legs, and a head, but it was stooped and walked with quick suddenness, its head bending to the air.

'Stay back,' warned Urgh from his somewhat tactically unsound position of being on the floor, 'or I'll spike you with this!' He considered picking up the barbed weapon and then settled for just pointing at it.

Somewhere in the distance there was an oink.

The little figure's head shot upwards and it glanced about furtively. 'We must hurry, or the hogs will be back. Come with me; you have nothing to fear.'

Urgh took another look at the figure. It wore a dark grey cloak with a very large hood from beneath which wriggled a pair of enormously long, flaccid, mangy ears. A thick hemp belt held the cloak around the figure but didn't hide the obvious pointed stick, which was clearly lurking under the cloth. Beyond this, the figure had no other obvious weapons except those teeth, which even now peeked sinisterly and squarely from within the dark confines of the hood.

Another oink sounded from somewhere in the forest nearby.

'We must hurry to the burrow or the hogs will be back. No time for any questions,' said the figure.

Urgh trembled as he stood up, wincing as his weight fell on his ankle. He was careful to keep a distance from those teeth, and cast his eyes at the ground for something which wouldn't hurt him to pick up. Casting his eyes about furtively was a skill Urgh was somewhat good at, what with his head arrangement and all. The figure moved forward again and held out its hand, which was grey and furry; then, very quickly, it threw back its hood.

It was a rabbit! Well, not exactly a *rabbit*. It had a rabbit's head; a very large rabbit's head. In fact, an incredibly mangy and ugly rabbit's head with eyes that looked in one-more-than-one different directions at once. 'I am Lord Nibbles, Bunnylord of the Rabbit Folk of Tulgy Wood, and I mean you no harm, goblin. If we do not move to our burrow quickly, the hogs will be back and you will end up like your friends.'

Like my friends? Urgh's eyes welled with tears. The BunnyLord, seeing his distress, took him by the arm and led him swiftly into the trees. The trees here were sparse but the undergrowth was thick. Brambles pulled at Urgh's chin, hair, and clothes as he moved through the wood. Beyond, the sound of oinks was beginning to build again, and soon it was obviously closing.

'Run!' shouted Lord Nibbles, and took off at great pace, bounding on his legs almost like he was hopping. Urgh found it

110

difficult to keep up—his ankle still hurt, and he became afraid that he would lose his guide and become quick relief for some particularly bloated hog. The noise behind him grew and grew. He risked a glance over his shoulder and saw, to his horror, that a huge crimson hog was just a few feet from him. He could just make out Lord Nibbles beyond a sycamore sapling and swiftly gave chase. He was sweating now, and the tears in his eyes were making seeing anything difficult; the salt stung him and his own sniveling was barely discernible above the grunting behind him. The dreadful little flap, flap, flap of the hog's stupid wings was at Urgh's shoulders; he was sure he could feel their breeze.

Suddenly, he came into a clearing in the trees and spotted a large dark burrow ahead, a partially closed iron gate being held by shadowy figures within. Nibbles was waving frantically to him. 'This way! Be quick!' he shouted. Urgh could see other Rabbit Folk crouched in the entrance, looking anxiously directly above and behind him. He glanced up and, for a split second, clearly saw a snout at his back—then all was dark—

—and he was in the burrow. The iron door slammed shut. The flapping receded.

'Have no fear, friend goblin, for the hogs cannot enter our burrow.' Urgh's eyes adjusted to the dark and he saw that it was a lady rabbit speaking.

'This,' said Nibbles, 'is my BunnyLady Floppsy and our little burrow. You have nothing to fear! You are perfectly safe. Honest!'

From the shadows, several rabbit-things emerged, hungrily.

It was later. Urgh eyed the bowl of greens, suspiciously. The other BunnyLords and BunnyLadies seemed to be tucking in, as if it could be their last meal, which was uncanny. This part of the burrow was bare save for the long low table they were all squatted at, noisily tucking into their greens with relish. Crude tunnels led away from this room. Urgh suddenly saw a fat juicy slug in the green and ate it, munching hungrily. 'I must go and see about my friends soon,' he said, dribbling green as he talked.

111

'Give the hogs a chance to move on, and we'll all go,' said BunnyLady Floppsy. The curiously mangy rabbit folk nodded in unison, suddenly stood up, looked nervously around, and then sat down and resumed eating.

'They call me BunnyLord Hoppy!' said the rabbit sat to the left of Urgh. He didn't look very hoppy—his grey fur was particularly matted, hanging in clumps down his chin, and his legs were at odd angles to his torso.

A new pair of rabbit folk came in, both looking tired. As they joined the merry group, BunnyLady Floppsy and BunnyLord Hoppy got up and left the room hurriedly.

'And I am called my BunnyLord Snufferty,' said the one on the right, bowing. The others bowed and smiled at the goblin.

'You have had a narrow escape, child of fires and smells,' said Nibbles, as he gnawed at an especially bushy bit of greenery. 'The hogs have come over the river. We have never seen them so far south at this time. Normally, the giants keep them to use in their fires all through the cold. This group must have escaped.'

'Escaped from the giants? I wouldn't like to have to do that,' said Urgh, uncannily. 'Do you think my friends will be alright?'

The group stared at each other in a way that suggested they were sure they weren't. 'Of course they are,' said Snufferty, unconvincingly. 'And, in the meantime, you are quite safe. We are peace-loving creatures who seek only to pass our lives in happiness and calmness, with plenty to eat and no predators to worry us. We strive only to continue our race and live in harmony with all living things. What brings a mighty handsome goblin such as yourself so far into the Great Forest?'

After Urgh realized he was talking to him, he began his tale, elaborating it as he went with his own impressions of Moaris and Sorry and Lady Carline, and concluding with their improbable escape—so he hoped—from the hogs by Moaris's cunning use of violence and shouting. The tiny group of BunnyLords and BunnyLadies were rapt as he spoke. 'So you see,' he said, at the end, 'I must get the message back and deliver it to the giants or the Wise Wench will not only be very cross, she'll also be VERY WRONG, and she can't be very wrong because she's the Wise Wench, which means that we are bound to get there, somehow, but, oh dear, I'm confused now.'

Urgh had become increasingly animated during the discussion about 'the plan'. So animated, in fact, that he had nearly killed one of the BunnyLords by swinging his arms about frantically while holding a fork.

'But, friend Urgh,' said Lady Floppsy—who had returned some time ago—'it is so dangerous, you cannot know what you are saying. The giants' tower is a terrible place. Giants pull things apart, or sit on them to squash them. They delight in tearing things up or eating them whole. They are very, very naughty and bad!'

'Nevertheless I *MUST* go, and soon! My friends will be worried about me.'

'Those are brave, heroic words, little goblin,' said Lady Floppsy.

Heroic words? Is that what being a hero entails? Probably not that easy, thought Urgh. *Plus, they probably aren't worried about me anyway*, thought his thoughts without asking him.

She continued. 'Then, we shall go with you. Our little band shall help the good goblins of the forest deliver their message, 'so cunning,' that peace shall fall upon the forest forever more. Such is a worthy risk.' Floppsy did a little bow and Urgh clapped. The other BunnyLords and BunnyLadies murmured their agreement and began to pat the little goblin on the back. 'But first we must all... prepare.' The rabbitfolk looked at each other in a curious way and then left the room leaving Urgh alone with his thoughts and worries.

It was some time before the rabbit folk returned. They'd all clearly been packing furiously and were out of breath. 'We are ready,' said Nibbles, proudly, tossing a few remaining greens in a large sack. Urgh beamed as he saw the other bunnies prepare, and soon the little troop was out in the fresh air again. Nibbles carefully sniffed the air a few times and looked pleased. 'It seems the hogs have gone. It is safe. Now,' he added as he walked back towards the goblins' campsite, 'we must pick up your friends' trails if we are to find

113

them.' Nibbles began to stride purposefully back through the woods where, a few short hours ago, Urgh had nearly been blown up. Urgh wondered what it would be like to be blown up, and whether it might not be quite the spectacle.

The morning cloud had given way to bright sunshine, and the BunnyLords seemed joyful, turning their faces up to the bright warmth, and snuffling their noses happily. Amongst these excellent creatures, Urgh felt safe and walked on with fresh hope that all would go as the Wise Wench said. His ankle felt a bit better and he smiled as he thought about his initial fear of the BunnyLord. *Now, they will be friends for life* he thought, unaware of just how right he was.

Only a short time later, the little group emerged next to the goblins' camp. All seemed undisturbed. 'Come,' said Nibbles, 'let us gather the goblins' belongings. We never know, one of his friends may yet be alive and glad of the things we bring.'

There was a murmur of agreement from the bunnies, and bedrolls, sacks of food, and weapons were all carefully gathered and heaved by them. Even the scary barbed thing without a name was carefully wrapped in thick hemp and carried reverently. 'Honor the things of our goblin kin,' said Floppsy. 'They are our friends, and though they may have fallen, they have fallen bravely; as bravely as any young bucklord would in battle.' Again, a murmur of agreement.

Nibbles had strayed to the edge of the camp to where Moaris and Sorry had fled. He was intent upon the ground when Urgh came over to him.

'Ah, it is a terrible thing to see innocent friends flee the hogs, for flee they did, as you said. They were in a great hurry, and I can tell by the droppings that there were many hogs. You must prepare for the worst, my friend, though your friend with wings may have flown away and be safe.'

Urgh's face fell, but he was determined to be brave. 'But I still say that the Wise Wench said we would succeed. We have the prophecy to fulfil, although, to be honest, I can't remember anything about noble BunnyLords in it. Perhaps it slipped my mind?'

Nibbles smiled and patted his new friend on the back as he walked towards the other BunnyLords and gathered them together. They held a brief conversation before seeming to agree something and stepped towards Urgh as a group. 'We have decided,' said Nibbles, 'that we shall help you in any way we can, even if we have to brave the giants' keep. We wrongly thought that all goblins were sneaky, violent swines that did little except set fire to things, shout, destroy, and pollute without conscience. Now, through you, we see that we were wrong, and now we see how our goblin kin really are, we have decided to be friends with you for all time, even if it means death. It is worth it for our new friends. May this be a sign that peace will reign across the whole forest and began with the friendship of goblins and rabbitfolk.' Nibbles held out his hand and Urgh shook it. A few moments later he was crushed by the embrace of the rabbitfolk and had to fight back a little tear of gratitude.

'I hope it shall, friend rabbitfolk. Never has a goblin received greater peace and friendship from a stranger—strangers, I should say! I'm sure the Wise Wench, the king, and all my clan will embrace our new peace and friendship. Let nothing stop it!' He hefted his sack over his shoulder and grinned.

'This way, my BunnyLords!' said Nibbles, as he led them off into the forest.

The path was clear, for Moaris had obviously taken the trouble to break as many branches as he could on his run from the hogs; *perhaps as a sign?* thought Urgh. Then he realized that Moaris had just been destructive, and was probably deliberately slowing himself down to increase the danger he was in. Here, the undergrowth was scant save for a few green ferns which had begun to show, and bluebells.

Suddenly, there was a call from ahead—a raven's caw. The black bird took flight above them, calling a warning to his fellows. Floppsy took a few steps forward and then bowed her head as she entered a blackened clearing. More ravens took flight, ending their feast for the moment.

Their feast was a corpse.

CHAPTER 7

The sling seemed regal enough now that Looti had sewn some *bantams rampant* into it, although as sewing wasn't her strong point they did look a bit like squids which the king liked. The king moved his elbow gingerly as he swayed in his palanquin. Above, the gob-boy shouted: 'King! Make way!' quietly, so as not to annoy him. The bearers walked very carefully through the village, taking care not to tip the king up, for he had decreed that if he suffered one more fall before the end of the adventure, he would declare a 'villagers-on-fire' day and burn selected servants, if not all of them. Looti walked seductively through the village, which had momentarily come to a standstill to watch the king coming through on some mission of terrible and vital import, apparently. Anxious goblins watched as the king and his new adviser followed the Wise Wench to the bottom side of the settlement. They seemed to be engaged in some serious conversation, and the Wise Wench appeared particularly animated. The villagers grew worried that trouble might be ahead and proceeded to hide behind each other for safety.

'But the rhyme of Coddly Darkarts doesn't mention deaths, does it?' asked the king, smugly.

'No,' answered the Wise Wench, with customary directness, before adding, 'well, only superficially.'

'So, I'm afraid I don't understand. Which one of them dies? I distinctly remember you saying one-one-and-one stand and fall, not one stands and falls.' He looked even smugger, which was not easy—only possible, in fact, because he was king and had therefore been carefully trained in the techniques of mastering various stages of smugness.[34]

'Irrelevant,' said the Wise Wench.

---

[34] Some goblin royal families specialize in looking smug or superior and have developed it into a high art. Most, however, are satisfied with bearing enormous weapons (usually vast spiked clubs) that enjoy frightful reputations for slaying goblins by touch, sight, smell, or even mere mention.

'Well, if it's irrelevant, then why did you mention it in the first place?'

'I have my reasons. The prophecy must be fulfilled, and just because it's a slightly different prophecy from what's actually happening doesn't make it not a prophecy.'

The king looked confused.

Looti looked confused.

The bearers looked very confused.

The Wise Wench carried on, striding purposefully to the front of the village where there was a small bald outcrop of stone with a dead crow nailed into it. Below, a stony path lead downwards below the village and away through a broken gate. She pushed her walking stick firmly in the ground. 'This is where our hamster shall be,' she said, loudly, to the crowd.

Everyone looked slightly embarrassed.

'Did you say '*hamster*?'' asked the king.

'Yes, our Iron Hamster.' She smiled and did a quick survey of the land about, gazing, and taking a few mental notes. 'We must repair our fortifications, which in essence probably means building them from scratch. These ramparts need rebuilding, the whole village needs a nice big wall around it,' she said, staring down at the tumbling mass of stones before her. 'And get the gate fixed. Oh, and place spiked spears facing outwards all the way around the village. Anything spiky will do, in fact. That way, when we are attacked unexpectedly, our hamster will be behind our fortifications.' The others stood by and looked at each other with quiet discomfiture.

'Well, that's settled then!' said the king. 'Hurrah! Our hamster shall be here!'

'*DON'T* be sarcastic!' snapped the Wise Wench. 'And follow me back to the Great Dragon Kettle. We need to talk.'

'Must we?' said the king, answering his own question. With a flick of his whip, he spurred his bearers on. 'Well, get on with it!' he shouted to those nearby, waving absent-mindedly at the goblins gawping at the tumbling ramparts.

'You're talking garbage woman! Bunkum! Rubbish!' said the king as he marched around the kettle. It was slightly later, but not later enough for the king, who wanted to have an afternoon nap. He stomped around the room. 'Rubbish, rubbish, rubbish!' he added, and, for regal effect, stamped his foot mightily as he said each word.

The Wise Wench sighed, patiently. 'It's *THE PLAN*,' she said firmly. 'The only plan.'

'What about the *first* one, then?' answered the king, testily, and smiling in the direction of Looti, self-righteously.

'First, what?' said the Wise Wench, watching disdainfully as he anxiously pointed a royal finger in the direction of her nose.

'*First* plan.' *Got you so called Wise Wench.* He folded his arms and continued as regally as his little fat frame could muster. 'You have already told me THE PLAN before, and now you've just told me a different plan, so it can't be THE PLAN, can it? It can be A PLAN, but not THE PLAN, because THE PLAN has already been discussed by THE WISE WENCH, or have you changed your mind?' He was feeling very pleased with himself, it wasn't often that a king got the chance to cross-examine the Wise Wench. In fact, it hadn't happened before as far as he could recollect, although recollection was not his strong point.

She frowned. This was getting difficult. The plan, after all, *had* changed, but that was hardly her fault. No, it was Queen Quench's fault. She thought for a while and wrung her hands while the king continued to pace about comparing plans and other plans and becoming generally louder and louder.

'The plan,' said the Wise Wench, 'the *final plan* is the one I've just told you. Telling you the initial plan was part of *the plan*. The plan was to confuse the issue by making the first plan seem like *the plan*, when, in fact, *THE* plan was not to follow the first plan.' She sat on the kettle and wrung her hands. It was getting harder every day to move the grubby playing pieces of the gods about the grimy, soot-stained board of life.

The king sat next to her and looked confused. They both looked at Looti.

Durth had been looking at Looti all the time.

Looti smiled, thinly.

'Well?' said the king, in answer to her thin smile.

'Well, what, Lord Mightyregalness?' said Looti.

'Well, what's the advice? As if I can't guess.'

She thought for a while longer and looked several times at the Wise Wench and once at Durth, who was smiling at her, hopefully, and dribbling. 'My advice is, Your Rotundity, that you should follow whatever advice the Wise Wench should give you.' She stood back and gave Durth a handkerchief, which he would never wash, ever.

'Well, that sounds familiar. What's the point of having an adviser if all you all ever do is advise me to agree with the Wise Wench,' said the king, disagreeably, and budged up against the Wise Wench.

'They're in your pocket,' shouted the Wise Wench, upwards, to no one in particular, then budged the king back, playfully.

'Oh, thanks!' came a voice from the heavens.

The king stood up. 'Do what you bloody like,' he said, and strode out mightily. *Bloody giants,* he thought to himself, huffily. *Bloody wenches. Bloody goblins. It's time I got rid of the lot of them, then I can be king without any subjects to get in the way of my kingness. Yes, that sounds like a plan. A PLAN! Hah!* He stomped back through the village, barging deliberately into as many of his subjects as possible. All bar one had the good sense to crash to the ground as he did, as though flattened by a pick-axe handle, while yelling appropriately loudly about might and permanent injuries.

Sadly the last such victim, Pumf, was not so wise in royal interaction when barged and remained stood. 'Good afternoon, Your Huffyness,' said Pumf, the new Poo-Pit Maester. He was entirely round.

The king walked towards Pumf and smiled a very sarcastic smile. 'What?' he said, regally.

'I said, 'good afternoon,' Your Lordshipness,' answered Pumf with a slight smirk on his face, a smirk he instantly removed and regretted.

'Durth!' shouted the king. 'DURTH!' he added, angrily, and stood imposingly adjacent to Pumf. A few moments passed, the king looked around. When he turned back, Pumf was gone. Satisfied that he had scared the living daylights out of his subject, and making a mental note to have the position of Poo-Pit Maester punishable by death at some future date, he resumed his walk to the Moot House. The village seemed very quiet indeed. As he looked around, he could make out just a few of his subjects; all hiding. He smiled and walked in, suddenly remembering why he enjoyed being king.

The room beyond was smoky and sweaty. A pair of sparrows fluttered up into the beams high above, where the smoke provided them with an excellent hiding place to nest. *I'll have those brought down and spiked for supper tonight. Then I'll set about passing some new laws.* King Stormgrunties climbed the ladder and resumed his seat on the high chair. Idly, his hands fell to caressing the handles. He dreamed briefly of milk and udders before realizing he was being watched.

Tongue smiled thinly at him, his eyes suddenly widening in terror as he stared at the door as it creaked open.

Stood there was a wizened, crooked goblin, its hair matted into long dreads, the face hidden behind a badly-severed stag's head, its antlers drooping flaccidly. The creature leant upon a mossy staff and smelt of damp and earth and stagnant ponds. 'Good day, great King Stormgrunties the many-many-and-lots-after-more-than-many-dead-King Stormgrunties-after-the-first, king of the Great Forest!' said the goblin—a female voice, as far as the king could make out, although it was so cackling that it was hard to tell. 'I think I should warn you,' it said in a sinister voice, 'that your village is doomed, unless you act!'

The king jumped, and the chair teetered, precariously. He smiled and rode out the rocking. 'And who, who, who are you, pray?' he said mightily, peering into the smoke and shadows.

'A friend' answered the figure.

'Bit odd for a friend to skulk in the shadows, isn't it?'

'Might be,' answered the goblin. 'But never mind that,' it added, with a hiss.

'Was that a hiss?' asked the king.

'No. Well, yes, a bit,' hissed the goblin, who shuffled about in the shadows. 'I have a bit of a sniffle,' it added.

'I see. Well, what do you want, *friend?*' said the king, with a skeptical grin.

120

'I come to warn you.' The stranger shuffled about on its feet, and droplets of water dripped from its sodden clothing.

'Warn me?'

'Yes.'

'Oh? What about?'

'The Wise Wench will betray you.'

The king did a double take. And then another. '*Pardon?*'

'You heard.'

'I'm not sure I did. Let me get this straight. You, a hissy friend who skulks in the shadows, comes skulking mysteriously in here, hissing and being mysterious, and tell me that the Wise Wench will betray me? Is that right?'

'Yes.'

'I see.'

There was a long, embarrassing pause as they looked at each other. Well, one of them looked at the other; the other didn't look at the other because he couldn't see her properly.

'I'm not sure I believe you, I'm afraid,' retorted the king, with utmost cunning. 'Although, she *has* been behaving pretty oddly, lately.'

'Well, you should do.'

'Why.'

'Because I'm a friend, as I said.' The figure crossed her arms, or its arms—he still wasn't quite sure what it was. 'I'm not fibbing, honest. She will betray you. Unless you act with regal decisiveness, which you will, the village is doomed. Don't forget who told you so.'

'And who are you, pray?'

'You know well, great king.'

The king scowled and thought, but all the thoughts were being pushed back into his head by how much was going on outside it. 'Well, thanks very much for telling me,' he said.

'Pleasure.'

'OK.'

'Right.'

'Thanks. Do pop around again. If there's anything else you want to warn me about, I'm always here.'

121

'Right, will do. I'll be off then.'

'Right.'

'Well, cheerio.'

'Cheerio.'

'Oh, just one more thing,' said the curious figure, as she blew dust from her upraised palm at him. There was a strong smell of lavender and suet. The room spun and the king's head was invaded by strange noises; he felt dizzy. A huge heifer was telling him things in his mind, whispering secrets, telling him *all* things. He coughed as he swallowed something in his mouth.

The something slipped down his throat and into his brain where there was plenty of space. The little crooked figure scurried up his great chair and began whispering things into his ear.

There was a pause, and the king was suddenly very sure he was alone again. He got down and marched towards the door, opened it very quickly, and ran off in the direction of the Kettle Hall, shouting for help.

By the door of the Moot House was a pool of water.

It was a little later. The king realized he was wet.

'Now, take a deep breath, and tell me *calmly*,' said the Wise Wench.

The bucket was full of water, after all. Or had been until she'd thrown it on him, and then it had rapidly become an empty bucket. He was outside, he was confused, and, now, he was exceedingly moist.

Looti dried the king with a large purple towel the Wise Wench had found.

The king caught his breath, lost it, then caught it again. Work had come to a standstill and all eyes were turned to him. 'I'm feeling confused, but, I think,' said the king, 'I think—' he added.

Everyone waited.

'—I just met—'

Breaths caught.

'—Queen Quench!'

More water hit him.

'Now, go through the whole scene again, calmly this time,' said the Wise Wench. They were back in the Moot House, the whole village seemingly trying to hide inside, which inevitably led to a tiff or several.

The king wiped his beard and hair; the water dripped onto his tunic and made a large dark stain which he wasn't sure he liked. He looked at the Wise Wench and the vast crowd which had gathered around him. He could clearly make out that smarty-pants Whippet smiling at him. *His days are numbered,* thought the king to himself, as he began to mentally pass a number of obscure laws about banishing people from the village because their names had one-more-than-one p's in them.

'Even a hint, Your Massiveness?' added Looti, and smiled at him.

The king thought suddenly about turnips, and smiled back. He opened his mouth.

There was a pause.

He shut it again.

'You were in your throne room and...' prompted the Wise Wench.

'Well, why don't you tell me?! After all, you're the Wise Wench!' snapped the king, and folded his arms. His chest was getting cold as the water soaked deeper into his tunic. 'Or are you?' he added, peering at her.

'Of course I am, but I'd...rather hear it from you,' said the Wise Wench, unconvincingly. She looked around and smiled, then gave a shrug of her shoulders. 'You have such a beautiful speaking voice, Your Grace,' she added, slyly.

The king looked pleased and stood up, shaking himself down, and gaining a regal air. Apart from the stain on his tunic. Something was whispering in his head about the Wise Wench, was it the Great Mole in spirit form? Perhaps. Suddenly what it said seemed to make sense and he regained his regal composure. 'Friends,' he said, to the tops of everyone's heads. 'Gather closer, for I shall tell you a tale of woe and fear. A tale few could have witnessed and lived through, but

123

which I, King Stormgrunties, king of the whole forest, have not only lived through, but lived through with dignity.' He effected a little wave, and the Wise Wench bit her lip.

'I was in my throne room, carefully considering our next move, and also wondering if now was the right time for a cut in taxation on pigs.'

Everyone smiled.

'When, suddenly, there was a sound like a bolt of thunder! The whole room shook, and I thought, for a moment, that Ramiclees, the Mole of the Apocalypse, had, indeed, finished his long tunneling to at last emerge into the forest through the Molehill at the End of Time. But it wasn't him, luckily. Or was it 'luckily'? Perhaps, only time will tell...but it was worse, in truth.' He paused again, for effect, but glancing up he noticed that, perhaps, he was overusing the pause technique of tale-enhancing as well as the references to obscure gods; one or more-than-one goblins were already looking bored. 'For, suddenly, before me appeared the most terrible thing ever beheld by any goblin! It was Queen Quench astride Cribmuncher, the Pig of Damnation, and she looked at me, and her baleful stare was wrath.' The king held up his fist and brought it down, suddenly, with a rather immature whooshing noise.

The Wise Wench frowned.

'And she suddenly looked at me and spoke. '*Beware,*' she said in her rasping voice, 'for I bring news of dread which only you, King Stormgrunties, greatest of all goblins are fit to hear.'

'Greatest of all goblins!' whispered Durth, in awe.

'Greatest of all goblins,' muttered the Wise Wench in disbelief.

"And, may I add,' said Queen Quench to me, 'that all we gods are sure that, upon your death—which shall surely be many summers from now—there will be a place at the head of the table of the Great Oak of the Gods for you, and that we shall be honored to share it with you, mighty Stormgrunties!' I should add that Queen Quench had a look in her eye, a look I should guess was fear!' The king smiled and looked very smug. Inside his head, the whispers went on.

Fear thought Durth in profound admiration.

Fear thought the Wise Wench incredulously.

'Yes, *fear,* my subjects, and, then, she begged my leave to tell me more. And, after properly adjusting my neckerchief, I gave her leave to speak on. *'Beware!'* she repeated. 'Beware, my lord and master Stormgrunties the Mighty, greatest goblin ever, for there is a traitor in the village, a traitor who will stop at nothing, a traitor who wishes to see the whole forest soaked in boring and left to rot. *And,* great and mighty king, the traitor is none other than THE WISE WENCH!"

Everyone jumped back, including the Wise Wench herself. Several goblins fell in an unruly heap. Only the king seemed composed. 'Durth Dimbits, you are to arrest the Wise Wench and take her to the gaol!' said the king, with great authority. Somewhere inside his head words of praise echoed emptily in the space.

Durth looked like a goblin caught in a dilemma. He looked at the Wise Wench, who was frowning, and he looked back at the king, who had folded his arms and was staring, theatrically, at the ceiling while blinking rapidly. Durth cleared his throat. 'Wise Wench,' he said, in a whisper, 'I arrest you in the name of King Stormgrunties, vanquisher of the gods. Do you mind?'

The Wise Wench frowned at the king. 'Lead on,' she said. As she slowly walked from the Moot House, she pushed a small bag into Master Whippet's hand and winked. Durth led her out and everyone, except the king, looked confused.

* * *

'This is ridiculous,' said the Wise Wench. 'Just go and fetch him.'

Durth looked troubled and shook his head. 'His Majesty said you were to stew here until you came to your senses. Sorry.' He pulled out a huge pipe, which he gave his undivided attention, desperate not to meet the Wise Wench's stare in case she might cast a spell on him and transmogrify him into a pound of turnips, or something worse.

An hour or so later, the gaol door opened and in walked King Stormgrunties, regal in his evening dressing gown, which was a

125

particular favorite of his, with its deep emerald material interwoven with pictures of frisky cows cavorting in fields full of scantily-clad milkmaids. It had a thick hood, which was up at the moment, giving him a slightly mysterious appearance. Behind him walked Looti.

Durth leaped up. 'Your Majesty!' he said, very loudly.

'Is the prisoner safe, Head Thug?' replied the king.

'Yes,' said the Wise Wench, leaning out through the bars. 'Although I am getting VERY BORED!' she added, vehemently.

'Well now, *prisoner,*' said the king smiling, 'you'll be pleased to know that I've scheduled the trial for tomorrow morning! No point in hanging about—ah, if you'll excuse the pun?'

'Excused.'

He ruffled his neckerchief.

'Trial for what, exactly?' asked the Wise Wench.

'Well now, I thought *you'd* know that?' smiled the king with a chortle, and looked on at Looti and Durth, regally, before bursting into peals of laughter.

'Well, perhaps you'd just tell me anyway, Your Majesty,' snapped the Wise Wench, and stood a little way back from the bars.

The king snapped his fingers and Looti cleared her throat.

* * *

At exactly the same time, Master Whippet moved away from the woods and up the garden path. He was very nervous, he'd once heard that the Wise Wench's cottage was protected by calamitous squirrels and worse. He shrieked inwardly at every crunch from the gravel drive but soon found himself at the cottage door. All was dark and quiet. He turned the handle and walked silently in.

Master Whippet struggled to light his lamp and was glad that he did so, for the Wise Wench had left one of her whisks just by the door and he almost fell. He picked up the whisk and looked around. Sure enough, right there on the table were the pair of jars he was looking for. *Exactly as she told me in the speakme bag message, of course*, he thought happily, remembering what had happened when he'd burnt it in the Kettle Hall earlier.

The fire had suddenly popped, and in its embrace danced an image of the Wise Wench. 'Pay attention, Master Whippet,' said the image, 'for Queen Quench has convinced the king that I am a traitor. He will have me arrested and sent to the village gaol where he will leave Durth Dimbits on guard, not daring to trust anyone else.

'When it is dark go to my cottage and get the one-after-one vials off my kitchen table. One is marked *danger* with a skull, and the other is a sleeping draught—you can't mistake which one is which. Then come back and hide outside the Moot House. You'll hear the king making some unnecessarily fatuous remarks in conjunction with his accusations. Don't think bad of Looti, she is but a tool of the gods. When they've gone, fetch some of your cider and put the sleeping draught into it. On no account open the jar marked *danger!* It's dangerous. Come back and pretend to be friendly with Durth. He won't be able to resist the cider and will soon be out like a light.' The image faded, and then popped up again. 'Oh, and, just to finish, I am *not* a traitor, so don't worry, and also don't worry about getting into trouble because the king will eventually be grateful for what you do.

'Oh, sorry, one last thing: be careful when you come out of my cottage; your shoe lace will be undone.'

Nervously, Master Whippet picked up the jars. One had a skull on it, the other a snoring figure. He smiled to himself, put them in his pocket, and walked out, taking care to shut the door and latch it on his way. As he began to walk along the path he suddenly stopped, stooped, and tied his shoelace.

* * *

'The king charges the Wise Wench with the following crimes. Providing what, on the face of it, seemed to be good advice, but which will, at some later date, doubtless turn out to be so many blessings from Noc and will poison us all; wearing a silly bonnet without leave; being clever—'

127

The list wore on, and on, and on. The king wore an oddly detached smile as the crimes were read out. '—smelling odd; having silly hair; not doing as she was told; correcting royalty in a smug and repetitive manner; changing her mind; having multiple plans without permission; not passing on messages from the gods properly; setting fire to monarchs in public places; not being respectful enough—'

'—AND, most important of all,' interrupted the king, rubbing his head, 'being a TRAITOR! The sentence for which is death.' The king stood back and frowned. 'And the worst thing of all is, you know the outcome of all this, don't you?' He smiled, triumphantly.

'Oh, yes,' said the Wise Wench and lay back on her cot. 'Oh, and Looti? *Moose.*' She closed her eyes and began to lightly snore.

* * *

It was dark when there was a knock at the gaol door and Master Whippet came in, clutching a large earthen pot. Durth stood up. 'I thought you might like a taste of last summer's cider, master Durth?' said Master Whippet. Over Durth's shoulder, he could see the Wise Wench wink at him.

'That's very kind of you, Master Whippet. I was just sat here alone with the accused, I could use a drop,' said Durth, agreeably, and pulled out another chair and tankard. Whippet admired Durth's famously enormous drinking tankard depicting dancing hens juggling ferrets. He knew Durth was fond of drink, and so did the Wise Wench.

'Now, Master Durth, tell me the tale of the time you and young Tuppy from Miffed met them giants in Stumpy.'

Durth sat down and smiled as Whippet filled his tankard. 'Well,' he said, 'it was just after the dreadful incident with the exploding sheep's boils over at Mess—'

'—weren't those the boils that started off on the sheep and then moved onto everyone else?'

The Wise Wench smiled on as the drinking and tale-telling blossomed.

'So that's how young Tuppy got that thing that burst in sunlight?' said Whippet, with genuine interest.

Behind the bars, the Wise Wench was shaking her head.

'That's right,' slurred Durth, as he slumped back in his chair.

Somewhere in the distance, something that sounded generally like a bull snorted very loudly.

Momentarily, Master Whippet held his breath and looked at Durth. He was, after all, feared and respected as Head Thug, and even though Whippet wasn't scared of much, he had respect for the Durth.

'It's quite all right,' said the Wise Wench. 'My sleeping draught never fails. I got the recipe from the Slumber Queen, Lady of Naps.' She smiled and Master Whippet looked around for the key.

'The one-after-one drawer down,' said the Wise Wench, and added, 'it goes without saying that you burnt my speakme bag, but then I knew you'd get it anyway.'

Whippet soon had the door unlocked, but jumped, nervously, when he heard what sounded like a cow in pain, mooing pitifully, somewhere in the distance.

'Don't worry, it's only the king talking in his sleep,' said the Wise Wench, and led Whippet out by the hand.

'Where are we going?' asked Whippet, nervously.

'We must hide until my trial.'

'You mean, we aren't going to flee?'

'Oooh, no! That would be boring. Now, come with me; I know where we can spend the night peacefully.'

The pair fled into the moonlight.

CHAPTER 8

It was no good. Lady Carline wasn't amongst the ravens, but then, even upset as he was, Urgh felt sure she would never eat any of his dead companions; she was too classy, for that.

'You must take this, stoically. Remember, we are here to help,' said Nibbles, as he slowly walked into the clearing. Urgh walked behind him but kept a hand on his friend's shoulder. The other bunnies slowly crept with them, bowing their heads, slightly.

The clearing ahead was huge; a vast, blackened circle where lots of trees had been hurled backwards and burnt. The ground was still smoldering in places, and, on the edges of the clearing where the ravens had been, were a few shards of blackened flesh.

'Courage, friend,' said Nibbles, as he held Urgh. The goblin stared at the flesh in disbelief. Who or what it was, it was impossible to say, but nothing could survive this.

The other bunnies moved reverently into the clearing and removed their hoods. They each consoled Urgh. 'The quest is over,' he said quietly. 'We have failed.' He sank to his knees.

Snufferty BunnyLord put a consoling hand on Urgh's shoulder. His final words were: 'It is not over friend, we will help you,' before the happy BunnyLord fell with a bolt through his neck.

As Urgh looked up in surprise, Lord Nibbles was also felled with similar bolts.

'Death to Craprabbits!' shouted Moaris, as he charged into the clearing with his axe spinning and slashing.

Urgh felt something strike the back of his head, spinning around as he fell to see a man-like ferret just behind him, bringing down a huge club. 'Hang on! This ain't no r—' said the figure, and then Urgh remembered no more.

'Chicken!' said Moaris as he pushed the body of one of the rabbits.

'No, it's a rabbit, mate,' said a voice. They all laughed.

Urgh stirred. He was lying in the middle of the clearing face down. Someone gave him a poke. He rolled over and opened an eye.

'Hello,' said Sorry. 'Don't worry, I'm quite safe!' he added with a broad grin.

'I think you've actually just slaughtered all of them,' said a cultured voice from somewhere in the trees nearby. 'If only you'd talked first and shot later, you might have had valuable allies instead of dead bodies. Typical goblins: attack first, just in case it attacks first, and ask questions later, not that you can ask questions later.' Silence answered Lady Carline's words.

From somewhere nearby, somebody mentioned carrots, potatoes, and parsley. There was suddenly a flurry of activity and voices. There were other figures nearby checking that all the BunnyLords were dead. Urgh could make out long weaselish faces of brown fur, and bodies with slender arms and legs. Each had a crossbow and a very long, pointed knife. 'Wotcher,' said one to Urgh, who stood up very crossly. 'Just what is going on here?' he shouted. 'These BunnyLords were my friends! They *HELPED ME!*' He looked helplessly on at the bodies. '*Helped me—*' he added.

Moaris came up to him and put a consoling hand on his shoulder, saying, '—No, Urgh, you are mistaken!' he said.

'Why?' *Idiot.*

Moaris looked a little perturbed. 'Well, because I'm very hard, and you're very soft! Oh!' he added, 'these are my mates, the ferret-folk. They are very, very hard!'

One leaned on Urgh's shoulder and grinned, revealing very long, pointed teeth. 'Ey up,' it said.

'They saved us from the hogs. Isn't it great!' said Sorry.

Moaris suddenly leered over, aggressively.

'Sorry, Moaris,' mumbled Sorry. 'They saved *me* from the hogs. Moaris didn't need saving.'

'That's right, Daisy!' said Moaris, with a grin. 'There we were, fleeing through the forest, with a huge balloon of hogs at our backs. And when I say 'fleeing,' I mean, of course, tactically withdrawing to a more aggressive attack point!' He looked at Urgh, daring him to disagree with him, looking a little dubiously at his expression of light defiance. 'Anyway, there we were, tactically soundly withdrawing to a more suitable and aggressive attack point, when suddenly up pops Bert Ferret and his gang!' Bert Ferret touched his cap. Urgh suddenly noticed they all had flat caps on.

'Then, whoosh!' shouted Moaris. 'The air was alive with ferret-folk bolts, all tipped with toads and frogs and wrens; primed to explode on contact with guff-hogs! Luckily for the hogs, because I was just about to get out my BEST weapon,' Moaris stopped and grinned, 'which I must have dropped just there!' He pulled a barbed thing from under the remains of Hoppy. 'This, my ferret-folk, is the Pokeyoupine!' Somehow, he picked it up and held it aloft. Sunlight flickered off its myriad points, barbs, tips, and spines.

'But,' said Urgh, 'what happened? I heard an explosion, a scream. And where have you been since?'

'Oh, that was me,' said Sorry, glancing at Moaris, nervously. 'I thought the ferret-folk were attacking us. Turns out they weren't, they were saving us. Can't quite work out why, though. As luck would have it, however, they're all scared of Moaris. Sadly, the more hogs they killed the happier they got, and pretty soon the air was alive with them. We had to fle— we had to *withdraw* to a new attack point behind a big wooden door and regroup. Anyway, what have you been up to, old mate?' said Sorry, patting Urgh on the shoulder before walking off, totally uninterested.

Urgh looked on incredulously. 'The message?!' he asked, suddenly.

Moaris held the speakme bag up proudly. 'Got it here, Tulip!' he said. 'And, now, it's time to go!' He walked around the ferret-folk and thanked each one with a sort of wrist burn which none of them seemed to like. But they all seemed privately pleased when Moaris led his fellow goblins off into the forest to resume their journey.

Urgh glanced at Lady Carline, who smiled sympathetically down at him. Well, did as much as a raven can to smile and look sympathetic, anyway. He shook his head, took one last look at what was left of his friends, and walked after his companions on the quest.

The Great Forest was not only becoming thicker, it was also becoming perceptibly *wetter*. The ground was thick and muddy, and the group often had to turn back to avoid a marshy pool or deep green bog from which frog eyes stared at them until Moaris threw stones, nails, sticks, hammers, darts, and bolts at them. The trees hereabouts had great green beards of moss which drank from the foul deep pools below. Huge webs of unwholesome smelling green fronds wafted from the branches and nearly touched the ground. Occasionally, these fronds would brush the goblins and make them shudder and think of the huge spiders of Huge Spider Wood.

Except Moaris, who sharpened his spider-spikes.

'It's a shame about the Magenta Death, Moaris,' said Sorry, grovelingly, as the little band picked their way through the Great Forest.

Moaris nodded.

'Why, what's happened to the Magenta Death?' said Urgh, still seething within.

'Apparently, it died.'

'Selfish swine!' shouted Moaris.

The little group came to a particularly twisted pair of ancient willow trees. The trees wound together as if in some dance, a pairing that had taken, perhaps, lots-more-than-one summers to perfect. They were beautiful and ancient. Urgh stood and wondered how many passing feet had come this way, how many other goblins had stopped to admire them in their perfect embrace?

Then he heard a chiseling sound and saw that Moaris was carving a picture of himself on them.

'Aaargh!' cried Sorry.

Urgh and Moaris looked around and saw that Sorry was backing away from the side of the tree with a look of horror on his face. He pointed up into the branches and mumbled incoherently. Moaris stood for a second in deep thought, and then suddenly drew out what seemed to be an enormous hat pin and leaped to Sorry's side. Suddenly, Moaris dropped to his knees and began sobbing.

Moaris is crying! Is the sky dropping? thought Urgh, suddenly, looking upwards to check. *No.* He slowly wandered around and saw why Moaris was weeping. High up in the trees hung a circle of goblin skulls and heads. Some of the heads seemed to be very fresh indeed. Lady Carline gave a squawk of horror.

Moaris pointed at the ugliest head, which was nailed in the middle by a giant nail. 'It's daddy,' exclaimed Moaris, 'and nunky Spadge!' he added, pointing at another hanging nearby and weeping.

Urgh looked up at the head of BigBad Chief Runty Miffed the many-one-and-many-more after the first dead Chief Miffed the Miffed of Miffed village. It looked somewhat surprised and lightly maggoty. His head was crudely nailed between a few other fresh ones, some of which Urgh didn't want to make out, but could see a very ugly girl with a smile on her face, and a goblin with magnificent nasal hair, which, as Urgh watched, wafted past him and brushed against his face. 'That must be Bulby Conkfringe,' he said under his breath, and bowed his head reverently.

'This is what giants do to goblins,' said Lady Carline. 'Come, we must finish the quest.'

'No, not yet,' said Moaris. He seemed to regain his composure and stood up again, directly under the ceaseless, unblinking stare of the head of his family. 'For the blood that has been spilt, I swear to my ancestors that it shall be avenged many-many-and-many-lots fold! We shall slay every giant we come across. No mercy shall be given, no quarter, no prisoners. 'Death, death, death' is all they shall hear from our lips, and our lips shall be wrath! Won't they?'

'Yes Moaris,' agreed his goblin companions with admirable haste. 'That was quite composed,' whispered Urgh to Sorry. 'It worries me deeply how reasonable he's being.'

'Perhaps we're rubbing off on him,' said Sorry, nodding in agreement.

Moaris pulled out a big axe from his sack and asked Urgh and Sorry for a leg up, which really, *really* worried them. An hour or so later, the branch had been felled and the heads given what little burial the goblins could give them. Moaris had remained silent all the way through the work and, after they were done, walked off to fetch his pack.

'Right!' said Moaris, as he came back with his pack. 'There's good news and bad news. Which do you want first, Daisy?'

Sorry looked at the forest floor. 'The good news, please, Moaris,' he mumbled.

'We're in Giantland,' he beamed, broadly, 'which means our quest is almost at an end. A quest, let me remind you, ending in an enormous, bloody apocalypse!'

'And delivering a message,' squeaked Urgh.

'Yes, if you like,' muttered Moaris, admiring his spiked weaponry. 'Well, aren't you going to ask me what the bad news is?'

'I daren't, Moaris,' muttered Sorry.

Moaris laughed, theatrically, and put an arm around each of his companion's shoulders—one more easily than the other. 'Well, that's because, brave Tulip and mighty Daisy, the bad news isn't for us, it's for the giants! And that bad news is...USSSSSSSSSSSSSSSSSSSSSSSSSSSS!' he shouted into the forest. 'We're coming for you, giants, and we're coming now!' Moaris continued shouting oaths and explaining anatomical injuries he intended to inflict until he ran out of breath and passed out, momentarily.

'Quick,' whispered Sorry, 'he's out! We can run while there's still chance.'

'No.' Urgh attended to his bag and watched to see if Moaris was breathing. He was.

Sorry stared into the darkness of the forest. Caught between a horror of choices, he stepped back, heard a distant howl, and decided now was not the right time.

Moaris roused, leapt up and looked about suspiciously. 'Right!' he shouted, 'let's go and kill lots of giants!' and marched off, purposefully. Sorry and Urgh exchanged glances, picked up their own packs, and trudged after him. Above them, Lady Carline flapped cautiously between the trees.

A little later, they were wading through mires up to their waists; progress was becoming incredibly slow. 'These bogs are becoming annoying. Thank goodness there aren't any gnats!' said Sorry.

Suddenly, the air was full of small biting gnats.

'You stupid idiot!' said Moaris. 'You've obviously never heard of dontthinkmegnats. They're common in Giantland, you bloody green-scum-filled-pond-brained sissy!'

'Pardon me, mighty Moaris,' stammered Urgh, 'but—'

'—what are dontthinkmegnats?!' finished Moaris, on his behalf. 'Dontthinkmegnats are, for your information, 'Mister let's-sit-down-and-talk-it-through sissy,' gnats which lie in hibernation in bug form. They sleep in the bottom of green bogs just waiting to be awoken by being thought about. They only awaken when there is something nearby to eat that thinks, and most things like that don't like being bitten by gnats.' Moaris looked at the bog and decided to push Sorry head first into it. 'So don't think of them again!' he added.

The day wore on, and after they crossed what seemed to be the many-loads-some-more-and-manyth boggy pool, Moaris found a marginally dry hummock of briars and fallen logs. He got out a very sharp knife and cut the briars back. 'This is camp!' he barked, and sat down, angry that he hadn't seen a single giant to kill all day. 'How far is the giants' keep, bird?' he shouted up into the boughs.

'Not far,' replied Lady Carline, curtly. *'Bird,' indeed! I'm a familiar. Rude pig.*

'Moaris?' asked Urgh. 'Tell me again how many things you've killed?' As the list began, Urgh, applauding and cheering the prancing Moaris, slipped his hands into Moaris's bag and took something out.

Soon darkness fell, and the goblins slept fitfully. At one point, Urgh awoke to hear Lady Carline talking to herself. At least it *sounded* like she was talking to herself, but every so often she'd pause as though listening to someone answer. A 'someone' Urgh couldn't hear at all, but some of the words got him thinking.

Urgh opened an eye.

136

Moaris was pacing about very hard. His tongue was lolling from the corner of his mouth. 'You lot get breakfast ready, and I'll go and scout ahead. I must—*look*—for something. And make sure it's a big breakfast, because it's going to be our last!' With that, Moaris stomped off into the forest muttering under his breath about the paucity of lampreys in a woodland location.

Sorry came over and began to help Urgh make breakfast. Urgh grinned.

'I don't know what you've got to be happy about,' snapped Sorry, as his bottom lip began to wobble. 'Moaris has told us this is our last breakfast! We're going to die!' His speech shot out like a huge, cowardly bolt, shot from some dark, very tight place it didn't want to be. He began to sob and mumble about giants.

'You needn't worry. I've been up all night thinking.'

'Thinking? You're always thinking. What is there to think about? 'Will we die horribly' or 'will we die *very* horribly?'' mumbled Sorry between gulping sobs.

'I've been thinking about the Wise Wench.'

Sorry momentarily stopped feeling sorry for himself and stared at him.

'Think about it. This is supposed to be a peaceful mission, isn't it? We're here to deliver a message. I think the Wise Wench knows about Moaris, and that's why she set up the prophecy of Codly Darkarts. Think about it! I mean it's impossible:

'And a lamprey shall smile on the west,
and be caught by him as a token,
that and many-one-less-than-many tearful cockerels,
one-and-one blue ewes made shall also be gathered by him.
Burn, burn, burn it, oh!'

'You mean...?' asked Sorry, not knowing what to say.

'Moaris is going off to gather these things to fulfill the prophecy, but he'll never find them. Which means you and I sneak into the giants' keep ourselves, sneak the message to them, and flee. I think that was the Wise Wench's plan all along, bless her. I wish

Lady Carline was here to confirm it but she seems to have flown off. Perhaps that, too, is part of the plan. Maybe she's distracting Moaris while we make good our escape to the giants' tower.'

'Escape *to* the giants' tower?' mumbled Sorry. 'Are you sure you have that the right way about?'

'A lot less dangerous than going in with Moaris shouting 'Death to giants!' in a giants' keep full of huge angry giants who take great pleasure in pulling things apart.'

'That's all well and good, but you've forgotten one important thing: the speakme bag.'

'No, I haven't,' said Urgh, as he pulled the bag from his sack with a flourish. 'If there's one thing Moaris Miffed is, he's easy to distract. I took it yesterday while he was going through his kill list again. I thought it would be wise and then I thought of the prophecy. Now, quick! Get packing! It'll be a while before he's back, and we want to be long gone by then.'

'But what happens when he finds us again?'

'We'll worry about that afterwards. And, anyway, who's to say he'll ever find us?' Urgh began throwing his sparse gear into his sack.

* * *

Only the one called Moaris can help solve the riddle. Bloody apocalypse. Burn, burn, burn it, oh! Damnation! What else was there? There was a list, definitely a list. Did it have stoats on it, or was it carrots? Why can't I get rid of this nagging doubt? That's the trouble with prophecies—we all have to go out of our way to fulfil them. Why did the apocalypse come after the list of things? Why can't they be straightforward? 'Moaris went to the mill pond and drowned some puppies. The end.' Perhaps I should just ignore it? Ignore a prophecy? That sounds dangerous. But I like danger. My head hurts. Perhaps I should just go in and slaughter them all now. No, that would never do. The Wise Wench might be ugly, but ignoring her is a bad idea, even though the Not-at-all-Wise Wench got hers.

Moaris found a snake and squashed it, but it was only a fleeting moment of joy before pesky thoughts came back, unwanted, into his mind.

Beheading, bloody apocalypse, and, oh, what else was it? Moaris stomped about, taking little care to keep his movements quiet. Death was all he expected from this day. He'd known it since he'd heard the fox bark just after the owl had hooted and that nightwrenk had wrenked.

Just as he was about to give up and attack the giants' stronghold, the memory of the prophecy awakened in him. He'd been dreaming about his own death. A glorious death, fighting with one arm behind his back, facing a wall of giants—an uncountable number of them. It hadn't hurt him, he knew that. He was a warrior, and warriors died warriors' deaths. They didn't die in tree-felling accidents, or by falling into holes, or by going 'ulp!' and suddenly falling over clutching their chests never to rise again. They died horribly, knee deep in bits of enemy. Such had happened in Moaris's dream.

And he certainly had died beautifully. Beautiful. It was the first time he'd ever associated something with that word. Beautiful was a sissy word, and yet—perhaps he'd been wrong all along?

The forest was even thicker here, and Moaris had to force his way through many walls of briars. The thorns pricked and pulled at his skin, cheering him momentarily. Despite this, forcing his way through the undergrowth was beginning to bore him so much that he was considering turning back, when suddenly he forced his way through a wall of thorns and crashed onto a broad muddy path.

He was not alone on the trail. A trio of huge giants had their backs to him and were engaged in some giant argument which sounded like it could be about what the butchest cheese to eat was.

Moaris smiled and held his axe firmly. Finally, the thought came to him. '*Only the one of the name of Moaris can help solve the riddle and all things shall be killed horribly by him in the bloody apocalypse.' Praise you, Lord Noc, and praise you more, Slash Corpsemangler, God of Slaughtering-Without-Dialogue.* He grinned and took a moment to adjust his stance, carefully parting his legs to the correct angle and tugging at his shirt until it tore slightly. 'Oy!' he shouted. 'I see many ugly heads, would you like me to help by removing them from your bodies!' He grinned.

The giants stopped arguing and looked around. They began to laugh.

'Laugh all you like!' said Moaris quietly. 'The joke's on you, tragedy-features!' Moaris paused for effect for a few seconds before yelling 'MIFFED!' and running at them. The speed of Moaris's charge took the giants by surprise, and before they had time to adequately get out of his way Moaris had plunged his axe deep into the middle of the middle giant. He looked at him with both heads in a mixture of mild surprise and disappointment, and then fell over, dead.

Moaris turned and roared, 'I can't hear you laughing now, bloat-face!' and shook his fist at the remaining giants. They both hefted huge nail-covered clubs and yelled.

The second giant took a few steps towards Moaris and swung its club in a great arc, its end vanishing into the tops of the trees. 'I'M GOING TO SQUASH YOU FLAT!' it said, in a matter of fact—if enormous—voice. The club itself looked to be at least one-more-than-one goblins high, and as broad as Porkly Tubwide, the fattest goblin Moaris had ever met.

Taking his axe in his left hand, Moaris took the initiative and ran forward. The giant's club came whooshing down but Moaris rolled to one side, dropping his axe as he moved. The giant leant forward and peered. A second later, a pointed stick was in Moaris's stronger right hand and he plunged into the giant's left neck.

The giant gave a roar and pulled back, taking the stick with it, its arms flailing at the wound until it fell back with a very noisy choke. Moaris walked past him. 'Next!' he added, with a grin.

The final giant looked worried. He'd never had to fight anything this small that fought back. He decided the chief needed to be warned about this intruder immediately. Sensing the giant's imminent departure, Moaris grabbed his stick, swung it high over his head and hurled it at the giant's shoulder. It hit home with a bone crunching strike. The giant gave a groan.

As it moaned, it turned and stared in hatred at the goblin, gripping its huge spiked club with white knuckles.

Moaris realized he was weaponless.

Then he smiled and realized he was *never* weaponless.

The giant came for him, swinging its great club and bellowing some very rude words. Moaris stood very, very still as the hulking beast came thundering towards him. He stayed as it roared and came closer, and closer. The club came down towards Moaris. He felt the wind before it whistle down at him, bringing certain death.

He stepped aside at the last second, grinned at the furious giant's uglier face as it bent over to look at him and elbowed it in the eye. The giant dropped the club and cursed.

Moaris stared at the club in admiration but realized it was beyond him to lift it.

Then he realized something else. He fell back and gave a very sudden, very strong sweep of his leg at the giant's shins. In its moment of blindness, the creature didn't see the kick coming and caught its full force. It fell forward with a crash straight onto its own spiked club and was still.

Clarity came to him in that bloody moment; a calmness as his plan formed. They were not *words* in the prophecy, they were simply *challenges*, and they were calling him names. Moaris Miffed never backed down from a challenge, particularly if there was any chance of it being bloody or involving death. He began whistling as he set about finding his axe to ensure the prophecy was fulfilled.

* * *

'This way! Quickly,' said Urgh. The camp was an hour behind them now, but the goblins had made scant progress because of a combination of briars and fear. They came to a small pond. Frogs lurked in the green waters and scattered—word of Moaris had spread quickly in frog tongue.

'What do you think he'll do when he finds us gone?' asked Sorry.

'He'll be gone for ages. By the time he realizes there aren't any lampreys between here and the next world, the whole adventure will be over. Hopefully.'

The goblins moved into a patch of faint morning sunlight which was winking through the pine branches. Nearby, a small pond of frogs were noisily announcing that someone was near.

Sorry began to laugh, saying, 'I wish I could see his face when he gets back to camp, and finds not only are brightly-hued sheep impossible to get hold of—'

'—and lampreys,' giggled Urgh.

'Lampreys!' choked Sorry.

'Not to mention tearful cockerels.' The pair collapsed into hysterics.

A few moments later the frogs went underwater, and started swimming away.

'Shh, now. We must be careful; there are still giants about,' Urgh placed a finger across his mouth and shushed.

Then he realized the frogs had gone.

Then he realized why.

'Oh no! It's not possible—' Sorry's words trailed away as he began to sob.

Moaris marched up dragging giants' heads and a huge sack. He stood in the clearing and splashed noisily at the waters' edge, accidentally killing a frog. 'Right!' he said, and began emptying the sack before his ever more hysterical companions.

'That's many-one-less-than-many tearful cockerels, right?!' He hurled them down. 'They look like they've been crying right?'

They did.

'One-and-one blue ewes!' He smiled as he threw the sheep out. Urgh and Sorry looked bewildered and amazed.

'And this is a smiling lamprey. Do you have any idea how tricky it is to find lampreys out here?! Especially cheerful ones. SMILE! He shouted at the creature as it wriggled in his sweaty palm.

His companions shook their heads in unison as Moaris stretched the lamprey's mouth into a leering smile. 'We have nothing to fear!' he shouted. 'And do you know why?'

142

They carried on shaking their heads. Their bodies followed shortly thereafter.

'It's because I am a hero of legend who has just killed one-one-and-one weak giants in less than a minute, and you are ex-sissies!'

They nodded, sissyishly.

'One-more-than-one ex-sissies who are now coming with me to the giants' tower which is about an hour's hard march from here. Ask me how I know that!'

'How do you know that, Moaris?' they mumbled.

'Because I've been there! And do you know what?'

'What do we know, Moaris?' they whispered.

'You're going there, too!' He grinned at them, and gave them each a friendly pat on the face. 'And do you know something else?'

They shook their heads.

'We're going in, but we aren't coming out!' He smiled and kissed them both.

CHAPTER 9

Master Whippet wasn't sure if he liked it, but the Wise Wench had certainly just kissed him.

'Oh, stop reading things into it,' said the Wise Wench, with a huge grin on her face. 'It was just because I was so happy that things are going to plan. Urgh and the others are about to deliver my message, the kettle is nearly finished, and we're about to spoil the machinations of Queen Quench. Probably.'

She moved the curtain, slightly, and looked outside. The village was coming to life now, and the goblins were heading out and talking. And fighting. And setting fire to things. Everyone was pointing to the Moot House, which had a small group of goblins decorating it. From their hiding place in a cottage the Wise Wench had commandeered last spring, the entire spectacle was unfolding.

'Besides,' continued the Wise Wench, 'Wise Women are forbidden from being breed-bound. It would just create—problems—in the relationship if one person knew everything and was always right[35].'

Master Whippet smiled, looked like he was about to say something, decided not to, and peeked outside. 'What do you think—sorry—what *is* going on?'

'They're getting ready to put me on trial.'

'How can they do that if you're not there?'

'It's that fathead's idea of justice. He's had another visitation last night. The king thinks I won't turn up so has taken measures. Queen Quench has told him that I'm going to turn up anyway but he doesn't believe her. What she doesn't know is that I've got *this*.' She held up the jar with the skull on it.

'And what is that, exactly?' said Whippet, as he stared at the vessel in confusion.

'The wrath of the gods!'

---

[35] No comment.

'Just put it up there and do as you're told,' barked Looti, as the mirror was moved to afford the king's chair a particularly fine view of itself. 'He'll love it.' She busied herself instructing the goblins in their duties, and telling them exactly what should go where, that she knew best, and was never wrong. She slowly worked her way through the items she needed. 'More-than-one large millipedes on the mantelpiece. Make sure Gwordoomdoomdoomdoomdoom is dusted. Brush up the floor. Take the twigs of many elms taken from not less than many-some-and-more paces from the village center and tie them over the king's chair. Lightly oil one-more-than-one piglets and place them with bows tied around their tails by a gathering of whelks from the west.' She was feeling very pleased that everything was going to plan and that the trial would be run according to strictest traditions. She didn't know what she'd have done without the Wise Wench's advice.

The Wise Wench's advice.

She'd found the speakme bag unexpectedly below her moose outfit only that morning. It was odd—she'd not worn the outfit for years, and couldn't remember how the word *moose* had got into her head. She could see that the bag had the Wise Wench's mystic prunes all over it and thought about giving it to the king, but something had persuaded her otherwise. Later on, she learnt it was because a small gob-boy was lying outside her house at that time whispering: 'Burn, burn, burn it, oh!' The Wise Wench in the speakme bag had not been very talkative—one might even say curt— but had been very specific in her instructions which Looti had followed to the letter.

'Now, one last thing,' said Looti, climbing into the upper cupboards almost more-than-one-goblins' high. From here she could see the king's chair and admired his courage in spending his days so perilously high. She pushed Tongue aside and reached into the cubbyhole. 'The Substitute Great Mole, exactly where the Wise Wench said he would be,' she said, gripping the mangy baby mole and staring into its blank eye sockets. She climbed down reverently and laid it at the foot of the Great Chair.

'Thank you, mortal,' said the Substitute Great Mole wisely and earnestly and in Looti's voice as it was placed[36].

The door opened and the king walked in, oblivious to the fact that he had a large pair of bull's horns on his head and that his key swung between his legs like some sort of demented iron sporran. He looked around and obviously approved; his entourage, which was considerable, echoed his movements exactly. He slowly checked things were in place as though he had ordered each item personally.

'Good! Yes, the starling looks well and truly frightened! Excellent! Ah, the mop's nicely clean. Good. I see you've hung the mirror correctly. Excellent, excellent.' He slowly and regally climbed into his chair and noticed he was wearing bull horns.

He adjusted his key and colored up.

Everyone stopped and looked, while desperately trying not to look like they were looking.

A minute passed, while the king fumbled for an excuse.

In the distance, dogs began to fight.

Suddenly the king smiled and looked back at the mirror. 'Ah good,' he said, 'I'm so glad I remembered to put that on in case of attack by cormorants.' He took the horns off and threw them away.

Someone yelped.

'Er, Majestic Correctness,' mumbled Looti.

The door flew open and a hooded figure in black stood there dripping.

'Not now, advisor,' he said, and gestured for the figure to enter.

* * *

The Moot Hall was very full now—everyone in the village was there. The king was pleased and looked at his subjects. Then he looked

---

[36] As we have seen before, beatific moles and other such creatures are able to take over the minds and mouths of lesser mortals with ease.

146

nervous as he beheld the darkly-hooded figure that stood near him, dripping water from her divine tunic. Inside his head the murmuring continued.

Looti stood up on a stool, whispered earnestly to the Substitute Great Mole, and called out in a clear voice. 'Blessed local scum and pointless dismal peasants all. Upon the advice of the Substitute Great Mole, His Majesty, King Stormgrunties the many-many-and-lots-after-more-than-many-dead-King   Stormgrunties-after-the-first; king of the Great Forest; be-keeper and guardian of the Great Mole; holder of Gwordoomdoomdoomdoomdoom, the Mop of the Dreaded Magpie People; ruler absolute of the Kingdoms of Mudge, Spray and Tottle-by-the-Mire; keeper of the Stoat Hat of Justice; Arch-magicmaster supreme; his Cunningtude Grace; the Honor of Tunt; slayer of Lucy Carter and her puppy, Snuffles. His Massive Mightiness has accused the Wise Wench—'

Smirks and giggles.

'—the Wise Wench,' repeated Looti, firmly, 'of *treason*. Because the Wise Wench has chosen not to appear to defend herself, her effigy is to be tried in her place.'

All eyes turned to the effigy.

It was crap.

It consisted of a long stick of wood, about half a goblin high, with a pumpkin instead of a head that had a big smiling face drawn on it—the king had personally supervised this section of work. Above it was slung a sheepskin with a bonnet clumsily thrown on top. To finish the masterful illusion, a small gob-boy had been chained to the effigy and had to say, 'I am the Wise Wench; the *accused*,' in a voice that was loud enough to be heard, but not loud enough to put the king off.

There was more stifled laughter from the back.

Looti continued. 'And for the—'

'—Wait a moment,' interrupted the king, regally, while looking around nastily. 'It seems to me that my subjects are finding this whole trial a little *amusing*. Perhaps they regard the crime of treason as something to giggle about? Perhaps they find the idea of a traitor *a bit of a laugh*? Perhaps they would like to see the village burned to the ground? Perhaps I should start by burning some locals?' He began humming to himself, aggressively. His Majesty waited for a few minutes. Then he waited some more until he was sure that everyone was very serious. 'You may continue,' he said.

'Thank you, Your Grumpiness,' said Looti, nervously. 'Wise Wench, how do you plead?'

The room burst into roars of laughter. The goblins rolled and hooted, pointing at the crap figure, and heaping abuse upon every facet of its creation—especially the face.

'NOT GUILTY!' shouted the Wise Wench as she marched into the room with Master Whippet walking meekly in behind her.

All eyes turned to the Wise Wench, who marched up to her crap effigy and tutted as she looked it up and down. She paid special attention to the head, gave the king a disdainful look, and pushed the figure out of her way. It crashed on the floor and the head splatted over several goblins nearby. It turned out to be quite tasty.

She gazed at the hooded figure and felt in her pockets to make sure that the glass vial was still there.

The king harrumphed several times and cleared his throat very loudly. 'So, you decided to join us, having broken out of the town gaol last night, and—'

'—It wasn't Durth's fault,' she interrupted.

'Well, we only have your w—'

'—It was yours,' she finished, and smiled at him.

'As I sai—'

'—So let him out of gaol, oaf!' she snapped.

'I give the orders around here!' he snapped back. Then he looked nervous and looked at the ground; it spun dizzily before him. His head was dancing with words, most of which he didn't understand. Something was not quite right, but he was king so it must be. 'Now, Looti, er, where are we?' he said, rubbing his temples.

The Wise Wench smiled to herself and shook her head.

'Lordship,' said Looti to everyone in the room, 'the Wise Wench stands accused of treason and has pleaded not guilty. Who accuses this woman?'

148

'I do,' hissed the hooded figure.

The goblins visibly drew back from the strange figure as she leant upon her lichen-soaked staff and rubbed her antlers.

'And your name is?' said Looti, nervously stepping back.

'Beryl.'

'Beryl? Not Queen Quench?'

'Well, that's my stage name so it'll do.'

The room became hushed.

'Queen *Quench*?' asked Looti. 'Queen Quench, naughtiest of the gods? Queen Quench who once took her pet dragon for a walk, which then slipped its lead and more-than-can-be-counted summers of darkness fell on the forest? Queen Quench who once tried to chop down the Oak of the Gods with Yuthor, Chopper of the Terrible Woodcutter? Queen Quench who has unleashed the Hedgehog of the Endless Thunderstorm on the forest?'

'Rumours and exaggeration, you know how these things get blown out of proportion.'

'Hmmm.'

The room stilled again, and Looti and the Substitute Great Mole whispered in the king's ear. They exchanged harsh, hushed words, but the king seemed to win the argument. The impression was entirely wrong.

'And what evidence do you have that the Wise Wench is a traitor?' asked Looti, firmly, while trying not to make eye contact with the god.

'Well,' said Queen Quench, in a thoughtful, yet still sinister and hissing voice, 'I am a god, and I saw her betraying you.'

'Ah, when exactly did this happen?' said Looti at the villagers.

'Next Thodsday.' The goddess shook her matted hair, wriggling worms fell out, devoured little holes in the Moot House's floor and continued downwards. Several goblins nearby were annoyed that they couldn't catch them as they looked juicy.

'Aha!' shouted the king, and wagged a finger at the Wise Wench before coloring up and putting it away.

149

A low murmur broke out amongst the crowd. The Wise Wench looked on, dispassionately, idly. She began cleaning her nails.

'But if she doesn't betray us until next Thodsday, she hasn't actually been a traitor yet, has she?' added Looti in a commanding voice.

'Well—' said Queen Quench, '—that's a good point. But not good enough, I'm afraid!' She roared and threw back her hood. Everyone in the room gasped, for Queen Quench had an uncanny, almost family resemblance to the Wise Wench herself, except she had a few more moles. 'I have you all together, and her—*HER!*—to die before me!'

The villagers held their breaths. The room was as still as the Topiary of Tranquility, just after the release or Yorkquin, the Duck That Stopped Time.

Queen Quench looked around, and then smiled, evilly. In the distance, a flapping, oinking sound could suddenly be heard. 'I suggest—*nay!*—foretell,' she said, facing the Wise Wench, 'that your little village is at an end. The hogs are coming! *The hogs are coming!*' She began to laugh and overact, fiendishly.

'You can cease that fiendish laughter and hamming this instance!' commanded the Wise Wench in a commanding voice.

'Who are you to command I, one of the gods, from commanding you, a mere mortal?!' Queen Quench was towering above everyone in the room now, and even the king, on his mighty chair, seemed dwarfed by comparison. Outside, thunder clouds began to gather, and, in the distance, came the dreadful oink and flap of vast numbers of approaching manic guff-hogs. The villagers began to panic and shout, pushing each other, and setting fire to various objects; a general crush developing as they all tried to make their way out of the one door at the same time. A few took advantage of the melee by stealing the odd object.

'Fools!' laughed Queen Quench. 'And to think this was only the start! You are all doomed already!'

'Silence!' shouted the Wise Wench.

Everyone was silent.

150

Except the hogs, who were now approaching the outer huts of the village.

The Wise Wench marched slowly forward towards Queen Quench and looked at her with a mixture of scorn, pity, and admiration. Everyone was very impressed by her multi-emotional visage and clapped.

The Wise Wench bowed. 'Fiend,' she said, 'you have been judged by the gods, and they say that you are *very* naughty. You are to be punished!'

'Punished? You do not know my power, mortal girl. I could crush you in an instant!' The storm gathered above the village, and lightning struck several trees which fell with mighty crashes. The oinking sound, which was getting steadily nearer, was almost drowned by the crackle of the lightning. Queen Quench was silhouetted, eerily, and all the goblins, bar the Wise Wench, averted their eyes. Except Dome Eyes, who was forced, to his horror, to stare on at Queen Quench despite his attempts not to.

'And you *will* be punished!' the Wise Wench roared above the storm, shouting so loud that she was momentarily forced to break off her tirade of condemnation to cough very loudly.

The oinking had almost reached the door. There was a moment's stillness before a sudden vast oink ripped through the air.

'Fool!' shouted Queen Quench. 'You are too late!' she strode to the Great Door, her hands upon its dirty handle.

The hogs began to bash at the door from outside.

'Not quite!' shouted the Wise Wench, and pulled out the bottle marked with a skull, uncorked it, and hurled it straight at Queen Quench. The god laughed when she saw it coming towards her, reached out a hand, and caught it, still laughing. She suddenly stopped and gazed into the bottle.

The merest noise—barely a wisp, the slightest little breath—emanated from within it. Noc's punishment was upon her.

Queen Quench fell to the floor clutching at her throat. The hogs ceased their battering and began to panic, flying in various directions, oinking and flapping in frenzy. Queen Quench stared balefully at the Wise Wench, gulped, and was gone.

The oinking outside suddenly ceased.

CHAPTER 10

Moaris marched off into the forest with a certain aggressive, squelching noise which his companions knew meant trouble. Urgh shook his head and looked totally dismayed. Sorry shook his head, as well.

'Stop it,' said Urgh, removing Sorry's hands from his head.

'Sorry, I panicked,' said Sorry.

Moaris gave a little glance over his shoulder and was pleased to see that his companions had at last learnt to begin to fight; they would need all the fighting skill they could muster very, very soon. He grinned broadly, and waved for them to follow.

'Excuse me, Moaris,' whispered Urgh, bravely, 'but Sorry and I were just wondering where on earth you got the lamprey—'

'—Smiling lamprey, chicken-features.'

'Sorry, *smiling* lamprey, great Moaris, and the blue sheep this deep into a wooded area?'

'Persistence and improvisation,' grinned Moaris, licking his bloody axe.

'But you were only gone an hour, and how come the sheep are blu—' Sorry changed his words as Moaris stared at him. '—which is really great, of course,' he continued, 'but not as great as you, Moaris.' Sorry decided to stop interrupting and began to clap. Urgh joined in.

'Do be quiet! The giants are very close,' said a voice from the trees. Lady Carline emerged, using her wing as a fan. She eyed the goblins, disdainfully. 'You goblins excel at making noise.'

'The giants are close? Great!' shouted Moaris, and gripped his axe.

'Yes, and they have excellent hearing. It's probably due to having that extra set of ears. Now, don't forget what the Wise Wench said about, for example, chimneys.'

'Yeh, whatever,' answered Moaris.

'Hang on, hang on,' said Sorry, looking at the raven. 'Why can't you just fly into the giants' keep and deliver the message for us?

153

I mean, you have wings and everything, and you can speak, somehow, even without lips, which, frankly, is pretty unrealistic, if you ask me.'

Lady Carline stared down at the goblins, coughed, and said, 'I don't think Moaris would be happy if I flew in and took all the glory, would you, Moaris?'

'Ey?' said Moaris, who was cutting his finger on the edge of his axe to prove how butch he was. 'Message? No, it must be me. Why? Who says otherwise?' He began looking about for a villain to blame and subsequently hurt.

Sorry and Urgh looked at the ground. 'No one, great Moaris,' they said together.

The raven flew onto Urgh's shoulder. 'Besides,' she whispered, 'every tale needs a hero, and a tragedy to work, doesn't it, Urgh?'

The little goblin nodded.

Soon, the group came to the path Moaris had found. The giant corpses were still lying there, looking extremely headless. Ahead, the path broadened and raised up on a huge timber walkway.

'Impressive, one little goblin against all those giants!' said Lady Carline. 'You truly deserve—sorry, *will eventually deserve*—a seat in the Great Oak's battlebranches when—sorry, *if*—anything untoward happens.'

Moaris. Moaris turned to his companions. 'I'll scout ahead in case of extreme danger.' He then stood, an inane wide grin on his face. A long line of dribble fell to the ground, drowning a microscopic mite.

His companions began to laugh nervously, their laughter growing into a manic thing, fed by Moaris's angry encouragement. 'All right, that's enough humor for one day, I think, and you can stop clapping; it's patronizing. This is the end, then, friends; just along that trail is the giants' keep. I shan't say I hope we will live, because we shan't, but I shall wish that Slash Corpsemangler smiles upon us, and allows us a glorious death. And that Mopwind, the Master of Pain, spares you from suffering during the torment to come. And that Dropsy, Lord of Tripping and Unexpectedly Dropping Things, turn his single, baleful, swollen eye away, looking for other folk to drop things in the forest, rather than fixing his single, hateful green eye upon us, and making our weapons slippier than the edges of a poo-pit!'

'Oh dear,' said Sorry.

Urgh looked at his feet and was thinking that he wasn't sure if he was afraid or not. Yes, Moaris was in charge, and, yes, their deaths did seem very imminent, but, yes, the Wise Wench had said that they would be okay. He felt into his sack for magic and was comforted that he had plenty left. His memory cast back to the eyes of the badly-drawn giant fox in the Wise Wench's sack and he wondered if he'd ever find out what it was for. 'Then let us go with Noc's noisy blessings and be damned to death!' he said, quite quietly. *Is this being a hero?*

Moaris smiled and for one part of one second regretted his companions' imminent violent demise. 'Charge!' he roared, and headed off up the path towards the giants' keep.

Urgh drew his little knife and charged after him.

Sorry skulked off back towards the forest.

Lady Carline watched Sorry creep off, nodded sagely, and flew after the others.

Moaris ran headlong up the trail, screaming giant-derogatory abuse at everything he could see. Bushes, worms, lichen, everything. Shortly, everything he could see was engulfed by an enormous timber tower which lurched out of the forest. Great circular turrets topped with wickedly-barbed ironwork stood at each corner. Ragged banners were everywhere; hanging and fluttering stiffly in the air. Directly ahead on the trail, a great drawbridge spanned a scum-filled moat which looked very deep. As luck would have it, the drawbridge was down, so Moaris and Urgh charged towards it.

'Wait, Moaris!' whispered Urgh, as loudly as he dared. 'I can't see Sorry! I think he's got lost behind us.' Urgh caught up with Moaris, who was carrying out a short tactical survey of the tower.

'He's a pointless, shoulderless, useless cabbage, anyway. We can do without the cowardly little runt,' shouted Moaris,

155

understandingly. From the bridge, the tower was indeed vast—taller by many times than the Great Tower of Miffed, which, of course, was now no longer the Great Tower of Miffed, but now the Great Demolished Tower of Miffed. To say the giants' tower was well-built would be a considerable exaggeration. It would be more accurate to wonder how it still stayed upright—something Moaris was planning to rectify.

As Urgh crossed the bridge, he glanced into the green waters of the moat and was stared at by the most gigantic pike he'd ever seen. *I wouldn't want to have to swim past that* he thought, very uncannily. He stared up at the banners, which soon resolved themselves into what could possibly be described as giant clothing drifting on ropes swaying around the keep. It was clearly being left out to soil, the lines of assorted unpleasant outer and innerwear displayed in their vast unpleasantness.[37]

'Moaris, please, wait,' pleaded Urgh, vainly, as he stared at the soiling lines. They rose from rusty iron wheels attached to pegs hammered into the ground on the outside of the moat and upwards to the rooftops and battlements. Urgh gave one a tug and felt it give, alarmingly. Following the line upwards he saw it pass directly by battlements filled with shadowy figures. *Perhaps not that way,* he thought to himself, disappointedly. He looked around to see Moaris already storming the building via the great outer gate.

Suddenly, a giant appeared in the huge gateway and made his way towards an enormous frying pan which he had perched by the

---

[37] Giants take smells far more seriously than goblins, which is probably entirely due to the fact that goblins (especially male goblins) can't really be bothered to go out of their way to do much. True, if a huge cowpat presents itself on the ground ahead, any self-respecting goblin is going to roll straight down into it to collect it properly. What they won't do, in almost every case, is go out of their way to do such things; they can't be bothered. It would, perhaps, therefore be more accurate to say that giants are more *professional* in their relationship with smells. A good giantess would travel far and wide to collect a particularly repulsive odour for her sweaty mate. This is why putting out clothes to soil where the elements and birds— which are encouraged to settle above giant homes—can properly batter them is such an important part of giant life, along with eating, shouting, and squashing things.

side. Before he could reach it, Moaris appeared and had hurled his pointed stick into the giant's left-left head. It hit. The huge creature roared and thrashed at the air for a few moments, before falling into the moat with a considerable splash. Thrashing followed as the huge pike made its intentions known, and, within moments, all that was left was bubbles and lots of blood. Moaris stood back with his legs wide apart and tore his shirt completely off. 'I'm rapidly coming to the conclusion,' he said calmly to Urgh, 'that the simpler a weapon is, the more effective it is. Miffed!' he yelled, and plunged into the castle.

Outside, it began to thunder. As the weather growled, somewhere nearby the cockerels that the giants kept for snacks began to crow.

Not far enough away to be safe, Sorry manage to hide just as a patrol of giants—fully almost-not-possible-to-count strong—returned along the path towards the castle. In the distance, he thought he heard a giant roar followed by a massive splash. The giants rushed off towards the sound.

The corridors of the keep were clearly designed to fool intruders. Its garish wallpapers and cunningly tasteless arrangement of furniture made the goblins dizzy. The stench within the keep was very, very considerable—a potpourri of sweat, meat, and other, less pleasant things. Moaris looked confused as he came to yet another door which was not only vast, but also seemed to be locked. So far, only one chamber had been open, and that had nothing in it but a big fireplace decorated with bas-reliefs of giants laughing and sitting on poultry. The door latches were very high, but Moaris had an array of prodding and poking implements that enabled him to open anything. Urgh walked up to Moaris and patted him, gently, on the shoulder. Moaris spun around and knocked him to the floor.

'Sorry!' said Moaris, and helped him up. 'Force of habit. Don't touch me again!'

'That's all right,' mumbled Urgh as he wiped the blood from his nose, 'but we must stop for a moment. What is it, exactly, that you want to do?'

'Kill everyone!' said Moaris, happily.

'Yes, but surely *some* "everyone's" have more priority than *other* "everyone's?"' What about trying to get to their chief first?' asked Urgh in a moment of inspiration.

'Yes, good idea! Kill their chief!' replied Moaris, and made to smash the door down.

'Wait, wait,' urged Urgh, desperately. 'If you want to kill the chief, you must get to him stealthily—he's sure to be guarded.'

'Good! The more guards, the better!'

'Yes, but what happens if one of the guards gets a lucky blow and kills you?'

Moaris didn't look impressed.

'Well, when I say lucky blow I mean a lucky blow from behind, unseen, from a distance, by a sneakily hidden giant, with an arrow. Several arrows. Poisoned, of course.'

'The skulking swine!' said Moaris, his neck steadily reddening.

'Precisely. Surely it's far better to stealthily make your way to the throne room, fulfil the *prophecy*, launch an open heroic attack on the chief, kill him dead, and *THEN* kill everyone?' Urgh smiled hopefully.

Moaris thought. It was a long job.

During this time, the giants that Sorry had cringed from only moments before had returned from the forest and noticed the blood. They'd decided they weren't at all happy about the situation, and had resolved by unanimous vote to disembowel whomever had killed poor Terry and pushed him into the moat. One giant offered a controversial and contrary suggestion in that what had actually happened was that Terry—who was a bit dim, even for a giant—may have cut himself shaving, tripped into the moat, and been eaten. But, plausible though this deduction[38] was, merely suggesting something

---

[38] Needless to say, there is no word for 'deduction' in Giant.

complicated caused a fight which was settled, in the traditional giant way, by strength of numbers.

Meanwhile, within the keep, Moaris had thought. 'Good idea!' said Moaris, and patted himself down. 'Wait, I haven't got the speakme bag!'

Urgh reached into his sack and brought it out.

Moaris took it back and looked cross. 'You didn't take this from me, did you?' He scowled, pointy yellow teeth baring. 'If, for one minute,' he said, testily, 'I thought you'd taken this from me with the intention of sneaking into the giants' keep, tossing the bag on the fire, and just delivering the message, I'd be cross. *Very* cross.'

'No, that wasn't my plan at all, Moaris,' lied Urgh, unconvincingly.

'Well, that's all right then,' said Moaris, pocketing the bag, aggressively.

Urgh looked relieved. 'In which case,' he said, 'let's go back to the room we just came through; you know, the one with that big fireplace? I have a feeling we can climb up the chimney and maybe it will link to the chief's room. I assume he lives at the top.' Urgh smiled as he remembered the Wise Wench's words: "*they used their cunning to enter the giants' stronghold by, say, entering a chimney, sneaking into the upper tower, and delivering the message to the giants' chief.*"

They went back into the previous room and crept towards the fireplace. Urgh stared upwards and was alarmed to discover that he could barely see a tiny circle of light far, far above where the chimney opened. A bird flittered over the opening and gave him an encouraging squawk. The chimney was made up of broad, rough pieces of stone ideal for clambering up. Momentarily, Urgh thought back to long summers of happy tree climbing, of lazy, hot days leaping from the boughs of sycamores into deep, cool pools. Then he remembered what had happened to him when everyone else found out about his odd habits and rubbed his head.

He suddenly heard the sounds of giant feet approaching. 'After you, Moaris,' he said, urgently, and stood back with some haste.

Moaris marched into the fireplace—which was much bigger than him—and spat on his hands.

'Oh, Moaris?' said Urgh, slyly. 'Perhaps you'd better hand me the speakme bag, after all? You never know, you may need weapons in each hand if the chief's hall is absolutely full of giants.' He held out his hand, nervously.

Moaris scowled and gripped the bag. 'How full?!' he snapped.

'Giants beyond counting. It's certain death!'

Moaris handed him the bag and started clambering eagerly up the chimney. 'Great!' he said, from the distance above.

Urgh clambered up just as the door opened and some huge giants marched in. They were arguing about shaving.

Urgh held his sooty breath.

The door below shut and the voices went away.

'Good,' he said to Moaris in a whisper. 'It's safe to go on.'

Moaris had already done so.

Urgh slowly and carefully made his way upwards, taking care not to look up since Moaris was disturbing an awful lot of soot. More than was necessary, he thought to himself.

They passed another floor, and had a quick glance in from the fireplace. It seemed to be a giant games room, although what violent games they were even Moaris, the most aggressive of all goblins, could not guess. There was an array of dried slugs, darts, clubs, hoops, rabbit heads, giant manacles, and a scoreboard, but the room was littered with more bizarre objects, too: a large pile of massive antlers with head straps; vast amounts of pointed sticks; a selection of grinning pot ducks; a massive leather bull; and a live donkey. Moaris was sure he'd get plenty of time to learn all the games later on, and particularly looked forward to riding the leather bull.

Alas, however, he was incorrect; his gaming days were already over.

The mumbling above was getting louder. Moaris picked up his pace while muttering aggressive words under his breath as he scrambled up the chimney. Before Urgh could protest, Moaris had disappeared through a fireplace opening above. As quickly as he could, he followed him through the opening and into the chamber.

Luckily, the fire was low and banked forward in the huge fireplace. The massive logs which the chief's fire-stoker had placed had yet to catch fire, and Urgh was able to follow Moaris's steps across them and into the room. The stench of sweat and nastiness was overpowering. He saw that Moaris was stood in the middle of lots of giants, his legs further apart than he'd ever seen, and that he kept slapping his bare sooty chest. Urgh leapt off the last log and stood by his side. Moaris had already begun his taunting of the giants.

'—and not only sissies! Giant sissies! Which makes you, without doubt, the largest sissies I've ever come upon! Sissies who cry at the sight of a graze and who weep at the thought of fighting. And let me tell you this: after I've killed you all, I'm going to plant you and grow you into giant flowers! Dancing will compulsorily occur each night at your graveside, and happy songs about peace will be sung liberally by choirs of—'

Urgh stood in awe while Moaris kept up his threats. The hall was gigantic and adorned with the heads of all living things. Well, deceased living things, stuffed rather badly. A huge table, made of many of the mightiest elms ever seen in the forest, dominated the chamber, and at it sat lots of giants. But it was the head of the table which drew Urgh's attention the most, for there sat the Chief of the Giants. *He's got one-one-and-one heads!* thought Urgh to himself.

'—with lacy nether garments, and those who visit your ruined tower will paint it pink and encourage pretty plants to grow upon it, and the plants shall be dried and used to scent the rooms of old goblin ladies—'

The giant's chief was studying them both with a mixture of surprise, annoyance, and hunger. He was able to do this, not through any particular skill, but through an accident of birth. He did, after all, have the necessary number of heads for such an event to occur. Should he wish, he could look on anything with a mixture of fear, amusement, and sarcasm.[39]

---

[39] Many scholars have said that giants are the hardest of all creatures to discern the moods of. They cite the many and complex natures of the personalities of the twin

161

Or sarcasm, haughtiness, and sarcasm.

Or sarcasm, condescension, and hatred.

His was a gift of the gods indeed.

'—these booties your bodies shall be attired in shall be made of finest pink material, and tied with bows with bells on, and they shall—' Moaris looked happier now than Urgh had ever seen him. He was almost dancing with the joy of the violence he was about to unleash and the abuse he was giving out to his countless future opponents.

The giant chief had a huge iron ladle lying next to his vast bowl of porridge on a low stool. The other giants looked nastily at the goblins and from somewhere under the stool came a giant growling and a giant purring.

'—declaring their undying love for fury animals. And a monument shall be made above the ruined tower and be decorated with red bows, shaped into HEARTS! Bowls of sugar, honey, and kittens shall be liberally—'

Urgh jumped as a huge ugly giant dog's head emerged and scratched behind one ear. Then scratched behind another pair of ears as its other head appeared.

'—and the tokens of love shall be placed about your fallen bodies and at all times gentle wind chimes shall—'

The chief stood up.

'—Now, funeral headgear! Firstly, your corpses shall have yellow fluffy—'

He looked at Moaris with all of his heads and snarled.

'—which shall have tassels, the edges of which shall be trimmed with silver puppies—'

---

heads and the dichotomy they present—particularly for the giants, who are regularly known to have violent, occasionally fatal, arguments with themselves. Everyone else says this is rubbish as all giants really want to do is eat and squash things. The chief, with three heads, is by no means unusual amongst giant-kind, and giants with as many as many heads have been recorded in the annals of goblin history, which sadly have all been burned, if indeed such things ever existed amongst creatures so averse to recording things beyond singing about them and/or cooking them.

He brought his huge ladle down on Moaris, who disappeared under it. He laughed to the other giants and leant over, peering at the floor. He pulled the ladle back with a grin, saying, 'MNARRRRRR!'

There was nothing underneath.

The chief looked around annoyed, checking under the furniture, and staring at his followers suspiciously. Then he looked closer at the ladle. Moaris was gripping it with one hand, and holding a pointed stick with another. 'Missed!' shouted Moaris as he poked the giant chief's right-right-right head. Then he added a final word, which predictably enough was 'Kill!' and dashed into the giants.

Urgh had been thinking, and suspected the moment would come when he found himself in the giants' throne-room with Moaris. He realized a fight would occur and had a plan.

A brilliant plan.

He pulled out a cabbage.

This was not just any cabbage, however. This was a magic cabbage.

A magic 'misty smells' cabbage.

He threw it onto the ground just behind Moaris, who was running below a chaise-longue, severing giant ankles with his axe. The giants, for their part, were busy pulling the furniture up and trying to get at Moaris so they could bite his head and other anatomical parts off.

They were failing badly.

The cabbage suddenly burst in a cloud of foul-smelling dust that enveloped the room. As the dust bloomed, Urgh saw a particularly ugly giant smiling at him. He had glasses on each head and grinned broadly.

Urgh stepped back towards the safety of the fireplace as the carnage continued. Moaris had started singing about the pending memorial carvings above each giant's grave by now, and what he proposed they depict was less than flattering. Urgh reached into his sack and pulled out the speakme bag. An axe suddenly cut the dust beside him and he screamed a proper terrified scream. Through the dust, he glimpsed the reflective rim of a pair of a pair of spectacles.

Beyond, he could hear the giant chief shouting, 'HE'S ONLY A GOBLIN! SPLAT HIM!' By the sounds of the other giants, they didn't agree.

They sounded scared.

Properly scared.

Urgh had to admire Moaris's violent mayhem and fearlessness, and resolved to tell him so afterwards, but put such thoughts on hold while he clambered into the fireplace, the speakme bag in hand. There was a sudden scream from the giant chief followed by the sound of scrambling close by.

As the cabbage and dust settled, a scene of carnage greeted him. Lots of giants were dead, and Moaris was stood menacingly before the prostrate chief of the giants, his huge stomach just in front of Moaris, who was holding his axe. Both were covered in gore, but the chief was lying on his back. Either side of Moaris, the giant's legs quivered.

'WAIT A MINUTE NOW, LITTLE GOBLIN! LET'S TALK THIS OVER, SHALL WE? LET'S BE PEACEFUL! LET'S BE FRIENDS!' The chief slithered back slightly along the bloody floor.

Peace? Urgh blinked as he took the moment in. *Amazing. So she was right all along,* he thought, and smiled broadly.

Moaris smirked. 'The time for talk is over!' He flicked a grin over to Urgh, and shouted, 'I understand Urgh. I understand the prophecy. Listen! Listen! It's stormy outside, the cockerels are calling.' Outside, noises echoed in confirmation of his words, perhaps as though a little afraid of him. He grinned widely at the remaining giants. 'And I, Moaris Miffed, son of the Miffed of Miffed, avenge my village. I am Chief Moaris Miffed, the many-one-one-and-many-more after the first dead Chief Miffed the Miffed of Miffed village and I am your bloody apocalypse!' He hefted his axe backwards, but as he did, the spectacle-wearing giant, who had clambered above the fireplace, leapt down behind him. Urgh shouted a warning but the giant brought an enormous mallet down on him, squashing him flat.

* * *

'Be silent. You're quite safe. At least for now!' she shouted at the gathering of weeping, shaking, hiding goblins. Then, the Wise Wench suddenly looked up, a grave expression crossing her face. A tear fell down her dirty cheek.

The distant storm growled.

'Poor Moaris,' she whispered. Then she looked up to the heavens. 'Don't forget our bargain!' she shouted and shook a fist. 'At the battle of the gods for eternity!' she roared, parting her legs slightly, and tore a bit off her blouse in tribute. 'And, for gods' sakes, don't let him get bored,' she added, with a chuckle.

As if in answer, the wind suddenly picked up. As it howled, it sounded almost afraid. The goblins nearby shook their heads. 'She's started talking to herself, then,' said a very round goblin that was a peculiar shade of ochre.

Everyone agreed no good would come from that little development.

* * *

Urgh looked at the giant with glasses, who lifted his mallet to reveal a very flat, extremely angry-looking Moaris.

A very dead Moaris.

Then the chief turned his heads to Urgh, who began backing into the fireplace. He turned to run but saw that the flames had caught behind him. His way of escape blocked, Urgh could see that every surviving giant was on his feet, and the huge dog with one-more-than-one head was at the front. It began to snarl.

They all began to snarl.

Urgh wiped sweat from his head and trembled.

'AW, LOOK! THE LITTLE BLIGHTER'S CRYING! MNARRRRRR!' laughed the giant chief, adding, 'WHAT WAS THAT YOUR LITTLE FRIEND WAS SAYING?' Soon, everyone was laughing.

Urgh backed all the way up to the flames but was finally unable to retreat any further without being alight. *So this is it,* he thought to himself, and fumbled for the speakme bag. *Looks like being heroic is just painful.*

The giants moved menacingly towards him and, very worryingly, began to laugh even louder as well as snarl. 'LET'S SKEWER HIM AND HAVE HIM AS A MIDDAY SNACK CHIEF!' said one from the back.

'NO, NO! IT'S 'LET'S SKEWER HIM AND HAVE HIM AS A MIDDAY SNACK' YOUR TRI-NOGGINNESS!" said another, and struck the first one with his corking mallet.

'HOW ABOUT WE TURN HIM INSIDE OUT AND USE HIM AS A MITTEN, YOUR HEX-EYED-MASTERFULNESS?!' said a really ugly giant at the back. Several giants agreed strongly with this proposition.

Urgh struggled to understand giant-talk but got the drift of it. He looked at the flames and wondered just how bad merely burning to death could be. He reconsidered a few seconds later when he felt the flames licking him.

'WHAT ABOUT I TREAD ON HIM AND THEN YOU CAN USE HIM AS A SORT OF DECORATIVE SKULL CAP, DESIGNED IN THE LIKENESS OF A GOBLIN, YOUR TREBLE-NOSED-BARBARITY?!'

'HMMM,' considered His Treble-Nosed-Barbarity.

'WAIT, WAIT, I KNOW! PAY ATTENTION TO ME,' called Ate Eyes, the smarty-pants giant with the glasses. 'WHAT WE NEED TO DO, YOUR TRIPLEFACED-TRIUMPHANT-FLATULENCE, IS TO FORCE-FEED HIM WAX FOR A YEAR AND A DAY AND THEN USE HIM AS A FAT GOBLIN-SHAPED CANDLE! GOBLINS CAN EAT ANYTHING AND NEVER POP I'VE HEARD! HE COULD GET REALLY MASSIVE!'

Everyone clapped.

Ate Eyes stood back proudly and, as he cleaned one pair of glasses, bowed slightly.

'Wwwait!' said Urgh, as loudly as he could.

The giants looked round angrily, annoyed that this goblin dare to interrupt giants busy congratulating themselves on a successful idea, a rare event at any time. Weapons were readied, and Urgh found himself momentarily wondering what a fine giant Moaris would have made.

If only he wasn't flat.

And dead.

He glanced over at Moaris; even in death he looked cross.

'Because I have something for you!' shouted Urgh. 'Something for you, personally, oh great one-one-and-one headed chief. Your, erm Regal Smellness.' Urgh held out the bag, which shook very violently in Urgh's violently shaking hand.

The chief moved cautiously forward and looked at it.

'CAREFUL, OH MIGHTY TRI-SLAP-HEADED ONE!' said a particularly smelly giant from the back of the pack.

'ROVERS!' said the chief to his dog. The dog looked up at the chief and sniffed the bag suspiciously a few times. It smelt odd. It smelt like magic. Magic was trouble. Rovers bared his teeth, twice.

Everyone looked at the chief. 'WELL?' he roared.

'It is a message from the goblins, Your Many-Wiffyness. You throw it on the fire thus, and...'

A pair of giants jumped out of a window as a precaution. The chief backed away slightly. Ate Eyes peered thoughtfully at the bag, suspecting trickery. He gripped his mallet and held it high above Urgh just in case.

There was a double splash from somewhere below, followed by thrashing and screams.

The flames sparked around the speakme bag, and in their twisting dancing embrace formed a figure—the rotund figure of King Stormgrunties, resplendent in soaked attire. Water dripped spectrally from the vision and vanished into the flames without a hiss. The king smiled and adjusted his regal attire. 'Ahem,' he said, clearing his throat.

Urgh waited.

The giants waited.

'Here comes the message, a message of great cunning and complexity, something you need to listen to carefully,' said Urgh.

The king smiled, coughed, stared straight at the giant chief, raised a pointed finger to the heavens, and said, in a clear, crisp voice: 'Surrender!'

CHAPTER 11

'It has begun!' shouted the Wise Wench, to no one in particular. 'Time to get back to work. Whippet, if you'd be so good as to accompany me? Oh, and King Stormgrunties, let Durth out immediately, will you?' She began walking away through the crowd.

'Erm, just a minute, Wise Wench,' said the king in between harrumphs. 'I'd like a few answers. Just what has *begun,* exactly? I may be as slow as the Tortoise on the Endless Staircase, but I really don't understand what the blazes is going on! As far as I'm concerned, you're still guilty of treason, and I'll be watching out for it when it occurs.' He crossed his arms, regally.

'Ah, thank you for reminding me,' she said, and rushed up into his great chair. The crowd gasped. They gasped even more when she slapped him and shook him. She forced his mouth open and stared in, shouting and tugging. 'Come out! I know you're in there. Come out, or I'll come in and get you!'

'Mmmmfff,' said the king, trying to get her off while still remaining regal.

She was gripping like a monkey as she pulled his nose out of the way and fumbled into his mouth. Looti was shouting from below, while the goblins looked on, their initial feelings of horror vanishing into amusement. 'What are you doing?' shouted Looti from the base of the chair.

'He's possessed! Queen Quench has sent her familiar into his head to control it! I need to get it out, but I can't see it in all this space.'

'Could we not trying burning it out?' said one of the villagers, helpfully. Everyone agreed it was a fine plan.

The Wise Wench shook the king's head very violently, and something stringy came out of his ear. It was like a sickly purple leech with wings. It grinned broadly, and flew off out of the building, looking smug.

Half a second later, a starling ate it.

The Wise Wench stopped and adjusted the king's ruff dutifully. His face was bright red. 'I'll just, er, get down now you're free of it.' The Wise Wench clambered down, awkwardly.

The king coughed, looked shocked, shook his head again, and rubbed his temples. 'Right, so, how does the milk get from the teat into the bucket?'

'Majesty?' asked Looti.

'Give him a moment,' said the Wise Wench.

'Ah, Wise Wench! Good, I was just about to send for you.' The king noticed the crowd gathered in the Moot Hall and stood up. 'And since when has my Moot Hall become a public gathering place?' he shouted. 'I'll give you one-one-and-one seconds to get out, or I'll have you all turned inside out and fed to the village cormorant.'

The gathering did as they were instructed.

'Right, so what happens next?' he said, royally.

The Wise Wench quickly stuffed something made of wool into her bodice. From the king's quick glance, it looked like a completely round, flat goblin. He wondered if it was a gift for him—he was very fond of novelty coasters but thought it might be a surprise gift so just smiled and nodded knowingly. 'OK,' said the Wise Wench, 'so Queen Quench saw what was happening between us and the giants, and decided to try to destroy us by driving a wedge between the villagers—namely, you and I—with a view to delaying matters while her guff-hogs, who had been driven away from Urgh, Sorry, and Moaris by the Ferret-folk, flew towards the village. Or maybe she just hoped they'd blow us all up?'

'Ferret-folk?' asked the king, quietly.

'Yes, ferret-folk. They are old friends of Moaris's. He once beat their chief in a 'be mean to sparrows' contest, and they've had respect for him ever since. Furthermore, any delay to THE PLAN could totally wreck things. Anyway, that's old news now. While all this was going on, I was warned by the gods themselves that she was up to something, which is how I knew everything that was about to happen.'

'*Who* was up to something?'

170

'Queen Quench.'

The king turned around in his chair, revolving and somehow becoming stuck all at the same time. 'And when does she appear?' he added, nervously, now facing away from her.

'She's already left,' said the Wise Wench, reassuringly. 'And don't try to remember when she was here. She hexed you with her familiar and when that left, all recent memory will have gone with it.'

The king suddenly nodded, dozily, in his chair.

'Including last night's sleep.'

'Ah, good. And what happens next?' yawned the king while unravelling himself from his chair.

'The giants have your message. What do you think happens next?' inquired the Wise Wench, rhetorically.

'Well, that's splendid news,' said the king, beaming regally. 'Now, all the forest shall have peace. Good old Boris, Flaid, and the other fellow with the funny head. They've come through and delivered our message of hope and clarity to the giants. I shall declare a public holiday. Advisor!' he shouted, and noticed that Looti was sat just below him. She smiled up at him. 'Ask the Substitute Great Mole to declare a public holiday!' he said, regally.

She consulted the mole.

'No time for any holidays,' said the Wise Wench.

'*Do they* surrender, by the way?' whispered the king to her, more in hope than for any other reason.

She looked crossly back and looked like she was about to scream.

'But what was in the glass bottle?' asked Looti, in a sudden attempt to defuse the situation.

'The wrath of the gods,' answered the Wise Wench, carefully picking up the bottle and recorking it. 'Now, if we've all had enough explanations, there's work to be done.' She marched out, her arm around Whippet.

The king looked very confused. 'But I don't understand any of this,' he said to Tongue, who was hanging nearby chewing a wasp, 'and I'm king!' He sighed, and his hands fell idly to caressing the handles of his great chair as his head began to throb louder.

'Shall I let Durth out, Your Migrainity?'

'Why not? He hasn't done anything wrong—at least, not anything I recall,' said the king, shrugging his shoulders.

* * *

It was a bit later. 'All right, lads, show her what you can do!'

'Mnar, Mnar, Mnar, Mnar!'

'I see. So we haven't been practicing after all, have we, lads?'

Silence answered him.

'I said, 'have we, lads?''

'No, Chief Thug Durth,' said the lads, in close harmony.

Durth stood back and looked angry. He walked slowly down the line of nearly-many thugs he'd personally selected on account of their loud voices. They'd certainly made plenty of noise when he'd volunteered them for an as yet unspecified dangerous mission the Wise Wench had asked for volunteers for. Noise which had further deepened his hangover. 'Right, we'll try it again, only this time we'll make it a little more interesting. If you don't impress the Wise Wench enough to make her clap, then I'll be forced to set fire to one of you. All right?'

He glanced at the Wise Wench. She was sat in Master Whippet's rocking chair and was looking idly on towards the Kettle Hall, keen to see the latest creation.

'After one-more-than-one then—'

The thugs picked up their megaphones, cunningly fashioned from pickled, vitrified puppy skins, and each over many feet in length, tapering from a toad's lips width[40] at one end to nearly one-one-and-one heads' wide at the other.

'—one—'

The Wise Wench rocked backwards.

'—one-more-than-one. And!'

---

[40] Easily verified by the fact that the mouthpieces were actually toad lips.

'MNARR! MNARR! MNARR! MNARR!' mnarr'd the lads with more enthusiasm[41].

Everyone looked at the Wise Wench. 'Yes, very good, very good. Very monster-like.' She clapped, more to appease Chief Thug Durth than for any other reason. 'But could you make it sound a little more menacing?' she added, absentmindedly.

'You heard the Wise Wench! More menace, lads! So, after one-more-than-one. One, and.'

'MNARR! MNARR! MNARR! MNARRR!!!' One of the lads began to cough. Another praised Lord Noc, accidentally.

'Yes, that's much better,' said the Wise Wench, cheerfully. 'Now, keep up the good work, and I'll soon be able to let you know about that secret, very dangerous mission.'

'Did she say '*very* dangerous'?' whispered one of the thugs.

The Wise Wench got up and walked towards the Kettle Hall. In the distance, the king appeared, still in his favorite palanquin. He'd had it liberally decorated with udders, which swung flaccidly below making it look like something out of a horrible nightmare. 'Wait!' he commanded, regally, from the distance.

Ignoring him totally, the Wise Wench walked inside.

It began to rain.

Inside the Kettle Hall, work was just beginning again. The sound of hammering, cursing, tea-making, and frobjit juggling was creating a symphony of its own. Master Whippet marched purposefully up to something covered by a huge tarpaulin. 'Wise Wench, I give you, the Iron Hamster!'

He pulled the cloth away. The Wise Wench's face lit up. 'Oh, bravo, Master Whippet! Bravo, indeed!'

She began to applaud, loudly.

Outside, it was raining hard. Water dripped down the udders hanging from the king's palanquin, and the king looked more cross than usual as Looti finished speaking to him before stepping out of

---

[41] Fear.

the regal carriage. 'What are those idiots doing?' shouted the king, pointing at the thugs with megaphones.

Everyone looked at the grass.

'Well?' he added, disagreeably.

'A secret mission, Your Vastness,' said Durth, under his breath.

'Secret mission? Why wasn't I told about this?'

Everyone looked at the grass and began to hum.

'Well?' he said, crossing his arms.

'Because...' whispered Durth.

'Because?' asked the king.

There was a sudden noise from the Kettle Hall—a squeaking and scraping of metal on metal. Everyone looked up as the door flung aside and, slowly moving along the rails, came a huge, very fearsome-looking, iron hamster, fully a-few goblins high and nearly one-more-than-a-few wide. It had huge, pointy teeth, horns, and big flappy wings. Apart from these minor additions, it looked, to all intents and purposes, like a massive iron hamster.

The king's palanquin bearers began neighing nervously.

'Because it's secret! Or, at least, it *was* secret.' The Wise Wench swung down from the belly of the hamster and left Master Whippet ably in charge. She moved up, surreptitiously, to the king. 'You remember this part?' she whispered, 'the part with the *visitors* we're going to have soon?'

'Visitors?' asked the king, leaning precariously forward then stopping himself.

'Yes, you know? The *visitors?*' she added, standing directly below his plummet path.

'What visitors?' he replied, stretching further out. His bearers leant the palanquin a little more towards the Wise Wench, their fear of the hamster quelled by the fact that the Wise Wench had got out of it.

'The visitors that will be chasing our heroes back into the village...'

'Oh, you mean the GIANTS!' said the king, loudly, and sat back.

'Giants?' shouted the thugs who began to surrender to each other.

The king shook his head. Everyone seemed to know what was going on except him. Master Whippet marched past with a gang of about lots-many gob-wenches, each carrying an iron rail. Nearby, Durth and his lads began to toil away at making iron pins for the rails, while the Wise Wench and Looti watched impassively. Within the Kettle Hall, work resumed to finish the great kettle in time. In the distance, Whippet and his girls began to strike up an old goblin work song, all about toil and an honest reward for a hard days labor.[42] The king began to think that being king wasn't as easy as it used to be, when all he had to do was make lots of speeches, and eat and drink lots of vittles. He fondly thought back to the day of his breed-binding, when he and his beloved had been tied together with ivy and sheep in front of the whole village. *How times change,* he thought. It had taken them almost a week to get free. He still had a scar.

'You'd still be there if I hadn't untied you both. How is Her Majesty, by the way?' asked the Wise Wench, who had sneaked up on him and was smiling.

The king looked troubled. 'As cross as ever.' Then smiled broadly, leant down, and ruffled the Wise Wench's hair. He laughed heartily and reached over to repeat the gesture, only to find she'd stepped out of reach. 'Life, eh? Full of surprises, little twists and turns, *errors* even.' He sighed very heavily and smiled thinly at her. 'My adviser and the Substitute Great Mole have been filling me in on things. It appears I may have— well it's possible I could have been— there appears to have been, erm—'

'—A totally farcical trial?' asked the Wise Wench, grumpily.

'Well, I think '*totally farcical*' is taking it a bit far!' he snapped.

---

[42] Well, sort of. 'Give me a hammer, a chisel, and stick, I'll work for you today. I'll give you an hour, or maybe a tick, burn, burn, burn it, oh! You might want to try the girls, they like it more. They work all the day from dusk to dawn, burn, burn, burn it, oh!'

'Oh, really? You don't think, then, that imprisoning the one person in the whole village you can trust above all others, based entirely upon the testimony of one, very bad god is farcical, then?' she bit, venomously.

'Well—'

'—And you don't think you were wrong in trying to get me killed?'

'Well, *possibly*,' he mumbled. 'Even though I can't remember any of it.'

'Pardon?'

'Well, more than *possibly*. I'd maybe even go so far as to say *probably*,' he whispered, then added, 'oh, all right, then! You were right and I was wrong, as usual. But just try to remember that I am only a goblin, after all. I don't have the benefit of your feminine intuition or your far-sighted gift of being able to pop off and talk to the gods whenever you fancy. I'm just a king, when all's said and done. Just a king and not a female!' He managed to turn completely around in his palanquin and turn his back on her.

'Well, I think you make a very good king. It wasn't your fault you were bewitched,' she said, and began examining her knitted figurines again, smiling as she saw one showing the king with his back to her with a bloody nose.

'P-p-p-pardon?' said the king, still with his back to her.

'I said, I think you make a very good king. One of the best, in fact,' she added, slowly putting her daisy chain of figures back into her bodice, and finding several very large, brightly-colored handkerchiefs pulled them out. 'You might need these shortly, in case of nose bleeds.'

The king suddenly turned around. 'Did you say it wasn't my fau—' he said and banged his head on his palanquin window. His nose began to bleed profusely.

The Wise Wench passed him the bundle of handkerchiefs and walked off.

CHAPTER 12

Wise Wench, you won't believe what happened. Me, Moaris, and Urgh were in the giants' keep. We were surrounded, and just as Moaris was about to hand over the speakme bag, they attacked us. We killed many of the horrible things, but they just kept coming and, in the end, we gave up. I think they had Moaris for lunch, and dear old Urgh, my lifelong friend, for dinner. They were ready to eat me, too! They led me to the kitchen and threw me into a huge pot.

It was then that I decided I must escape and warn you. I grabbed the side of the pot and kicked it for all I was worth. The boiling water hit the cook and blinded him, but I had to fight his many-more-than-a-few—

'No, no, no. It must be more realistic,' said the Great Mole, wisely.

—his few giants. All I could find were some salad tongs—

'No! *Realistic!* Think properly,' scalded the Great Mole, scaldingly.

—a big rolling pin, but I put up such a fight that one-one-and-one of them lay dead and the others fled for help. It was then that I saw the window was open and I escaped. I haven't eaten for weeks.

Sorry scratched his head and thought a little more. From high up in the oak, he could still see the giants' creaky tower. He hadn't dared run home yet because there were patrols everywhere. He thought he heard one of them talking about flattening a goblin. *Which one? Am I bothered?* At least he hadn't seen that pompous bird since he hid.

Wise Wench, you won't believe it. We got there, but it was a trap. They killed Moaris with a really vicious sieve, and then squashed Urgh, my dearest lifelong friend—almost a brother. 'I'll have to cry at that point. Crying will make it look good. That and pleading for food, piteously,' said Sorry to himself, deviously.

I haven't eaten properly since we set out. What I wouldn't give for a bag of juicy whelks. I tried to catch the speakme bag but the giants tore it up. I grabbed the pieces and threw myself onto the fire with what was left. My whole body is covered in burns.

'Burns? That won't do. They'd have to be real, and I'm not burning myself just for this,' Sorry whispered to himself as he puzzled over his plan.

I haven't eaten properly for days. Bonfires are great. Burn, burn, burn!

Sorry sat down and thought some more. The sun was slowly sinking behind the trees. The tower, now a dark silhouette, looked even more fiendish and barbed than in the daylight. Its clothing banners were wafting eerily in the breeze. He tried to remember what the Wise Wench had called it—she knew everything, after all.

'She knows everything,' said the Great Mole, wisely, nodding at the goblin in a glove-puppet way.

The words echoed in his head. *She knows everything. She knows I'm up a tree hiding when I should have gone into the castle with the other one-more-than-one. She knows.*

Nearby, another giant patrol was returning. There were many giants in this one but, luckily, no dog. The one with the dog had scared Sorry the most because he thought it knew he was up the tree. These giants stopped only a few yards beneath Sorry's hiding place.

'I THINKS THERE WAS JUST THE PAIR OF THEM,' said Bront, a giant dressed in red.

Pair? Is that one-more-than-one? I hope so, thought Sorry.

'HE SAID THERE COULD BE MORE,' said Bront's right head to his left.

Noooooooooooooooo! Think about bonfires! Bonfires, crackle, crackle.

'OH YEH, AND WHAT WOULD YOU KNOW ABOUT IT, QUAGMIRE-BREATH?!' said the left.

'WILL YOU STOP BICKERING? MNARRRRRR!' said a very nasty-looking giant whose left head was much larger than his right.

'YEH, BE QUIET,' squeaked his right.

Bront sat down and started to pick his noses.

'ANYWAY, THE CHIEF SAID THE FLAT ONE WILL COME IN HANDY TO COVER ONE OF HIS BALD SPOTS,' said the last giant, who had no distinguishing features apart from having two heads, being eleven foot tall, and carrying a huge mallet with the word 'maim' written five times on it, none of which were vaguely close to being correctly spelt.

The giants laughed. Hidden above them, Sorry tried not to think about being mashed and more about looking like a branch and thinking about bonfires.

'SO WHAT'S HAPPENING TO THE ONE WHAT'S ALIVE?' said Bront's left head. His right was still sulking and refused to speak. 'SOMETHING VERY NASTY, I HOPE!' it added, by way of definition.

One that's alive? So it's true.

'ATE EYES IS MAKING HIM INTO A CANDLE FOR THE CHIEF. HE'S IN THE DUNGEON NOW,' added one of the giants, cheerfully.

'WELL, AT LEAST HE WON'T BE IN THE DARK!' roared Graunt. The giants began laughing hysterically and repeating the word 'DARK' very loudly. Eventually, they meandered away from Sorry and back towards the keep, leaving behind a vicious aroma of garlic.

In the tree above, Sorry was praying to Noc. The Great Mole looked at him solemnly and whispered: 'You know what you must do. If you don't do it, she'll find out. She knows everything. Imagine how much trouble you'll be in.' It looked profound and enigmatic, as well as a bit flea-bitten.

'I could just be honest and say I was too scared to help.'

The Great Mole looked down his nose at Sorry, who suddenly shook a fist at the heavens. 'All right, I'm going!' he whispered, vehemently, and climbed out of the tree and after the giants, the Great Mole encouraging him as he went.

Urgh was feeling sick now. Ate Eyes was running down through the castle as fast as he could, swinging the goblin about. The jogging motion was making Urgh feel queasy, slung, as he was, over the

179

giant's shoulder, then between his legs, then in front of him. He'd left all his magic and belongings in the chief's hall, and was feeling very sorry for himself.

'SO!' said Ate Eyes. 'JUST HOW MANY CANDLES DO YOU THINK YOU CAN EAT, ODD FACE?!'

Urgh considered for a moment, 'I could probably nibble one-more-than-one,' he said, hopefully. 'Goblins can eat lots, you know.'

Ate Eyes stopped before a particularly huge barbed door made of black iron. Stood before it were giant guards carrying what Urgh thought must be some sort of huge meat mincer each. They came to attention as soon as Ate Eyes stopped.

'I KNOW. WELL, LET'S PUT IT ANOTHER WAY!' said Ate Eyes, holding Urgh to his face. 'HOW MANY CANDLES DO YOU THINK WE HAVE IN THE CASTLE?!' The stench of the giant's breath made Urgh reel—he must have been eating garlic constantly with every meal since birth.

And then had garlic ice cream for dessert, followed by garlic coffee.

'Erm, a few?' said Urgh, hopefully.

'NO, A FEW MORE THAN THAT. GUESS AGAIN!' grumbled the giant as he signaled for the guards to unlock the door.

'One-more-than-a-few?' Urgh realized this horrid giant could actually count in goblin.

The door slid open with a terrible scraping of iron on iron. Warm air blew up a long dingy staircase with the biggest spiders webs Urgh had ever seen. His eyes widened, and he thought about creepy crawlies. He really didn't like creepy crawlies.

'NO!' Ate Eyes watched Urgh as the little goblin surveyed the webs for any sign of life and a huge grin crossed both his faces. 'MORE-THAN-CAN-BE-COUNTED,' he laughed and headed down the stairs gripping the goblin while saying, 'AND YOU'LL BE EATING EVERY SINGLE ONE! DO YOU KNOW WHAT THIS PLACE IS, LITTLE GOBLIN?!' he added, as he marched into the dark.

'The wine cellar?' replied Urgh, cockily. He was sure that the Wise Wench was telling the truth, and had worked out that

180

somehow he would escape and return to the village intact. At least he hoped so—mindless optimism wasn't his strong point. He wondered where his friend Sorry had got to. Perhaps he had been captured, too? And what about Lady Carline? Perhaps she would rescue him. How would a bird save him? And Sorry? Probably not since Sorry was such a coward— in all likelihood he was hiding up a tree.

'NO, IT'S CALLED THE TERRIBLE DUNGEON OF WOE!' said the giant with both mouths. 'THE TERRIBLE DUNGEON OF WOE AND MASSIVEST SPIDERS!' He laughed and thrust Urgh up into a huge web. The foul threads brushed over the little goblin's face and he yelled out, which just made the giant push him further in. Suddenly, Urgh came into a small opening in the web and there, in the center, surrounded by countless young, was the biggest spider Urgh had ever seen. It was even bigger than spiders he dreamt about and ran away from.

'PERHAPS YOU'D LIKE TO STAY HERE WITH QUEEN FRIGHTENINGLEGS! OR SHOULD I LET YOU GO?!' laughed Ate Eyes.

Urgh screamed to be released but that just made the giant push him closer to the terror in front of him. He could see the spider's foul bloated belly and her cluster of eyes! He could even hear her young scuttling about on her belly. Then, suddenly, he was pulled out of the web, and could smell again the foul garlic-gorged breath of his tormentor. Even that foulness was more welcome than the smell of the spider's den. As the giant laughed and marched on downwards he kept pretending to push Urgh back into the webs. A few moments later he tired of the amusement,[43] tossed Urgh into a cobwebby corner and stomped upwards and out, slamming the door angrily and saying, 'I'M OFF TO GET MORE CANDLES! I'LL BE RIGHT BACK! MNARRRRRR!'

The cell was damp.

Every corner of the ceiling was full of cobwebs.

---

[43] Giants are well known for their short attention spans—so short, in fact, that those who have tried to measure the span have found themselves squashed. In theory, therefore, there is no actual proof of this fact, it just is.

Cobwebs with *things* in them.

Urgh knew what the things were and shivered as he huddled into a corner. He wasn't quite so sure about the Wise Wench now, and he was even less sure about escape. He jumped as something scuttled, just at the edge of his sight, under the straw-covered palette he was sat on. He gave a gasp and drew his legs up as close to him as he could. Then he gave another gasp as he realized he wasn't alone.

A goblin crawled out of a pile of straw in the corner of the room.

A very, very old goblin covered in warts, with a great, grey wispy beard which seemed to be dancing to some sort of song only it could hear. And, perhaps more importantly, he was wearing a pink dress with a big yellow bow. A very faded pink dress that he looked to have been wearing for decades. Part of Urgh quietly sympathized with the poor old goblin as he stared down at his dirty smock. 'You haven't, by any chance, been working for a goblin called Moaris have you, stranger?' said Urgh despondently.

'I like chutney,' it croaked. 'I haven't had any chutney for years. Have you got any for us?'

'No,' said Urgh, nervously. 'Sorry,' he added, apologetically.

'No chutney,' said the other goblin, who began to sob, uncontrollably.

Urgh went to console the old fool. 'Did you say *us*?' said Urgh suddenly jumping up and looking at the webs.

'That's right,' sobbed the old goblin cradling his head in his arms. 'Now none of us has any chutney.' The sobbing grew worse and Urgh realized he was having a very bad day.

It got suddenly worse. The door above crashed open and a large crate of giant-sized candles fell into the room. 'HERE'S LUNCH, AND IF THESE AREN'T EATEN BY NIGHTFALL, I'LL GRATE YOU RAW AND FORCE-FEED THEM TO YOU!' Ate Eyes shut the door, locked it, and marched off, laughing gigantically. The guards followed him.

'*None* of us?' asked Urgh. 'Don't you mean neither of us?'

'No, none. There's just you, me and Lynel,' said the old goblin looking fondly at the wall by the door.

182

'I see,' said Urgh, seeing nothing and anxious to change the subject. 'Excuse me for asking,' said Urgh, 'but why have you got a dress on?'

'It's not a dress,' snapped the old goblin.

'Not a dress?'

'No.'

Urgh looked awkwardly at the old goblin in the dress, and raised an eyebrow.

Or should that be lowered an eyebrow.

Perhaps brow isn't even the right word.

'It's my uniform,' said the old goblin who then winked at the patch of lichen on the wall.

Urgh began to wonder whether he was actually dead and had been taken to the stomach of Gilcrint, the Absurd Megalo-Stickleback who took a countless number of days to pass the door at the middle of time, where nothing ever made any sense.

'You see,' said the old goblin, 'I was captured by the giants when I was a gob-boy. Their chief wanted to have me boiled and used as a salad accompaniment. But I was quick-witted in those days and noticed he had a daughter, and so I did a little jig for her.'

'And that saved your life?'

'No,' mumbled the goblin, 'that just made him cross. It was Lynel here who saved my life,' said the goblin gesturing to the lichen-covered wall. Urgh peered. He could still only see lichen and stone. Perhaps Lynel was invisible.

'He persuaded her to keep me as a doll, which she did, and we played together for many summers. She was very kind in a giant[44] way. But summers went on and she grew tired of the little doll she called Grumpy, and eventually she left me, forgotten in her toy box.'

'Oh, I see,' said Urgh. 'The gaol was her toy box.'

'Don't be stupid! The toy box is upstairs. I only got out of it yesterday—my back's killing me! They threw me down here to rot.' The old goblin leant against the wall and started stroking the patch of lichen. 'Just you and me now, Lynel,' he whimpered.

---

[44] Violent.

Urgh couldn't see anything apart from lichen-covered stones. Very large stones. He lay down and tried to remember that the Wise Wench was always right. Soon, sleep took him.

The forest was beautiful in the sunlight and the air was a carnival of insects. It was hot but Urgh was shaded by the huge green canopies overhead. He wasn't quite sure how long he'd been walking. In fact, he couldn't remember getting up or, for that matter, how he'd escaped from the giants.

No matter, he thought, and sat down lazily in the forest and listened, contentedly.

A moment later, Urgh heard something nearby and his eyes shot open. There, before him, leaning next to a gnarled sycamore, was a very old goblin with a long wispy beard and an even longer wispy nose. He wore a long black coat, buttoned up as if the day were cold, and he seemed strangely familiar.

'Who are you?' asked Urgh, as politely as he could.

'Your father,' answered the old goblin.

Memories flooded back into Urgh's mind. He'd never known his father, and was widely held to be a foundling, particularly in view of his head situation. But his mother had once told him the true story, the story of a handsome goblin prince riding a magnificent war-pig who came to call on her one summer; of how the prince had left her suddenly, left her with a little gob inside her. Left her sorrowful for all her days, waiting, waiting for her prince to return. He never had. That was perhaps why she was so horrid.

'Sorry about your head, but it runs in the family—seems to have jumped a generation with me though. You'll, perhaps, find out about your family, one day, if you're lucky,' he added, almost as an afterthought.

'S'alright' mumbled Urgh, as he got up. The old goblin backed away, fearfully.

'Wait,' said Urgh.

'I cannot stay long, son,' said the old man.

Son.

'But I have something very important to ask you to do. You won't want to do it, but you must. Now, listen to me very carefully—'

The old goblin began whispering in his ear.

'—YOU WON'T WANT TO DO IT, BUT YOU MUST!' Ate Eyes offered Urgh another candle. The goblin was now wide awake, with his father's instructions still ringing in his head. He tried to fight the giant off but was no match for him. The wax tasted vaguely of lard and actually, on reflection, was quite palatable[45].

'Lynel says 'well done, sir!'' said his fellow prisoner to the giant while pointing vaguely at the wall.

Ate Eyes ignored him and continued to feed Urgh candles. After a little while, the box was empty. 'WELL, YOU'VE HAD YOUR DINNER, AND NOW I'M GOING FOR MINE, BUT I'LL BE BACK SOON WITH SUPPER!' Ate Eyes laughed hysterically and left. Urgh lay face down on the palette and began to tremble as he remembered the words his father had spoken to him in his dream. At least he wasn't hungry.

* * *

The giants were still laughing by the time they reached the broad timber drawbridge over the wide murky moat.

'DARK!' cheered Bront, as they walked in. They all roared again, with the exception of Bront's sulky right head.

---

[45] The ability of goblins to eat and digest practically anything has been put to several—sometimes extremely bizarre—tests, as you can imagine. Chiefs have tried various experiments with their subjects, often involving very large, very inedible living creatures, extremely large rocks, things with spikes, snaky things, and countless other strange objects. The only stumbling block is the width of a goblin's mouth, which can be very large indeed, and, in some cases, even stretchy. The great goblin demi-god of gluttony, Fatwell Massivemiddle, Porklord Lord of Pork, once allegedly ate an entire mountain over a period of several weeks. His extraordinary eating prowess has also birthed tales of him eating ships, whales, forests, and countless naughty goblin children.

Sorry crouched in the undergrowth not far from the moat, and looked. The tower was vast, larger even than Miffed Tower, and his mouth fell open as he took in its barbs, its statues of gargoyles gripping its crooked timber flanks, and its awesomely high soiling lines, festooned with soiled garb. Somewhere above them, he fancied he saw a bird flying oddly, as though searching. He stared at the lines, wondering if they would hold his weight, and then saw how close they were to the waters of the moat and the battlements. As if in answer to some yet-to-be-asked question, he saw a vast toothy pike flick the waters with its huge mouth full of huge pointy teeth. 'Lord Noc! Giant fish!' he whispered, miserably, under his breath. Suddenly, there was a tremendous splash and Sorry saw another pike, as big as a house[46], leap out of the water and grab a heron which had strayed too close. Sorry blinked and the awesome fish was gone. *I'm not going anywhere near them*, he thought, somewhat ironically it would transpire.

He stared into the gloom of the castle entrance but could see no one. The stench of the giants competed with that of the tar and pitch the tower was treated with. *Hmmm*, thought Sorry, sniffing. The word *bonfire* kept popping into his head, leaving no room for any other words, so he ran across the bridge and into the keep.

The entrance hall was huge, with great oak double doors, the outer faces of which had more barbs than Sorry had ever seen in his life. Near the doors was an enormous double iron collar and chain. Beyond was a wide opening with more doors. 'One-one-and-one shut doors I see,' muttered Sorry. 'Alright, we'll let Noc decide. Ip, Dip, a pound of fish, to eat your lips, and I, choose, you! Burn, burn, burn it, oh!' sang Sorry, quietly under his breath, as he pointed to the doors in time with the words of the rhyme. His finger finished pointing at the middle door. Quietly, he walked up to it and listened intently.

Somewhere far above came the sound of raucous singing. Sorry wasn't sure, but he thought he heard lots of swear words. They sounded like swear words, anyway. *Dungeons mean down*, he

---

[46] Pile of things that someone lives in.

186

thought, adding a quick image of a really huge bonfire. He looked closer at the door. A large iron latch hung high above him. He looked around for something long to flick it with, and his gaze fell on a large mallet which lay near the entrance. He walked up to it and gave it a tug. His arms nearly came out of their sockets. He couldn't even move it, let alone pick it up. Grumpily, he decided to look further around and soon noticed a pile of very long fishing rods piled in a corner near a pair of especially smelly wicker baskets.

A moment later, the left hand door opened and a pair of giants walked in. Sorry dove into one of the baskets. It was full of fish. Very large fish. He held his breath as the giants came closer and crawled deeper in, taking a few nibbles as he did.

'MUST GET THESE FISH IN THE KITCHEN, GRUNT, OR SHE'LL BE CROSS,' said one of the giants, and the basket Sorry was in was suddenly raised. He crawled in amongst the fish and tried to look as dead and fishy as possible.

'SHE'S ALWAYS CROSS! I WISH I WAS UPSTAIRS WITH THE CHIEF INSTEAD OF DOING GUARD DUTY DOWN HERE WITH YOU. SO, IS IT TRUE THEN?' said the other giant.

'WHAT?' said Grunt, irritably.

'THE CHIEF'S BIG ANNOUNCEMENT? GORG MUCH-CHINS SAYS HE'S TOLD ALL THE GIANTS TO BE READY FOR WAR. HE'S HAD ENOUGH OF LIVING IN THIS BLOODY SWAMP AND HE'S GOING TO MOVE THE KEEP.'

'WHERE TO?'

'THE MIDDLE OF THE FOREST. THAT'S WHY WE KILLED ALL THOSE PESKY GOBLINS THE OTHER NIGHT. THE CHIEF SAYS IT WAS A SORT OF TEST, AND IT WAS SO EASY HE'S DECIDED TWO THINGS AT ONCE.'

'TWO THINGS AT ONCE? WHAT A GREAT LEADER HE IS! SO WHAT ARE THEY?'

'WELL, FIRST, HE'S DECIDED TO WEAR THE DEAD GOBLIN AS A FLAT CAP FOR THE REST OF HIS DAYS, AND SECOND, HE'S GOING TO KILL ALL THE OTHERS.

'WHAT VISION! WHAT A GREAT LEADER!' they agreed, reverently, as they booted open a door and were subject to a tirade of verbal abuse from what Sorry assumed to be the cook.

The kitchen was full of smoke, which Sorry was very pleased about. The brief journey he'd had here so far had been unpleasant enough, and he wondered if facing the Wise Wench would have been so bad after all. At least smoke meant fire. *Fire, heh, heh,* he thought. He took another bite of fish while he considered his options. Somehow admitting to the Wise Wench that he was a coward and a liar seemed a relatively easy task compared to sitting in a basket full of big fish on their way to being cooked while surrounded by giants. He glimpsed through the wicker sides of his hiding place.

A small group of female giants toiled in the chamber, cooking foods and soiling clothing. The place stank more than anywhere Sorry had ever been to in his life and his jaw dropped in awe at the number of smell-stories that must be here. The giant who was the cook was really ugly.[47] She wore a bloody dress stained with decades of gore and was very cross about it. Suddenly, she noticed the guards with the basket.

'WE'VE BROUGHT YOU SOME FISH TO COOK, MISTRESS FOULMOUTH,' said one of the giants, bravely, as he placed the basket on the table.

The cook opened her mouth and a long rioting crowd of words—really bad proper swear words—streamed out without pause. A frying pan of great size flew across the room at the guards, who simultaneously ducked and fled.

The cook then screamed some words at one of her assistants—the very, *very* ugly one. Sorry didn't know what the words meant, but he gathered and felt their inference. A bowl was duly passed to the cook.

---

[47] *Really* ugly.

188

It transpired it was not the correct one and the cook violently uttered an entire paragraph of giant swear words without pause for breath and threw a carving knife at her assistant who dodged, expertly. The knife spun in the air and stuck straight into the basket Sorry was in. Its blade stabbed deep into the basket, missing him, but only just.

The cook complained of feeling frail in a curiously, cuss-word-strewn, way.

Sorry reddened with embarrassment—he'd never heard such filth.

The assistants just nodded in agreement. 'SHALL I GUT THE FISH NOW?' asked the prettier one.[48]

The cook intimated that it would be appropriate and hurled a ladle full of hot fat across the room at them by way of encouragement.

Sorry looked around. The assistant was very close. All he could see was the meat cleaver and the chopping board. She picked up the basket and swung it the short distance onto the table and turned it over.

The fish and Sorry fell out. For a moment he was in front of all the giantesses, completely exposed and surrounded by knives, things with blades, and big things that grated.

The giantesses seemed more interested in squabbling, or, perhaps more accurately, being verbally abused by the cook, to notice. Sorry dropped from the table, slid under a cupboard, and then snuck through a gap in a very warped door nearby and into the room beyond.

Outside, the cook screamed and began hurling pots, pans, and cutlery about the place, indicating her concerns about the task at hand not being dealt with rapidly enough. Crockery smashed and fat flew, knives hurled and glass broke.

The room Sorry was in was dark, but, through the gap, he could make out shapes. As he did, and as he also noticed the smell, his face broke into an enormous grin. He was in the fuel store! The

---

[48] In truth, this is a fairly charitable description of her.

189

place was crammed with kindling, fat dry logs, tar, chopped sticks, and flint and steel. He paused for a moment, then began touching things. In his mind, thoughts fought their way to the top and beat each other into a plan. *Better not,* he thought, vainly.

He grinned even wider, almost splitting his head in half with glee as he piled kindling under the logs and barrels of tar. He paused, praised Noc, and then began striking the flint and tinder together. They sparked immediately—they always sparked immediately because Sorry was a firestarter, a *goblin* firestarter. As the flames began to grow, raptures of joy almost bent him apart as he began tittering.

Not far away, Urgh wondered if there were any candles due anytime soon. He was getting hungry again, and food took his mind off what his father had told him to do. He wasn't sure if it even was his father, yet when he'd met him, it seemed so clear.

Above him, the sounds of giant carousing echoed down, along with the angry screams of the females he'd heard nearby. He heard more pots crashing and giants shouting. A few moments later, something passed the top of the stair into the dungeon with a growl. Chains were moved and, somewhere far off, he heard machinery moving, slowly ending with a massive thump.

The outer gate was closed.

Urgh sat in the dark wondering if the Wise Wench was losing her touch.

Wise Wench, I got into the tower—honestly I did.

'You did indeed,' whispered the Great Mole, encouragingly.

But there was a fire, what could I do? The giants were everywhere, I had no choice but to escape. Sorry grinned at the flames, and almost singed his eyebrows as something popped and the fire began to bloom.

'She'll know,' whispered the Great Mole into his ear.

Then he noticed it had gone very quiet outside. Before he could move, the door had crashed open, and several giants stood kissed by the dancing light of the fire he'd lit. 'FIRE!' they shouted in

190

unison. 'GOBLIN!' they screamed immediately afterwards in close harmony.

Sorry ran. He dashed from cover to cover as he darted from the kitchen, the Great Mole telling him which way to go. From somewhere nearby there followed a grinding of distant machinery and a loud thud. He found a set of stairs creaking their way upwards and was about to dash up them to find a window when a group of giants ran down with buckets. He crouched below the stairs behind a huge pile of gigantic false fruit which crowded a grill at the floor. The figures ran by shouting about fire and generally panicking.

'It sounded like 'fire!' said Urgh.

'We heard nothing, didn't we, Lynel?' said the old goblin.

Urgh stared upwards into the gloom as the pandemonium began. He started screaming for help.

It was then that Sorry heard the voice.

The voice he recognized—it was coming from behind the grill nearby.

It was Urgh shouting for help. He must be in trouble—he might be in deadly peril.

Perhaps I'd better just leave.

He looked sheepishly at the Great Mole, who glowered judgmentally at him. 'Oh, all right,' said Sorry. He pressed his head to the grill. 'Urgh, are you in there?' he whispered. Around him, the shouts were growing.

Urgh got up with a start; someone had spoken his name. He looked across at the old goblin, who despite the clamor was stood still staring at the wall, lovingly.

'Urgh, you ugly stoat, are you down there?' It was Sorry's voice.

Sorry, beloved Sorry.

Sorry who he was going to wed.

Sorry who he would shower with hot kisses of love and adoration.

'Yes, I'm here!' he said feebly, and clambered to the grill. 'It's you! I knew you'd come to help! I just knew you weren't a sniveling, cowardly, worthless wretch who would sell his grandwench for a moldy turnip.'

Sorry frowned. 'Where's Moaris?' he asked, quietly.

'Dead.'

'I thought so. Horribly?'

Urgh nodded, solemnly. 'Exactly how he wanted it to be. I've delivered the speakme bag message, though.'

'So why are you in here? And why are the giants talking about a battle?' Sorry stopped as a giant ran up the stairs crying about conflagrations. The smell of burning chased the giant upstairs.

'I don't know about that. Sorry, the message—it was just one word, surrender!'

'Surrender? No wonder they're so cross. I think they're going to attack our village.'

'Then we must get back and warn them.'

'I have a plan! Let's not do that. Let's go and live in a dark part of the forest where no one is and avoid all the trouble.' The Great Mole thought about saying something and announcing itself but loitered instead behind his back, gripped by some unseen force.

Urgh tried with all his might, which was inconsiderable, to move the grill, then he tried to slip through and got his head stuck. Sorry helpfully shoved him back. 'Is there a key outside?' asked Urgh, hopefully, from below.

Sorry took a tertiary look round. 'No,' came the reply.

'There's a guard at the top of the stairs. He might have it.'

'Guard? Guard? Do you mean one of the giants? One of the very tall, very strong giants with one-more-than-one heads and dogs to match?'

'Yes! Hurry.'

Sorry looked around for a moment. *Wise Wench, he was trapped in the cells, what could I do? I tried and tried to find the key but couldn't. Poor Urgh, he was like a brother to me and now he's dead. But at least I escaped to warn you, eh? I haven't eaten for weeks.* The Great Mole looked at him, sternly.

'The stairs should just be over to your left. If you're very quiet, you might be able to pinch the key in all the commotion,' whispered Urgh, hopefully.

In that commotion, smoke was billowing from the kitchen as several sooty giants ran by, remonstrating with the guards. Sorry waited and then slunk by, keeping to the stained wainscoting and slipping from cover to cover. Not far away there was another door. Luckily, it was propped open by a mountainous pile of boxes full of candles.

A giant ran past shouting, 'HE DEFINITELY ISN'T HERE!' and vanished into the kitchen with a bucket.

Sorry looked up above the boxes and suddenly noticed a large ring of hefty keys hung high above him by what was clearly a gaol door. The keys were vast—almost as big as he was—and out of reach. Beyond was the glint of light and the airy chamber that was clearly the entrance to the tower. He flicked a glance at the keys and then thought about outside and how safe it was. Then he thought of his friend below: trapped, miserable, and awaiting a certain, painful death.

He marched past the keys, determined to escape.

He had barely stepped into the room beyond when he heard growling. He looked around and noticed he had come through the middle door he had originally seen when he came in. Triumphantly, he looked to the exit hall with the drawbridge.

The drawbridge was up.

And a dog sat in front of it.

A massive dog with one-more-than-one heads thought Sorry.

Luckily, it was chained, but it still began to bark furiously and slaver hungrily. It darted at him, snarling and barking.

'SOUNDS LIKE THE DOG'S SEEN SOMETHING!' shouted a hoarse voice from above. Giant running footsteps followed.

Sorry's heart fell and he considered walking towards the dog to end his misery. The thought of how much it would hurt him made him reconsider—imaginary pain in any quantity generally had that effect on him. He skulked back into the doorway and hid behind the boxes. A giant arrived in the entrance hall, found it empty, and slapped the dog. The dog bit him. More than once. With a yell, the giant ran back upstairs announcing various quite complex swear words.

Sorry glanced upwards at the keys again—they were truly huge. Inside the cell, Urgh clambered wheezily up the stairs. 'Are you there?' he whispered.

Wise Wench, I was so close. I was just outside the cell door but the keys were too big to move. 'That bit's true, heh,' whispered Sorry to himself. *What could I do? I tried and tried to move them but I was too weak. I hadn't eaten for days by then, and now it's been weeks.*

Sorry became aware that he was being stared at. He glanced down at the Great Mole and scowled before pushing a box under the keys. 'Yes, I'm here, old friend. You didn't think I'd leave you, did you?' his whisper didn't seem entirely genuine.

Silence answered his question.

He clambered onto the box and grunted as he tried to move the keys off their hook. With his prowess and mighty shoulders, the task was not inconsiderable, particularly for muscles totally unused to any kind of effort. After an age, he unhooked them and they dropped onto the box with a dull thud. Sorry Moth-Ripper stared down at the iron keys. He tried to lift them and failed, feebly. 'I can't pick up the keys, they're too heavy,' he said.

There was a whimper from inside.

'But don't worry,' said the Great Mole, 'we'll think of something.'

'We?' said Urgh.

'That's right, me,' answered Sorry.

The Great Mole looked up at him and then at the keys. 'Come, Sorry Moth-Ripper, we'll try together,' whispered the mighty glove-puppet. He gestured at the keys and gripped with all his might, signaling for Sorry's right hand to do the same. They heaved and groaned and praised Noc, and slowly, slowly, the keys rose and one drove into the lock. With a final twist of flesh and glove-puppet, they turned the key. It worked. The Great Mole and Lord Noc had

194

guided him! That, or he was just lucky. There was a groan from within and, after a mighty struggle, it opened inwards.

The Great Mole, its work done, slipped back to safety as Sorry clambered down. Urgh ran for him and hugged him, patting and grabbing his friend, his rescuer! 'My friend, you came to rescue me! You aren't a sniveling back-stabbing coward after all. Oh, true friend, am I glad to see you!'

'Gerroff, fathead!' yelled Sorry, and kicked Urgh on the shin. 'You might not be so pleased when I tell you what's happening. The giants know I'm here.'

'Not a problem.'

'They have dogs.'

'We can sneak past them.'

'And they've pulled up the drawbridge.'

I wouldn't want to have to swim past them...

'And the moat is full of—'

'—massive pike.'

'Yes. Oh, and one more tiny thing. I've set fire to the tower...a bit.' Sorry looked up at the pluming smoke, heard the distant screams, and modified his description to, 'well, quite a lot, actually.'

'That's perfect,' said Urgh. 'I think I know a way out, but it won't be easy. Now, hurry!' He grabbed Sorry. 'It sounded like there were one-more-than-one of you outside. I thought for one minute Moaris might not be dead, but you're alone, aren't you?'

'Absolutely totally alone,' lied Sorry, unconvincingly, the Great Mole remaining, for now, hidden in his pocket.

Urgh frowned, then smiled, and turned to the old goblin below. 'Quick, follow us and you'll be free.'

The old goblin shook his head, 'Not without Lynel,' he said, and sat down.

'Suit yourself,' answered Urgh, then led the way back to the room with the chimney, ducking and hiding to avoid the giants whose dogs seemed to have run away from the flaming bits of building which was now well and truly on fire. 'This is the way me and Moaris went. It leads to the roof. We might be able to escape that way,' said Urgh who began climbing.

195

The climb was made worse by the smoke from below, but through it, Urgh could see Sorry smiling. He was sniffing the air delightedly. 'This place stinks of pitch and tar—it could be the biggest bonfire ever!' he said, laughing.

'It won't do us much good if we're in the middle of it,' snapped Urgh, coughing.

Sorry smiled back broadly and they soon came to the top floor. They heard it before they came to it. Shouting; giant shouting. Sorry and Urgh reached the noise and crouched at the back of the chimney. The fire had burned low and there, sat next to it, ignored, was Urgh's magic sack. 'The chief's room!' whispered Urgh, as he clambered into the fireplace.

'Are you mad?!' whispered Sorry.

The table had gone, and in its place were many, many giants. Possibly an uncountable number; maybe more. They were all lined up in neat rows and were stood very much to attention. Urgh thought that the ones in front must be the captains or head thugs because they had various creatures pinned to their cloaks.

Various creatures that were alive.

Urgh cringed as a bat pinned to the lapel of a very red-faced giant struggled and tried to fly away. The giant smacked it with the flat of his hand and mouthed something at it.

'YOU ARE ALL STINKING SCUM!' roared the chief. 'YOU MAKE ME SICK TO LOOK AT YOU. MAGGOTS, WORMS, LUGS, BEETLES, AND THRUSHES, THE LOT OF YOU. ONE LITTLE GOBLIN GETS FREE AND YOU CAN'T EVEN CATCH IT! DO YOU HAVE EYES? HAS LORD NO-EYES TAKEN YOUR WITS AS WELL AS YOUR SIGHT?! MNARRRRRR!' He began flinging things across at the giants, including axes and swords. A few giants fell to the floor.

'CAN'T YOU CATCH ANYTHING?!' he screamed at one of the fallen. 'DOES YOUR MOTHER PUT BUTTER ON YOUR HANDS AND SING YOU LULLABIES?' He was blue with rage now, but the last remark made one of the giants giggle. He marched over to him at an urgent pace, picked him up bodily and threw him out of a window. There was a loud splash, some gurgling and thrashing, then all was still.

'NOW, THE BRIDGE IS UP, YES?' he shouted.

'YES, SIR!' they screamed in unison.

'SO THEY CAN'T GET OUT, YES?'

'NO SIR!' they added.

'AND THE TOWER IS ON FIRE?'

They nodded in nervous agreement.

'THEN I'LL MAKE THIS VERY SIMPLE. UNTIL THAT GOBLIN IS CAUGHT, NONE OF YOU ARE LEAVING THE BUILDING. IS THAT CLEAR?!'

The giants nodded in agreement, and then one of them spotted Urgh, dragging his sack into the fireplace. He pointed, yelled 'GOBLIN!' and threw an axe.

It hit the giant next to him and stuck in the back of his left head.

'Come quickly!' yelled a cultured voice from above Urgh and Sorry.

'Lady Carline!' shouted Urgh.

Sorry had already sneaked up the chimney and onto the roof when he heard the commotion below. Urgh raced up the chimney, giant heads leering below.

'CLIMB ONTO THE ROOF!' shouted the chief below.

As Urgh emerged through the chimney, the wind was stronger. The roof sloped away at acute angles on all sides and was covered in bird droppings, making it incredibly slippery. Sorry looked more scared than he had ever seen him, which was saying something. Below, flames licked the sides of the tower, and giants were leaning out of the battlements; some had already started to climb down. And up.

The drop was vast.

Really, really vast.

The moat was like a tiny circlet below. A raven flew past, scrawking loudly. 'Where've you been?' yelled Urgh. 'I've been trapped.'

'I know,' she answered.

'And now the giants' tower is on fire.'

'I know that too,' she answered.

'So where have you been?'

'Waiting up here for you.'

Urgh wiped soot from his face. 'So what happens next?' he shouted.

The raven glided off the edge of the roof and headed towards the forest.

'Well done! Oh very, very well done. Great plan,' cried Sorry as he looked at the drop. 'So all I have to do now is grow wings!' he added and proceeded to sob and say, 'wings' under his breath in a baby voice.

Urgh wandered carefully around the roof looking for inspiration. Above him, vicious looking pigeons circled. There didn't seem to be much. The roof was ankle deep in pigeon pong and precious little else. Smoke billowed upwards from below. Then his eyes suddenly lit up and he smiled.

He saw the clothes put out for soiling blowing in the wind, the threads snaking down across the moat to the ground.

All around the clearing was the Great Forest. It looked so fine, friendly, and inaccessible. Urgh led his crying companion to the edge of the roof and pointed to a giant billowing pair of underpants. 'Those underpants, my friend, are our salvation[49],' said Urgh.

Sorry wiped his eyes and looked at the undergarment. They were certainly huge, alright. Then his eyes noticed the line they were hung on. It was on a sort of pulley that went right down to the ground on the far side of the moat; the line he'd seen earlier—the line that flopped into the moat. Obviously the giants pegged their washing out and then reeled their washing up when it was properly soiled. All they had to do was clamber into the underthings one at a time and reel themselves down to the ground.

The ground.

Far, far below.

---

[49] I know, sorry, but I have, in truth, waited my whole life for an excuse to write the words 'Those underpants, my friend, are our salvation.'

'I can't do it,' said Sorry, heroically.

'Yes, you can,' said Urgh, as he gently forced his friend onto the parapet where the rope went through a pulley. Urgh pulled the rope slowly up and the huge underpants came towards them.

'No, no, no,' muttered Sorry as his eyes looked towards the ground.

Urgh pulled the gigantic netherwear over the parapet and motioned for his friend to climb in.

Sorry continued to shake his head.

'It's a simple choice, Sorry,' said Urgh. 'You either climb on board those undergarments and I reel you down to the ground, or you stay up here and burn to death.'

Burn to death. Sorry remembered how painful fire was and reluctantly climbed into the underwear. The stench was not inconsiderable within. The drop loomed below him as the material stretched to accommodate his mercifully feeble form.

Outside, the giants were climbing towards the roof.

'Put one leg on either side of the gusset; it'll be safer,' said Urgh. 'Now, don't forget: once you're down, you'll have to reel me down. It's too far between the clothes and the rope above for me to reach.'

A goblin thumb appeared from between the buttons on the front of the underpants, and Urgh took firm hold of the rope, slowly reeling it down. His friend was surprisingly heavy and it took all of his feeble strength to lower Sorry slowly downwards. When he was halfway down an alarm was shouted, and giants leant from the tower waving spears and assorted hardened vegetables towards the escaping goblin. As they did, the poorly-made battlements outside collapsed and they hurtled into the moat. As the pike played with the giants who had fallen into the moat, Urgh pulled Sorry quickly on, the underthings kissing the water near the end. Mercifully, the fish were busy dinning on giant, and within a short while, Sorry came to rest on the ground. He got out and looked around. The moat stood behind him. The tower was now halfway ablaze. *Wise Wench, I managed to get to the ground but poor Urgh got caught. I couldn't release him, and the giants found him. He was my closest friend.*

Then he looked up and saw giants climbing on the outside of the tower towards his friend. *I'll have to cry, then. Crying will help convince them. I haven't eaten for months.* Sorry smiled to himself and marched toward the forest.

The Great Mole 'ahemed.'

Angrily, Sorry moved back and grabbed hold of the reel, waving to his friend and smiling.

High above, Urgh sang a nursery rhyme to take his mind off the drop.

And the smell.

And the flames.

In truth, the flames were very impressive.

From somewhere below, a floor collapsed, sending sparks and flames and smoke upwards, completely obscuring his view. When the smoke had gone, Ate Eyes was stood on the roof with him. 'LOOKS LIKE IT'S TIME TO LIGHT THE CANDLE!' he shouted, and grabbed for him.

It took a moment to weigh the odds. Urgh looked at the soiling line, flung his sack as hard as he could, and leapt, reaching for the line, which he missed by some considerable distance. He plunged down, past climbing giants, through smoke, and down towards the moat. The sack slapped into the edge of the moat, and Urgh plummeted right into the water next to it with a massive splash.

From above, he could hear Ate Eyes laughing as the water engulfed him.

He spluttered and tried to swim in the thick water. Something vast and sleek swished past him. He broke water a few seconds later to see a gigantic, open mouth tearing across the moat at him. It was only a few feet away, then it was only a few inches away. Urgh had a strangely consoling thought that his sack wasn't wet, then saw inside the pike's massive maw. He closed his eyes and waited for the end.

He never saw the plummeting giant hit the water right in front of him, and kill the pike instantly. He just felt the wave slap him across the water and suddenly became aware there was something solid behind him.

Land. He'd been washed up on land by the wave.

The giant was flapping in the water as more pike appeared. Urgh pulled himself out, grabbed his sack, and ran. He could hear Sorry shouting and crying ahead of him, and then his friend suddenly stopped and began laughing and jumping up and down. He caught up with him and turned. Behind them, the giants' tower was beginning to collapse. He saw the drawbridge crash down and smoking and burning giants rushing out. Some braved jumping into the water. Others higher up were jumping from battlements before they collapsed, and, on the roof, he saw Ate Eyes fall into the burning building. A few seconds later, there was a terrific groan and the whole building leant and then fell; a roar of flames and smoke dropped angrily to the ground, spilling giants and burning timber as it steamed.

Sorry stood motionless, a huge grin tearing his face in half. 'That's fantastic!' he said.

CHAPTER 13

The Wise Wench had put some large wax and wicker figures just outside the kettle hut. One looked like a village full of goblins, the next an evil looking hamster, and the last was a big fat giant. The king looked on intently. He appeared to be very tired.

'I'm sorry, Wise Wench, it still isn't clear enough. Just why do we need the hamster, and why do the rails have to go right through the village?'

The Wise Wench sighed and looked on at Looti. Looti sighed and looked at the palanquin bearers who just looked at their feet. In the distance, the sound of goblins shouting 'mnarr, mnarr, mnarr,' echoed across the meadow. The Wise Wench turned very red and threw chalk at the king. 'As I've explained times-beyond-counting now, the hamster comes through the village and frightens our foe. It rolls on the rails, and goblins inside push it—just like the Great Dragon Kettle. It's the last thing they'll expect.'

Everyone present agreed that being unexpectedly reinforced by a giant iron hamster with wings was a pretty unlikely turn of events. The king looked on blankly.

'Oh, just trust me! I know what I'm doing!' shouted the Wise Wench as she stomped off into the Kettle Hall.

'Reckon it's her moon time,' whispered one of the bearers. They all nodded and looked like they expected trouble.

Inside, work was virtually complete on the magnificent kettle. Master Whippet was busy polishing all the knobs and looked very proud. The Wise Wench climbed up and stood by him admiring the handiwork. The gob-girls and wenches—all of whom were covered in soot and grime—stood about looking pleased with themselves. 'Now there's just one more crucial thing to do, Master Whippet,' she said, and, bending down, she opened what seemed to be an oven.

'Yes, I was meaning to ask you about the oven, Wise Wench,' said Master Whippet, respectfully, as he peered in. 'What's it for?' His words echoed within.

'The pudding!' said the Wise Wench as she led him away.

The king turned his head upside down to see if that helped him understand. It didn't. His key slapped him for his impertinence. He understood that the hamster was needed to frighten the giants away, but what he didn't understand was why they would need frightening away since peace was about to be made with them now they had surrendered. If they *had* surrendered. He had, after all, been told by the Wise Wench to use the word *surrender* in her message—well, more a singular statement, in fact.

Perhaps the hamster was a joke.

He began to laugh.

Everyone began to laugh.

'Oh, yes, yes, yes, it's all very clear now,' chortled the king, his stomach rippling and his chins wobbling. 'Yes, perfectly clear,' he smiled at Looti. 'A joke that'll make them laugh and we'll all be best of friends,' he added, chortling.

The Wise Wench walked past with Master Whippet.

'Very clear now,' shouted the king after her. 'Very good joke!' He laughed, waving his key at her and winking.

Joke? thought the Wise Wench. *How ever did he get there?* She gave a shrug of her shoulders. 'That's right,' she said. 'Joke. Well, cheerio!' she waved, and walked off into the forest.

The words 'mnarr, mnarr, mnarr,' echoed feebly from the meadow behind.

An hour or so later, the Wise Wench led Whippet into her cottage.

'Special, you say?' said Whippet as he followed her in.

The Wise Wench stooped over, picked up an escaping whisk from near the door, and hung it back on one of the beams. 'Tea?' she asked, smiling, and made her way over to the stove. Whippet looked around. He'd only seen the place in the dark before and was amazed at how many things were cluttered in various cupboards and shelves. He remembered the smell, though; that vaguely interesting, but not quite clean, smell that all old people seemed to generate

203

about themselves when they have so many stories. Rather like old-gob-boy-green, the color old goblin males somehow find and cherish when they reach a certain age and then refuse to wear any other color; a color that is totally impossible to find or tolerate at any other time.

In the middle of the room sat a curious collection of objects including an udder. 'One of the king's?' asked Whippet, casually.

'No. In fact, that udder and the things around it are the reason we're here,' answered the Wise Wench.

The curious collection of objects included a map, several drawings of evil-looking cows, a drawing of something metallic like a big iron jug with a lid and straps, and a diorama of a curiously tortured landscape with several wax models of the evil-looking cattle. A small group of figures—including, he noticed, one with an upside-down head—were arranged at various points on the diorama as though prepared for battle. Arrows pointed liberally from these figures into the cows. There was also a curious smell of brimstone.

The Wise Wench tossed a large cloth over the diorama and smiled thinly. She filled the kettle and put it on the stove, then reached up and produced a large wicker basket filled with dainty cakes made in the likenesses of winged monstrosities. 'Terror cake, Master Whippet?' she asked, and proffered the basket.

'Don't mind if I do!' said Whippet who tucked in. They were delicious, if a little terrifying-looking—particularly the one with the fins.

'Yes, the udder is special,' said the Wise Wench and, reaching under the cloth, drew out the pale fleshy udder. It flapped about, flaccidly. 'Tell me, Master Whippet, have you ever heard of the Very, Very, Very Horrible Meadows?'

Whippet shook his head, eyeing the udder suspiciously as though it might leap up and try to throttle him.

'Goodness, have you never stared at the distant mountains and wondered why occasionally they smoked?'

'Not really,' said Whippet, guiltily. 'They seem so far away they aren't relevant.'

'Well, they're about to become relevant,' snapped the Wise Wench. 'And how about fire-breathing heifers?' she added, in all seriousness.

Again, Whippet shook his head as she handed him the drawing of the iron object.

'In that case, my desire to get you to build a pressure kettle for the milk of the Fire-breathing Heifers of the Atrocious Conflagration in the Very, Very, Very Horrible Meadows might come as a surprise to you. Another terror cake?' she added and passed the basket.

'Just where are the Very, Very, Very Horrible Meadows, oh Wise Wench?' asked Master Whippet as he finished the last crumbs of his final terror cake—one that had horns, flappy tentacles and many legs.

'At the very edge of the Great Forest, Master Whippet,' she answered, picking up some knitting. Whippet saw she knitted what looked like identical Wise Wenches arguing while a pair of kings looked on, unaware their bottoms were on fire. 'It is a place,' she continued, 'so terrible and hot, that it is a hot and horrible terrible death to try to cross it; a place where the very air is yellow and foul, where fire shoots out of the earth itself. Unless you know where to go, exactly, then it's not quite so bad.'

'And you've been?'

She suddenly stood up, looking west, and smiled. 'No. Well, yes—a bit. But speaking prophetically of fire, the heroes have escaped from the giants' tower and it's burning. Lots, heh, heh. The biggest bonfire ever seen in these parts has just been somewhat improbably made by a very small, cowardly, devious, somewhat irritating, narrow-shouldered goblin. It burns so brightly I can see it. The forest will never be the same again, I suspect. Nor, indeed, will either of them.' She sat down and carried on with her knitting.

Whippet stood and leant outwards. In the twilight he could see a faint glow a great distance away above the forest. 'What does it mean Wise Wench?'

'It means the first part of the plan has succeeded, but now the most dangerous part begins,' she said, her knitting needles clinking furiously. 'Well, can you build it or not?' she added, nodding at the drawing and then frowning as she dropped a stitch.

'I think so. I don't quite understand why you want one with straps on, though,' he added and looked at the drawing again. It was a complex device and looked very heavy.

'Because someone is going to carry it for me.'

'Someone? Do you mean you are going to send some fool off to milk one of these...whatever heifers? Isn't that rather dangerous?'

'Very, but I have goblins in mind. One-more-than-one should suffice. The important thing is that it must be ready for Turnipday or we're all dead.' She put her knitting down and stared over at Master Whippet. 'We must get the milk of a Fire-breathing Heifer of the Atrocious Conflagration for the Great Dragon Kettle. To do that, we must journey as swiftly as possible to the Very, Very, Very Horrible Meadows, itself an arduous trip, and we must do it before the full force of the giants arrives!'

'Or?'

'Or every goblin in the forest will be killed by the giants.' She sat back. 'More tea?' she added, and reached for the pot. 'Yes, it must be Turnipday or the plan will fail. That's when they get back, you see,' she added.

'*They*, oh Wise Wench?' asked Whippet, apologetically.

'Oh do come along, Master Whippet. *They*, the one-more-than-one returning heroes, being chased by—' She suddenly stopped, politely moved Whippet back from the fire, and stepped away herself. '—giants who will be very angry. That bonfire is what's left of their tower, or will be. They'll begin to think once-more-than-once about goblins and how easy they are to kill after that and what Moaris did to them. That fear and doubt is a powerful weapon for us.' Suddenly a cloud of soot fell down the chimney and into the room, covering the hearth and the area where they had just been. '—Urgh, the hero of the village, or soon to be hero of the village, will be in front, remarkably. They will arrive here at one-more-than-one minutes past many-o-the-clock the day before Turnipday with a horde of giants behind them.'

206

'Hmmm,' said Whippet, trying not to imagine a horde of angry giants. 'Then I'd better get cracking.'

'One moment,' the Wise Wench said as she smiled and opened the door. 'Your Majesty wants something?' she said into the darkness outside and stepped back, knowingly.

The king was outside astride Cribmuncher, his resplendent noble riding pig, glorious with its train of living poultry. The king was in the process of beginning to knock and stopped, a confused look on his face. He dismounted, leaving Cribmuncher to nibble on some apples that had somehow been piled exactly where he was looking. The king entered, looking carefully about for traps. 'Yes, I want some information,' he said. He looked at the table and Whippet with suspicion.

There was an awkward silence.

'Yes, I know. I'm glad you answered my summons,' said the Wise Wench. 'Terror cake, great king?' she added, handing him what was left on the plate. 'Look, we've saved the best until last for you. The only one left in the tureen is a representation of Longparts the Catastrophe Megalo-turbot, stylized in marzipan and tuna. His propensity for havoc, of course, is well known to us all.' She winked knowingly at no one in particular.

The king looked at it dubiously but ate it anyway. 'Your summons? I received no such summons. If I had, I wouldn't have come.' He smiled and crossed his arms, theatrically.

'I know, which is why I sent my message subliminally,' answered the Wise Wench, tartly.

'Aha,' said the king, 'and that's where you're wrong, because I only just thought of coming here, and dashed onto my special evening pig to reach you. We galloped. It can't have been more than not-many minutes ago since the idea of visiting you even came to me.'

Outside, Cribmuncher munched his apples while his escorting poultry pecked at what he left.

'I know,' said the Wise Wench, somewhat smugly.

The king looked suspicious and peered at her.

'The pictures of the moon,' said the Wise Wench.

'Pictures of the moon? Have you gone mad, woman?' The king smiled his most knowing smile.

'Nope. You've been seeing them all day, and pictures of my cottage, and little corn dolls of me, lying subtly at the edges of your vision. And, I think you'll recall, hearing my name whispered on the wind while you were suckling your favorite heifer as it was going dark tonight. That was Gipp, a sensible gob-boy, up the tree next to you. Doing as he was bid.'

The king scowled at her and went very red. 'How dare you summon me here without asking me!' he shouted. Then recalled a number of other images and curious objects he'd seen earlier that day—a carved wooden parrot, a balloon with mouse tails, an enormous badger made of pine cones. Damn the woman! The king looked over his shoulder wondering what else she might be making him do without him knowing.

'The Wise Wench was just telling me that our young heroes will return soon,' said Whippet, quietly, in an attempt to change the subject.

'Fascinating!' shouted the king, grumpily.

'Yes, apparently they'll be back at one-more-than-one minutes past many-o-the-clock on the day before Turnipday,' he added, smiling.

'One-more-than-one minutes past many-o-the-clock, you say?' said the king, sarcastically. 'Very precise for you, oh Wise Wench. And what, exactly, will they have to say for themselves at this hour, pray?' he added, glowering at her.

The Wise Wench smiled and paced around for a few moments, then came to a decision and smiled more broadly. 'They will say: 'Your Majesty, I bring terrible news. Your Majesty's leg seems to be on fire!"

The king's face dropped.

* * *

The fire crackled and spat as the fat fell on it. The chickens were nearly cooked now, and a slavering group of goblins looked on hungrily. Nearby, the whole village sat around in a huge circle of competing fires[50]. Dome Eyes stood up and scratched himself, intimately.

'Don't do that, dear,' said Straggly, his breed-bound, and threw a small rock at him. 'Just be glad you've been let out early from the village wolverine.'

Dome Eyes gingerly brushed his wounds, looked around for a suitably large revenge rock and found one nearby. It was a good few heads in size. He reached over to pick it up.

'So, what about these giants?' said Smells, an appropriately unpleasant-smelling goblin nearby.

Dome Eyes grunted as he tried to lift the rock and gave up after half a second of effort. 'What giants?' he said, cursing that he couldn't pick it up and fling it at Straggly.

'Giants, dear,' answered Straggly. 'I've heard rumours they are coming this way. The whole village is murmuring about it.'

Nearby, there could be heard lots of murmuring.

'See?' she added.

'Well, if there are lots of giants coming this way then why don't we all just f—'

'—You are probably all wondering why the king has called a moot?' cried Looti in her most commanding voice as she stood up in the midst of the villagers, her perch enabling all to see her. She gripped her pelican-shaped megaphone awkwardly with both hands. It was, in truth, too big for her but often the only way to be heard above so much prattling and murmuring was to take extreme measures. There was a general murmur, and a smacking of male goblin chops.

Dome Eyes, like everyone else, suddenly stopped what he was doing and looked up, which he seemed to be doing most of the time anyway. Looti was dressed in a magnificent purple robe of the finest silk, and about her neck she wore a necklace of chicken claws to protect her from the unwanted attention of the dreaded Barnvelder,

---

[50] The art of goblin bonfire duelling being a sensible and less painful way of settling disputes through skill *and* of having fun doing it.

209

the Cockerel That Preferred the Company of Women. Nearby, a small gob-boy began saying, 'Royalty and Wise Wench only. Scum not allowed,' through a small megaphone every few moments to keep the crowd back.

'His Vast Circumference will be with us in a short while. Be careful to pay attention to *all* he says, not just the good bits. You will learn well that his wrathful gaze is as bad as the wrath of Lord Noc. So just watch it.' With that she stepped down off the trapeze and gave a wink to a small huddled band of goblins nearby. They got to their feet and blew a fanfare on their tortoise trumpets[51].

* * *

'And why would I want to do that, pray?' said the king sarcastically, while carefully checking the corners of her cottage for subliminal messages.

'It's quite simple, really,' said the Wise Wench. 'The villagers are a cowardly lot. They would sell their own mothers for a pound of turnips—some for just *a* turnip, and a rotten one at that.'

'True,' said the king, disdainfully.

'So what do you think they'll do when they learn about giants coming this way?'

'Run off, if they have any sense,' answered the king, regally.

'Exactly, and that would not be good for the...*current version* of the plan.'

The king looked at her, suspiciously.

'The whole village must be here in readiness for the—*coming events*—and if they've all already fled the giants, they wouldn't be around to fight them, which they must be for the plan to succeed. Do you follow?'

The king's blank stare answered her question.

'So, how do we keep goblins in one place?' she continued, enthusiastically.

---

[51] Trumpets made from tortoises.

'That's easy! Just have them all killed,' answered the king, and smiled, assuming it was time to move on.

'True, but the giants would surely see through a ruse where all the goblins they saw were actually dead and hung from poles?'

The king had already lost interest but nodded so the conversation would end quicker.

'So, Master Whippet, give the king the benefit of your fine brain. As well as just having them killed, what other way could we keep all the villagers together?'

'Fear,' answered Whippet with the most obvious answer.

Nearby, the king was thinking about udders.

'Good! Fear, yes, and what also about bribery? There is never a better reason for a goblin to stay put than the reason of having a soon to be full belly, or a belly so full that movement is impossible without the risk of it exploding.'

The males mutely agreed, then the king silently insisted that as king he should silently agree first. Whippet mutely conceded the honor.

'So, perhaps a combination of these things would be the surest way to keep the villagers together?'

'If you like,' said the king, testily.

'Good, that's settled then,' said the Wise Wench, and she went for her coat.

'Hang on, hang on! What's settled then?' said the king.

'The moot. The moot you've arranged requiring one-more-than-one days of feasting and eating and bonfires and entertainment on pain of death.'

The king looked confused. 'And when does this start?' he said, examining his royal fingers.

'About not-many minutes ago. We must rush or we'll be late. Looti has already gathered the locals together. We'll need to sneak in through your back door and out of the main door, regally, when we arrive to make a proper entrance.'

'I do not *sneak*,' said the king, sneakily.

In the distance, trumpets sounded.

211

'Any minute now,' sighed Looti. Nearby the fanfare wheezed into another hour and the goblins were looking bored and winded. One had passed out.

The Great Mouth flew open and the Wise Wench came out of the Moot House, shaking her head. Behind her, on Cribmuncher, now specially decorated in the magenta cloth of partying, was the king, resplendent in his alternate red and green striped dressing gown of the fungiver. He smiled, regally, as he was brought to the stage in the center of the ring of fires. All eyes stared enviously at his greatness.

His Majesty grinned broadly. 'Friends!' he roared, staring at the trapeze, suspiciously.

Loud cheers, some concerns.

'Friends!' he said again.

Slightly less loud cheers, concerns growing.

'We stand at the edge of greatness!'

Scattered cheers and the odd murmur.

'Soon we shall see the return of our heroes from Giant Land!'

More cheers and a chorus of loud belches from the older female goblins who were allowed to be rude at public occasions.

'I declare a special festival shall be held!'

Cheers from all concerned, backed by a vigorous wind-breaking session from the aforementioned goblins.

'A feast I alone am responsible for conceiving. Starting right now, we shall celebrate the festival of the Heroes and Hamster. I declare that to honor our heroes, on each of the following one-more-than-one days and nights, we will hold a moot. A very special moot, for at it we shall eat one of my own very special hogs!'

The king's hog looked upwards at him, nervously.

'And there will be ale—*free* ale—and cider!'

Everyone looked around thirstily and began to run towards the approaching huge barrels, held aloft on appallingly-constructed wheelbarrows.

'At the end of the festival, the Iron Hamster shall be paraded into the village ready for the arrival of our one-more-than-one heroes!'

Everyone had stopped listening and was fighting over the alcohol. The first near-fatal injury of the moot was recorded, followed in retaliation by the next.

'Did he say one-more-than-one heroes?' said an unusually attentive very purple goblin at the back.

'And the day of our returning heroes shall be known as Heroes Return Day, and on that day we shall honor our heroes not only with a feast fit for a king, but we shall also show our respect at that time by refraining from lighting fires anywhere in the village. This respect will be shown, on pain of death, starting at festival's final evening!' *Then we'll see how legs can catch on fire! Oh yes indeedy, so called Wise Wench.*

The Wise Wench carried on shaking her head, but as the king began to get off the stage she elbowed him in the ribs.

'Oh, and one last thing, meaningless subjects and scum! I hear that, very sadly, the village wolverine has escaped and prowls the edges of the village. Anyone who escapes—erm, heh heh, I mean *goes out for a stroll* beyond the confines of the village—will meet a terrible, messy and bloody, very painful slow death and then be eaten while still alive. I think they've stopped listening,' he added to the Wise Wench.

'Don't worry, word will soon spread,' she said, and patted Looti on the shoulders. The adviser moved off to gossip.

'Pass the potatoes,' said the Wise Wench. It was later.

The king's table was laid on the stage at the center of the circle of fires. Only the Wise Wench and the king sat at it. Looti stood nearby nibbling at a salad.

The king seemed lost in thought as he stared at his adviser, his mouth wide like a turbot's.

'So you approve of my choice, then,' said the Wise Wench, watching him.

The king colored. 'Satisfactory,' he mumbled dismissively under his breath as he swallowed a whole turnip. 'I must remember to ensure my future advisers are always suitably callipygian and bathykolpian.' He stared very smugly at her and brushed his shoulder, regally.

The Wise Wench looked at him dubiously before ladling some more sprouts onto her plate. 'Praise Noc,' she said and reverently cast one behind.

A small band of very brightly-dressed goblins slowly began to approach the king's table. Even from here, the king could hear their bells jangling.

'Oh no!' cursed the king as he saw them. 'It's those sodding mummers. They'll want to do one of those awful plays!' He deliberately cast a potato onto the floor. 'Oh dear, I've dropped something,' he said deviously. 'I'll just have to get under the table to reach it. I could be some time. Days even,' he added and began to climb out of his seat.

'Your Majesty dropped this,' said a goblin servant who was stood under the table.[52] He proudly polished the potato on his tunic, leaving a large gravy stain, and reverently placed it back on the royal plate.

'Oh, thank you so much,' said the king, sarcastically.

The little troop had by now reached the table and stood smiling and jangling. The king gave them a disdainful look. They were all dressed in bright yellow mummer's tunics, and had an uncountable number of tiny bells sewn into their garments. Each wore lace bonnets into which were sewn pictures of their favorite types of root vegetable. They smiled at him.

The king imagined himself holding an axe over their heads.

'Nope,' said the Wise Wench sympathetically to him. 'You can't have a moot without mummers. It's tradition.'

'Yowr Majestwy!' said the middle one.

---

[52] The honoured position of tablemaester, or undertable operative or manager, is greatly prized by goblins. So much so, in fact, that the post is usually the subject of a fight or bonfire to the death to establish who gets it and all the leftovers.

The king cradled his head in his hands.

'It is our pleasure to pwesent our little pway. It is a complex storwy, and verwy, verwy long.'

'How long?' growled the king.

'It is an act in almost uncountable parts, your Divine Wounditude!' simpered the lead actor.

The king frowned so deeply his face nearly fell into itself but then he seemed to recollect something and smiled widely. 'Your name, inane common person?' he grumbled, hungrily.

'Fickle, Yowr Massiveness,' he answered, and then clapped his hands and the actors scattered to their respective places. 'We pwesent Gobwins—Our Storwy. Act One!' shouted Fickle to the assembled, disinterested drunken mob. 'The stowry of how Lord Stomper slew the Black Duck of the Pond of Death using only his wits and his beawtiful beawtiful singing voice. So, let us sing, sing, sing!' The little troop began pirouetting and started to sing.

CHAPTER 14

'Bravo! Bravo, indeed!' said Lady Carline, as she landed on Urgh's shoulder. 'Bravo to you both! You see, being heroic isn't so hard, it just takes courage.'

'I have a feeling our heroics have only just begun,' said Urgh, as he rung out his breeches.

'Well, that's true, which is why the Wise Wench has such faith in you. Both of you,' she added, somehow seeming to smile at Sorry

'Don't you understand, misery guts?' said Sorry to Urgh. 'We're free, free, free! Big fire!' He gave Urgh another feeble, disingenuous hug and then returned his stare—and love—to the massivest bonfire he'd ever created. Suddenly, there was an explosion in the fiery remains of the giants' tower and a cloud of billowing smoke boiled upwards. Amongst the confusion could be heard swearing and barking—lots of barking.

'I'm afraid we're not free,' said Urgh.

Sorry began crying.

'RELEASE THE HOUNDS!' shouted a really, really cross giant in the distance.

'Time for you to run, chaps,' said the raven, as she took to wing.

Sorry stuck his thumb in his mouth and began to burble as the barking got louder.

Urgh shook him and reached into his sack. 'Stop blubbing,' he snapped and smiled confidently as he brought out a pile of false noses made of papier-mâché tied with twine. 'We've got nothing to worry about, I have my magic noses.' He tossed a few of his noses on a nearby rock. They burst into clouds of pepper. 'Now, let's get home!' he shouted, dashing off into the forest.

Sorry followed, momentarily torn between fear of any kind of pain and staying to watch the burning tower. Fear and cowardice once again won the day, and he ran as fast as his scrawny legs would take him into the darkness. As he caught up, Urgh began to throw

216

more noses behind them as they dashed into the forest's somber embrace.

They had run well into the night before they felt safe enough to stop and briefly sleep. The barking had ended, and the goblins assumed the hounds had swiftly returned sneezing and hungry to their masters who had immediately given up the chase. Goblins are very good at self-delusion and power-napping[53].

Urgh stirred and gave a yelp as he woke. The sycamore towered above and about him, its great boughs seeming to cradle the goblin, or—to his feeble, sleepy mind—grip and grope him. Its roots, which seemed warm, inviting, and stuffed with goose down when he first lay in them, had apparently changed overnight to be cold, aggressive, and filled with spanners, anvils, and small, armor-clad, restless gob-boys and girls.

He looked up. Above him, the wan sun was sneaking a glance at him through the boughs. The day had that slight chill which promised that it would soon warm and become uncomfortable. Not, however, as uncomfortable as Urgh who, having failed to rise, fell back against the roots and banged his head. He gave another yelp.

A huge bush slapped him. Behind it was Sorry, looking, as ever, on the verge of crying. 'Will you stop yelping. THEY might hear you!' he snapped, and continued shivering and feeling very sorry for himself nearby. 'I'm hungry,' he added, helpfully. 'Do you think this will burn,' he added, staring hopefully at the damp bush.

'No, and not as hungry as me,' snapped Urgh, pulling leaves from his smock. Then he drew a little map on the ground in front of them. The map showed the giants' keep, the forest, and the village.

'So where are we?' said Sorry as he held his stomach and made slight mewing noises.

'Here,' said Urgh, pointing to a twig near the giants' keep.

---

[53] And, indeed, any kind of sleeping for that matter as they are so lazy. It's said that certain tribes of goblins can sleep while walking, or even running, although it can have obvious dangers unless the path they follow is really, really good.

'What, next to the ant?' said Sorry, looking up and imagining an ant scaled up. Such an ant would block out the sun, in a similar manner to Mothmass, the vast Moth which Blotted out the Sun, had.

'Yes,' said Urgh, irritably. He also held his stomach. It gave a gurgle.

'Praise Noc,' said the goblins, bowing their heads.

'Which means we've still got a long way to go, so we should head on, and besides, you're right: THEY could still be chasing us,' said Urgh with an air of urgency. 'Where's Lady Carline?' he added, 'She might be able to see.'

'Have you got any food in that sack?' asked Sorry, trying to sneak a peek.

'No.'

The pair despondently stood up and began to walk.

* * *

Bliss at dawn. A thin mist skulked around the village, groping the ruinous scene it revealed. Unconscious goblins littered the village brown. Empty and broken barrels, smoldering fires, and detritus were scattered across the barren, shattered landscape.

The first night of the moot had gone without too many hitches. A few deaths, true, and quite a number of accidental acts of arson[54], but most goblins were still alive. A few gob-boys and girls—including Spoilt—had escaped the child pit, but as they had their guards held prisoner, no one had so far noticed or cared.

The king drunkenly opened one bleary eye.

In front of him was a giant chicken.

He closed his eyes, shook his head, wished he hadn't, and opened them again.

It was still there.

---

[54] For the sake of clarity, it's important to note that the words *fire* and *accidental* (or any derivatives, slang, or associated meanings) never appear in the same sentence of spoken Goblin.

'Yowr Majesty!' said the gigantic poultry. 'So, our little epic enters the one-after-one day. The dawn wises and, with it, wises the curtain on act one-after-quite-a-few!'

'What curtain?' grumbled the king under his breath.

'It's just acting talk,' explained the Wise Wench. 'He's putting it on, like his fake voice.'

'And with it,' continued Fickle, 'comes a celebwation of fire.' Suddenly behind him, a burning goblin dressed as a moth arched across the sky and splashed into the Poo-Pit with a big squelch.

'That reminds me,' said the king to Looti, 'let it be known that I need a new Poo-Pit Maester.'

Looti smiled demurely, nodded, and wandered off to tell everyone.

'Any opinion?' said the king, sniffing a kipper and looking at the Wise Wench.

'Not really,' she said, closing her eyes.

A pair of goblins dressed as chicks marched forward juggling goblin babies between them. 'Once, there was no such thing as fire!' shouted one of them. 'But then, along came a goblin, and soon fire was born!'

'One moment, if you please?' added the other actor. Ignoring the flying babies, he suddenly marched over to the king and took his costume off. 'By ancient rite, Your Circularity, I beg leave to try to impress you[55].' There was a series of bumps.

'If you must,' answered the king, nonchalantly.

The actor drew a bottle from his pocket and began liberally rubbing himself with it.

---

[55] The ancient goblin rite of trying to impress the chief into liking you goes back years without counting (which, in truth, is not hard). All goblins can claim the rite, unless they try to do it too often and fail, in which case sundry and varied punishments are available to the leader. In general, rather like those of their chiefs and kings (and occasional queens—although generally gob-wenches avoid the idiocy of rule and prefer to pull the strings from a sensible distance), these acts tend to be quite self-destructive and almost always doomed to failure, as long-term injuries, death, or other serious consequences are the usual result of even the most successful attempts to impress.

'What's that he's rubbing all over himself?' asked the king out of tedium.

'Rubbing alcohol,' answered the Wise Wench with unerring accuracy.

'Oh. Is that a firestarter he's sparking?' added the king, with sudden minor interest.

'Yes,' sighed the Wise Wench who leant back a little. There was a sudden spark and the goblin became a ball of fire. The smell of burning hair and screaming followed it as the goblin burst into a squealing fireball and began dashing about looking for the duck-pond.

'Next,' said the king, wearily.

The actors suddenly reassigned their roles and the act commenced once more, this time without the discarded infants, which the king had to admit to himself made it much less of a spectacle, even though he would never ever admit such a thing to peasants.

As the singing began with gusto, trumpets, kazoos, and horns were produced by smiling players dressed as fiery bantams. Not far away, there was a loud splash and sizzle. 'Basted, the Flaming Chicken marched away to war, her siege coop gave a roar, her battle chickens were white as snow, a-burn, burn, burn it, oh!' sang the enthusiastic troupe, almost in tune.

'They are *definitely* coming back tomorrow, aren't they?' said the king through spread fingers at the Wise Wench.

She nodded sagely and began joining in the song, in truth, not only to encourage the actors, but also to annoy the king.

The day had moved on. Very, very slowly. Suddenly the king noticed it had all stopped. Silence prevailed at last[56]. He thought about opening his eyes, remembered what had happened the last time and kept them shut. He was damp. Very damp. 'Is it over?' he

---

[56] In truth, it's never truly silent anywhere where groups of goblins are, which is one reason, perhaps, why they have no word for silent. Or fluffy.

mumbled, in the direction of where he'd last seen the Wise Wench seated.

'No, they're all waiting for your reaction to the end of this part.'

'Which part?'

'Act several, Your Flabby Wetness,' added Looti, helpfully.

'I'm not opening my eyes. Perhaps they'll go away if I ignore them?' It was more a question than a statement of fact. 'Are they still there?' he asked, hopefully.

'Yes,' said the Wise Wench.

Someone handed the king a cloth. He began wiping his face.

Looti delicately mopped the king with a sponge. At the forefront of the re-enactment of the flaming apocalypse—the grand finale of this part of the show—he had borne the brunt of the dousing that ended that act. He sighed as he was mopped and noticed that the whole area was knee-deep in mud. Damn, he'd opened his eyes anyway.

The Wise Wench put her black umbrella down and smiled.

'Act several?' said the king, and his lip began to wobble. He bit it very suddenly, remembering the beatings he got from his father, the awesomely violent Lord Grumpy Stormgrunties the Terrible, for showing signs of weakness—which in truth were numerous. He once had the entire village burnt down when someone sneezed without permission. *That was true leadership* thought the king. *He wouldn't have any truck with actors, but if I can only bear it until tomorrow— yes, by tomorrow—all this will have been worth it.* His lip began to bleed profusely.

'But think of it this way: we're nearly half-way there,' said the Wise Wench as she handed him a bandage and gave a watery smile.

The king shrugged his shoulders and gingerly dabbed his bloody lip. *Not quite half-way there* was all he could think. He gazed absentmindedly across the festival field. It was littered with the debris of goblin partying; discarded bones, broken empty barrels whose interiors had been licked dry, and full-sized papier-mâché crocodiles from act the-one-after-quite-a-few-but-not-lots. He clapped. Once.

The actors all bowed gratefully. 'And now we must prepare for act many-and-a-few-more, Your Bleedership,' said a very green

221

goblin actor. 'In this act, the Queen of Sheep saves the Kingdom from Mushbad, Demonlord of Rude-Shaped Fungi. While we do, Moribund here will entertain you with his songs.'

A large group of goblins appeared bearing luminous ochre fungus costumes while another began to push forward through the throng. Finally, he reached the front. A goblin dressed as a giant green duck now stood before the king and began to quack, dance, and sing.

The king sighed. 'How many days of this drivel do I have to put up with, advisor?' He looked at the duck through his fingers.

'Just over one, Your Potent Largeness,' said Looti, and she smiled very sweetly.

'And how many more acts?'

'Lots-more-than-many-and-one, I'm afraid,' conceded the Wise Wench who stared westwards. In the background, the singing and quaking continued with great enthusiasm.

'Perhaps I can cheer, Your Majesty up?' said Looti, bringing over an enormous bucket of cider.

'How?' growled the king between gulps.

'I have some candidates for the position of Poo-Pit Maester, Your Milky Magnificence.' She bowed. 'Shall I start bringing them over?'

'If you must,' he answered, watching her wave an arm towards a crowd. It was answered by the appearance of a shuffling, very unpleasant-looking thing with hair on one side of its head. The king smelt it long before it spoke.

'This is Grilt, potential Poo-Pit Maester, Your Multiplechinosity,' said Looti, and she batted her considerable eyelashes.

The king scowled at the grotesque shambling ruin before him. 'Speak,' he said, diplomatically.

'I'd be rightly honored and nidorously grateful to be considered for the job, Your Looks-a-Bit-Like-a-Toadiness,' said Grilt, now clearly visible as a part-bald, terrible-smelling goblin with sweat rings under his vest.

The Wise Wench scowled at him.

'And just why do you want this post, unpleasant-smelling common person?' said the king, regally.

Grilt shuffled uneasily. The king sighed and scratched a large udder on the arm of his chair.

'Erm,' said Grilt, uncomfortably.

'Well, peasant, do you like pong, at all?' said the king, helpfully.

'Yes, yes I do, Your Uddertude! I like it a lot, and feel that I could do a lot with it if given the opportunity.' Grilt smiled.

The king looked absentmindedly at him and smiled officiously. 'Yes, well, scum,' he said, 'we have several other dismal nobodies to interview today. If you haven't heard from us by the end of the week, you may assume you haven't been successful on this occasion. However, don't let this put you off applying for any other village posts in the future.'

Grilt sighed, put the cow-pat back on his head and walked off.

'He seemed quite promising,' said the king, quietly.

'Yes, Your Sweatiness, and he did seem well-qualified in the smell department,' added Looti.

'Hmm, yes, I've decided to dispense with the remainder of the interviews and appoint—'

'—Useless!' snapped the Wise Wench and she folded her arms.

'And just what do you mean by 'useless'?' snapped the king back who folded *his* arms.

'I mean he's no bloody good,' snapped the Wise Wench, and she somehow managed to fold her arms right behind her back.

'I see, I see. So you think that's an end to it, do you? Well, let me tell you that I'm king around here and I make the decisions.' He sat back and tried copying the Wise Wench again. There was a dull, painful-sounding grind of bone popping out of joint and the king gave a yell. Looti dashed to his side and cradled his head in her arms.

'My Sweetness,' cooed Looti and soothingly stroked his head. 'Are you injured?'

The king began making strange noises—a sort of cross between mooing and sighing as she cradled his arms.

'And besides,' snapped the Wise Wench, unfolding her arms and smiling, 'his name doesn't begin with a P. You can't have a Poo-Pit Maester whose name doesn't begin with a P. You couldn't have Roger the Poo-Pit Maester, or Harold the Poo-Pit Maester, it just wouldn't work. It's got to be Pilt, Patricia, Puckle, Pod or Pongwelllots. The villagers would never stand for it any other way. How could they put their trust, their sacred trust, in a goblin whose name is deficient in the P-commencement department? There would be revolution.' She sat down and ordered cockroach crumpets.

The king stood up painfully and nodded in agreement. 'Next,' he shouted. An unfeasibly short goblin came to the table, and then proceed to vanish under it.

'Name,' said Looti.

'Puppington Pap-Pinch, Your Wobbleness,' he said, and apparently bowed.

'Hired,' said the king, and he turned to more weighty matters with butter on them while trying to ignore the squabble of actors prancing before him as their play wore on, and on, and on.

* * *

They seemed to have been running all afternoon when Sorry darted for the opening in the thorny hedge and pushed himself through, pausing for breath. Briars and needles pinched and cut him. Urgh was not far behind, crushing Sorry's hopes that he'd started flagging and would be eaten as a useful distraction to his own escape.

Nor were the dogs, which had somehow picked up their trail once more.

Lady Carline had reappeared, warning them of their impending death by being eaten while still alive, and they had been running ever since. The light was beginning to fade, making running more difficult in the already gloomy forest. The goblins had fallen over several times but had mercifully not broken, sprained, or severed anything.

Yet.

'Will they never give up?' muttered Sorry, gasping for breath.

'I don't think so,' wheezed Urgh, as he leant by his companion.

'You know they won't. You can't delay for long,' said the raven, helpfully.

A pair of howls came from the distance, and again, the horn sounded. But now a murmur of giant shouts could be heard.

'Do you have any more noses?' whimpered Sorry.

Urgh shook his head. 'Nothing that will help unless they get really, really close, and I don't want to have to find out if my magic is strong enough then, unless I can help it. They're already getting too close for comfort.' He looked around for inspiration. They were amongst a thick, thorny hedge of brambles, a skirt of nettles, nearly as high as the goblins, was on the far side. Somewhere nearby was the sound of running water.

'How far away is the village?' gasped Sorry.

'Still a long way off, I'm afraid,' said a raven voice from high above.

'Then we need to lose them, but I don't know how,' answered Urgh. Then he saw the reeds. He grabbed Sorry by the hand and led him forward. There was a large, green pond surrounded by the reeds which were thick and high; a stream danced lazily away back into the forest beyond. Big, juicy, winged insects swept over the pond and buzzed. Sorry snatched one and bit it in half. It bit him back and he yelped.

The horn sounded again, and this time, Sorry and Urgh heard the voice of a giant admonishing someone and could pick out the words.

'Well?' muttered Sorry.

'Don't you remember the story of how Prince Whiff escaped from the Terrier of the Gods?' said Urgh, hopefully.

'Nope.' Sorry shook his head.

'Prince Whiff was hungry, and had stolen the dog food of the Terrier of the Gods. This understandably made the dog pretty cross and he chased Whiff. The chase lasted days beyond counting, with the hound pursuing the great goblin hero, who couldn't work out how the terrier was following him, until Whiff realized that it was his own smell-story which gave him away. His smell-story was so long it was reaching out to the dog and pulling at him. Whiff used his cunning and swam below the deep waters of the River of the Gods and the hound lost his smell. The long chase was over, and Whiff was revered for it.'

'And how did he breathe? Did he become a fish?' Sorry added, angrily.

'In a way,' said Urgh, breaking off a pair of reeds and blowing through them. 'He used reeds to breathe through while he swam.'

'Oh,' said Sorry.

'Don't you see? If we do what he did, we might lose the giants. It's magic.'

'Lose the giants,' said Sorry, hopeful. 'But getting wet will make me lose my smell-story; it's more precious than anything to me. And I can't swim much, why would I need to?'

'My story is precious too, even more so now,' agreed Urgh. 'But heroes must make sacrifices.'

'They're coming!' shouted Lady Carline, and she flapped away into the trees shouting 'Quickly!'

Sorry dived into the stream. It was very green and very slimy but the thought of escape from being dinner helped him block the slime and what might be in it from his head. Urgh soon dived in after him. The pair swam upstream, Urgh helping Sorry as much as he could. They tested their reed breathing tubes as they slunk below the chilly waters to fully quench their smell-story and crawled along the stream bottom. It didn't take long for fear to help them get the hang of it.

They swam and crawled for longer than either of them could count[57] before emerging by a clearing in the forest circled by a knot

---

[57] Not long.

of very ancient beech trees. A huge unkindness of ravens took wing as the goblins arrived. 'I can't swim anymore,' coughed Urgh, 'but we need to get away. The dogs are bound to pick up our smell-story again—it'll only delay them. Can you see them, your ladyship?' Urgh shouted upwards.

'I can see torches far away in the forest,' answered a distant voice.

The giants thought Urgh glumly and shivered. Then they heard arguing, distant shouting, and acts of violence permeating even the blanket gloom of the forest. After a few minutes, the shouting headed away from them. Sorry almost cried out with happiness. 'I think they're going the wrong way,' he gleefully whispered.

'It looks like it,' said Lady Carline. 'Yes, they're heading away,' she added.

'Then let's keep moving while we still can,' muttered Urgh as he squelched on.

They marched on into the growing darkness, the night hours bringing only weariness, hunger, cold and the occasional childish prank. It seemed an eternity before the sky slowly brightened. The morning brought rain—very heavy rain—as the companions trudged silently on towards home.

Behind them, however, something was still following them.

* * *

The whole table, the king and Looti were covered in tapioca. The Wise Wench put down her umbrella again. She was spotless.[58]

In the gloom, the little band of mummers stood back and waited for the applause. The king had lost count of how many acts he'd seen, his misery gaining a single joyful speck of opportunity by remembering his part at the end of the play. *The payment, heh, heh.* He still felt like he'd died and gone to Hell[59]; a Hell occupied by

---

[58] For a goblin.
[59] Or at least, the goblin version of it. In truth there are countless version of what the afterlife might be like for bad goblins, all of which are pretty nasty and

endless singing and dancing. He stirred himself as he realized the sun was rising on the final day. 'It's going to be a very clear day,' he said to himself, cheerfully. Then the clouds arrived and almost instantly it began to rain. *Oh well, good for keeping trousers wet,* he thought smugly to himself.

A few scattered handclaps echoed from the other goblins nearby.

The king suddenly stood and applauded wildly, whistling and cheering. 'Get me the Head Thug,' he said to Looti. She gave a wave to Head Thug Durth. The actors looked worried.

The fires were slowly dying now. The hog had been devoured and the goblins were looking fat, drunk, and, to some extent, bored with eating pig. The king gave a little harrumph to himself and winked at his adviser.

Looti clicked her fingers and, across the devastated party field, the last fires were extinguished by goblins with buckets.

The king smiled at the Wise Wench. 'Oh, goodness me. All the fires have been put out, and the entire village is being doused. And it's raining. What are we to make of the effect that will have upon prophecy?' The king gave a mock gasp and began to laugh.

Durth bowed before the laughing king and approached the royal table. He gazed at Looti's dress. She had chosen a very low breakfast gown with yellow sequins in and had forsaken the chicken claws for today, as all goblin girls knew, was Barnvelder's Darkday, when the chickens came calling him.

The king smiled and mouthed the word *wrong* in the direction of the Wise Wench before shifting his gaze. 'Ah, erm, yes. Well, I have a mission for you, Froth,' he intoned, wisely and very correctly.

'Durth, your Majesty,' corrected Durth Dimbits.

'If you like,' sighed the king, admiring his chief thug's uniform, emblazoned with the thugs' motif of a pair of huge fists closing in on a surprised-looking goblin face.

---

generally perpetually damp, painful and infested with big things with pointy mouths that eat goblins while they are still alive, or at least still alive in a dead way, if you see what I mean.

228

'Yes, Lordship?' bowed Durth, and gave Looti a wink. She winked back. Durth staggered vaguely and held on to the royal table for support.

'I wish you to find me a crossbow,' purred the king. 'Not just any crossbow, mind, but an especially *large* one. I wish the bow to be loaded and brought to me. I'll be using it.'

'Ah, the *payment* for the festival of the mummers' dance,' added Durth with an evil smile.

'Yes, the *payment*,' repeated the king, licking his lips, 'where the king may, should he so wish, kill in cold blood any actor or thespian who has displeased him in some way.'

'Just the one mind,' the Wise Wench reminded him.

'Well, yes, just the one. *Traditionally*,' he added with an evil grin.

One of the entourage of actors walked up to the table and bowed very low, his hands behind his back, theatrically. It was Fickle.

'Don't say, 'burn, burn, burn it, oh!" said the Wise Wench with a very serious look on her face. 'His Majesty will be most displeased.'

The king smiled fiendishly at the actor.

'Youw majestwy!' said Fickle, revealing he had a glove puppet on each hand— a sheep and a wolverine. 'To pwotect us from evil spiwits, we must turn to our fwiends and guiders, the glove puppets, who alone bwing us messages fwom the gods. In the absence of the Gweat Mole, may we ask the substitute Gweat Mole to begin the Long Dark Day of Dummies?'

Looti smiled, bringing forward the Substitute Great Mole. It looked about regally before issuing its instructions into the adviser's ear. 'The Substitute Great Mole says you may begin,' uttered the Substitute Great Mole via its intermediary.

The king smiled. He had a feeling today was going to be a *very good day*.

* * *

229

Behind them, enjoying every minute of the chase, and just waiting for the cruelest moment to strike, was the giant chief's hound. It had never lost the scent but wanted the kill for its own. It knew it was being followed, however; its own considerable scent had given it away but it managed to stay ahead of the hunting giants behind. The pursuers were not going to get a share of this feast, however, not until the hunt was over and it had satisfied its hunger and considerable capacity for naughtiness.

As the Great Mole had promised to Sorry as they ran, the companions began to notice more familiar types of tree. Even the friendly larch, so common around the village until they'd burnt them all down, began to appear, and even some friendly blackened stumps. They were getting closer to home. The goblins marched on with renewed vigor, setting fire to a handful of bushes on their way, confident that each tree-stump would be the last and that, any moment now, the Wise Wench would appear from behind one with some sort of pie. They halted at what they thought was midday under the boughs of a great elm tree.

'I'm fearfully hungry,' said Urgh.

'What did you have to talk about food for? I'm so hungry I'd forgotten I was hungry.' Sorry sat down with his back to him and sulked.

Some time passed.

'Sorry, what do you think will happen now the Wise Wench's plan has failed?' said Urgh.

'Don't know, don't care. Just want biscuits.'

'But it's never happened before has it? I mean, she's never wrong. Until now that is.' Urgh looked puzzled. 'She said our message would bring peace between us, but it's done just the opposite. I think it's made things worse—if that's possible.'

'Perhaps she was lying,' muttered Sorry and he started staring at Urgh.

'Gosh, I never thought of that. The Wise Wench lying? That is scary!' He glanced at his companion whose eyes were wide and terrified. 'Oh, come on, Sorry, it's not that bad. She can't be the first gob-wench to lie.' He looked at him closer—and realized he wasn't

230

quite looking back at him. Urgh frowned. 'You're not looking at me, are you?' he said, and turned around.

A dog with an extra head was not far away. Urgh could see the dribble slowly running from its mouth. It bared its teeth. Sorry drew his little knife and handed it to Urgh. They both looked at the knife, which was fine for peeling potatoes.[60] Then they looked at the huge, slavering dog. The dog snarled and began to bark and rush at them.

Sorry and Urgh ran, screaming 'Help!' in the hope that someone would. Lady Carline suddenly swooped down, trying to distract the monstrous hound.

The dog, ready and happy to give chase, bounded happily after them, barking and ignoring the bird. The hound deliberately got close enough to let the goblins feel its breath, gave one a nip, and then sank back a little.

This is it! We're going to die thought Urgh as he fumbled in his sack for the jar—his last chance.

This is it! I'm going to die thought Sorry, and he suddenly noticed Urgh's shoelaces were untied. *Wise Wench, it was awful. We were just about to get away when Urgh fell over his laces! The dog killed him instantly and must have stayed to eat him. I haven't eaten for days.* Sorry tripped his friend and leapt over him.

Urgh, surprised by the sudden fall, went onto his back. The dreadful hound leapt straight onto him, mouth open for the kill. Urgh felt its breath on his face. It gave a terrible, long howl as its slaver dribbled onto Urgh's face. *Noc protect me*, he thought, and reached into his sack for his hornet gourd. He plunged the gourd into the dog's left mouth and squeezed it. It popped open, releasing its contents.

Countless hornets burst into the giant dog's mouth. The hound gave an appalling howl and dashed into the forest, trying to bite what was stinging it and failing badly.

In the distance, horns sounded. Somehow, they sounded cross.

---

[60] Not that goblins bother peeling potatoes.

Nearby, the hound dashed into a tree with a terrible bang, whimpered pathetically, and was still.

'Oh, well done! Oh really, really well done,' said Sorry. 'Now you've gone and let the giants know exactly where we are AND you've killed their chief's favorite pet.'

Urgh stood up and parted his legs slightly. 'Don't tell me I've made a mistake ever again!' he yelled at Sorry, who cringed apologetically. 'Understand?'

Sorry did, and nodded in agreement.

'Well done, but quickly. Quickly!' shouted Lady Carline.

Horns sounded again, and distant dog-barks struck up.

'Er, excuse me, Urgh,' said Sorry, 'but I think we should perhaps run.'

'One moment,' said Urgh, as he tore at his shirt and stared at the hound. 'Miffed!' he yelled at the top of his voice. It was too well made to tear. He looked slightly embarrassed and undid a button for effect. 'Just what I was about to say,' he said. 'Damn, I must have tripped on these,' he added, as he tied his laces

Lady Carline glanced reproachfully at Sorry, who would have shrugged his shoulders if he had any. The goblins ran off into the forest, an anxious raven swooping behind them. 'Not far now,' she said. 'There's no place like home.'

* * *

It was early afternoon. The sun was dancing bright in the sky. The king was wearing his turquoise celebratory mummer-slaying costume, decorated with pictures of dead or dying actors fashioned from dried grass and kindling. Somewhere nearby, a fight was occurring.

'They should be back soon,' said the Wise Wench, 'but I fear they will have to rush. They have quite a chase on their hands.'

'Soon?'

'Well, relatively soon, figuratively speaking.'

The king grinned broadly at her and looked at her patronizingly. 'Let me fill you in on the facts. Your facts. Facts you told me as facts. Our one-more-than-one returning heroes will be

232

retuning here at exactly one-more-than-one minutes past many-o-the-clock after daylight sinks. Ages away. So you see,' he added, haughtily, while aiming his crossbow at the crowd—all of whom ducked—'I have plenty of time. Sometimes, my dear, you'll realize that always being right and being smug about it will get you into trouble. Adviser! Announce me. I'm about to speak.'

The Wise Wench rolled her eyes.

Looti, who was dressed as a heifer, hefted up the megaphone. 'The king is about to speak. Pay close attention, one and all,' she shouted.

'Friends!' he shouted.

Everyone stopped fighting and looked up.

'Soon our one-more-than-one heroes will be retuning, and the mummer's gift will be taken.' He patted his crossbow benevolently. 'To prevent any chance of injury, sparks, or danger, no fires may be lit, even when it gets dark, or I will be very, very cross. Well, what are you waiting for, get on with enjoying yourselves!' He happily started aiming again. He saw one particularly annoying-looking mummer dressed in bright orange.

How he hated bright orange.

He happily took aim; his joy multiplied as the actor spotted him and began running off holding his hands over his head and screaming.

The king began to chortle regally.

'Happy day, Your Globeness?' said Looti.

'Indeed, Mistress Adviser,' he said, and he began to laugh out loud, while playfully pretending the bolt was firing.

'Just the one, mind,' said the Wise Wench.

'Adviser, take note,' said the king, accidentally squeezing the trigger. Suddenly the bow fired, as if by itself.

'It wasn't me!' shouted the king, somewhat untruthfully.

Then he realized he was the only person in the area with a crossbow.

A figure near the Moot House dropped with a yell.

'I think that might have been the new Poo-Pit Maester, Your Butterfingeriness,' said Looti, and she began to run with some urgency towards the victim.

'Good, he won't count,' said the king, and he handed the crossbow back to Chief Thug Durth to be reloaded.

After a few minutes, Looti came back, panting. 'Yes, I'm afraid it was Puppington Pap-Pinch, Poo-Pit Maester,' she said, gasping.

'Puppington Pap-Pinch, *former* Poo-Pit Maester,' corrected the king. 'For, even though young Puppington never got to carry out his duties—'

'—because you shot him—' interjected the Wise Wench.

'—because of his *accident*,' corrected the king, 'we must still show him the respect he deserved, even though he never actually earned it.'

Durth handed him back the loaded crossbow. The king beamed and started waving it about again.

Everyone on the festival field ducked.

'Let the mummers come out from their hiding places, for they have one final chance to impress me. Great shall be their reward if they do so, and gentle and not painful in any way shall be the consequences of any failure. Here, look, I set aside my bow out of reach.' He did so, slyly. 'We've plenty of time to enjoy ourselves. It'll be ages before any giants arrive. Darkness shall be upon the village before anyone unexpectedly returns.'

Not far away somebody screamed 'Giant!' and the party field erupted into chaos and terror.

* * *

Urgh and Sorry were still running. They hadn't stopped all day.

Neither had the giants.

Now the place was alive with larch and ancient oak, great sycamores, and bent birch amongst countless burnt stumps, and, every now and again, the pair caught sight of acts of mindless vandalism. But the air was full of hound bays and barking, the sound of hunting horn, and giant laughter.

Urgh suddenly stopped.

A gob-boy was hanging from a tree next to the path. The gob-boy coughed and swung his left arm up. 'Mucky quite a way that way,' he said, then swung the right one and added, 'Stormgrunties not far that way.' It held out a hand for payment.

Urgh nervously fumbled in his pack, found something with hairs on, and handed it to the youngster. 'Thank you, stout signboy. But listen, you'd better—' he stopped as Sorry put his hand over his mouth.

'—Listen, stout sign,' Sorry said. 'We have some friends following us—pretty big friends actually. It would be a great lark if you were to tell them we'd gone to Mucky. *Not* Stormgrunties. Do you understand? Mucky.'

The gob-boy sign nodded as Sorry led his companion along the path towards their own village. A few minutes later they happened upon another surprised-looking old goblin smoking a huge pipe. Urgh and Sorry halted. 'Mister Smellpipe!' they yelled. 'My friend Smellpipe,' added Urgh.

The old goblin bowed. Urgh grabbed him.

'Where have you young scamps been? Scrumping, no doubt,' said the old goblin, and he blew a huge, foul-smelling ring of grey tobacco at them.

'No, Giant Land, actually. In fact, we've been in the giant king's keep,' said Urgh, nervously looking over his shoulder. 'We burnt it down in fact.'

The old goblin began to laugh.

'We haven't got time for this,' said Sorry, urgently.

Barking started again.

Nearby.

'And the worst thing is, we have a horde of angry giants and dogs just behind us, so you'd better run,' said Urgh, as urgently as he could.

The old goblin laughed harder. 'Oh, I know all about you young lads. You've been out with giants, all right. Giant sacks of scrumpin' apples, and giant blackberries, and then, I bet, you've been peeking at all those goblin girls swimming!' The old goblin wheezed and had to sit down.

Not far away, he heard a gob-boy scream out. 'They went that way, to Stormgrunties!'

'Oh dear,' said Urgh, and he shook his head.

The baying grew louder. 'Time to go,' said Sorry, running off along the path.

'He has a point,' shouted Lady Carline, following him.

'Mister Smellpipe, what do you think that is?' said Urgh, pointing in the direction of the dogs.

'Wind?' said Smellpipe, straining.

'Mister Smellpipe, I know you think it's the wind but it isn't. It's a horde of angry giants and their dogs, and if they catch you, they'll kill you, so run home as fast as you can. It's us they're after.' Urgh smiled and shook his hand before dashing after Sorry. Smellpipe continued to hold his sides and laugh.

A few minutes later, he was still laughing when the giants, holding their dogs on great studded leashes, came into the area. He then stopped laughing.

In the distance behind them, Urgh and Sorry heard screaming. They dashed on, knowing how far they were away from home. They passed Old Muck Farm and Mucky Bottom, Knobbly Log and Smell Bog.

Sorry suddenly pointed. Ahead, on its slight rocky promontory, was home. 'The village, praise Noc! We've made it!'

As he did, the giants came into view behind them, laughing as they led the hounds.

'Run like Quicklegs the Particularly Swift Hare!' screamed Urgh, spurting so fast he even outran his cowardly companion for once.

Another scream echoed from the village as they ran towards it.

Urgh yelled. He could almost feel a dog's breath on his back. Sorry was screaming. The edge of the village came into view, its happy houses and its merry Poo-Pit just a slight uphill run. They reached the bank and Sorry tripped as they reached the gate at its foot. Urgh ran back towards his companion and tried to lift him. It was too late.

The giants towered above them. They slowly began to walk towards the stricken goblins, dogs pulling at their leashes, snarling and biting the air.

Suddenly, they looked up as the king's voice filled the air. 'That's not fair! You said many-o-clock!' he shouted.

Then *it* appeared.

The Beast.

The Beast from Beyond, towering over the figures below from its perch atop the rocks above them, with its black wings and its terrible pointy teeth and fire gouting from its belly. A hamster, a hamster of nightmares. A vast iron-skinned monster squealing as its mouth slammed open and shut menacingly.

The dogs stopped barking and began to whimper.

The giants began to shake.

'Come and have a go, if you think you're hard enough!' shouted the king from a safe distance through his megaphone.

The foul, vast hamster's wings began to flap. 'Mnarrr! Mnarrr! Mnarrrrrr!' it said, horrifically.

The giants backed away. 'PERHAPS WE SHOULD TELL THE CHIEF ABOUT THIS,' said one of them, wisely.

'GOOD IDEA!' said another, shaking.

They withdrew, strategically and rapidly, back towards the forest to report home.

Urgh got to his feet, and, through his stinging eyes, he could see the huge Iron Hamster. He had half a mind to run but then saw the Wise Wench's head pop out of it. The king walked a little way forward and smiled down, benevolently.

'Your Spherity!' shouted Sorry.

'Wise Wench!' shouted Urgh.

The goblin adventurers began to race up the bank to embrace their friends. Lady Carline flew onto the Wise Wench's shoulder and whispered something.

The hamster sat, fiercely. The smoke low now, and its great groans near still. A door in its iron belly opened and several goblins with megaphones got out, congratulating each other.

'Not bad at all, lads. Not bad at all,' said Durth, coming over to congratulate them. 'Nice mnarrrrrrrs!' he added.

The Wise Wench and Whippet got out and left the door open. A tiny spark followed them, and, picked up by the wind, landed straight on the king's trouser.

Urgh and Sorry finally reached the top of the bank. The villagers, having seen the truth about the hamster, decided not to flee but came towards the heroes and mobbed them, screaming and hugging them, bearing them aloft towards the king.

The king smiled regally.

The spark became flame on the dried grass and kindling of his attire.

As the crowd parted, Urgh and Sorry bowed and crawled towards the king.

'Your Majesty,' said Urgh, 'I bring terrible news—' Urgh noticed the flames rising from the royal posterior and added, '—Your Majesty's leg seems to be on fire!'

The king looked down at the flames, sighed, and ran towards the duck-pond.

CHAPTER 15

The mob surrounded Sorry and Urgh and cheered. 'Welcome, our heroes,' shouted the villagers. 'We love Sorry,' shouted a few of them.

We love Sorry.

He smiled at Urgh, who was crying.

In the distance, the king gave a sigh of relief as he finally put his burning leg and bottom in the duck pond, the noise of his cry almost drowned by the crowd of cheering villagers. The sun slowly began to sink.

The Wise Wench put a consoling arm around Urgh who sobbed deeper. Great heaving moans echoed from him as he gulped down snot which had nowhere to go but back[61] up his nose. The Wise Wench produced a huge, red, spotted handkerchief and led him away, raven on shoulder, leaving Sorry on his own with the crowd. He set eyes on Looti.

Looti. Dressed as a heifer. But no ordinary heifer. Sorry tried to remember the old story he'd heard about a cunning, beautiful cow who plotted the destruction of her herd by raising an evil calf, but which instead became a legendary cow hero who fought in many unlikely bovine-battles. Or had he made that up? He swayed momentarily, then he began to sway considerably as she grabbed his hand and led him after Urgh and the Wise Wench. Outside, Durth and his men were laughing as they shouted 'Mnarr!' through their megaphones. The actors vanished into the mob unscathed.

The king arrived in the midst of the departures looking moist and confused.

Inside the Moot House, the noise of the cheering villagers was no more than a murmur.

Urgh was still sobbing.

---

[61] Or, more accurately, down.

Sorry was already getting a little bored, but soon cheered as Looti handed him a huge mug of goblin ale so creamy it was all head and no beer.

Just the way he liked it.

'Wwwww—' said Urgh, heroically getting a grip on the situation.

'—Take your time. I know what you're going to say,' said the Wise Wench.

'Yyyy—'

'—Yes, I do,' she said, and smiled broadly.

'The speakme bag,' he said, finally.

'Yes, I know.'

'It wasn't.'

'Yes, I know that, too.'

'But, you said—'

'—I had too, I'm afraid.'

'But why?'

'Young Urgh, haven't you guessed yet? The giants intend to kill us, kill all of us, and the only way to defeat them is by cunning, not might. I have provoked them into a hasty attack which has failed. They will now go back to their chief and tell him what has happened. He will get very cross and eat a few of his most faithful henchmen before deciding to mount a serious charge, but by that time, we will have our weapon ready.'

'Weapon?'

'The Great Dragon Kettle.'

'Kettle?'

'Yes, kettle. Our Dragon Kettle, the kettle that breathes fire. With this mighty weapon, we shall scare the giants from the forest forever. Well worth facing a few giants for, don't you think?'

Fire, thought Sorry nearby, his head filling with images. He got all excited.

'But Wise Wench, why the...' asked Urgh, nervously.

'...Elaborate plan?' she answered.

'Yes.'

'Because,' she said, and she narrowed her eyes into a scowl.

'Then you know?'

'Oh yes, I know everything,' she added, and glared at Sorry crossly. 'Aren't you hungry?' she said to him, crossly.

He colored.

'They did very well, both of them,' said Lady Carline.

'I know,' said the Wise Wench, softening her stare. 'Quite a bonfire,' she added, patting Sorry on the head.

The door burst open, and the king squelched in, water and duckweed dripping from his royal posterior. He scowled at the scowling Wise Wench. 'Good, I have witnesses. Right, pay attention, everyone. Adviser, get everyone to pay attention.'

'Pay attention to the Moist-Yet-Mighty One!' said Looti, and she smiled and winked at him as he clambered into his high chair. Water continued to drip, and a toad fell out of his trousers and hopped away. The Wise Wench smiled, thought about laughing, was instantly aware of the result and so didn't. The king managed a watery smile back. There was a long pause.

'Sorry, it was a spark from the Hamster,' said the Wise Wench, apologetically, and she shrugged her shoulders.

'We'll deal with that in due course. Now, you quite categorically stated, *and I quote*, that at *exactly* one-more-than-one minutes past many-o-the-clock on the day before Turnipday these,' he stared at Urgh and Sorry below him, 'inconsequential nobodies would arrive being chased by giants. Well it isn't even anywhere near that time now.' He stared at the clock to make sure time itself wasn't tricking him in some way, still smarting from the subliminal message thing. 'Well, what have you got to say for yourself, woman?'

'I lied,' said the Wise Wench, haughtily.

Lied! Oh, that makes her dangerous, thought the king, wondering if he should have her quietly removed or met with some improbable sausage-making accident.

'I'd see it coming,' said the Wise Wench, grumpily. 'And besides, I don't like sausages. I had to lie,' she added, as if that was explanation enough for now.

'I'm properly cross about that,' said the king. 'Next time you intend to lie to me, I expect you to tell me. And another thing, the next time you summon me without me knowing, I want to be made aware of it the day before. Understand?' *That felt good.*

'Let's get you out of those wet things,' said Looti, leading the king to a side room.

Sorry noticed that the king was scuffing the ground with his foot as he followed her.

"Wise Wench, you were telling us about the plan,' said Urgh.

'Plan B.'

'Oh?'

'Plan A was to deceive everyone into believing that the message we sent to the giants would bring peace to the forest, but we can never have peace.' The Wise Wench grimaced as she stared at the closed door Looti and the king were behind.

'Why not?' said Urgh, looking disappointed.

'Because, young Urgh, we are different. We are very different from the giants, and they will always hate us for that. They won't rest until they have cut down every tree in the forest, and it becomes one big wet meadow where nothing could ever burn. Plus, they get very cross very readily, so even if we had a partial peace, it wouldn't last, not that we ever could in the first place. They just aren't sufficiently mentally developed yet to understand that getting along with each other would be better for us all.'

Sorry and Urgh looked confused.

'The only way to keep them away is to make them fear us, and the only way to do that is to give them, as Moaris would say, a good kicking.'

'I'm awfully hungry,' said Sorry.

From the side room there was a sudden thud, followed by a quiet moo. The Wise Wench looked over, shook her head, then rummaged amongst a series of knitted objects within her skirts, and produced an unlikely knitted figure that looked like someone with a crown embracing a cow grabbing a key. She put it in her pocket and gazed up to the heavens. 'The things I do for you.' She then turned to the heroes, and scowled at Sorry. 'Of course, you haven't eaten for days, or was it weeks or years, I forget?' She handed him a gigantic bag of whelks. His momentary self-doubt whisked away by hunger, he smiled so wide she wondered if his head might split into one-more-than one halves[62] and shot under the table so he wouldn't have to share them.

Suddenly the door burst open and Durth Dimbits marched in carrying a huge tray. Sorry glanced up from under the table. 'These are the sandwiches you ordered, Wise Wench, and the cake,' he added, smiling.

'Ah yes, the heroes' cake,' she said. 'Cake fit for heroes. Cake more fit for heroes than the Great Heroes' Cake of Gluggluster, the cake made especially for heroes but which turned out to be hollow and had within it Ropit, the poisonous devious Netherworld Apricot.'

Everyone in the room bowed their heads.

'Cake?' said Sorry, hungrily, from under the table, tossing the empty bag aside.

'Mother Crumblies' cake,' corrected the Wise Wench.

They tucked in as Durth stood back, proudly looking at the new heroes. 'Forgive me but I wouldn't have expected a pair of big sissies like you to have it in you. I must say I'm impressed.'

Sorry and Urgh smiled in between bites.

'Even if you are both wearing dresses.'

They looked down at their attire, soiled from days of the chase from the giants. 'They're not dresses they're smocks, smocks with flowers on, Moaris made—I mean Moaris gave them to us,' said Urgh haughtily. From nowhere, the Wise Wench produced a pair of small sacks bundled full of clothes. She smiled.

'Tell me: how did Moaris die?' added the Head Thug with a worried look on his face.

'Horribly,' they said in unison.

'Ah, great! Just how he wanted to go.' Durth smiled and walked out, a tear forming in one eye.

The king came in wearing a fresh pair of trousers; a really very bright pair of orange breeches. 'How I love orange,' said the king,

---

[62] This does happen from time to time amongst goblins that are so happy or laughing so hard, as we have mentioned.

hypocritically. 'Ah, cake, and Mother Crumblies' cake! I always love a bit of cake!' The food began to be devoured as a matter of urgency. After they had finished, Looti entered and served up huge mugs of mead, and everyone except the king toasted the heroes.

'Now, to business,' said the Wise Wench.

'Ah yes, *the plan*,' said the king, who tried to look very wise. Unfortunately, he just succeeded in screwing up his face and looking vaguely cross-eyed.

'No,' said the Wise Wench. 'We need to pause for clarity's sake. The plan isn't the plan anymore. We have a new plan which I shall, for ease of reference, refer to as the *proper* plan.'

'*Proper* plan?' all of them said to her.

'Yes,' she answered.

'But—' said the king who then harrumphed, loudly.

'—No *buts*. The *proper* plan is about to enter its most crucial phase,' said the Wise Wench testily, taking an exaggerated theatrical step towards the door.

'Hang on, what's that dreadful smell?' said the king, wrinkling his considerable nose at the enveloping farmyard stench that had suddenly entered the chamber.

'That, Your Majesty,' said the Wise Wench as she threw the door open, 'is just what I was about to tell you. Behold, Zephyr, the fastest pig ever seen in the forest, ever!'

There was a considerable oink, followed by the arrival of an enormous grinning sow which took almost a minute to enter. She tossed her head haughtily and gave out a proud oink. She was almost pretty for a pig—an effect emphasized by an enormous pink bow tied to her head. Clinging to her considerable curly tail was quite the most repulsive goblin anyone had ever seen; so ugly, in fact, that Sorry uttered 'Eurgh!' under his voice, glancing at his companion nervously as it slipped out.

'You remember Porkscratch, your regal pig-worrier and hog-sire?' The Wise Wench winked at Porkscratch, the really repulsive goblin who had just entered.

Porkscratch reddened humbly.

'Of course I do,' said the king, barely able to conceal his admiration for the sow that had entered his royal court. 'One of my finest insignificant scum,' he continued, 'but I don't recognize the pig—and I know my hogs, as you know.' The king scowled at the Wise Wench and added—switching his gaze to Porkscratch—'And I don't like deviousness in my underlings. Therefore, I intend to immediately dismi—'

'—No, you won't dismiss him,' interrupted the Wise Wench. 'The frankly repulsive Porkscratch here acted on my express instructions, and has been doing so since last summer, in fact. I commanded him to breed and train me the fastest pig ever seen in the Great Forest, and he has done so.' She nodded at the vast sow, which had become a significant part of the room. She grinned at the Wise Wench, attractively. Perhaps *attractively* is a bit far-fetched.

The king stared at them both suspiciously, but couldn't help but admire the massive, grinning pig before him. He checked his stare and returned to scowling as soon as he realized everyone was looking at him.[63]

'And before you ask, great king, he's been working in secret under my instruction, feeding Zephyr here a special feed and a brisk potion of my own devising. In fact,' she added, chuckling, 'you nearly walked in on us on the last Splatday in Dung when we were oiling her for the winter, but luckily, aware that you would walk in on us unexpectedly at one point, I took steps to stop you, and so—'

'—Hang on,' growled the king. 'Splatday in Dung? Wasn't that the day I was struck by a plummeting meteorite?'

The Wise Wench looked a little taken aback and smiled. 'Might have been,' she said, bashfully, folding her arms as she spoke.

'So now you can cast stones from the sky, can you?' He thought about folding his arms and then stopped, remembering what had happened last time.

---

[63] From an early age, goblins pay very careful attention to their leaders. It's safer to, just in case they do something unpredictable to you—which of course they do often.

'Well, not quite. In truth, it was young Pappy. She's a good gob-girl and frightfully accurate at throwing rocks. It was her, up a very tall tree nearby.'

'Nearby?'

'Well, quite-a-few-and-nearly-many gobfeet away. As I said, she has a fine tossing arm.'

'I'll have her killed.'

'No, you won't.'

The king frowned and leant over. 'That rock really hurt,' he whispered to her. He then looked at the sow again, admiring her oiled flanks, and began wondering what she'd taste like boiled. 'So, tell me: what is this fabulous beast for, exactly?'

'Exactly?'

The king took an involuntary step back in his chair. 'Approximately will do.'

The Wise Wench moved behind Urgh and Sorry, and put a heavy, consoling arm about them, tightly. 'Well, great king, as you know, to feed our fire-breathing Dragon Kettle, we must get milk from a Fire-breathing Heifer of the Atrocious Conflagration in the Very, Very, Very Horrible Meadows and get back in time to defeat the giants. To facilitate our journey in a suitable amount of time, we need haste to get there. Zephyr here is that tool. Young Porkscratch here has been slaving night and day to hone her haste, refine her rapidity, and polish her promptness. We leave tomorrow!'

'How improbable!' muttered the confused king.

"The real adventure begins here,' she added.

Real adventure, thought Sorry and Urgh at exactly the same time.

In the Great Oak of the Gods, Hoggy-Uncannythoughts, the Demigod Understudy of People Thinking Things at Exactly the Same Time, smiled and rubbed his blackboard clean for the day.

'Yes,' said the Wise Wench at them both. 'All is prepared. We leave tomorrow morning for the Very, Very, Very Horrible Meadows!'

She smiled and moved over to lock the door, placing the key in her knitted woolly bodice.

'Well, good luck with that,' said Sorry, attempting to leave the room and trying to forget the word *we*.

'Oh, we won't need any luck,' she answered, scratching Zephyr behind an ear.

'We?' whimpered Sorry.

'Yes.'

Sorry began to cry.

'And will you?' said the king, astutely.

The Wise Wench didn't answer.

The king looked worried. 'I said, and will you?' he snapped.

'The only way we can succeed is by crossing Terrifying Pass,' she answered in a non-comital way.

'Tttttttttterrifying pass?' said Sorry, looking terrified.

'Yes,' she answered.

He looked at the locked door and, defeated, lay down to sob. Not just a quiet little whimper, real gut sobs, true bawling. He kept repeating the phrase 'Why me?' as he banged his head on the floor.

'I can't go on my own, it's too dangerous. Sorry and Urgh will be accompanying me. I need someone to carry the milk, anyway,' said the Wise Wench. 'My beloved familiar and confidante, Lady Carline, will be my representative in the village while I'm away. You may consult her as you would consult me.'

'I'm not asking questions of a bloody bird,' whispered the king under his breath.

'But, how dangerous will it be? I mean, will all of us come back?' said Urgh, patting his sobbing friend on the shoulders, or approximate place where they should be.

'Oh, very. Terrifying Pass is well named, and, once past that, we shall have to reach the meadows. Not to mention how deadly the heifers are to milk, and then...ah, but I'm getting ahead of myself. Anyway, you're both coming, so get used to the idea. And don't think about trying to escape, Sorry. I have given Durth special instructions and extra powers to do particularly horrible things to you when—sorry, if—you try. As for your other question,' she said, patting Urgh on the head sympathetically, 'well, we'll just have to see. So have a good rest and get ready for the morning. Porkscratch, you'll have Zephyr prepared and oiled ready for her journey with supplies and all for the morning?'

He nodded proudly, patting the huge pig, lovingly. She grinned at him, piggishly.

'Thank you, master Porkscratch. You know it's a great shame you chose piggery as your profession. I have a feeling you'd make a damn fine Poo-Pit Maester.' She unlocked the door, held it open for him, and he and Zephyr trotted out after her. Lady Carline followed, staring haughtily at the king as she did. The door slammed shut.

Sorry suddenly entered a new, even darker, phase of self-pity.

'Don't worry, Sorry,' said Urgh. 'We're heroes now. We have nothing to fear from a few big fire-breathing cows, and I know there are a few stories about Terrifying Pass, but it doesn't sound too bad.'

'Not too bad? What about the story of the Magenta Bat of Slopey Ridge, the bat that bit the head off the goblin hero Reg? And what about the Wobbly Cliffs of Terrifying Pass, the cliffs that trip up the unwary and toss them into the chasms below—chasms occupied by goblin-eating jelly? Oh, and then—no, no, nothing to worry about at all. I wish I'd let the dog eat me.' Sorry shouted the last words, petulantly.

'It seems that we have no choice, anyway,' added Urgh, consolingly. 'I'm going to see mother. I'll see you here tomorrow morning.' He walked out.

Urgh's mother! Gods, I suppose things could be a lot worse, thought Sorry to himself. He waited a while and then snuck towards the back door. He smiled and, as quietly as he could, opened it.

Durth was stood there with a huge, barbed whisk. He smiled back and walked in.

Urgh's mother's hovel lay at the edge of the village under a copse of former elm trees—now elm stumps—all admirably burnt. She had moved to the edge of the village when Urgh was a child and the other gob-boys and girls had begun to tease him about his head arrangements. It had made her pretty cross. She had a bit of a reputation herself amongst the locals, but we'll come to that shortly.

Urgh had a small pet ferret called Grip, which was his childhood companion. Now old in years, Grip still managed to see off the odd unwelcome guest. In fact, in infirm old age, Grip saw everyone off, and as Urgh came to the green garden gate, he saw Grip staggering towards him arthritically. He smiled as he went through the gate and saw the old ferret shuffle happily towards him. 'Grip my old friend, it's me, your friend,' said Urgh happily. Eventually it reached him.

And bit him.

Urgh gave a yelp and tried to shake it off, kicking his leg out until finally the cantankerous old thing lost its grip and fell off. 'Blind old git!' he said, rubbed his ankle and ran to the house.

The cottage door was opened and Ill Maid, his beloved mother, stood there scowling and dribbling. In one hand she gripped bloody sheep's innards and, in her other calloused arthritic appendage, a very sharp cleaver. In her crooked lips she held a pipe which spluttered some sort of unpleasant pollutant into the forest air.

'Mummy!' shouted Urgh, happily.

'What do you want, ugly?' croaked his rancid mother, aggressively, waving the innards as she spoke.

'I've been on an adventure—an amazing, dangerous adventure—and now I'm home to tell you all about my travels!'

She staggered back inside and slammed the door shut. A bolt slid in place with some finality.

Grip stared up at Urgh and wondered if he might be edible. Somewhere in the distance, starlings began to fight.

Urgh walked up to the door and knocked loudly.

'Bugger off,' came the warm response from within.

'But, mummy, I have lots of adventures to tell you about. Don't you want to know what your only born has done?'

'Nope,' came the comprehensive reply.

Urgh knocked louder.

There was a knock on the cottage door. The Wise Wench got up and opened it. Master Whippet stood outside, looking vaguely embarrassed. He handed her the flowers.

'Why, they're beautiful Master Whippet,' said the Wise Wench, and she planted a kiss on his cheek. 'Come in.'

Whippet looked bashful and stared at the floor as he said, "I'll miss you', is all I wanted to say—' He turned to leave.

'—Haven't you something else for me?' she said, staring at the enormous object he was struggling to grip.

'Ah yes,' he answered. 'There was something else, Wise Wench,' added Whippet, and he lifted the huge metal milk-churn up onto a table. Painted on the outside was a picture of an udder with a skull and crossbones cunning emblazoned on top.

'Perfect,' she said, smiling warmly.

He blushed.

"Dangerous milk. Keep away!' It's exactly as I wished for, as usual. You really are a treasure.' The churn had little straps attached to it so it could be worn as a pack by someone without shoulders.

'I'm afraid it's mighty heavy,' said Whippet, apologetically.

'No matter. I have a willing volunteer,' said the Wise Wench, before leading him into her workshop. There were a pair of packs hung up by the table, which was covered with an assortment of gear. A couple of inflated pigs bladders, a pair of oars, a lot of food and fruit cake, a shiny new lantern, some bandages, a large yellow and red striped flag, a strange metal hat, some rubbing oil in a jar with a picture of a chicken with a black line through it, a huge net, an enormous picture of a very mean-looking fox as big as a tree on a roll of canvas, some chalk, what appeared to be a folding megaphone, a hefty vice, and a tuba.

'Well, that's a surprise,' said Whippet, sitting in the chair by the fire and blowing the tuba.

'It's no easy matter, Master Whippet. It's a dangerous adventure. Preparation is key.'

'But surely you know the outcome?'

The Wise Wench turned suddenly and mouthed for him to be still. Then she began checking in all the cupboards and drawers before, satisfied that no enemy was within them, she leant close to him. 'No, I'm afraid I don't,' she whispered. 'The gods allowed me to see most of it but, for some reason, there are parts of the adventure that are unknown.'

'Unknown? To you?'

'Yes, I suspect the worst.'

'Queen Quench!' said Whippet, and he checked out of the window.

'The same. But name her not within these walls. Young Urgh is something odd, something very odd, and although I know he is a hero and hasn't got an evil bone in his body, I fear him.'

'You fear him?'

'I do, a bit.'

Urgh could hear the birds through the open window. He watched his mother devour the last of the cake he'd brought her, the reason he was allowed inside. She ate it in the same way a crocodile might swallow a stickleback. A long line of dribble began its journey southwards from her mouth towards the almost impossibly dirty floor—so dirty, in fact, that Urgh wasn't sure if there was a floor there at all.

'Mother, I have something important to say,' said Urgh, earnestly.

His mother went back to knitting the shark costume and glanced up, hatefully. 'Not interested,' she snarled. The dribble wavered about gracefully before latching itself onto a wolverine that lurked under the sofa.

'When I was at the giants' keep, I had a dream.'

She suddenly met his stare and said, 'Have you got any more cake?'

'No. I dreamt that I met my father.'

His mother looked up, her face a symphony of conflicting emotions and memories. She walked up to him, removed her shoe, and smacked him with it. 'You haven't got a father. You were a foundling. I found you in a particularly large cowpat. How I wish I'd

251

left it undisturbed, but it had such an intriguing smell-story. And so I rummaged in it, and there you were.'

Undeterred by the verbal abuse, Urgh continued. 'I knew it was him, I just knew it. But he asked me to do something I don't want to do. He said I wouldn't want to, but he also said if I didn't then something terrible with fleshy flappy things and teeth would come for you, and that the forest would be swamp without fire forever, and lots of worse things.'

'Good. Now, if you've no more cake, I'll bid you good riddance.'

'But, mummy,' said Urgh, his lip wobbling, 'he said I had to kill the Wise Wench.'

The king marched out into the royal chamber beaming and adjusting his underpants.

Sorry was squatting and rubbing various parts of his anatomy gingerly. There was a vague smell of garlic.

'Ah, yes,' said the king, as he eyed Sorry up and down suspiciously, before he wandered over to Looti. 'What am I supposed to do with that scum? I mean, he makes the place untidy with his commonness.'

Looti smiled. 'Why not invite him for tea, Your Rampantness?'

'Well, erm, Scurvy,' said the king, not entirely accurately, 'what about dinner? I'm powerfully hungry.'

'No, thank you,' said Sorry, who continued rocking backwards and forwards.

'Well, never mind, young lad. Why don't you pull up a chair, put some lip butter on your troubled parts, and tell me all about the giants.'

'I'd rather not,' said Sorry, wimpishly.

The king scowled, grabbed Sorry, and twisted his arm up his back. 'Oh, but I insist!' he said, and he slammed his fist on the table, cheerfully.

Sorry grimaced, saw the valuable rings of gold and silver on the king's fingers, and, recovering his deviousness, said, 'Well, Your

Bullytude, I don't know what the Wise Wench has told you already, but I was really there. You see, after I took charge from Moaris.'

'*You* took charge?' answered the king, dubiously.

'Oh yes, he was obviously not up to it, so I gave him a good kicking. Anyway, where to begin? Gosh, a hero's tale is hard to tell. It'll probably take all night! You've got lots of food and ale I see, I'll need them! I hope you don't think I'm a bighead, but, actually, it was me that did everything.'

Another day dawned. Outside the cockerel called and the sun glimpsed the land.

The door suddenly slammed open. An overpowering smell of sprouts entered, followed by a figure. 'Where is he?' snapped the Wise Wench as she marched into the Moot House. Whippet followed her in, heaving a pair of heavy bags and the milk churn. He gasped and wheezed as he set everything down. Sunlight streamed through the door and lent the smoky atmosphere an unearthly quality.

The king was asleep in his great chair, while Looti was curled up nearby. They'd got bored with Sorry's story after a few minutes and fallen into a slumber. Sorry stood nearby looking deeply depressed. The king opened one eye, expecting the giant cockerel he'd been dreaming of to be there. He smiled when he saw it wasn't and gave Looti a gentle nudge with his peasant-poker.

'And no, you didn't,' snapped the Wise Wench, prodding him with her fattest finger.

'Didn't what?' said the king.

'Don't lie to me. Where is he?'

Who?' said the king, attempting to hide in his high chair while answering her regally.

'Urgh. Ah, new trousers AGAIN I see,' added the Wise Wench, climbing up and prodding him in the stomach.

'How dare you prod the royal tummy,' said the king, and he growled. 'What's that smell? It smells like off sprouts.'

The Wise Wench growled louder. 'Yes, and never mind about them. They're for the quest.'

The king stood up and growled very loudly.

The Wise Wench pulled a megaphone from nowhere and growled through it. Outside, several villagers began packing.

The king thought about growling some more but stopped himself. The Wise Wench began opening cupboards, drawers, and sacks, angrily, in her search. Above, the king began to look worried and angry at the same time.

'He was supposed to be here before me. Why isn't he?' shouted the Wise Wench at everyone. Sorry shook his head. 'Durth!' she shouted.

The door opened and Durth, flanked by a pair of under-thugs, came in. Durth looked around and drew his battle hedge-trimmers. 'Having trouble, Wise Wench?' he said, and he approached Sorry, opening and closing the shears aggressively. Sorry backed away into the corner.[64]

'No, no trouble, Durth,' she said. 'But go and find Urgh for me. He's fallen out of the proper plan.'

'Right, find the prisoner and punish him,' said Durth, who, from nowhere, produced a corkscrew of immense length.

'No, no, Durth. Just find him and bring him to me. Like you did at the start of the book, remember?'

'Book?' answered Durth, confused.

'I mean *adventure*. Now, on your way, and don't break him or I'll be cross. Bring him straight back here.'

'Alive?'

'Preferably. No, no, wait Durth,' she added, hastily. 'I mean *definitely* alive. Now go. Try his mother's cottage first!' The Wise Wench marched about, wringing her hands and looking worried.

The thugs looked collectively anxious and held a quick game of rock-paper-scissors which the uglier of the under-thugs lost. He stepped forward, sheepishly. 'Do we have to go there, Wise Wench?' he said, nervously. 'She's a bit scary.'

---

[64] Accidentally upending Lord Vix, the Occult Washboard, and fatally injuring him.

'Very scary,' added Durth, helpfully. 'She's not called Eyesore for nothing.'

'I thought she was called Ill Maid?' answered the under-thug.

'I'd heard it was Horrid, or was it Monster?' interjected his colleague.

The Wise Wench waved her arms about dismissively. 'Yes,' she growled, 'and her name is Ill Maid. Well done. Many out of many-and-one, top marks for being clever.'

The thugs marched out reluctantly. One of them beaming, self-importantly.

'I thought we'd finished growling?' said the king from on high.

'Will you stop interrupting events?' snapped the Wise Wench, and she shook the royal chair.

'Calm down, woman,' said the king, as quietly as he could. The Wise Wench shot him a fouler glance back so he began inspecting the floor for cracks. 'What's the problem, anyway?' he added for good measure. 'You know where he is, don't you? *Don't you?*' he added, nervously.

The Wise Wench didn't answer.

Nearby, Sorry was rummaging through the packs she'd brought with her, looking for the sprouts. 'What have you got oars in here for?' he asked, incredulously. *Was that a tuba I saw*, he thought. *Nah, can't have been. A tuba! The idea.*

'No, it's what have WE got oars for?' she barked. 'Anyway, stop interfering. You'll find out soon enough.' She ripped the bags from him and sat in the corner looking, for the first time anyone had ever seen, perturbed. As she moved away, Sorry felt sure he heard a little parp from some wind instrument within.

Outside, a spectral mist lurked beyond the sun's groping fingers. The birds flew nervously over the village and the locals[65] set about their daily chores careful to keep away from Durth, who, with his thugs, ran at some speed across the village brown, down the fallen ramparts towards the edge of the forest. They sped on, passing

---

[65] Well, the ladies, anyway.

Mother Scarecrow, who was fixed by twine to a post. 'Keep off, you crows!' she shouted at them as they passed.

Then they ran down Noggy Bottom and up over Squelch, leaving the village behind.

'Hut! Hut! Hut!' shouted Durth, in time with his jogging.

His assistants wondered what he was talking about but dare not ask him.

'Hut! Hut! Hut!' cried Durth, more urgently, and pointed towards a rancid hut at the edge of the village, lovingly shrouded in tree stumps and muck heaps. A curious noise echoed from ahead; a mixture of feral grumbling, snarling, and hissing. The assistants nodded and drew out a huge hat pin each. Durth noticed that one had a hat pin with barbs. He made a mental note to promote him.

As they came closer, they could make out Ill Maid's famous muck-heap[66] into which she threw everything, and which, it was said to local children, could get up by night and wander about the village and forest looking for things to swell its bulk—almost always goblin children. It had swollen and towered to almost several-many-and-almost-uncountable feet high. The thugs looked up admiringly at its festering flanks.

Suddenly[67], an elderly ferret dashed from the undergrowth and moved towards Durth who marched straight up to the myopic creature and booted it across the garden. It gave a yelp and landed in the rhubarb. The assistants noted the rhubarb for later. Durth gave a silent wave of his hand and signaled to the door. He crouched,

---

[66] A whole mythology has grown up around goblin muck-heaps, which are a source of great pride for their owners and the reason for several battles. In a world where a goblin's worth is measured by his smell-story, having a truly nidorous muck-heap is something that any self-respecting goblin wishes for, if he can be bothered. In truth, as making one is quite hard work, they are usually stolen, which is not easy; perhaps the reason why would-be thieves are discovered and fights and battles are the inevitable result. Just for the record, and the sake of clarity, there is no word for self-respect in Goblin.

[67] As a further point of fact, the word *suddenly* is included here for dramatic effect. As anyone who keeps venerable ferrets knows, they don't do things quickly as they age.

crawled his way through the runner beans to the side of the door, pointed at it and then he waved at his assistants.

One smiled and waved back at him.

Durth waved again, this time more aggressively and pointed again at the door.

He continued to smile.

'Kick open the door!' shouted Durth.

'Oh right, sorry,' said the under-thug. He marched forward and kicked the door down. Durth rolled in and, with a single graceful movement, drew out the corkscrew and stood, legs slightly apart; he thought about tearing his shirt in the manner of his hero, Moaris, but events stopped him. He saw Ill Maid only momentarily before her ladle hit him and smashed him across the room, removing his favorite tooth.

When he woke up, Ill Maid was sitting on his assistants while her wolverines nibbled them. 'More for the heap, little children!' snarled the considerable gob-wench, joyfully.

There was no sign of Urgh, the prisoner-in-waiting. Sizing up the peril his beloved followers were in, and the fact that he'd be next on the list, Durth quickly realized that—most regrettably—he'd have to tactically withdraw to a safe distance. However, after a quick glance at the exits—a barred window and door, sat before which were his opponents—he decided on a different strategy. He stood up suddenly. 'Hello, gorgeous!' he said.

Ill Maid stopped bouncing up and down and stared at him, one tooth peeking out of her mouth, alluringly. 'Are you trying to be funny?' she said. From somewhere inside her, a growl emerged.

Durth wondered if she somehow kept reinforcements inside her stomach—there was certainly plenty of room—before grinning and scabbarding his corkscrew. 'Not at all. You're a damned attractive wench.' He tried to ignore the stains. 'Which is one of the reasons we're here.'

'*One* of the reasons?' she croaked. She stood up, still keeping on top of her foes.

'Yes, we've one-more-than-one reasons for coming to your,' he stared at the blood-caked ruin that he was in, 'charming rural idyll.

The first is to seize your revolting son who has been accused of, erm, cannibalism.' *Hah, that'll get her on my side. Everyone knows how much she hates her child.* 'And the other reason, of course, is to look upon your loveliness.' He wasn't quite so sure about the last part, but the first part went well, he thought. 'And, my goodness, look at the size of that leopard!' he added, with great cunning, pointing past her and outside.

Ill Maid turned long enough for Durth to dash past her. 'Run, lads, run if you value your lives!'

The lads did, and joined in his escape, running at full pelt back to the village. As they passed Mother Scarecrow, they came upon Urgh happily whistling as he carried a colorful sack made of patched leather, cloth, and parts of squirrels. Durth rushed at him, his followers wheezing mightily behind, and leapt on the escapee, grabbing him with one of his favorite painful head-grips known to the goblins as the *deadly both ear-pull cheek-pinch-tug back.*

Urgh yelled.

'Now listen,' said Durth, calmly, squashing him. 'I know you are the village hero, but I've been sent here on a mission.'

'Mission?'

'Yes, to stop you from escaping.'

'But I wasn't trying to escape. I was—' He stopped and looked at Durth, who looked more cross than usual. '—Yes Durth, I was trying to escape. You're absolutely correct—as always. Sorry.'

Durth grinned. 'Not here,' he said, 'he's with the king. Good. So are you going to come along quietly, or do I have to use this?' Durth drew out his siege corkscrew.

'Quietly,' said Urgh.

'Oh, good,' said Durth, disappointedly and not entirely truthfully. He released his grip and signaled to his thugs who also helped Urgh on his way back to the Moot House.

The king paraded about the throne room, theatrically. 'So, let me get this right,' he said. 'You know everything? *Everything?*'

'Yes,' answered the Wise Wench while staring at the door

'Except?'

'Except nothing.'

'Oh, I see,' enthused the king. 'So sorry. I was under the impression that you *didn't* know something. Didn't know something rather important. But obviously I was wrong. Silly old king. Bad, naughty king.' The king began slapping his own bottom in a rather comical way. Titters broke out across the room. The Wise Wench continued to scowl. 'All right, where is he, then? This great hero who so much depends on—like starting the journey right now,' snapped the king.

The Wise Wench crossed her arms.

'Let's look, shall we?' The king began bounding around the room, lifting things up and staring under them. 'Is he under the bucket? No. Is he in the hen bath? No! Under the Enchanted Potty? I'm afraid not. I'll tell you what: we'll play a game. You tell me when I'm getting warm when I get closer to him.' He proceeded to make even more exaggerated movements across the room, all the time looking back at her for guidance.

She said nothing.

'What, not playing my little game? But you're the Wise Wench, after all. *The* Wise Wench. Or, perhaps, you're an impostor!' The king suddenly stopped and looked worried. He stooped down and picked up an unfeasibly large magnifying glass so big he could hardly lift it. He dragged it over to the corner full of mummified kittens in their display cabinet. 'Am I getting warm yet?' he said, sarcastically, before dragging it over to the door. 'Warm?'' he said, laughing.

The door burst open, knocking the king over. Durth and his assistants marched in, holding the prisoner.

'Very warm. Hot, in fact,' said the Wise Wench, looking very relieved, and she marched up to Urgh and pinched him. 'I was just saying to the king, we were just waiting for you to get ready.'

'Yes, I'm ready,' said Urgh, nodding at Sorry.

'Then, with his grace's permission, we will be off.'

The king had stopped staring at the Wise Wench and was peering at Looti through the magnifying glass.

'I said, and with his grace's permission, we will be off.'

He continued to stare.

'Ahem!' said the Wise Wench. The king suddenly came to attention and smiled. Then he realized everyone was looking at him.

'Erm, yes, not too much butter on mine,' he said, obtusely.

Outside, winsome oinking heralded the arrival of Zephyr and announced that it was time to go.

A short while later, the villagers had, on pain of death, gathered around the Moot House to cheer. Durth had been quick to tell them that the heroes were soon to depart and the cheering wouldn't need to last long.

The Great Mouth suddenly opened and the king came out, mounted on his favorite pantomime hedgehog. He looked magnificent in his red and green stripy pants of office, with their large colorful pictures of hungry bats fighting over sugared puppies. His stomach grumbled contentedly. Behind him stood Looti carrying a large pile of trousers, all neatly pressed. The Wise Wench came out next, carrying a small pack and scowling. Lady Carline sat on her shoulder and nodded as the Wise Wench whispered to her. Urgh followed her with a similar pack, and at the back came Sorry, struggling with the huge milk-churn. He was already sweating.

Finally, sauntering out of the Moot House came Zephyr, lightly oiled and gracefully clipped. She bore a howdah on her back, a rope ladder helpfully dangling at her perfumed flank.

'Don't forget about the new peril,' whispered the Wise Wench to the king. 'The villagers *all* need to be here when we get back. I mean *if* we get back.' She patted Sorry on the shoulder and gave him a little affectionate pinch. 'The proper plan must proceed!'

'Don't worry,' winked the king, and he turned to the crowd. 'Friends!' he said.

'Bottoms!' shouted one of the very old goblin wenches at the back, assuming this was a new public occasion to be rude on.

'You all know what happened yesterday, and the great peril the village is in. Without my masterful plan, all of us would surely be dead!'

The Wise Wench looked at the floor.

'Yes, my idea of the Iron Hamster was a great one; one worthy of a great king, a noble lord, surely the mightiest of all chiefs! But now I have a deed to command. I command that the Wise Wench, and her one-more-than-one brave but very common and ordinary companions, head out from this place on a mighty voyage across the forest. They may never return.'

'Yes, we will,' whispered the Wise Wench to him. 'Well, mostly,' she added, staring at Sorry crouching on the floor.

'I do not command them merrily, nor with a light heart.'

At the rear, one of the old goblins blew her nose without using a handkerchief.

'But command I do, for now we know that the giants will be back. Aye, and back soon. Stay still everybody!'

The scattering goblins froze. Several goblins had begun finalizing holiday plans with immediate effect and started moving home to pack, urgently. It was suddenly very quiet for the first time ever.

'But alas!' said the king, looking momentarily in the Wise Wench's direction. 'We have it on great authority that they have already set up camps around the village—just out of sight mind you, so they cannot be seen. There they squat, horribly, with their enormous cheese graters, just waiting for goblins to come fleeing to them. Grate, grate, grate. Any goblin trying to flee the village now will meet them shortly and soon be grated, squashed, and eaten while alive, or fed to their terrible dogs and eaten while alive. Or worse.'

'Well, how will *they* get ou—' shouted a particularly hairy goblin from the back, pointing at the adventurers. He was quickly stuffed into a sack and led away by Durth, who waved at the Wise Wench and gave her a thumbs up.

The king continued. 'So we must—on pain of death—remain here and be ready for them. Dutt and Whappet here will soon be organizing all of you pointless peasants into working groups to prepare the village defenses. You shall not rest, nor sleep one moment while this toiling goes on, on pain of a death worse than death. I shall personally bring my royal shovel to aid you, and she shall not be still. Let us put aside our fear of borborygmus noises.

261

Let us cheer our heroes as they absquatulate and are away to their almost certain deaths, and let us prepare for battle!'

Everyone stood quietly, still trying to work out how they might escape and what the long words meant. They were used to the king making up such words and soon forgot, however[68].

A trumpet sounded from nearby as the Wise Wench led Urgh by the hand up the ladder onto Zephyr's howdah. Sorry clambered up awkwardly from a sitting crouch as they set off, causing the Wise Wench to mouth a long word under her breath, look at the king, and nod. Sorry soon found that it was only a one-more-than-one goblin-sized howdah, so he was forced to grip Zephyr's few remaining back hairs which were, of course, quite oily. The king gave his pantomime hedgehog a hefty tap with his crop. Below, one of the sweaty goblin bearers gave a squeak.

'Don't forget what I said. You have exactly one-more-than-one-and-some-and-a-few days, remember!' shouted the Wise Wench.

The king winked at her, then looked at the crowd. 'Well, get on with it, scum!'

Durth began to pull goblins out of the crowd by their ears, Whippet absent-mindedly pointed to some as he stared at the departing adventurers, tears welling in his eyes. Zephyr broke into a canter as she vanished over the hills and into the Great Forest.

---

[68] Kings, chiefs, important sire-wenches and other goblins of rank like to remind everyone how clever they are by using very long words occasionally; sometimes (in fact, generally) making them up as they go along. Some have their own word-wards, word-inventors, and word-advisers to find or make up particularly obtuse words for them to slip into polite conversation with people of rank, or just to show off by using in front of pointless peasants to feel superior.

CHAPTER 16

Durth stood in the watchtower and smiled. The wind played with his spartan hair as he fumbled with his megaphone. Despite his most heroic efforts, his hair refused to provide anything but the least covering for his bald head. It began to rain. He sighed to himself, placing his palm firmly on his pate. Below him, the villagers were scurrying in this direction and that, hastily working. Occasionally, goblins shot a nervous look up towards the tower. Behind Durth's field of view, the older goblins were laughing, while making pretend comb-overs with their hands.

The ditch at the top of the rise was coming along well,[69] while the silhouettes of goblins on top—his own idea to make it look like there were more goblins defending Bliss—had now been painted, though not terribly realistically, to be honest. The goblin maids were busy nailing them to the top of the outer wall that the village squatted upon, and which was beginning to be repaired[70] with larger stones and sod. Spears had been fixed pointing away from the village gates which lay surrounded by walls at the bottom of the rise the village sat on, and the sheep were, at last, all shaved and painted. Durth smiled to himself and spied Master Whippet busy constructing an ingenious one-one-and-one catapult. As he looked on, a pair of mules laden with huge stones and sacks of smell came through the gates and up towards the siege engine, led by some of his under-thugs.

Durth suddenly scowled as he spied one of the commoners leaning on his shovel, whistling. He loaded his crossbow—the very one he'd lent the king—and took aim. His shot went considerably astray, but, luckily, found another goblin who gave a yelp. Durth put that down to his devotion to Lord Noc, and picked up the megaphone. 'Get some work done, you slug!' he shouted. 'Pick up

---

[69] For goblin work, which—let's be honest—isn't known for its haste or quality.

[70] In general, even goblins are not stupid enough to believe that walls are effective at keeping anything out. In their experience, whatever is outside simply finds a sneaky way to get past said wall, rendering it useless, but these were desperate times and they needed a futile piece of symbolism.

that shovel and dig, dig, dig, dig! Yes you! Dig! Now!' His face and neck reddened as he yelled, but the commoner quickly picked up his shovel and began to dig, furiously.

Quite why he'd decided to dig a pit for no reason in the middle of the village no one had time to ask.

The king could hear the labor and rain through the Great Mouth which stood slightly ajar, propped open by one of his boots.

Looti smiled at him as she played with the golden bracelet and purred. 'This really is beautiful, Your Titantummyness,' she said, in her deepest possible voice, and edged closer to him.

The king shuffled somewhat uneasily and swayed slightly at the scent of her perfume—a heady mixture of lavender, sage, and onion. He looked down at her and colored slightly. 'Well, erm, yes, erm, erm,' he said, regally. 'It's been in the family for longer than anyone knows, you know. Originally belonged to Great, Great, Great Grandgob Gusset Stormgrunties. Her husband, Spherical King Muffrood Stormgrunties the many-some-and-then-one-more, had it made for her on her many-many-and-manyth birthday.' He paced and stuck a finger in his mouth before smiling. 'Well, actually, it wasn't her many-many-and-manyth birthday, we just tell the peasants that to impress them[71].'

'Which birthday was it, exactly?' purred Looti as she leant into the king, her velvet green and yellow striped gown, sewn with pictures of green ducks herding cattle, rubbing gently against his hairy arms.

'Her not-manyth. She died a month later, crushed to death by a falling pig.'

'What, she was riding and fell off her pig?'

---

[71] Goblins have, as we have already established, pretty poor memories, and unless something is repeated in song, mime, or glove-puppetry (or any other local variation), it tends to be forgotten. Certain enlightened rulers have used this memory loss to implant stuff that becomes fact, such as monarchs living forever, and the fact that if you kiss toads on the lips they explode.

'No, it was a plummeting pig. It had been raining pigs all that year.' The king looked saddened. 'It hasn't rained pigs for many a summer.' He sighed.

Looti held the bracelet aloft again. 'It is so very, very beautiful.' She gazed at him from the corner of one eye. 'May I...could I...try it on?'

The king coughed, coughed again, and then had a long coughing fit. 'I shouldn't see why not,' he wheezed, and he reached for the nearest royal pouf to sit on.

Looti sighed, slid the golden bracelet on her left wrist, did a pirouette around the king, and began to dance, caressing the bracelet at every opportunity. 'Oh, it feels so fabulously expensive!' she purred. 'I bet she was very grateful. Why, if a king gave this to me, I'd be so very, very grateful! I wouldn't know what to do in appreciation.' She finished, put her hands on her lap and leant, expectantly at the king.

He frowned and tried to look past her.

She leant closer.

'Ahem, erm, well, yes. You see, the problem is...the problem is that, technically, it...erm...it belongs to HER Majesty. The problem being that if she, as it were, spied it on your wrist, then, erm, she'd be rather, erm, cross. Crosser, in fact, than the Very Cross Little Old Man of the Bacon Barn in legend.' The king rubbed his tummy as if remembering some painful wound. Then he rubbed his head, ankles, shins, hips, ears, chest, nose, fingers, mouth, and, finally, his royal posterior.

'And I suppose moo couldn't bring yourself to do that, even for me. Moo?' She mooed very quietly, as if she only wanted the king to hear.

He colored again.

'I'd be ever so grateful. Ever so ever so ever so grateful to moo,' she whispered.

The king sighed. He'd never had this trouble with Kringe. All Kringe ever wanted was bowls of slug porridge and to have royal child's archery practice day off. Part of his duties were to be the target. 'I suppose, if you were to wear it indoors, say inside the Moot House, as a sort of—'

'—You mean, if you *commanded* me to do it, at your *command*—'

'—Exactly. If I told you to do it, even if you didn't want to,' said the king, grinning.

'Then I would have to do as you said.' She leant forward and puckered.

'Now, what was that moo were saying about gratitude?' said the king, in his deepest voice.

The sun rose and a hot day bloomed. The king was mounted on his favorite false hedgehog again. It was beginning to look a little worn through overuse. The paint had flaked in places, and the odd needle had broken off, but the head was still intact, as were the struts underneath. His bearers, their heads shaved for the coming All Sharks' Eve, heaved the king along through the village behind Durth, who was busily giving the king a guided tour of the defensive works. Looti trailed behind, eyeing the key the king always kept on his belt. She didn't know what the key was for, but she would find out.

Soon.

The king himself was resplendent in his orange and aquamarine striped pants of office ready for the celebrations. His ruff was especially ruffed and cunningly decorated with ceremonial seaweed and shark fins, and his coat of green velvet—embroidered with pictures of geese engaged in siege warfare against a castle of other, evil geese—was so clean it shone. It was already making the king uncomfortable in the heat, however, and sweaty stains were blooming. About his neck, he wore a shark tooth on a leather thong. 'Ah, yes, Durth,' said the king, as they approached a line of goblins digging a pit, 'and what, may I ask, is going on here?'

Durth beamed as he leant on an old gob-wench who creaked as she shoveled up more dirt. 'This, Your Impending Sharkiness, is an idea I had only yesterday. You see, I suddenly had this great idea, Your Majestic Pre-Fishness. Why not dig a great big pit and the giants might just fall in it when they walk past?' Durth stood back proudly, his legs slightly apart, his hands on his hips.

There was an embarrassed silence as everyone, bar Durth, instantly saw the flaw in his plan.

Looti whispered in the king's ear and he smiled. 'Yes, yes, I've just thought of a way of making your totally flawless plan even more flawless. Why not cover the pit with trees and rushes, and then the giants might think its solid ground, fall in, and, well, hopefully break their necks.'

Durth thought for a while. There was a smell.

'*And,* Your Prominence—' said Looti under her breath.

'—Ah, yes, and not only that, but we could place a likeness of a goblin, engaged in a rude and offensive giant-insulting gesture in the center. They are bound to be annoyed and head straight for him to tear him to bits!' The king sat back. There was a groan from the rear bearers.

Durth thought some more.

'So, I'll leave that with you, then,' prompted the king, and he poked one of his bearers with his hedgehog prod; a thumb-thick gnarled staff of elm that ended in a pretend finger. The bearers groaned and lifted the king on.

Durth looked confused for a moment, and then walked away.

After a short time, the royal party[72] came to the great one-one-and-one catapult with its extra buckets. Master Whippet was supervising the loading of the great stones and smell. He stopped and walked over to the royal party, noticed his dirty hands, and held them behind his back. 'Overlargeness!' he said, and bowed.

'Ah, Master, erm—' stammered the king.

'—Whippet,' said Looti.

'Yes, Whippet,' said the king, who stared at Looti for a moment.

Whippet coughed.

---

[72] You could—as you may already—argue that a royal party must consist of more than one member of royalty, but goblins don't see it that way.

267

'Ah yes, Master Whippet, and what sort of thing is this?' The king pulled out a large magnifying glass from a shelf in the hedgehog and closely examined the catapult.

'This, Your Forgetfulness, is a catapult, but no ordinary catapult. It is a one-one-and-one catapult; a catapult for throwing a few more times as many things as a normal catapult!'

'Oh, bravo, Master Whippet. Bravo!' enthused the king, and he began to clap very loudly.

Everyone else began to clap, just in case.

Within a minute, everyone in the village was clapping. The clapping went on for several minutes, with everyone whistling and cheering. Eventually the king, smiling through the applause, waved for everyone to stop.

Several more minutes later, they did.[73]

The king smiled broadly and waved at his subjects. He stared at Whippet. 'Just one question,' he said, imperiously.

Whippet stood, shoulders back, proudly waiting for the question.

'Why?'

Whippet's face dropped. Everyone stared. He began to cough, and tugged at his shirt collar. A bead of sweat ran down his forehead. Silently, he praised Lord Noc. 'Why?' he whimpered.

'Yes,' the king said, narrowing his eyes considerably.

Everyone continued to stare right at him.

'Erm,' he mumbled.

Everyone waited.

'Erm,' he coughed.

Everyone still waited.

'Erm, because the Wise Wench told me to,' he croaked.

The king leant forward and scowled. Then slowly a smile crossed his face and he began to chuckle. 'Well,' he giggled, 'if she says to build a big catapult, then we must build one, I suppose.'

---

[73] Goblins always find it safer to overly-enthuse when in the presence of royalty; wearing false smiles, laughing, and being overtly keen as much as possible for as long as possible.

Everyone looked relieved.

'You may continue,' said the king, and he signaled to the passing, confused-looking Durth while cracking his stick on a bearer's head. 'You, Head Thug. Get all your men together. I'm going to give them a task. Oh, and, by the way, they may try not to do it, so I want you to tell all the thugs that if they see any thugs attempting not to do the thing I'm going to ask them to do, they should kill them.'

'Kill them. Good,' sneered Durth, aggressively. 'And what is the task, oh king?'

The king leant forward, his movements answered by a slight whimper from the bearers below. 'Well, I'm not going to tell you *that*, am I, peasant?' The king tutted for some time, long enough, in fact, for him to still be tutting as Durth returned with his thugs.

'*Left*, one-and-one, and one-one-and-one, and *right* one-and-one and one-one-and-one! And HALT!' shouted Durth.

The thugs halted.

One-and-one rows of many goblins stood in the sunshine, chests out, before the king who surveyed them regally. 'Thugs!' shouted the king.

They all jumped.

'Great thugs, one and all! What a fine sight you are! How broad your shoulders, how strong your arms, how frighteningly repellent are your faces, and how unnecessarily barbed your weapons.'

Durth's chest stuck out so far he almost burst. His teeth protruded from his top lip and he went into a broad gap-toothed grin parted by a half-eaten worm.

'And it's because of that very barby-broad-ugly strength that I've decided that you are all going to volunteer for something.'

Everyone started to leave the field in a hurry. The thugs, confused by their orders, then began rounding each other up until the entire group was in a large scrum. Punches were exchanged. 'Stay still when you are being volunteered to die by the king!' Durth yelled, and he bowed to the king, certain that, as Head Thug, he wouldn't have to volunteer for anything.

269

'Thank you, Dirt. Now, brave, brave thugs. The mission is this: I want you to head out, in groups of one-one-and-one, and patrol the edges of the Kingdom looking for—yes, you guessed it—looking for giants!'

There was a scared murmur. Knees began to knock and lips began to wobble. The whole scene reminded the king of the story of how the Lord of the Jelly People marched his army to ransack the Castle of Queen Blancmange, only for him to fall in love with her as the castle fell into a big soggy pudding. How he loved the heroic tales of the old heroes.

'When seen, you are to—on pain of a fate worse than a fate worse than death—report it to Durth here, and we shall prepare for...whatever we have decided to prepare for.' The king grinned at the dirty mass of limbs and wounded goblins before him. 'But it's not all bad news and work, lads, oh no!' he shouted proudly. 'I am your king and a gracious and unbelievably wise and mighty one at that—greatest of all, I hear you say!

Silence greeted him.

'I hear you say!' shouted the king petulantly.

'You are the great king of all,' they said, or at least enthused to a similar effect.

He continued. 'So, by royal decree, I pronounce that if you capture anyone attempting to leave the village, you may punish them in any way you see fit! Dismissed.' The king waved his hand nonchalantly in a regal, half-hearted wave, and walked off back towards the Moot House with Looti close behind, checking that he still had his key.

Durth took in a deep breath. 'Right, lads, you heard the king. Any way we see fit, heh, heh. Now, you 'orrible lot—'

Looti followed the king into the Great Mouth, keeping a careful eye on the key. The sun was huge in the clear sky, and everyone was wandering about the village with their hands over their heads—just in case.[74] Looti put her hand in the king's and gave a sigh.

---

[74] The goblin apocalypse begins with the sky dropping on their heads, squashing all the goblins flat. After this, various local-themed dooms are prophesied, including

'Oops, I must be more careful. I nearly knocked that *great big key* off your belt,' she said, and she stared straight at him.

The king jumped back and instantly and nervously checked the key. It was still there. He gave a quick sigh of relief. 'Don't say things like that!' he snapped.

Looti stepped back and looked suitably hurt, then pretended to cry. 'Have I upset my little bull?' she sniffed.

The king harrumphed a few times under his breath and narrowed one eye, somehow managing to raise the brow on the other without having them both unexpectedly fall off his face. 'Erm, um, well, no, no, of course you haven't upset your little bull.' He gave a little laugh, 'It's just that, well, that key is rather important—sort of a family heirloom.' He had a sudden vision of what his father would do to him if he lost the key. Lord Grumpy Stormgrunties the Terrible would undoubtedly have fashioned and delivered something truly awful as punishment, something to top the other punishments he had delivered to his beloved gob-boy to toughen him up for life as the king. The king brought out a bright purple handkerchief and handed it to her. She blew. He sighed and put it back in his pocket.

'It must be a very, very important key to make my king snap so at his humble adviser,' she said, in an incredibly irritating, childish voice.

The king colored. 'Well, yes, yes it is, it is,' he said, putting a consoling arm around her shoulders and then quickly withdrew it. As he looked outside, he saw his subjects going about their daily business with their hands over their heads. He followed suit and stared upwards nervously at the huge glowering sun through the windows, so close he could almost touch them. 'Is it me or is the sun closer to us?' he said, trying to change the subject.

---

the consumption of the lands by an apocalypse goat bearing a tolling bell about its neck that signals the end of all thing, that the world is rolled up like paper and burnt (all goblins, of course, believing the world is flat), and the world being swallowed by a vast sky bat that lurks behind the moon, and spat out the other end. Some secluded tribes and cults believe this last eventuality has happened before.

'And what is it for, exactly, my little bullsy-woolsy?' she said, as subtly as possible, her eyes widening and her mouth opening into an astonished gape.

'Well, its, erm, it's for the royal treasury in my house,' he smiled, and walked back out towards the hamster. 'Anyway,' he added as she followed him, 'we must prepare for tomorrow's festivities. There's a lot of work to do.' He slunk off for a snooze, feeling his key as he went.

Looti smiled to herself. For a moment, all was still, save for the wailing of gob-brats and the distant smell of smoldering seagulls.

CHAPTER 17

Sorry felt sick, bouncing about on the back of the pig was making him want to heave. Everything passed at a blur, but the Wise Wench kept her hands on the reins as Zephyr hurtled through the forest. The Great Mole surreptitiously told Sorry not to worry, calming his brow with its wisdom and gentle strokes of its paws as he gripped Zephyr's back bristles for dear life.

The forest was a little too still for Sorry's liking. As a child, he'd heard some pretty terrifying stories about the things that lived deeper in the forest. Tales that had kept him awake at night; things he told other gob-boys and gob-girls to frighten them—the hinky-punks, Stray Sod, taterfoals, and the Terrible Woden.

Some of the things had even put him off his food. Briefly. As if in answer to some blacker time, his stomach gurgled. He tightened his belt and crawled closer to the howdah behind Urgh, his knuckles white as he gripped with all his might. He lurked behind the howdah and suddenly smiled.

'Yes,' whispered the Great Mole, 'you're right. This way, when an ambush occurs, Urgh will get snatched first.'

Directly in front, Urgh gave a broad smile and began whistling *The Mermaid and the Gently Poetic Cockroach*. His spirits were up. He was village hero and was with the Wise Wench. Nothing could go wrong.

Then he remembered the axe in his pack.

The axe for a specific purpose. He stared at her back. Was this the right moment? No, he knew it wasn't. How could she *not* know? Did she know? She must do, she'd be expecting it and kill him first, but then the Wise Wench never killed anything, at least as far as he knew. His head began to get hot and he tried to stop asking himself questions he couldn't answer. It didn't work; as usual his head was giving him thoughts he didn't really want.

The Wise Wench continued to lean forward, gripping Zephyr's reins as the pig cantered and galloped ever forward at an alarming pace, leaping obstacles and oinking haughtily at the forest.

The Wise Wench yelled, her skirts blowing behind her in the breeze. 'This is the fastest any non-plummeting goblin without wings has ever gone!' she shouted.

'*Winged* goblins? Surely not?'

'Dear Urgh, there is more bizarre terror in the forest than you can ever know!'

'Winged goblins! I wouldn't want to meet any of those,' said Urgh, nervously.

The Wise Wench shot him a glance over her shoulder. *Uncanny*, she thought, alarmed. *Really uncanny, and that's not the first or last time either. He's been saying and thinking uncanny thoughts all the time. He's seeing far too far ahead. How is that possible?* She wrinkled her nose and stopped Zephyr very suddenly. Urgh, who had by now stopped whistling, barged into the back of her. Sorry flew over the top of the howdah and vanished into a bush with a yell. The Wise Wench climbed down and fumbled in her woolen bodice. Opening it, she pulled out her long line of knitted objects drawn into a long daisy chain and scowled, muttering about 'netting' and 'wings' and 'have I got the right adventure?' under her breath. Then she smiled, put the knitted daisy chain back and walked under the nearest tree—a huge alder, its great green canopy shivering.

It started to rain.

Urgh quickly followed her under the tree and threw down their packs. One crashed to the floor and both oars fell out.

'Be careful, dullard!' snapped the Wise Wench and she narrowed her eyes, aggressively.

'Don't see why we have oars, anyway,' mumbled Sorry under his breath, picking himself out of the bush.

'What?' she snapped, leaning forward and putting her hand to her ear.

'I said, what do we have oars for?' said Sorry, while heroically inspecting his shoes.

'We have them for *later*,' said the Wise Wench, and she crossed her arms. 'Honestly, you're nearly as bad as his imperial bullhead, the king!' she scowled. 'Well?' she added at Sorry.

He jumped, saying, 'Well what?'

'Well, get a fire going. This rain will last all morning.'

Fire, fire, fire! thought Sorry, gathering some kindling and within nanoseconds having a roaring blaze. He gazed into it, lovingly.

'Come over here,' said the Wise Wench to Sorry. Above them, Urgh was climbing up the tree.

'Must I?' spluttered Sorry, nervously, eyes still hypnotized by the dancing flames.

'Yes, now,' she said, putting an arm around his shoulder region. 'I have something for you, something you'll like.'

Sorry began to shake a little.

She shook him. 'Stop that, ungrateful oaf. Now just stand still and let me be *nice* to you for once!' She reached into her bodice once more. 'Freeze,' she added, gripping his absence of shoulders with a gnarly hand as he tried to escape. 'Now, I want you to have this.' She handed him a small leather bag. 'Be very careful with these. They're magic fire-starting marbles.'

Sorry opened the bag and looked inside. Within were countless tiny colored spheres. He looked at the Wise Wench, pleadingly.

'Yes, go ahead,' she crooned, indicating for him to hurl one against a stone.

He did so. There was a curious swallowing sound as the sphere broke and then it erupted into a ball of transient flame before swallowing itself, leaving a black smear on the ground. He began clapping and crying at the same time.

The Wise Wench smiled. 'I thought that would make you happy. They're yours to keep...forever.'

Sorry stopped, put the bag down. 'Hang on,' he said

Above him, Urgh was wafting about on a slender branch. 'I can see miles!' he shouted. 'There are some big mountains far ahead, and smoke! Lots of smoke.'

'I know,' whispered the Wise Wench.

'But before that are some...'

'...Moors and hillocks,' she shouted up to him, attempting to change the subject and not look at Sorry who was still staring at her and the bag suspiciously.

'Why are you suddenly being nice to me?' said Sorry, looking about for enemies, traps, dangers, and murderers.

'Oh, stop being so suspicious. I just thought you might like a gift, that's all,' lied the Wise Wench, unconvincingly.

Sorry stared at the bag, torn between his favorite possible gift ever and his innate cowardice and fear of pain.

He snatched the bag up but promised to increase his alertness—nothing was going to surprise him.

'You're welcome,' scowled the Wise Wench. 'Don't save them for too long, though. It's not good having such magic and not wasting it pointlessly in a matter of hours.' She stepped to one side as Urgh plummeted past her and hit the ground.

The rain carried on and on. Sorry had a mouthful of marbles and was playing about nearby. Urgh was still rubbing his head. He could see the Wise Wench fumbling with something in her bodice. She was staring at a knitted figure of someone with a crown and key next to a green figure wearing a dress with a gold bangle on. 'That fathead will get himself into real trouble,' said the Wise Wench to a squirrel that had dashed down a tree near her. The squirrel wasn't quite sure he'd heard what she said. It looked over its shoulder just as Sorry brought down the oar and squashed it.

'Got you!' shouted Sorry. 'Fresh meat for supper!' He picked up the dead squirrel and bashed it against the tree a few times to make sure it was really dead, then he bashed it a few more times, because he was nasty. The Wise Wench scowled at him. He suddenly realized he'd swallowed the marbles. He burped. A fiery little feeling filled his throat, then a great gout of flame roared out. He fell down, blinked, and then collapsed into gales of joyful laughter. He could breathe fire! And, suddenly, he loved the Wise Wench forever.

'Who, what?' shouted Urgh. 'Was that you?'

Sorry nodded, proudly. 'I can breathe fire! It's my most secretest best wish ever, and now it's come true!' He tried to burp again and continued to do so until he was almost sick. Swallowing another of his magic marbles he tried again, successfully. He was in raptures of joy and thought about swallowing the whole bag just to see what would happen, but then some strange impulse stopped him.

'Sorry, what were you saying, Wise Wench?' said Urgh, standing well back from his burping friend.

'Never mind,' she said, as she stepped out from under the tree. 'It's just about to stop raining.' She paused to kick the stones into the small fire Sorry had made and began to march off again, leaping swiftly onto Zephyr and leaning forward to hand her mount a truffle. Zephyr clearly liked it and gave a snort.

Sorry and Urgh followed her onto the pig and they shot off again. She led them steadily uphill, and deeper into the forest. After a short time, they picked up an old badger trail and headed along it, the route heading between thick briars and patches of twisting elder. After an hour or so they left the trail and started to head steeply uphill, where they passed the mildewed ruins of several crofts, some of which appeared to have been burnt long ago. The Wise Wench shook her head and sighed as she passed the last of these, and proceeded to push their way through a thick laurel hedge. Quickening their pace, Zephyr galloped uphill and came to a halt at the edge of a short steep muddy bank over a stream.

Sorry relaxed his grip and put his hands on his stomach. It gurgled, oddly. In the distance he thought he heard something; a roaring noise. He looked alarmed. 'I've never been this way before, Wise Wench. What's that strange noise I can hear?'

The Wise Wench smiled, put a finger to her lips, then made a rather frightening beckoning motion and slid down the bank.

They followed her. After a short while, the land grew rockier and soon great green cliffs were visible. The Wise Wench struggled as she clambered between these and pretended to nearly fall when she slipped on a small stream which danced between mossy banks. Eventually, they came to a cliff face which plunged down a long way before arriving at a cove at the banks of a huge river. The river waters clashed, collided, conceded, and rushed on before joining again in endless revelry. The noise was deafening.

'That, my friends, is the River Runny!' she shouted, and bowed.

Urgh remembered a song about the River Runny and, after a few seconds, he began to sing softly, as though to himself. 'Oh, where have you come from, oh, oh Runny Man I see? And where are you going and what shall you see? I can't say I'm that bothered, really. Burn, burn, burn it, oh!' Urgh stopped when Sorry threw the dead squirrel at him.

The Wise Wench looked as though, for once, she approved.

'You can't sing, so don't,' said Sorry, nastily, scrunching up his face until it almost—*almost*—resembled the face of the Gurn of the Gods, Bentface, the Unpleasant-Looking.

'For once, the foul, groveling, selfish, greedy, little wretch is right. You can't sing, so don't. And, anyway, you've got the words wrong. Everyone in the village put 'burn, burn, burn it, oh!' into every song just to annoy the king, long, long ago.'

Urgh looked crestfallen but managed a watery smile. 'Well, all I can say is I'm very, very, incredibly glad I won't be swimming in *that* river,' he said, with almost preternatural uncanniness.

The Wise Wench stared at him in awe for a moment and then looked away.

They continued to canter above the river for the remainder of the day, the scenery changing little, with rocks and moss a constant companion to the trees and the fierce, rapid-strewn, incredibly dangerous river below. As night began to fall, the group came to a halt in a narrow bowl of soft grass beneath a pair of huge oaks. Nearby, another tree had fallen and was leaning over the cliff starring at the river below. Soon the camp was made with Sorry's magic marbles and fiery burps, and a little fire danced between them. Sorry shaved the squirrel and put it on a spit over the flames while Urgh began cutting bread with his little knife and massacring some carrots and a turnip. He fed Zephyr some turnip. The Wise Wench seemed lost in thought. After a time, they ate supper and the Wise Wench passed around a small gourd of strong blackberry cordial brewed the summer before. It was very strong and sweet. The little group sat back and watched the fire cavort and jig in the breeze for a time before falling into a deep slumber.

Urgh woke. The morning mist clung to the river below. The fire had long since died and a cold clamminess came over him. He was suddenly aware that someone was watching him. He peered into the trees, squinting, when a shaft of sunlight fell across him. Sorry and the Wise Wench were nowhere to be seen.

Then he heard the noise.

A twig crack.

'Wise Wench? Sorry? Are you there?'

No response.

Urgh drew his little knife and gripped the blade, taking one-more-than-one huge heroic steps forward, before adding one-one-and-one, slightly less heroic steps backwards. He thought he heard a distant flapping sound and, for a moment, his heart was stone.

Then the hand grabbed him.

He turned around and lashed out, narrowly missing Sorry's head.

Sorry fell back in surprise and Urgh dropped the knife. 'Sorry,' he said.

'Sorry!' said Sorry, looking indignant, until a line of dribble fell from his mouth, when he just looked babyish.

Urgh helped him up and wiped the dew off his coat. 'Anyway,' he said, 'where have you been?'

Sorry stepped back and scowled. 'Fishing,' he said, looking notably fish-bereft.

The Wise Wench huffed and wheezed her way up from the river, carrying a pole with nearly lots-many-and-one-less salmon on. 'For supper later!' she said. 'But now we must get moving.' She climbed onto Zephyr's huge back, up into the howdah and, following her, they continued their journey.

'I'm looking forward to supper,' said Sorry hungrily, eating a fish head to stave off his hunger. He stared up at the Wise Wench who was scowling at him. He waited for the admonishment, eyes closed. When he opened them again, she was just smiling at him.

'Enjoy them, Sorry. You enjoy them as much as you like,' she said, her eyes slightly cloudy.

It was later. Sweat trickled into Sorry's eyes and stung them. He gave them a quick rub with one hand as he gripped Zephyr's back with the other. The Wise Wench was guiding their trusty steed over the numerous tree roots which snaked out from the rocky ground. Inexplicably, she suddenly put a large tight meshed net over her head. Urgh's collar itched and he wished the flies would leave him alone. He tried not to think of dontthinkme gnats.

Immediately, a massive cloud of the gnats appeared and swarmed about them.

'Oh, great, was that you?' shouted Sorry, knowingly, at Urgh.

They picked their way steadily over the roots and, after the gnats had given up the chase, halted briefly to catch their breath. The Wise Wench looked weary and let the reins go loose. They all stopped and panted. 'I can't remember a hotter day at this time of year,' said Urgh, wheezily. All eyes fell on the Wise Wench.

She paused and thought for a brief moment. 'About lots-many-and-nearly-too-many-to-count-less-one summers ago, a day like this presaged a summer that was so hot that pigs melted, birds caught fire in mid-flight, and hay burnt as it was being reaped.'

Her companions pulled incredulous faces. 'Begging your pardon, Wise Wench,' said Urgh, 'but is that, strictly speaking, true?'

The Wise Wench scowled. 'Of course it's true, young upstart!' she snapped and, as punishment, got them moving again. Sorry and Urgh exchanged skeptical glances.

The afternoon was the hottest Urgh could recall.[75] His whole body seemed to be immersed in warm lime marmalade, or at least that's the thought that came to him by way of comparison, and that seemed to raise his morale slightly. Sorry imagined himself about to burst into flame at any second, and he became quite worried about the fact, but then he thought it might happen to Urgh and he began staring at him, hopeful of spontaneous combustion at any moment,

---

[75] Which, knowing how short goblins' memories are, is not saying much.

280

wondering how great it would be as a spectacle. They steadily headed on uphill, through deep oak and over ever-larger rocks and roots until the sun finally began to sink behind the horizon and offered them a rest from its embrace. At the Wise Wench's insistence, they carried on a little further until they unexpectedly came to a small clear pool. Sorry and Urgh dived in while the Wise Wench contented herself with wetting an enormous spotted handkerchief and dabbing her neck. Zephyr walked straight into the water and stood grinning, piggishly.

Sufficiently cooled, they set up camp and ate their meagre supper in the dying rays of the sun, which glowed orange and cool behind the oaks. Urgh seemed lost in thought, while Sorry had taken to biting his toenails. The Wise Wench looked at him, disgustedly. 'Do you have to do that in public?' she snapped, bitterly, then corrected herself and said it was perfectly acceptable to do so at his time of life.

Suddenly there was a cry nearby, and a huge flapping sound.

Sorry and Urgh startled. The Wise Wench reached into her pack and brought out a net—a very large net.

There was a moment's silence before the goblins realized that they were not alone. Several really green horrible-looking humanoids stood at the far end of the clearing looking back at them. They looked a bit like goblins, but they were even more repulsive. They were dressed in flea-bitten furs and carried great spears. They had wings—well, 'wings' is perhaps a kind description. 'Flaps of leathery wan skin held awkwardly between odd-jointed limbs' would be more accurate. The Wise Wench stood forward. 'Well, get on with it,' she snapped.

The green group looked a little surprised and the fattest, baldest one took a tentative step forward, bending one wing back.

'Oh, come along. I haven't got all day. Get on with it,' she shouted, hoarsely.

'Erm,' the fattest, baldest one said.

The Wise Wench sighed. 'All right, I'll do it for you. Your name is Plummet. You are the chief of the 'Winged Ones', gobgoyles living in the mountains who are the result of an unpleasant

281

coupling between a lonely gargoyle and a very, very wide gob-wench long ago—a story I shan't elaborate on now for the sake of brevity. You have been watching us since yesterday and you want us to surrender and hand over all our valuables, weapons, and jars of pickle. Is that right?'

Plummet nodded.

'And then you were going to say that no harm will come to us if we go along peacefully, weren't you?'

The crooked-winged gobgoyle looked confused and tilted his head slightly.

'Which isn't true because, the moment you get us back to your village, you intend to put us in your biggest cooking pot and stew us with potatoes, carrots, and your tribe's holy symbol—the turnip. So the answer is no. I am the Wise Wench and, if you come anywhere near me, you will regret it.'

Plummet continued to stare. Then he realized that someone was telling him, a chief, what to do and he reddened before shouting 'Charge!'

The winged ones flapped and flew straight at them. The Wise Wench calmly held her net up purposefully while Sorry screamed and Urgh reached for his magic sack and pulled out a big fat dead spider. The winged creatures flew just above their heads, jabbing out with spears. One tore Urgh's shirt. He answered by throwing the spider at a winged thing. It struck him and sticky webs burst out. Spiders began scuttling about them and the creature soared away, brushing the spiders off and screaming in terror. The goblins turned in time to see the other winged ones soar up and prepare for a dive. The Wise Wench smiled. 'Don't worry. The chief is about to get tied up,' she said. She looked at Sorry. *I wish I could change things, little goblin, but I cannot* she thought, sadly. Without warning, one of the winged ones hurled a spear. It flew straight for Sorry who looked at it with a mixture of surprise, fear, and wonder. For that moment alone in his life, he emulated the Giant Chief.

Urgh hurled himself at his companion to try and knock him out of the way. As he did, the spear struck him in the back and he fell.

The Wise Wench's jaw dropped. 'What?' she mumbled, before she realized the winged ones were falling at them, all aiming straight for the old lady. She fell to one knee.

It creaked.

Then, just as the spears were aiming at her, she hurled the net up. It struck the gobgoyle chief who became suddenly entangled in it. He fell to the ground like a stone and was still.

The other winged ones gave each other frightened glances and decided it was time for a strategic withdrawal back into the mountains. They flew off over the trees and disappeared.

The Wise Wench stood up shakily, stared at Sorry, and then at Urgh's body. Sorry began to tremble when he saw the confused look on her face. She took a few teetering steps towards him, leaning heavily on her stick. 'I don't understand. Why are you still alive? I'm glad, of course, but...oh Urgh, what have you done? *How* have you done it?'

Urgh lay on the ground with a spear in his back.

'But that's not what happens!' yelled the Wise Wench in increasing desperation, her eyes narrowing, and her lip wobbling.

Sorry stood for a moment in fear and confusion. Then the Wise Wench began to sob. This confused Sorry to the point of collapse. His tiny brain hardly able to cope with the sight. Her, the Wise Wench, who had been his object of terror since he was born, sobbing. Filled with compassion, and a little guilt, he slowly stepped over to her and put an arm around her. Her sobbing grew.

'That's...not...what...happens,' she moaned, interrupting each word with a gulp and sob.

'Well, perhaps it didn't happen then,' he said, trying to be helpful. 'Perhaps he's alive and we're dead. Perhaps we've gone to the Special Cake and Pudding House in the Great Oak and what's happening here is just a dream.'

Sorry thought about what he said and almost convinced himself it was true until the Wise Wench shouted, 'But that's not what happens. You die, not him. You die pushing *him* out of the way. Your act of heroism that sees you given a seat by the Fireplace of the Gods. Bless you! But you haven't done it, *he* has.'

There was a groan behind.

They both stopped. The Wise Wench staggered towards Urgh.

He groaned again.

Sorry gasped in a breath.

As gently as she could, the Wise Wench turned Urgh over. The spear had gone straight through the little goblin's shoulder. Its point, together with a few splintered bones, stuck out of the front.

He groaned again.

The Wise Wench held him very tightly and looked up to the heavens. 'Oh, Lord Noc, grant me the strength of your healing hands to pull this spear from this, your somewhat repulsive son, and let your hands and smells guide my actions.' She looked down at Urgh. 'This is going to hurt a lot,' she smiled.

Through his giddy pain, Urgh thought he felt his mother cradling him. Then he felt something really, really painful and fainted.

The spear came out easily. 'Quick, your shirt!' shouted the Wise Wench at Sorry.

I'm supposed to be dead. Sorry stared miserably at the floor. So that was it; I'm expendable; little more than pigswill at the bottom of the trough. Nothing but an ant, under the feet of Greatboots.[76]

His shirt was lifted roughly off him.

To his indignation, the Wise Wench began tearing strips off it. 'Hey, that's my—'

'—Shut up and get me some water or I'll have to DO something to you' she shouted. Sorry jumped to attention and, grabbing the cook pot, plunged it into the pond. Green duckweed clung to the surface as Sorry slopped the pot over to Urgh and the Wise Wench.

---

[76] The legendary ant slayer who wandered for all his days seeking out ants to step upon.

Plummet the gobgoyle had stayed silent during this time, taking in all he heard. He decided to continue to pretend he was unconscious.

'And you can stop pretending to be unconscious,' said the Wise Wench to him. 'I know—' she paused, '—almost everything, and certainly everything about you.' She wrapped the makeshift bandage tightly around Urgh's shoulder and soaked water onto it.

Time passed.

The bats swooped over and around the small campfire by the pond. The Wise Wench cast a casual eye at them as they fluttered around catching bugs, flies, and grump-moths. Sorry sat with his back to her at the edge of the firelight. He'd been sat there since after their fish supper, and had refused to talk to the Wise Wench. Plummet had spent the entire time trying to pick a thread in the net and escape, but it had confounded his efforts—so far. Urgh lay quite still by the fire, his shoulder tightly wrapped.

The Wise Wench must have dozed for a while because, when she looked up, the first faint light of dawn was coloring the sky above.

Urgh stood near her looking up at the fading stars.

The Wise Wench shot up and grabbed him.

'Beautiful, aren't they?' said Urgh.

Then she noticed that the bandages were gone. She touched his arm gingerly, then had a closer look. Pulling back his torn shirt she noticed that the wound had gone. He was completely healed. She coughed. This would be the first and, she hoped, only time she would ever be in this position. The words stuck in her mouth at first, almost getting as far as her teeth before popping back down her throat. She tried again, harder. Finally, in a low drawl, they slid out. 'How did you do that?' she said, and sat down, exhausted.

'Do what?' said Urgh, matter-of-factly.

'Get better so quickly.'

'Get better from what, exactly?' he said, even more matter-of-factly.

'Do you not remember the—?'

'—I remember pushing Sorry out of the way of that spear. Then I must have hit my head on a rock or something. The next thing I knew, I was here, next to the empty net.'

'Aha!' said the Wise Wench, noting Plummet had indeed escaped as she knew he should. She suddenly looked very pleased. She took a cautious step to the torn net and prodded it with her longest, dirtiest finger. 'So the gift hasn't left me, Noc be praised!' She uttered a silent reverence to him. 'So our prisoner has escaped and, one day far away, will unexpectedly come back for vengeance. Good.'

'What do you mean, oh Wise Wench?' said Urgh, curiously.

'Oh nothing, nothing at all. Everything's as it should be. Plummet has escaped and won't be troubling us until next winter. Noc is in his tree, the king is on his hunting stool, and we need to be getting along!' She walked slowly and carefully around the pond towards the slumbering Sorry, and rubbed her chin with her hand. 'The only thing is,' she said to herself, under her breath, 'what do we do with you?' She thought for a few seconds before pushing the sleeping goblin into the pond.

He awoke with a splutter and an ear full of duckweed. Sorry scowled at the Wise Wench.

'Yes, I know, you're still not talking to me. Well, I can't say I'm too worried about that. Now, get your packs and let's be off. We have a long way to go today.'

They climbed all the next day, through sparser and ever smaller trees, cantering on and up with the Wise Wench keen to make up what she called 'completely lost time'. Lost, apparently, because she had intended spending less time fretting over a dead Sorry than a live Urgh. Sorry had sulked all morning but had begun to speak over a late brunch of fruitcake and thick, peppery, worm sausages from the Wise Wench's own, feared, smoke house.[77] By mid-afternoon,

---

[77] It was particularly feared because—allegedly—she kept a pair of knockers that skulked in the smoke within, fed the fires, and killed and smoked intruders. The duo could—allegedly—see in the dark on account of their great big staring eyes

the tree-cover had almost gone and they were in the open, somewhere no goblin liked to be caught. Childhood tales of gobhawks, frightfullies, henkies, and giant, naughty badgers put paid to any desire to run across meadows or through open fields. Open spaces—where the sky looked closer—were to be feared and avoided.

The Wise Wench gently pulled Zephyr to a halt at a small pile of stones. As her companions watched her, they suddenly realized why she had stopped. The stones were a low cairn on an open hillside of hummocky grass and heather. On the cairn, someone had chalked a pig with a pair of figures on its back and lots of eyes. Sorry instantly sulked. Here, the land lay open all about them and the view was as high and wide as any of them had seen. Yet it was not the broad spaces that they stared at, it was above; high, high above, at a line of white peaks that lay ahead. A line of great mountains wearing a bonnet of cloud. As they strained their eyes to look for any way across them, a great wall of ice fell from one of the peaks into the valley below. A full minute passed before the noise, a huge roar of falling snow, reached them.

'Oh, great,' said Sorry, weakly.

'We have to make our way up that ridge of rock to the side,' said the Wise Wench, pointing vaguely in the direction of the mountains. 'There, on that overhang, we must make a brief climb to the pass.' She smiled. 'It's a long way,' she added, somewhat unnecessarily.

Sorry stared at where she pointed. All he could see was a wall, higher than the highest pine by many times, and he was sure that the wall wouldn't want him to try to cross it, or else. He sighed and got down.

'It won't be easy,' she added.

---

which could hypnotise their prey into being still while they were chopped up, hung, and smoked, while still alive! Eurgh! It was untrue but so good at keeping visitors away that the Wise Wench was glad she'd spread the rumour in the first place, which, of course, she knew before she'd started.

Won't be easy thought Sorry, sulkily. *After all this and now we come to 'It won't be easy', like all the rest of it has been. Like the giants' keep and the chase and the gobgoyles were. Won't be easy...*

What are you thinking about, Sorry?' asked Urgh while scratching behind Zephyr's ears.

'Nothing,' said Sorry, sulkily.

'A minute's rest, lads, then we must press on,' said the Wise Wench, gazing at her companions, questioningly.

The wind scratched and tugged at Sorry's brown hair as he bounced miserably over the moorland. Far ahead, the mountains loomed, as impenetrable as ever. He cursed under his breath.

'Language,' shouted the Wise Wench from the front.

Sorry muttered something about 'trout' under his breath and carried on cursing.

Urgh had been staring at the mountains and feeling his pack to check that the very sharp axe—the axe with a very special purpose—was still there. Every time he felt it, he stared at the Wise Wench guiltily, yet she didn't look back once. His mind was doing somersaults over his quest. Of the long list of everything he didn't want to do, killing the Wise Wench was at the top of the list. Well, killing anyone for that matter. Then he remembered that the Wise Wench knew everything and tried to stop thinking about it, and the more he tried, the more it kept popping into his head. But his father had said it was the only way. Only by killing the Wise Wench could the gods allow the forest to remain. Fail, and the sky would fall, and it would be *his entire fault.*

He thought about his mother waiting expectantly by the fire for her prince to return, pounding raw meat with her fists.

He realized that the Wise Wench was staring at him. She wore a very puzzled look and frowned. She leant close to him. 'What were you just thinking?' she asked.

'Oh, nothing,' said Urgh, somewhat untruthfully.

She gazed into his eyes and frowned again. 'I can see you're lying yet I don't know what about. There's something very, very odd about you. And I'm not just talking about the fact that, unlike everyone else in the forest, you always look up to the sky without fear. At least, you used to until very recently, but now you do have fear in your eyes. Perhaps that has something to do with it—you constantly stare at the heavens.' She seemed to come to a conclusion and spurred Zephyr on.

Up to the sky thought Urgh, and yet she doesn't know what I'm thinking. Or is she lying? He became more worried than ever.

By the day's end, they had reached a small hill of broken stones and gorse, bowed by Lord Noc's benevolent gusts. They made camp on the hill's far side out of the wind and ate a meagre supper, brightened only by the appearance of a very healthy slice of sherry and smoked grub fruitcake.

Sorry and Urgh slept fitfully that night, aware that it was All Sharks' Eve and they hadn't brought their costumes. The lack of a costume left them horribly exposed to visitations from the ghosts of sharks past. The wind picked up and the strange noises of the moor made them nervous. Creatures they could not name slinked between hummocks and groughs, and night birds with odd calls stalked the land. They imagined each was some vengeful shark bent upon feasting.

The Wise Wench and Zephyr slept on, snoring contentedly against each other.

CHAPTER 18

The Great Mouth swung open and the king came out, resplendent in his green shark costume. In the firelight, he looked almost menacing. The entire party field was full of fires, feasting, and fighting. He was held aloft in the special palanquin for All Sharks' Eve. It was designed like a huge blue boat with a figurehead of a rampant, water-breathing, blue cow at its prow. The bearers, each dressed as rather ordinary grey sharks, struggled to carry him out across the field in the village center. Looti, clad in a skimpy girl-shark outfit of magenta and yellow, glided out after. Her eyes kept glancing towards the key as her plans continued to ferment.

The villagers all clapped and whistled as the royal party emerged, everyone from the youngest gob-in-arms to the oldest, wretched goblin-hag had turned out, and each had made a special effort to look their best and most shark-like on this, one of the most holy of days.[78]

The bearers' struggled on with the king until they reached the stage in the middle of the village brown. A huge flagpole painted with pointy teeth had been erected, and on this was pinned a gob-boy holding a megaphone. He shouted as the king adjusted his fins. 'Offers,' shouted the gob-boy in a very high-pitched voice, 'are invited for the post of Poo-Pit Maester of the village. Applicants shall be experienced with all modern manner of pong-related devices, and ideally have no sense of smell. Applications are particularly welcome from anyone who doesn't mind not having any friends at all. Goblins whose name does not begin with 'P' need not apply. Applicants should speak directly to His Realistically-Shark-Like's able assistant,

---

[78] There isn't a goblin phrase for 'making a special effort' and, in truth, they don't really make much of an effort at all if they can help it—the males, not at all. So, when we say 'making a special effort,' it generally means making *any* kind of attempt. Thus, in this case, various pathetic, feeble and laughably un-shark-like costumes and accessories had been attempted, but all were frankly rubbish and generally involved simply wearing some sort of false shark fin and, in rare inspired cases, pointy teeth.

Looti, Adviser to His Majesty King Stormgrunties the many-many-and-lots-after-more-than-many-dead-King Stormgrunties-after-the-first, king of the Great Forest. Offers are invited—'

The king turned to the crowd and smiled as the gob-boy continued repeating the message. Looti gave a little reverent bow as the Substitute Great Mole arrived. The crowd fell silent in awe of the beatific glove puppet.

The Substitute Great Mole spoke quietly to the king who smiled and nodded before clearing his throat. 'Friends!' he cried.

Vast applause, cheers, and harroos from the goblin maidens answered him.

'Friends!' he added, regally. 'The Substitute Great Mole reminds me—not that I need reminding about anything of course, so great am I—that this evening is All Sharks' Eve, the day when we celebrate the fact that sharks don't have legs or live on land. In this respect, we owe our thanks to the sound judgement of that most holy demi-god Lord Leg, the Giver of Legs, in refusing the shark such appendages.' The king turned to Looti and led her forward. 'The adviser shall speak the lore of Lord Leg. Adviser,' the king ushered his palanquin back to allow Looti center stage.

She smiled and cleared her throat. 'And lo,' she shouted, commandingly, 'Lord Leg gave legs to the hedgehog! And the next in line was the noble shark, and the Lord Leg spake, and he did say, 'So, noble shark, why doth thou wantest legs?' And the great lord shark said, 'My Lord Leg, giveth me legs that I may run upon the grass and playeth ball games. Let me run through the dewy morning and play with the babe-in-arms. Let my song fall on the boughs of trees and let my whistle light up the meadow.' And the Lord Leg did smile at the shark, and sayeth he, 'I am mindful to think that thou is trying to trick me, lord shark. 'Run in the meadow? Playeth with the babe?' If thou wish to do this, why then hath thou got a huge mouthful of pointed teeth?' And the shark said, unconvincingly, 'My lord, my mouth is so large to allow me to sing louder, and my many teeth are so that people can see my smile from far away and know how happy I am.' And Lord Leg looked at the shark and his look was wrath. And he said, 'Methinks that thou are trying to pull a fast one upon me, lord shark. Are not thy teeth for rending and biting, and are not thy muscles and fins for swimming? If I gave your kin legs, it wouldn't be fair to the others. Therefore, I shall make thee stay in the sea, and that shall be thy domain. But right impressed am I with thy trick, and so therefore I shall make thee lord of the sea, and all things shall fear thee.' And the shark smiled, and bowed, and swam off. And lo, it was late in the day and Lord Leg was ready for his tea, yet he had refused so many that day that he had a large pile of legs left. And so he sought out the Queen Millipede to end his work the quicker.' Looti bowed and stepped back.

The king stepped forward. 'Let us pray,' he said, shuffling about as everyone bowed their heads. He loved this bit, facing the tops of everyone's head. 'Oh, Lord Leg,' he said, loudly, 'we thank thee for thy gift of our legs, and we thank thee especial on this day for the fact that thou was wise enough to make sure sharks didn't get them. We honor thee in this, our eve of feasting, and we pray that our own legs and feet do not suffer thy wrath and fall off. Unless, of course, I should command it.'

The crowd uttered an oath and the king broke into a broad grin. 'Therefore, friends, let All Sharks' Eve begin! Bring on the seal-pups!'

The villagers cheered.

'With a snap, snap, snap, and burn, burn, burn it, oh!' sang the mummer in the shark costume. He bowed low, and the king could see that his fin was about to fall off. How he hated mummers, and how he hated singing, and how he particularly hated singing mummers. The king wondered if the payment might not be applicable after an event, or perhaps as a down-payment for future performances.

The party was in full swing, with dancing and cheering and whooping. Goblin maids danced, the escaped children squealed, and the older goblins ate with their mouths open.

Looti coughed, and the king looked around. How beautiful she looked, how regal and shark-like in her outfit. The Wise Wench had been right; she was a fine choice for adviser, so much more...*female*...than Kringe, and so much more pleasant. He almost lost himself in thought before he noticed a small, bent, ugly thing next to her.

It smelt.

'Ahem, Your Majestic Fishiness,' said Looti, indicating the bent thing. 'This goblin would like to apply for the post of Poo-Pit Maester. Step forward, pointless nobody,' she said to the goblin by her side. The old goblin did so.

The king eyed it up and down in a disinterested way. 'So,' he said, 'you'd like to be my new Poo-Pit Maester, would you? Well, let me tell you something first. Being Poo-Pit Maester is one of the most important jobs in the village. A happy goblin has a happy smell: that's my motto, always has been, always will be.' He smiled regally, and noticed Looti was mouthing a silent moo at him.

'Anyway,' he coughed, 'haven't got all day, you know. We've only got a few minutes before we have to burn the sharks' legs. So let's have it out. What's your name, dismal scumbody?' said the king.

'Roger, Your Aquaticness. Roger Eweworrier.' He bowed.

'Oh dear,' said the king. 'Oh dear, oh dear. No, no, no, that won't do at all.' He stuck his tongue from the corner of his mouth. 'Well, I'm sorry, Roger, but in light of new evidence, and having consulted extensively, I'm afraid to tell you that the post has already been offered to someone else.'

Roger looked crest-fallen.

Looti leant over and whispered something in the king's ear. He smiled and adjusted his collar. 'Now then, Roger,' he said, 'having consulted with the experts, and taking everything into account, I have decided to break against tradition and appoint you.'

Roger beamed, looked like he was about to say something, but stopped as the king poked him.

'Now,' continued the king, 'I can give you your first duty. You are to go around the village telling everyone of your appointment, and, more importantly, the new name that goes with it. I declare that from now on you shall be called Percival PartyPants, Poo-Pit Maester. Welcome aboard, Percy.'

Percy beamed.

'Now, go away. Quickly. There's a good chap.'

Percy waddled off, shouting to his friends. Looti handed the king a great torch and indicated the large pile of unrealistic-looking fake legs in the exact middle of the village brown. A crowd was gathering and they had begun chanting. 'Burn the legs! Burn the legs! The shark must swim not walk to bed! Burn, burn, burn it, oh!'

Smiling, the king stepped forward with the burning torch, wondering quietly to himself if he should use real legs next year.

It was very late. So late, in fact, that it was very early. The leg-based fire had died, drowned by the rain that was now pounding down. The few standing goblins were, to be truthful, not so much standing as leaning. The king was amongst these folk, leaning as he was, precariously, on his adviser Looti, the pair of them being propped at an alarming angle on the table. The table was strewn with empty cider jugs, plates of crumbs, rude and uncomplimentary carvings of sharks, and half-eaten insect legs. There was a general hush over the field. Momentarily, there was a beautiful glow over the horizon and then the sun glimpsed over.

Some distance away from the village, a group of under-thugs peered into the dawn gloom. 'I felt sure I heard something,' whispered one and scrunched up his face.

Suddenly there was another growl out in the dark.

The brave goblin group of voluntary heroes decided it was time to go back and warn the others. They turned and came face to shin with a giant. Suddenly, more came out of the gloom, leading ferocious, very, very large dogs.

'MNARRRRRR!'

The goblins tried to run.

'WELL, WHAT DO WE HAVE HERE?' said the ugliest giant. He picked the goblins up and had a closer look, then swallowed one of them whole. The remaining goblins began to scream very loudly. 'CHIEF!' shouted the giant. 'I THINK WE'VE REACHED THE VILLAGE!' and then swallowed another. 'DOES ANYONE HAVE ANY SALT?' he added.

The giants parted as the chief arrived, flanked by lots of other giants, each leading huge dogs. The chief clicked his fingers and the giant handed the last goblin to him. The chief grinned with one head, grimaced with another and whistled with the last. Then he held the goblin up to one of his mouths.

The goblin yelled.

'SHUSH, NOW! SHUSH!' said the chief, quietly, and he began to walk back into the forest, the other giants following nearby. A few minutes later, they arrived at the giants' camp, a huge clearing that had been made by pushing over trees. Lots of giants sat about. The goblin couldn't count that well but he could see some-over-a-lot of giants, all armed to the teeth and ready for war. Many of the giants had painted a stylized deceased many-headed dog on their helmets, armor, or battle-trunks. They stirred when the chief arrived, and the dogs growled. In the gloom by the edge of the camp, the goblin thought he could make out some large, bloated shape, unmoving.

The sun suddenly danced into the clearing, illuminating the terribly ugly occupants with frightful effect.

The chief set the goblin down in the middle of the camp right by the fire. Its glow made him uncomfortable, but not as uncomfortable as the giants did. The chief stared at him and laughed. His breath stank of garlic. 'NOW, LADS, WE'VE FOUND A LITTLE GUARD HERE. WHAT SHALL WE DO WITH HIM?' the chief smiled as sundry, sometimes quite complex, suggestions shot out.

'LET'S EAT HIM, RIGHT NOW!' shouted one.

'NAR, LET'S CUT HIM IN SLICES AND USE HIM FOR PAPER.'

'I KNOW!' shouted another. 'LET'S SEE IF WE CAN PULL HIM INSIDE OUT!' The giants began to laugh heartily. Even the dogs yelped, happily.

'I'LL TELL YOU WHAT WE SHOULD DO,' said a voice. 'LET'S LET HIM GO!'

The goblin's mouth dropped wide open.

Everyone looked around for the offending voice. Ate Eyes walked forward, smiling. He strolled up to the chief and whispered something in his ear. The chief grinned a very wide grin of very bad teeth and the pair of them began laughing.

'YES, LET'S LET HIM GO. AND QUIETEN DOWN, YOU RABBLE!' shouted the chief to the growing crescendo of objection. 'LET'S LET HIM GO AND LET'S GIVE 'IM A LITTLE MESSAGE TO TAKE TO *HIS* CHIEF. NOW, LITTLE FELLER,' he said with his right head, while winking with the others at the goblin, 'THIS IS WHAT YOU'RE GOING TO DO. YOU'RE GOING TO GO AND TELL YOUR CHIEF THAT I WILL ACCEPT HIS SURRENDER IF HE COMES OUT ON HIS HANDS AND KNEES AND BEGS ME. AND NOT ONLY THAT, BUT HE BRINGS ME THE *DOG KILLER*. ALIVE! UNDERSTAND?'

The goblin nodded so much his head nearly fell off. Behind him, Ate Eyes nodded smarmily.

'THAT'S LOVELY. ALL RIGHT, OFF YOU GO,' said the giant's heads together, and put him down.

The goblin needed no other invitation. He ran off into the growing sunlight as fast as he could, screaming all the way.

'OH, AND SAFE JOURNEY!' shouted the middle head. The others looked at it distastefully and scowled.

'JUST WHY ARE WE LETTING THAT TASTY MORSEL GO AND WARN THE GOBLIN SCUM WE'RE COMING?' said the right head, angrily. The left head nodded in agreement.

'BECAUSE, FATHEADS, WHAT WOULD YOU PREFER? A QUICK GAME OF SQUASH OR A WHOLE VILLAGE FULL OF SLAVES AND SNACKS TO LAST US ALL SUMMER? MNARRRRRR!' The middle head looked smugly back at Ate Eyes as the other giants smiled evilly and licked their multiple lips.

CHAPTER 19

Sorry and Urgh awoke, drenched. Rain was hammering down from the great grey clouds above, which seemed determined to be their companion for the day. Nearby, the Wise Wench slept on under an umbrella, which had somehow put itself up during the night and kept the rainwater off her. Zephyr lay dry below a tarpaulin next to her, its edges hung with garlands of shark teeth and fins. The Wise Wench yawned and smacked her chops contentedly, then opened one eye. 'If you look in the bottom of my pack, you'll find a pound of bacon. I brought it especially for today! Don't worry, Zephyr, it's not a relative.'

Sorry, hungry as ever, greedily reached into the Wise Wench's pack. *I wonder what else is in here?* he thought to himself, shiftily. Cautiously, he had a sly look around. There was more fruitcake, the pigs' bladders, a pair of gourds, and then he saw the long daisy chain of knitted figures.

The Wise Wench's reminders. But what's it doing in here? Sorry saw it was quite bulky. Perhaps she'd put it here for safety? 'Oh dear, it's slipped right down to the bottom of the pack,' he muttered, casting a wary eye at her as he carefully began pulling at the daisy chain as figure after diorama after figure emerged. He saw an unkind figure of a goblin without shoulders that had fire in his hands. *Is that supposed to be me?* A winged thing pushed a spear through the middle of the figure. Next came a pair of figures on the back of a smiling pig with a shark nearby, some bacon, and an umbrella hanging from the pig.

Then he saw the *horrific something* next on the chain. He almost choked in terror at what he saw.

The Wise Wench suddenly pulled him backwards. 'Nosy,' she said, and, fumbling inside her pack, threw the bacon at him. 'I thought you were hungry,' she snapped, and carefully rolled up the figures before hiding them back in her bodice.

Sorry realized he was never going to see it again; didn't *want* to, in fact. The knitted figure he saw stuck in his head and wouldn't move. *Shark-fins and bacon*, he thought, glancing around himself. *It must be next! We're doomed! I must escape! It'll kill her. I'd hate it to kill me. It can kill them, but not me, the dreadful, fearful, terrible thing.* He began to blubber and cluck.

The Wise Wench leaned over and whispered in his ear. 'That will teach you to look at things you shouldn't.'

Sorry continued to blub all the way to and through breakfast, still weeping as they set off on their mount.

The day moved on. The land ahead was peppered with huge boulders now, their sides smoothed and caressed by uncountable summers of sun and winters of ice and snow. These great stones reminded Urgh of grey guardians, marking the way to the pass that lay far ahead. They reminded Sorry of *the beast* he had seen in the knitting. Urgh shielded his eyes from the sun and looked up towards the mountains. The wall ahead was now softening, and a ridge was visible; a very narrow ridge—or so it seemed from below—and yet one the Wise Wench had said was 'sort of' safe.

Her words echoed in his mind. 'Sort of' didn't inspire much confidence in him because 'sort of' safe, turned upside down, could mean 'sort of' very dangerous. Nearby, Sorry was shaking and making the most peculiar clucking noises. Urgh was a little worried about him, but, then again, he was also a little fed-up with his whining. He decided to leave him alone for the time being.

Zephyr leapt over another boulder and squealed with delight.

In the early afternoon they had begun to leave the moorland behind and were crossing fields of boulders. The going was hard and they had to let Zephyr rest several times. Her howdah had to be taken off to allow her a really good scratch from time to time. At one of these stops, Urgh raised a concern as the mighty pig rolled on her back and oinked.

'She's going to be terribly tired for the return journey,' said Urgh with genuine anxiety. He'd already grown very fond of the vast pig; her speed, her loyalty and the way she always, always, smiled, even though he wasn't quite sure if it was a smile or just wind, or just the way she looked.

The Wise Wench cast a glance towards the river, still not far away. 'She'll be fine,' she said, and tried to hide her concerned look.

We won't be thought Urgh, guiltily, and thought about the axe. He walked over to Zephyr and scratched behind her ear; she grinned, appreciatively.

A short while later they came around a great nose of rock, pointing outwards from a grey cliff-face. They suddenly got a good view of the ridge leading to the pass. The stones above became lesser cliff faces, and idly tossed between these were several slopes of loose stone and scree. It was above one of these that Urgh could make out the ridge, a black, jagged line of rock which led upwards into the mists.

'Right, that's the easy part over,' said the Wise Wench laughing. 'Now, let's get doing some serious work. Time is already short!' She gave the reins a flick and Zephyr began almost leaping from stone to stone, heading as quickly as possible for the scree slope.

*Easy part...*Urgh thought that the Wise Wench, for all her wisdom, could do with a few lessons in tact.

East Part. So now we die, thought Sorry. 'Wings and fearsome dragons? We're all doomed anyway. We are but the underthings of the gods, and they care not if they soil us. Wings and dragons! We're finished this time. Press on, my lad, and press on. Death rides its dreadful giant black starling and will take us, cluck, cluck, cluck,' said Sorry to himself and followed, a look of resigned despair burdening him.

Urgh looked at him oddly and shook his head. *Poor lad, the strain has got too much for him, and who can blame him, what with him being supposedly dead and then not dead. This journey! The giants! I never thought I'd see the day.* Urgh smiled to himself as he watched his friend carry on clucking quietly.

The evening saw them reach a great bowl in the cliffs, directly at the foot of a scree slope. The cloud had come in even thicker during the day and clung to the mountain above, hiding the upper reaches in mystery. Here, their every move was echoed and amplified, making the younger goblins uneasy. As if realizing their unease, the mountain sent a small trickle of stones down the slope, which clattered and clacked before coming to rest above.

'We'll camp here for the night and get an early start,' said the Wise Wench, officiously. A few moments later, her words were echoed back and forth, giving her an even more mysterious quality. She smiled, somewhat evilly, at Sorry and Urgh, who had begun to unpack, taking the howdah off first. Zephyr rolled on her back joyfully.

Supper was a miserable affair, with Urgh and Sorry unable to avert their eyes from the ever-blackening gloom above. They shivered, and not just because of the cold. Momentarily, Urgh began to whistle *The Farmer and the Frightfully Big Lusty Woodlouse* before being shushed by his companions.

After a short while, the Wise Wench began to snore and Urgh hutched his way over to Sorry, who was talking to himself about the merits of thatch over slate while clucking. Urgh leant close to his friend. 'Sorry, forgive me for saying this, but you've been sort of talking to yourself since the morning. Why?'

Sorry shuffled uneasily, touched his nose, and whispered, 'Forbidden knowledge.' He then winked.

'Forbidden knowledge? What do you mean?' whispered Urgh as quietly as he could.

'Eh?' said Sorry, loudly. The Wise Wench stirred, muttered something that sounded like 'watch out for its rear end, Urgh,' and began snoring again.

'I've seen the future.'

'Future?'

'The Wise Wench's list. Her daisy chain of figures. I saw it when I was fishing the bacon out. It showed something...bad.'

'Bad?'

'Really bad.'

'When?'

'Soon. Very soon.'

'What?'

'Can't say,' whimpered Sorry.

'Why not?'

'Because it's really bad and saying it might make it come here quicker. Names are like that.'

'Really bad? As bad as Dando and his Dogs?'

Sorry nodded feebly. 'Worse. I think about running but it's out there. Now. The thing. My only hope is that she's started not knowing things, like when I was supposed to be hit by the spear that hit you. She said I'd only been brought along to get in the way so you wouldn't get hit, but you did. It didn't happen! She even cried.'

'Cried!' said Urgh, in growing alarm.

'Yep! She said she doesn't know things about you, that you defy her knowledge, and it worries her.'

Urgh looked at his feet and thought about the axe in his pack.

'Go to sleep now,' shouted the Wise Wench. 'I need to dream quietly about what's happening in the village. Things are about to heat up.'

They did as they were told, minds full of their own woes.

When they awoke, she was behaving strangely.

The Wise Wench put her foot on the scree slope. Rocks moved about. She ran up a short way and ended up further back than where she had started. She scowled at the rocks and wrinkled her face up. 'OK, lads, best get those packs off Zephyr. She won't be able to go on. And leave the howdah here. We'll go on foot for...as long as it takes from now on.' It was dark but moonlight illuminated them. As the duo were loading up, the Wise Wench moved over to the pretty pig and kissed her, handing her a handful of apple pieces. 'Have no fear, beauty. You've served us well. Without you, we'd never have got so far. When it happens, take care and flee as far as you can. May fortune and the Great Sow guide you.' She then whispered something to her.

'Are you all right, Wise Wench?' said Urgh, concerned.

'Of course I am. Why?'

'You look like you've been crying.'

Urgh went over to Zephyr and rubbed her chin. 'I'll miss you, pretty pig, but we'll be back before you know it,' he sniffed. He wondered if she would be alright. Sorry scratched his neck and wondered what she would taste like roasted with those apples in her mouth. The Wise Wench interrupted his thoughts by thrusting the iron churn onto his back and strapping it on.

'Hmm,' said the Wise Wench, quietly. 'Well, it's a while since I came this way. Still, best foot forward!' she shouted, and ran at the slope. Sorry and Urgh exchanged sideways glances at each other before watching the athletic mixture of black knitted skirts and bonnet hurl up the scree, cursing and shouting. Zephyr began struggling up behind her, her trotters slipping on the loose stone, her smile momentarily bruised by effort. The Wise Wench went back to her and whispered something else in her ears, rubbed her down with the oil she'd been keeping for this precise moment, chuckling as she saw the picture of the hen with a black line through it on the jar. Then she gave Zephyr a gentle push away and turned back, rushing up the slope.

'Dragons and calves,' muttered Sorry to himself. 'I don't hold no truck with either calves or pigs. Both 'as profit in 'em as far as I can see. Cluck.'

Urgh stared sympathetically at his companion before rushing up the slope after the Wise Wench. 'I think he's gone mad,' he said, earnestly.

The Great Mole sighed as Sorry carried on talking to himself. Behind them, Zephyr looked confused and sad. She vainly tried a couple more times up the slope and then settled back to eating what was left of the apples.

Urgh took one last look back at his friend.

Sorry took one last look back at his lost supper.

Then they headed away uphill.

The slope was a hard climb for all of them. Fast as a step was taken, the slippery rocks below tugged their legs back downhill. It didn't help that it was still dark, but the Wise Wench was insistent that the day would be full and the quicker they started, the better. Sorry took this to mean that the *terrible something* was soon to be upon them. He looked about for escape routes but the more he thought about escape, the more he thought *it* might come upon him when he was alone. At least with companions he might get away while they were being eaten while still alive.

By dawn they had made excellent progress and, as the first of the sun's rays glimpsed at them, they had climbed to the foot of the first cliffs. The sunlight showed another, steeper scree slope above, which wound its way out perilously under the cliff.

The Wise Wench pulled Sorry up and round from the edge of the cliff. She seemed a bit uneasy. 'You lads carry on up. I've got to adjust my, erm, undergarments.' She smiled thinly as Sorry and Urgh marched off, the Great Mole glancing back furtively.

When they were out of sight, the Wise Wench checked the large fox picture was still in her pack, and, happy that it was and that it was easy to get at, marched on. Urgh and Sorry had not got far ahead and she soon caught up and passed them, heading up over scree and towards more solid-looking ground above. Soon, she was well ahead.

Urgh shook his head and was about to call for her when he heard something. Or thought he heard something; a distant clucking. He paused and waited but all he could hear was the quiet debate that Sorry was having with himself.

Urgh laughed and decided he was wrong. How could chickens get up here, anyway?

Time moved on. The cloud was low and flew past the Wise Wench in small gusts, adding to her air of mystery. She had squatted on a small cairn under a high cliff, but, here, the land was flatter, although very rocky. Little grew here save the yellow lichens of the huge stones which piled one on another like some vast fortification. Urgh thought about the giants' prison and gave a shudder.

'Urgh, you just scout on ahead a little, will you?' said the Wise Wench, pointing vaguely under the cliff.

Sorry squatted nearby quietly clucking to himself. 'They're coming,' he whispered.

Urgh did as he was told and picked his way over the stones. All seemed eerily still. The trail was broader here, and someone had marked the way with cairns which he followed, eventually coming to the edge of a steep cliff. He reeled as he saw the drop. Goblins don't mind heights if they aren't high enough to have a big drop with them. This one had a very big drop. He held onto a large stone and gave a little gasp.

Then he heard it again.

Clucking.

This time, there was no mistaking it.

Vast, deep clucking.

He peered into the gloom.

Suddenly, a grey shape appeared, then another, and another. Huge horrible shapes on spindly legs with great claws. They were chickens, but these were no ordinary chickens. They were *changed chickens*, massive chickens touched by an evil hand. And they had teeth! Great pointed teeth, and horns, and great black leathery wings. Urgh gasped. He knew what they were. He'd heard the bedtime stories and had to check under the bed and in the cupboard to make sure they weren't in his room as a gob-boy, but they were with him now: his childhood horror.

'Ayeeeee!' yelled Urgh. 'Fell-Poultry!'

He ran.

CHAPTER 20

'Ayeeeee!' yelled the dashing goblin. 'Giants!' he added, very loudly.

The goblin under-thug had been running for a while now, still sure that, at any moment, he would be eaten while still alive by some unseen giant hound behind. The rain had begun to fall, and in some feeble hopeful corner, he thought that might put the giants off. He soon spotted the village slumbering on its mound ahead and redoubled his efforts to reach safety. He had decided to tell the king the news and then hide down the village well for the rest of his days. The goblin ran past the end house and along the muddy lane, its edges enclosed by briars flapping in the wind. He pushed on through the first gate and leapt another. Then, he ran down over the old stone bridge and, taking a short cut over Bog Kettley's Meadow, he ran through the cows, scattering them. As he got closer to the village, he began to shout.

The king yawned and stretched. Looti, who had been propped up on him, fell to the ground with a crash. Unconcerned, the king looked about him. The field was littered with sleeping, snoring, and mumbling goblins, all slowly and quietly stirring. The area was littered with fins and false pointy teeth of some size and quantity. The king smiled. How he loved days like this. He stood on stage and, in his loudest possible voice, shouted, 'Good morning, scum! Now, I don't know who is going to do it, but I want breakfast, and I want it now!' He sat down, held up a knife and fork, and waited, impatiently.

Then he heard someone screaming.

The under-thug ran straight through the middle of the village brown screaming 'Giants!' over and over at the top of his voice. The villagers, alarmed by this sudden pronouncement, started joining him in screaming. Others started to dig holes to hide in. Even Looti began to squeal. Only the king remained composed as ever. He blew his nose on his regal yellow handkerchief, embroidered with pictures of haddock knights fighting over a pair of fine hunting pelicans, and adjusted his shirt. Then, he casually stood and surveyed the crowd of screaming, digging peasants and picked out the dashing under-thug, whom he signaled with a finger.

Durth suddenly shot out of his house wearing only his bright turquoise underthings and carrying a huge spear. He ran towards the king to protect him from the *assassin* he'd just seen running into the village shouting oaths of defiance, or it might have been that—his hearing wasn't great these days so he'd decided as usual he was right. The king needed protecting! A moment later, the dashing figure was on the ground, pinned by one of Durth's favorite grips—the stag-beetle.[79] 'Don't worry, Your Roundness. I have him!' shouted Durth, extra proudly.

The under-thug toiled underneath Durth's grip and then went still, he suddenly recognized he was close enough to the king to be expected to grovel and unsuccessfully tried to bow very low. The king looked him up and down. 'Let him go, Dirt,' he said, calmly. 'This is no assassin or foe. Why, this is the very inconsequential nobody I've been expecting to arrive unexpectedly for some time. So, the giants are here are they, my lad? Who'd have thought time would have flown by, one-more-than-one weeks next Thodsday already? Well, well, well. Has the Wise Wench been gone for one-more-than-one weeks already?'

'Nope,' said Durth, panting. 'Your Majesty,' he added, for safety.

The under-thug wanted to speak but couldn't, instead he whimpered and waved an arm back towards the forest. The king smiled, stepped down and put a calming hand on his shoulder. 'No

---

[79] As we may have mentioned before, goblins love giving things names and go to quite ludicrous degrees to ensure they know what a thing is called. In truth, this is a useful tactic since goblins, as we have established, get bored pretty quickly and tend to forget about things. This is especially handy when things they may forget are potentially useful, such as a good spot to fish (often called a yum-spot), a good place for kindling (often known as a 'heh-heh'), and things like fighting holds and weapons. The annoying news for the females is that a male goblin is far more likely to remember the name of his luckiest whelk, truncheon, or sleeping undisturbed spot, than he is his breed-bound's name.

worry, lad. The Wise Wench is due back at any moment.' He looked around expectedly in the direction of the mountains and then at Durth and grinned. 'Master Durth,' he said, 'prepare the Kettle and rouse Master Whippet. The Wise Wench will be back at any moment, her mighty quest over!' He put his arm around the trembling under-thug and said, 'I'd nearly lost track of time, you know. I could have sworn that the Wise Wench had only been gone a few days—'

'—She has, lord,' interjected Durth.

'—and yet here we are. She's been gone over one weeks and we've hardly missed her. It's Thodsday, and now is the time for attack—'

'—It's not Thodsday for another one-after-the-one-after-one-one-and-one days, Your Wrongness—' said Durth.

'—and yet here we are, the final battle. Let trumpet sound! Let the minstrel sing the song of victory. Let pyres be lit and let the banners of war be unfurled.' The king suddenly paused and looked at Durth. His face suddenly fell. 'Not Thodsday?' he said, quietly.

Durth shook his head.

'Not for one-after-the-one-after-one-one-and-one more days?'

Durth nodded, gravely.

The king sighed. 'Well, that's just typical of a giant and a woman!' he shouted. 'You can always rely on the one to be early and the other to be late!' He paused and thought for a moment. 'Still, I must be off!' he shouted and ran across the meadow to his house to get packing.

Looti gave chase.

The place was strangely empty when they went in. 'Get packing, my round bundle of joy. We're going to leave the village right away!' the king shouted up the stairs.

Looti burst in. 'You're not leaving?' she snapped.

The king looked thoughtful and found his heaviest backpack. 'Well, yes,' he said.

She narrowed her eyes and scowled at him. 'And what about the villagers?' she snapped.

'What about them?'

307

'They are waiting to be saved.'

'Not possible.'

'And what about the Wise Wench? What did she tell you?'

There was a knock on the door. Whippet stood there holding a bag. He grinned, feebly, and handed it to the king, who snatched it and shut the door in his face.

'What's that, great king?' asked Looti, her concentration momentarily taken by the swinging pendulous key at the king's waist.

'A speakme bag,' said the king, scowling at it and moving towards the fire. He had a small, violent, internal debate. 'She expects me to toss it on the fire right now, I suppose. Well, I'm not having it!' he yelled at the heavens—well, *rafters*, actually. In answer, a small pile of dusty mouse-droppings fell, dropping into the king's open mouth. He gulped them down and pushed the bag onto the timber beam on top of the fireplace.

'So, you have to put it on the fire to hear its message!' said Looti.

'I don't *have* to do anything!' snapped the king, petulantly. 'You don't think I care about what she says, do you? Her opinions are irrelevant!'

'Are you going to throw it on the fire?'

'Nope! Over my dead body. Anyway, it's not just a message. I did one for the giants' chief. It's sort of like being there, but not.'

'I bet it's important.'

'Not as important as getting away from the giants. Have you ever seen a giant? They aren't pretty. And they definitely aren't easy-going. Nope, I've been tricked by her before. She told me the giants would be ages, one weeks after she left actually, so she either lied or she's losing her touch, both of which make her, as I have said once before, irrelevant.' The king swirled haughtily, and, as he did, his key swung, knocking the bag off the mantle. It bounced off a curiously strategic alignment of logs and ornaments and onto the fire.

The bag erupted into a thaumaturgic cloud of colorful fire. In the flames, the cackling image of a scowling Wise Wench suddenly popped into being. 'Irrelevant, am I?' she said. 'Well, let me tell you something. If I'd have told you there was no way we'd be back before the giants came, I know you would have snuck off, which is why I didn't. Anyway, all you have to do is stall them for a few days. Use your initiative. I know you'll succeed.'

The king smiled knowingly. 'No. I'm sorry to contradict you, Wise Wench,' he said, 'but it's not a few days; it's one-after-the-one-after-one-one-and-one more days. Anyway, listen: I'm king, and I decide what happens and what doesn't.'

'So you're not up to tricking a few giants for a few...for a while, then?'

'Of course, I could do it easily.' The king looked like his regal pride had hurt and that some peasant would have to suffer accordingly.

'Good, that's sorted then,' smiled the Wise Wench.

The king looked like he was about to say something, smiled, and stopped. 'Anything you say, oh Wise Wench.' *Obey her to her face—maybe—but as soon as the fire dies, I'm off,* thought the king, deviously.

The figure in the fire frowned. 'Oh,' said the vision in flame, 'and that idea you just had about sneaking off, it won't work. There are several giants waiting on the bridge you were intending to escape via. You'll all be killed.'

The king scowled and had a sudden thought.

'And that won't work either.'

The king frowned even deeper but then suddenly smiled.

'No, nor that one. And, before you ask, I'm not dead yet,' she snarled. 'At least, as far as I know, although if I'm right, we're about to be in the most terrible peril with some fell-poultry, but luckily I've...anyway, that's not relevant. And don't think I don't know what you're up to with the adviser. I've secreted several bags like these in strategic locations and I've left word that they are to be given to HER MAJESTY if you show the slightest sign of leaving, or the merest hint of cowardice, so get out there and face them. Bravely, Your Devioustude. And, by the way, don't forget Lady Carline is there to help.'

'I'm not asking the advice of a bir—' began the king. The fire suddenly popped and began to smoke and die.

309

As the image and flames sputtered, the Wise Wench seemed to lean out of the hearth. 'Don't forget,' she said, 'how stupid giants are. Good luck, great Kin—'

The fire perished.

The king looked thoughtful. He considered leaving anyway but didn't dare risk HER finding out. His head hurt. He walked about for a while then said: 'Oh, Lord Bigsbrain, Giver of Good Ideas, give me a good idea,' under his breath. Then, suddenly, his eyes fell on the cards, lying on the table. Her Majesty must have been playing solo dead-cockerel's bluff. He began to smile and turned to Looti. 'Well, at least we have a few cards in our hand. Foresight, young Looti, foresight, as well as iron discipline and an absolute disregard to the seriousness of the situation we find ourselves in. Decisive action is required! Go and fetch me my orchestra, immediately!'

'Immediately, Your Conducterment,' said Looti, following him as he strode out purposefully.

It was later.

Durth was stood on the outer wall above the Southern Gate which, on his orders, had been closed and barred. A wicked array of spikes and especially sharpened cutlery had been fixed on its outer face around the barbed spears already there. Durth played with his megaphone, nervously. At his side were a few village guards, the others having been summoned by runner as soon as the escaping under-thug had appeared, and were safely hiding nearby. Beyond, crouched the mummers and orchestra, quietly nervous at the coming performance but reassured that, for once, the king would not be exacting *the payment.*

King Stormgrunties appeared from the Great Mouth, held aloft on his war palanquin that was painted deeper than the deepest black and arrayed with polished steel barbs. From a distance, his carriage looked like a huge, evil porcupine—exactly the effect its owner wished for. His bearers were resplendent in black leather, the same clothes worn by Looti, his adviser. They slowly made their way over to Durth, their leather creaking with each movement.

Durth looked out again at the group of giants' that had emerged some distance away at the edges of the forest. He could see at least several of them camped by the old bridge which stood over Gurgle-Brook.

The king arrived and climbed the short ladder onto the wall to stand at Durth's side. The Chief Thug handed the king one end of a hugely thick rope and pointed to the group of giants, then towards the arrayed mummers hiding with their various silhouettes of monstrosities—or parts thereof that they had made or scavenged from the shark festival—just out of sight of the giants. 'Now, you pointless oafs,' said the king warmly to the ensemble, 'when I give the signal, you will begin your act as Durth has been instructing you.'

Durth looked both proud and a little weary; some of the actors rubbed various bits of themselves that had got in his way when he was cross.

'One slight change of plan,' added the king. 'I want the various noises and protestations, growls and roars to be performed *contrapuntally.* That'll make it sound even more menacing.'

The actors stared at Durth nervously. 'Well, you heard the king! When it's done, do it contra— just how he said to.' Durth crossed his hands, closing the subject.

The king surveyed the giants regally and then uttered a loud, condescending 'bah.'

His subjects answered with bahs of their own until it sounded like a herd of sheep had gathered.

The king frowned at his subjects, shushed them, and said, 'I can't see their chief.' He signaled for Durth to hand him the megaphone and, in a clear commanding voice, called out, 'I am King Stormgrunties the many-many-and-lots-after-more-than-many-dead-King Stormgrunties-after-the-first, king of the Great Forest, ...' The king paused as a big rock flew his way. Luckily, it crashed into someone else, so he continued, '...be-keeper and guardian of the Substitute Great Mole, holder of Gwordoomdoomdoomdoomdoom, the Mop of the Dreaded Magpie People, ruler absolute of the Kingdom of Mudge, Spray, and Tottle-by-the-Mire, the keeper of the Stoat Hat of Justice, the Arch-

Magicmaster Supreme, his Cunningtude Grace the Honor of Tunt, slayer of Lucy Carter and her puppy Snuffles. His Massive Mightiness.' He paused for breath and smiled and winked at Durth before continuing. 'You are on my bridge and must pay the *special toll* due to your extreme ugliness.'

The giants had heard every word and had begun to scratch their heads at the titles, which meant absolutely nothing to them. They decided to throw some rocks as those usually cured things. They hurled a few at the little goblin, but most just hit the walls or other goblins, much to their annoyance. One of them, a fairly smart giant, had sent for Ate Eyes who arrived from the chief's breakfast camp, wheezing.

'Ah,' shouted the king on spying the approaching giant, 'I see another ugly juggle of faces has joined the band. Well, what do they call you? 'Pretty,' perhaps?' The king laughed at his own joke, indicating that everyone else should do so. Soon the air was filled with nervous forced laughter, violently encouraged by Durth.

Ate Eyes colored and shouted, thinly, 'MY NAME IS NOT IMPORTANT, GOBLIN!'

'Something embarrassing is it?!' shouted the king, merrily. Some of the goblins nearby began to laugh properly. The king stuck his chest out and laughed, as loudly as he could. Unfortunately, he then began to cough, loudly. After he had finished, he stared at the group. 'Anyway!' he roared. 'I have a message, but I don't deal with underlings and dismal nobodies and peasants. Get your chief and I will talk with him. Otherwise, I shall have no choice but to unleash the—something—on you.' At this moment, the king shook the huge rope he held and, on his instruction, the noise orchestra began to use kazoos, megaphones, rattles, and musical saws to deliver a curious, other-worldly racket. As they did, the other mummers came forward with cut-out fins, pointy barbed tentacles, and fake dangly claws which they paraded from behind the wall so the giants could only see the silhouette appendages. As the king tightened his grip on the pretend monster, the orchestra redoubled their efforts—loudly humming on their kazoos and 'mnarr'ing into their megaphones while those with musical saws made admirable glissando. The king nodded approvingly as the cacophony increased and pretended to tug on the rope as though holding something.

The giants looked nervous. They had heard stories of the thing that had teeth and wings. They looked overhead, then underhead, then over and under the other head. Ate Eyes clenched his fist and shouted 'WHO DO YOU THINK YOU ARE, TELLING GIANTS WHAT TO DO? YOU'LL SURRENDER NOW OR I'LL–'

'–or you'll what? I'll tell you what you'll do. You'll fetch your chief double quick or I'll make sure you're the first that IT comes for.' The noise and waving of cut-outs reached fever pitch and the king pretended to be tugged violently by the rope.

There was a short discussion and Ate Eyes went back to the chief's camp. The other giants remained, nervously, and backed away a few paces to the far side of the bridge, just to be sure.

The king smiled conspiratorially at Durth. 'Now, Durth,' he said, in a whisper, 'get Whippet to bring the Hamster to the front of the village. Have the children blow up as many pigs' bladders as possible, and get me a bacon sandwich, I'm absolutely famished. In the meantime, adviser, I suggest we pass the time in some calm and useful pursuit.' He led the way back to his Moot House, regally waving his hand.

Time moved on.

Looti surveyed the board. Her great badger was cornered by the king's cormorant. She still had her turbot-and-toadstool, but that was pinned in by the king's shark. Finally, she decided on her move, bringing her badger sideways, taking the king's ferret, his allocated masterpiece for the game. 'Splat!' she said, happily.[80] The king knew

---

[80] Splat, also known as Master Dung's Doomsday, Farmyard Apocalypse, or Naughty Creature's Ruin amongst others, is a curious goblin game with countless local and regional rules. The playing figures tend to be similar—sharks, great badgers, turnips, poultry, pigs, squirrels, and other locally-sourced animals—and the general concept of taking over the Farmyard of Ruin by cornering an allocated masterpiece is almost always the same. Of course everyone cheats, has their own

he had lost again. Looti had a fine mind, not that he was remotely interested.

'Adviser, who's king?' asked the king.

Looti reconsidered her move, making the fatal error of moving her great badger into play.

'Splat!' shouted the king with finality, and he pushed all the pieces over.

'So, when you were looking at the cards back at your house, you were thinking about bluff then?' she asked, trying not to notice the key. 'Using the fins and bits of odd looking wood as silhouettes to make the giants think we have a monster. You are so much more clever than anyone ever.'

'Exactly,' he smiled. 'As even the irrelevant scum in this village know well, goblins are too small to fight—well, at least too small to fight fair[81]—so we have to cheat, lie, and bluff our way through the cauldron of misery we call life.' The king finished his last mouthful of bacon sandwich and allowed his napkin master to wipe the royal mouth corners. The king stood up, yawned, summoned his palanquin, and headed back to the battlements.

The giants were still stood by the bridge below, watching. The king got out his yellowest handkerchief and waved it at them. They made several rude noises in response. 'Well, how common,' said the king, happily.

The guards stood at the battlements now, and upon his instruction, gob-wenches took turns in moving the silhouettes of goblins that had been nailed to the walls.

Whippet ran across the village brown and up the ladder to greet the king. He bowed. 'The Hamster is ready to move at any

---

local variations and is generally prepared to come to pinching and blows to win. It is the noblest of goblin games that doesn't involve pigs.

[81] Goblins are, without doubt, the nastiest and sneakiest fighters. Those who can be bothered to listen to the old songs may find a whole deviant array of tricks, techniques, and dirty fighting methods. From throwing sand in eyes, to rotten eggs, through stabbing opponent's feet from behind cover of a dozen comrades to pelting opponents with rotting fish heads to soften them up, the goblin is endlessly resourceful at cheating.

moment, Your Cunningness,' he grinned. 'Also, your Potentness, the children have inflated many-some-one-and-one-more pigs' bladders.' Whippet signaled over to the village brown where several children lay, exhausted.

The king continued to waft his handkerchief at the giants, who were now making obscene gestures with their upper arms and fingers. 'Well done. I want it all ready to go at a moments' command.' Suddenly, he spotted movement and grinned. 'And get those annoying children back in the pit. Aha, here we go. Now we've got trouble.'

The chief of the giants emerged, wearing a tiara on each head to signify he was the boss. He scowled and shouted, 'I HEAR THAT YOU WANT TALK. WELL, LET ME TELL YOU SOME—'

'—Oh, do shut up!' shouted the king through his megaphone. 'I've not walked all the way up here to listen to your small talk about badgers and the depredations of pole cats!'

The chief's faces reddened in anger.

'Now, which one of you ugly heads is in charge?'

'I AM!' they all said in unison, and then realized that one of the giants at the back was smirking. The chief pointed at him, and his middle head said, 'TAKE HIM AWAY AND PICKLE HIM!' to a nearby guard.

The smirking giant's smirk faded. He fell on his knees, begging, 'NO, NOT PICKLING!' before being led away.

'Having trouble?' shouted the king with some amusement.

'NO!' snapped the middle head.

'So, which one of you pretty faces is really in charge?' shouted the king once more, taking the pretend rope leash as he leant further forward on the wall.

'I AM!' shouted the outside heads.

The king put down his megaphone and sarcastically began drumming his fingers on the battlement. 'I never have trouble letting everyone HERE know who's in charge. ME! I'm waiting. My fingers grow cold,' he sighed.

315

Behind him, the goblins were torn between admiration, fear of what the giants might do, and greater fear of what their deranged mad king might do first.

The chief's heads had a short conference, couldn't decide, and had to play a quick round of duck-goose-duck to settle things. At its end, the right-hand head smiled and looked up. 'I'M IN CHARGE, SHORTY!' it snapped. A couple of giants patted him on the back and repeated the word 'SHORTY' while laughing.

'I may be smaller than you, but at least I don't have a face that would make my nose run away in fear,' laughed the king. 'One-more-than-one such face, in fact!'

Cheers from the goblin villagers.

'We may indeed be shorter than you, but we are many, as are our strong sons and stronger daughters. You are merely enormous and ugly!' The king tore his shirt open slightly.

More cheers, and a trumpet call.

'THAT'S NOT TRUE!' snapped the giant chief, and, after calling backwards into the crowd, a pair of very, very ugly giants emerged. One had an extra, useless stunted head between his two normal ones, and the other's right head sloped upwards unnaturally. 'BEHOLD MY TWO SONS, SLOPEYFACE AND WIDE! NOW, LEARN TO FEAR, LITTLE GREMLIN! MNARRRRRR!!'

'Well, what a fine example of giant beauty and strength we have here! Slopeyface. Hmmm, Slopeyface. I'll wager that a giant maid would rather set fire to herself than have to kiss those slopey lips. I know I would. And as for Wide there, well, you do have a way with names! Spot on! That's one thing I like about giants—nothing!'

Vast cheers. The king removed a pretend hat and doffed it.

The giants shuffled about a bit, and there was a horn cry. Rocks were picked up. Moments later, over a countless-and-then-more giants stood in a long line, with half as many great dogs. All the giants had unnaturally pointed and barbed weapons which suddenly reminded the king of Moaris. The giant chief stepped to the front and said, clearly, 'IT'S TIME FOR ME TO PUT MY BATTLE CAP ON AND PREPARE FOR WAR!' He lifted out the squashed, and by now, somewhat decaying Moaris and waved him at the king. 'WELL, LET'S SEE NOW. LET'S HAVE A LOOK AT THE HAT. HMMM, IT LOOKS VERY FAMILIAR, DOESN'T IT? COULD IT BE—OH NO!' shouted the chief with mock horror. 'OH NO, IT'S THE LAST LITTLE GOBLIN I MET! BOO HOO!' he began to pretend to sob. The giants began to laugh.

Looti held the king back.

'SO NOW, WHERE IS THE *DOG-KILLER*? I WANT HIM. *NOW!*' shouted the chief. His giants cheered. 'I WANT HIM BROUGHT TO ME ON A PLATTER, AND YOU, BIG-MOUTH, CAN CRAWL TOWARDS ME WITH HIM BEFORE I EAT YOU AND DEAL... VERY HARSHLY INDEED WITH HIM!'

The king regained his composure, long enough to see Durth, who, in anger, had snuck over the wall, and was sneaking towards the giants. He quickly glanced back at the chief. 'You don't come here into MY Kingdom making demands. I'M the KING, and I MAKE THE DEMANDS!' shouted the king.

Durth was creeping closer, quickly slinking from cowpat to cowpat across the meadow.

'GET READY TO ATTACK, LADS,' came the response.

The king waved a key and shook the rope. 'Do you know what this is, dad to one-more-than-one monstrosities?' said the king.

The giant chief stared at it. 'A KEY? AND. SOME ROPE' he said, uncertainly.

'Oh, bravo, bravo,' the king clapped before continuing, 'no, not rope. A leash! And do you know what they are for?'

'NO!' shouted the chief. 'I'M NOT BOTHERED WHAT IT'S FOR! ENOUGH TALKING, IT'S TIME FOR SLAUGHTER! LADS, GET READY TO CHARGE, AND SAVE THE LITTLE FAT ONE FOR ME. I HAVE SOMETHING SPECIAL IN MIND FOR HIM.'

Durth was getting nearer to the giants, his eyes fixed on their chief, and his headgear in particular. The king noticed Durth gripped a short spear and, even from quite a distance, could see he looked very, incredibly cross. The bullocks nearby observed him idly, although each was careful to keep their distance from him.

'Well, you should, because last time you came, a certain pet of mine had got out. Your lads met one of them.' The king turned to the crowd behind the walls and gave a quick wink.

The giants began to look uneasy, well aware of the story of the thing with wings.

'And it seems to have got loose somewhere. I'm sure it'll turn up somewhere.' He began to look around in an exaggerated manner, carefully observing corners, under boxes, and checking beneath his hands.

'WE AREN'T AFRAID OF YOUR PET MONSTER!' lied the giant chief, and put his hands on his hips. 'IN FACT, WE LAUGH AT YOUR PET MONSTER!' He signaled for his men to laugh, and weakly, they joined him, while looking nervously about.

'But that's not what this key and leash are for!' shouted the king. 'You see, the one that's escaped is just the baby. You know, the tiny *baby monster* your men saw. I have the mother here!' he waved the leash, whispering, 'now everyone, get monstering.'

Suddenly the silhouettes began to parade about, fins danced, odd shapes lurched and a chorus of kazoos and mnarrs echoed and other odd noises echoed.

'And I'll just bet that she'll be very angry when she finds out her baby has gone,' he finished with a shout.

'DID HE SAY 'MOTHER'?' said one of the giants.

'So, I'll tell you what, chiefy,' continued the king, haughtily. 'I feel very sorry for you, what with you not even getting one decent head out of one-one-and-one, and with you having sons that look like cart accidents. So I'll tell you what I'll do. You have until dawn tomorrow to withdraw from MY Kingdom. Until dawn tomorrow or I'll let her out. And will she be mad. Oh, and just one more thing. Do you know what she eats?'

The chief shook his head, nervously.

'Giant!' The king shook the rope and doffed his imaginary hat. 'Anyway, I'd love to chat all day, but I've got important things to do. Cheese to be eaten, cormorants to be greased, swans to be rubbed, and the like, so I'll not see you here bright and early tomorrow morning. If you know what's good for you! Good day!'

The giant chief gave a little, absentminded wave.

'Oh, just one more thing,' shouted the king glancing towards Durth. 'As a visitor, I feel I should give you a gift.'

The giant chief inadvertently smiled, and as he did, Durth suddenly appeared a little way ahead of him and held the spear back. 'Miffed!' he yelled, and hurled it. It flew through the air with the barest of whistles, and struck the giant's third head right in the eye. It gave a yelp, and fell dead on the giant's shoulder. Durth tore his shirt open, turned and then ran back as fast as he could to the village, a hail of huge, slow, easily-dodged giant spears and rocks falling about him.

The giants picked up their injured chief and went back to their camp.

The king climbed down the ladder and strolled through the cheering villagers back to the Moot House, hand-in-hand with Looti.

High above at his home, the lace curtains twitched.

CHAPTER 21

The great black feral chickens were just behind Urgh! He could hear their foul clucks and taste the appalling stench of their breath, the odor of the *Farmyard from Beyond*. He ran at full pelt, screaming, but they came closer and closer. From somewhere distant, he heard a pig squeal and his heart sank, but then his own terror drew him out of his misery into a new place of fear and despair.

He remembered the tales of nasty farmers who mistreated their chickens, geese, and other farmyard birds, and he knew how the stories always ended: with the farmer in bed, unaware of the dreadful cluck, cluck, cluck coming up the stairs; not seeing the baleful eyes filled with hate, and not knowing the black wings that flapped, flapped, flapped until the sudden snap of the dreadful beak and then, after, the terrible, terrible egg that would be laid.

Snap! The beak snapped at Urgh's back, tearing his shirt. He squealed and gave a loud oath to Lord Noc before glancing back to see a vision of terror; a chicken of calamity at his shoulder, its terrible wattle swaying evilly at his back. He reached into his magic sack for his special don't-chase-me smell spell in its special magic cow's nose.

Then he fell.

He'd fallen on a small stone and his ankle twisted. He yelped. The chicken put a great claw on his chest and crowed, terrifyingly. It lifted its head and prepared for the final strike with its deadly beak and its pointy teeth. It's fearfully engorged wattle danced erect above its terrible face. Some of the other poultry—dreadful palsied things with great mangy feathers and crooked claws—rushed in for the feast.

Then there was a noise.

The chicken stopped.

The noise got louder and, as it did, a mist and a curious feral smell, like that of countless foxes and wolves, gripped the air.

The other fell-poultry stopped and looked up.

'MNARRRR!' said the noise. 'I am the Grey Fox of the Fallen Wood. Shall I feast on fresh meat today?'

The great chickens clucked quietly under their breath.

Urgh looked over the top of his chin and could just see a badly-painted fox on a huge canvas looming upside down from the mist. He looked back at the giant chicken before him. It seemed nervous. Behind it, the others widened their eyes.

The fox gave out a great echoing scream, which sounded remarkably like a woman's voice yelling through a megaphone. As it did (or, rather, as she did) the air was filled with the sounds of bursting fire as Sorry hurled some of his marbles at them.

The chickens scrawked and fled. Urgh watched as they ran in the most ungainly way possible, with legs at angles and heads pitched forwards. They fled in poultryesque terror.

The Wise Wench put the picture down, and Sorry, who had stood on top of a huge rock holding up his section, let that go. The picture crumpled on the ground. The Wise Wench folded her portable megaphone back up and grinned.

'That's the problem with poultry,' said the Wise Wench. 'They're stupid. Stupid and short-sighted. They remind me of the king. Come along, we haven't got much time. We only have some-less-one days to get the milk and get back to the village.' She marched off along the path as fast as she could.

'Hang on, hang on!' yelled Urgh. 'What about our faithful steed? Won't they go back for her?'

The Wise Wench turned. 'Don't worry,' she said, 'she's already far away and, anyway, I took the precaution of lathering her with poultry repellent before I left her. She's quite safe. Anyway, come and look at this.' She indicated for Urgh to join them. He moved over and his jaw dropped open upwards as he saw the broken acrid boiling landscape beyond. A twisting ridge led towards it.

'Now, let's get moving into the poisonous land beyond. Our quest is reaching its end.' She seemed almost cheerful as she put the words *poisonous* and *land* together.

'Oh, great,' said Sorry, miserably, and followed them.

'I don't believe there's any such thing as poultry repellent,' said the Great Mole, cynically. As he did, the Great Mole put a consoling arm around Sorry's non-existent shoulders and whispered something to him. They began to laugh.

'You're right, Great Mole. Why *didn't* she rub it on us?'

The Wise Wench whispered to herself and followed the others down the steep path. The route was so steep, Urgh thought he might end up falling over the top of his head and back down the mountain. It was hard going. The wind howled about them and increased in fury the higher they got. They caught glimpses of the tortured, burning land beyond, and Sorry, at least, was cheerful at just how fiery the land might get. They wanted to stop, but the Wise Wench forced them on. Sorry seemed happier than Urgh had ever seen him. He was merrily engaged in a singing lesson with himself and seemed oblivious to aching muscles. Surreptitiously, he even allowed the Great Mole to play with his fiery marbles.

The path broadened as it reached a plateau and, suddenly, after several hours' hard slog, they reached a great cairn. The Wise Wench stopped near a painted arrow on the ground which had a picture of goblin with an uncountable number of chins. The arrow pointed to a very narrow pathway which descended sharply. Urgh was too exhausted to worry about that and flopped down on a large rock. Sweat stung his eyes and it was some time before his vision cleared. The Wise Wench stood on the path a little way below. Beyond her, the land fell shallowly down an ash-covered slope and into a wide, flat expanse interrupted by the occasional huge bowl-shaped opening in the ground. Foul yellow mists emerged from each of these holes and Urgh, for some inexplicable reason, was sure the holes had no bottom. The land about them was grey and featureless, save for the occasional struggling thorny bush which had unluckily landed here and taken tenuous root. In the center of this grey land rose a black peak with half its top open in a vast gaping maw. Mist came from it, and Urgh became afraid.

Then he noticed the cows. Huge blackened cows as tall as a young oak staggering about on impossibly spindly legs and picking out lichen patches from the parched earth. Grey unhealthy-looking udders swung under each, save one. *That*, thought Urgh, *must be the bull*, a massive creature with horns as big as a house. Even from here, far away, it looked menacing. But there was worse to come. Suddenly, one of the great cows looked up, an expression of surprise and fear crossed its face and, with a rasping praise to Lord Noc, fire gushed from its backside and mouth. It burped, shook its tail, and began eating again.

'Well, THAT'S something you don't see every day!' said Sorry, happily.

'Right, you lads, get the milking gear out. It's time for what will probably be the next-but-one-to-one last great test,' said the Wise Wench.

Next-but-one-to-one last? thought Urgh. *Oh great. So what else is coming that's worse, and why am I so damn smart that I think of these questions, and why am I asking me?*

The Wise Wench got some chalk out and sat before the smooth slab of stone at the top of the pass. Urgh and Sorry sat down. 'I bet this involves danger,' said Sorry to himself. The Wise Wench drew a rather pathetic stick figure with several legs and an udder. Urgh put his hand up.

'Yes?' said the Wise Wench.

'Erm, pardon me for being critical, your Wise Wenchlyness, but what is that supposed to be?' said Urgh, pointing and frowning at the chalk figure.

The Wise Wench scowled. 'That, artless fool,' she said, impatiently, under her breath, 'is a heifer. Can't you see its udders?' She pointed at the poorly-drawn udders beneath. Urgh shrugged his shoulders. Sorry wished he could do that.

The Wise Wench drew a stick figure with a flag at the head end, and another figure at the other end. Sorry immediately noticed the figure at the head end didn't have any shoulders. She crossed her arms and looked at Urgh. 'What is going to happen is this. Urgh, you will be at the udder end, milking the cow, while Sorry will be at its head, keeping its attention up with this flag.' From her pack, she produced a large yellow and red striped flag and handed it to Sorry. 'And I will be busy with this.' She got out the tuba.

'I want to die,' said Sorry, miserably, and took the flag.

'You won't have to,' whispered the Great Mole from his pocket and began to whisper.

'Do you think he's up to this?' said Urgh, assuming Sorry was talking to himself. 'And, if you don't mind me saying, what are you doing while we milk these terrible cows? I mean, it's very nice to have a musical accompaniment but what use is it?"

The Wise Wench wrinkled her face up. 'One thing at a time, and yes, he is up to it. Well, probably. How would I know about him?' She crossed her arms again. 'Now, the thing you've got to watch out for is the tail lifting. When the tail lifts, she's about to explode, so whatever you do, BACK OFF! Understood?'

Sorry and Urgh nodded. 'Go on, tell her,' whispered the Great Mole to Sorry.

'Now, while you are doing the easy bit, I'll be doing the hard part,' said the Wise Wench as she picked up the small tuba and blew it.

In the distance, the bull looked up, startled. It scratched the ground in front of it, snorted, and bellowed.

The bellow sounded just like an enormous tuba.

'If you don't mind me asking, oh Wise Wench,' said Sorry, stroking the Great Mole's fur sneakily out of their sight, 'what was the plan *before*?'

'Before what, pointless one?'

'Well,' said Sorry, smugly, 'I mean, I'm dead, aren't I? Technically no longer with you. Fallen out of the story. What were you going to do upon that eventuality? I mean, for the purposes of argument, there are technically only one-more-than-one of you here now...technically. I mean, you couldn't wave the flag and play the tuba, could you?' Urgh thought he had an academic point and made it succinctly.

'He has and he did,' said the Wise Wench to Urgh. 'But I'm not prepared to answer you.'

'Why not?' asked Sorry.

'Female prerogative,' she answered, testily.

'Oh, great. Thanks for that,' said Sorry, glumly.

'Right,' said the Wise Wench, 'down we go to our destiny!'

'Do we die at all?' asked Urgh, nonchalantly.

'Nope,' said the Wise Wench, helpfully. 'At least, those of us who should still be in the story don't, as far as I know. As for the others,' she said, staring at Sorry, 'I really can't, in all honesty, vouch for their survival chances.'

Urgh wished he'd started asking plain questions some time ago.

The air in the meadow below was foul and reeked of devotions to the Lord Noc, although it smelt a tiny bit like eggy-bread, one of Urgh's favorite snacks. Urgh and Sorry marched purposefully but with caution down across the meadow, aware of the tuba playing on the far side where the bull was. The sounds echoed over back and across the foul field, amplified and changed. As they walked, grey clouds of ash danced around their feet. Some stuck to their trouser legs. Sorry crunched across a large patch of lichen and, in the distance, one of the smallest heifers looked up. It began to slowly pick its way towards them. Urgh looked across at the herd. There seemed to be about several-and-some females, some of which were clearly younger than the others. He spotted the one coming towards them and said, nervously, 'I think we should try for that one. It seems much smaller than the rest and, perhaps, won't be so much trouble.' Sorry nodded, absentmindedly.

'We need to be careful,' whispered the Great Mole to Sorry. 'You heard what she said: you've dropped out of the story. *Us*. It's all about *us* being safe and warm and full of food and making big fires, always.' Sorry nodded.

'Who are you talking to?' asked Urgh.

'Just myself,' he answered.

In the distance, the tuba playing grew louder. The Wise Wench had skirted around the edges of the meadow, picking her way between large pumice stones to lead the bull away. She had finally reached a spur of rock above the bull and began playing properly. From her vantage point, she could see the huge horns, several-some-and-one-more goblins' wide, and smell the foul breath snorting out from the bull's great flat nose. It stank of sweat, sulphur, and badness. The bull, annoyed that another was trying to muscle in on his heifer harem, tried to pick his way towards her.

Seeing her plan working, she played louder and edged further away from her companions.

Urgh came to the edges of a small rise in the rock, where a gaping hole came ripping from the very earth below. Here, truly, was the exit from the domain of Lurky,[82] whose eyes never see the sun, and whose soul is the same. Urgh picked up some of the ash from around the ground and threw it in, muttering, 'Oh, terrible mole, Lurky. Stay down your pit, today. The light above will blind you, burn, burn, burn it, oh!'

Sorry removed the heavy churn and gave a sigh. Instantly, cool air struck his damp back and he smiled. 'Now might be a good time to flee,' said the Great Mole, 'but, sadly,' it added, 'I don't rate your chances of success, my dear friend. Get a mouthful of fire marbles, just in case.' As Sorry stuffed his mouth with marbles, the pair peeked over the foul hole. Beyond it, the heifer had separated from the main herd and was nearby, but not yet far enough away from the bull to risk trying.

Seeing the youngsters below, the Wise Wench stood up, and blew as hard as she could into the tuba. A huge rasping note came forth.

The bull looked up, bellowed, then began to clamber awkwardly towards her.

'Look,' said Urgh, 'you get some of those lichens and try to entice the heifer towards us.'

'Why don't you do that?' snapped Sorry, speaking clumsily, his mouth crammed with marbles.

'Because I'm going to milk the Noc-damned thing,' he said, and scowled.

Sorry considered for a moment, and then quickly picked his way over to the lichen. He scraped a little into his hand, stood up

---

[82] The Mole of Darkness. Amongst giant, apocalyptic moles, he was badder than bad. His fur was pestilence, his claws oblivion, his snout death, and his mole-hills abomination. So they said.

and mumbled, 'Nice lichen for the moo-cow, nice moo-cow. Come and get it! Only some-and-one gold pigs a pound!' Suddenly, there was a vast explosion as some heifers simultaneously expunged, flames gushing from before and behind. The noise ripped from one side of the meadow to the other, crashing from rock and cliff, amplified and re-amplified, as the terrific exploding wind was unleashed on the land about.

A few moments later, the air was still, and they began munching again.

Sorry stood up again and dusted his clothes off. The smallest heifer had seen him, and began, very cautiously, to advance further. He eyed up escape routes and realized that, wherever he ran, he would have to pass something dangerous.

Above, the bull had reached the Wise Wench's cliff just after her, and was angrily following her above the meadow. It seemed remarkably agile for a bull as big as an oak.

Now a good way from the others, the heifer stopped and glanced about nervously. Urgh came out from his hiding place and began making soothing noises as he slowly, slowly walked towards it, indicating for Sorry to do the same.

Sorry decided it was the perfect time for a swift tactical withdrawal and ran. Sadly he tripped the moment he turned round and slammed into the ground. The heifer stopped as Sorry fell, but then caught the smell of lichen and took a few very large steps forward, reaching the petrified goblin on the last and towering above him. Sorry stood, unable to move, as a colossal drooling tongue reached down and licked him.

His shirt sleeve came off, and so did most of the skin on the back of his hand. As he yelped, a gout of flame erupted from his mouth. The heifer mooed and licked him again.

'I think it's in love,' said Urgh.

Sorry stayed still as he smoldered. The smell-story from the creature was indescribably strong, a lifetime devotions to Lord Noc clung to it. Sorry sniffed in admiration and, unable to resist, rubbed his hand on its snout. 'There's a smell-story to tell your grandchildren about,' said the Great Mole in admiration. Hair stuck in great tufts on the cow's flanks, while its back was raw with sores. Its whole body made a never-ending symphony of noises, from the gurgle of its deep stomach to the taught, stretching noises of its foul grey udders. It was mostly black, but had a few white patches, making it a rather comical calamity.

Urgh quickly dashed to the back of the great beast and came Urgh-to-udder with the end of his quest. A huge bursting mass of vein and skin, stretched taught. He opened the churn and took an udder in his left hand. 'Well done! Feed it some more,' he whispered.

Well done? *Prat*, thought Sorry as he looked around. He could only see the colossal cow, and its terrible rasping tongue, quivering above him ready to bring abrasive wrath upon him. He desperately reached to the ground.

Rocks.

Ash.

Great.

'Noc be praised, lichen!' He grinned, and scraped some up before holding it over his head and squealing, as quietly as he could.

Urgh pulled the udder.

A squirt of hot liquid shot out and landed on his boot.

A hole appeared in it.

Urgh managed to get out the words, 'That's amazing,' before the pain struck. 'Gnaaaarrr!' he sobbed. He grabbed the udder, and, taking careful aim, pulled again. A squirt of liquid shot into the churn, sizzled, and was still.

A tongue lashed over Sorry's hands, delivering more rasping pain, and then the terrible sniff, sniff, sniff of its great nose on his hand, eager for more to feast on. Sorry was distracted to the point of joy by the fiery udder, torn between desperately wanting a go and desperately wanting to escape without further injury. He was jolted back to sanity by the sound of the Wise Wench screaming.

The Wise Wench had begun to run. The bull, just a few lengths behind her, began to give chase.

Squirt, another line of milk flew into the churn. Urgh began to pull harder. His hands soon began to suffer on the caustic teat.

The Great Mole reached back and scraped some more lichen up for Sorry; very little this time. He screwed it up in his fingers and held it at fingertip. The cow took it gently.

A splash, as the churn began to fill more.

The Wise Wench threw the tuba away and broke into a sprint. Well, a sprint for a gob-wench of her age—perhaps more of an arthritic lope would have described it better. The bull crashed after her, scattering ash and rocks before its charge. The tuba was squashed flat by the bull's great hooves and it dashed on, its prey just a few feet ahead.

The Wise Wench saw the opening she was looking for on her right, a short cave marked by an enormous painted arrow. She dashed in just as the bull made a toss with its horns. A rock, fully one-more-than-one goblins' high, smashed off the cave wall. The Wise Wench sighed, smiled to herself, and checked her knitted figures. Immediately after a knitted bull were a pair of huge orange balls of fiery wool engulfing a goblin. A rain of flaming sprouts accompanied the scene. She smiled, reached into her bag and pulled out a bag of sprouts. 'But not just any sprouts. Magic sprouts, sprouts with a titanic magik[83] effect,' she muttered as though reciting a list while trying to hold her nose. She carefully tossed her bag of curiously arcane-looking sprouts out of the cave. Nearby, she heard the bull sniff and then munch, a smile and look of trepidation growing on her face as the eating increased. She reached deeper into her bag and pulled out a metal hat, which she immediately donned.

Splash, the churn was nearly full, and Urgh began to relax. He grabbed another teat and began to pull, while whistling *The Lonely Miller and the Talking Cauliflower.*

Sorry looked up; it hadn't taken it this time. From somewhere very close, there was a rumbling noise. Inside the cow itself, in fact.

---

[83] Magik with a 'k' is, of course, far more powerful that magic with a 'c.' Magiq with a 'q,' however, well that's something else entirely but we haven't got time to discuss that right now; our heroes are still in danger.

'Praise the gods!' prayed the Great Mole. 'We're almost there.' He smiled up at the colossal cow; it had a startled look on its face, almost as if—'Duck!' he shouted, and pushed Sorry to one side. A gout of flame enveloped him. His fur smoldered, the mole swayed in pain.

As the flames receded, Sorry cradled him, tenderly. 'Great Mole, you're injured!' he added, improbably.

Nearby, Urgh was nowhere to be seen. He'd dived away at the last second.

'Don't worry about me, lad,' said the Great Mole, bravely. 'I'll be fine!' The pain too much, the Great Mole fainted.

'Great Mole, speak to me!' he said, feebly, and began to cry. Sorry staggered a few paces and leant on the cow's thick leg, cradling his beloved celestial companion. Suddenly, Urgh stood up, very blackened, gave him a thumbs up, then he grabbed the churn. It sloshed, and some of the destroying milk splashed out and sizzled on the ground.

'That's enough, lads! Well done, and well done, Sorry, you've saved a hero's life, and that makes you a bigger hero, you and the Great Mole,' shouted the Wise Wench from the cave in the distance.

They looked over. All they could see was the huge bull, staring into a shallow cave and munching. Urgh sealed the churn and hurled it on his back, patting the cow's udder, gingerly. Then, he led Sorry away, his companion sobbing over his injured mentor. 'So that's who you were talking to! How clever of him to come along with us. Praise the Great Mole! Let's hope he survives!' said Urgh, sympathetically.

'You lads, get away quickly now. Something very dangerous is about to happen and I don't want you in the meadow,' came the voice from the cave. 'RUN!' she shouted at the top of her voice.

Urgh and Sorry ran. Sorry had started running when he heard the word *You.*

Inside the cave, the Wise Wench gripped her metal hat tighter to her head and prayed.

There was a moment's pause.

Sorry and Urgh ran faster.

Behind them, they could hear some titanic stomach noises.

They sped uphill away from the meadow.

All went suddenly quiet as the cows stared at the curious expression the bull wore.

Urgh and Sorry leapt over some stones; Sorry carefully holding the Great Mole in reverent respect, Urgh heaving the great churn. They leapt for cover behind the cairn near the painted chin figure. Urgh looked at it again in puzzlement. It seemed relatively new, and now he looked at it closer, it looked like one of the Wise Wench's knitted figures. The meadow stretched behind them, grey and somber and frightful and still. They peeked over at the bull. It stood, resolute and fearsome at the cave mouth, no longer chewing.

There was another moment's pause as a deep rumbling noise echoed from within the vast creature once more. Then, suddenly, the whole hill shook. They glanced out to see that the bull had run off, as quickly as possible, back towards the herd. The heifers, sensing some unseen danger, began to explode and moo. Soon, the whole meadow was ablaze with balls of fire and gouts of flame.

'GET DOWN!' shouted the Wise Wench.

The whole valley erupted in a pair of gigantic balls of fire.

The dust had still not settled, but the flames had stopped. Sorry was stood laughing and bouncing up and down making childish noises of delight. Urgh looked up and gave a quiet gasp of despair: the Wise Wench was somewhere below in that inferno. He dashed forward into the cloud of ash ahead, screaming, 'Wise Wench!' at the top of his voice.

There was no reply. He marched into the cloud and, immediately, his eyes began to stream. He held his hand up and couldn't see it. He began to panic. He did what he thought was a turn, and began to move back. Suddenly, there was no ground under his feet and he fell.

Then a hand grabbed him.

A scrawny hand with lengthy nails and a long, black, knitted sleeve.

The Wise Wench's sleeve. Through the ash, Urgh suddenly realized there was nothing else around but the Wise Wench—just a big empty space of ashy air. She hauled him back from the cliff edge and led him out of the clouds back to the cairn, where they sat and coughed and laughed for some time. Eventually, they calmed down and dusted the ash from themselves. The Wise Wench seemed unharmed, save for her black bonnet, which was very singed at the back. 'What happened?' asked Urgh in a hoarse voice.

'Sprouts,' she said.

'Oh, I see,' said Urgh, but didn't.

'No, you don't,' she said. 'In their wisdom, the gods made all things equal so that none could dominate the Great Forest. Does not the humble rabbit feed on the grass, and does not the fox feed on the rabbit, and does not the fox-eating terror-ghump hunt the fox, and does not the terror-ghump fear our ghump-traps? And do we not fear the giants?'

'And what do the giants fear?' interrupted Urgh.

The Wise Wench patted the milk churn. 'All things have a weakness, even the hell-cattle of the terrible meadows. Now, let us have a look at the Great Mole. How wise he is to have slipped along on our adventure,' she said, staring pointedly at Sorry.

Sorry handed over the stricken dead-mole-cum-glove-puppet reverently, his mind still spinning with images of more explosions than he'd ever, ever hoped to see, ever. 'I'd like to live here,' he said, absent-mindedly.

The Wise Wench spilled water on the Great Mole to put him out and chuckled. 'Nothing stopping you.'

The air cleared and the cattle became visible once more. The boiling, choking land began to settle and the huge bull stomped on the remains of the tuba. 'Perhaps not,' added Sorry. 'How is he?' he added, stroking the Great Mole.

'He'll live, but he is badly hurt. How did he get injured?'

Urgh and Sorry stared at each other momentarily, not sure if it was wise to answer a question from the Wise Wench—after all, reality might fold up. Eventually, Sorry picked up the courage talk.

'Saving me. He pushed me from the exploding cow. He injured himself helping me. I just can't understand it.'

'It's an odd thing to do,' said the Wise Wench, patting Urgh on the shoulder and placing the Great Mole in her bodice. Within, Sorry caught a glimpse of what looked like a knitted nose. 'You must just be very, very important Sorry. Important enough, in fact, not to die when you should have. One-more-than-once.'

Urgh smiled and said, 'I expect it was touch and go for you at one stage!'

'No, not really,' said the Wise Wench and, checking the arrow on the ground by the painted chin figure, she began heading in the direction it pointed.

I guess we're about to find out what the thing with chins is, thought Urgh.

Later, they huddled in a cave and shivered. The wind howled outside and the meager fire was giving scant light and even scanter heat. Urgh hadn't been able to find much firewood for good reasons. Firstly, no tree grew within a day's walk from here, and one-after-one-edly, he had something on his mind. His father had told him that, tomorrow, the Wise Wench would fall over in front of him when they reached the edge of the forest just beyond the stunted elder, and that he must do what he must do then, or the terribleness would happen. He wished they'd found Zephyr, or at least what was left of her, but there was no sign of the huge, curiously attractive pig anywhere.

The Wise Wench rummaged in her pack and pulled out the last of the fruit cake, while glancing at Sorry and smiling. She handed it to them and the goblins hungrily wolfed it down. Urgh looked at her. She was so clever. If only he could tell her that he was going to murder her the day after, he felt sure she would know what to do, but then, if he told her he was going to murder her, she'd know all about it and might do something horrible to him, and then his father's plan would fail, and he couldn't return to the forest, and his poor gentle mother, what would happen to her?

'I said, 'what do you think, Urgh?'' said the Wise Wench.

Urgh screwed his eyes up and tried to remember what she'd been talking about. He couldn't remember and sighed.

She frowned. 'Well?'

Sorry chortled a little and covered his mouth. Then he covered his eyes, nose, and knees before giggling some more. 'She's talking about getting home.'

Urgh jumped up. 'How long has it taken us to get here?' he said to Sorry.

Sorry shrugged his shoulders.[84] 'It feels like forever,' he said.

'Well, not quite forever. Ages certainly.' Urgh looked pleased with himself. 'So how are we going to get back with Zephyr gone? It'll take ages.' He stared at the Wise Wench, questioningly.

She smiled. 'A good question,' she said, 'and one that deserves a good answer. And an answer that answers other questions about chins painted on stones. And one for which the morning will bring the whole truth.' She turned over and closed her eyes. Sorry did the same.

The whole truth? I wonder how much of the whole truth she really knows, thought Urgh, and lay down to sleep. He couldn't, his mind kept racing with his dilemma. He loved the Wise Wench— well, as much as any goblin can love another—but if he didn't kill her, his father had said the whole forest would end.

The morning cloud clung to the slope they had camped on. A grey clamminess was in the air and Sorry and Urgh's clothes were sodden. Only the Wise Wench seemed happy, her knitted black clothes somehow fresh and dry.

They were soon heading quickly downhill, bounding over great boulders before eventually coming to a long scree slope which swept down and ahead of them into a valley below. The Wise Wench stopped at an arrow which depicted a goblin lady swathed in black with a goblin with an upside-down head carrying a churn of great size. Sorry frowned at the picture and felt extra sorry for himself as he hefted the churn. 'Now,' she said, 'I'll go first. This slope is a bit

---

[84] Place where his shoulders might be.

334

tricky, so be careful, but we haven't got far to go now before—' she said, and suddenly stopped herself. She glanced into Urgh's pack to check that the oars were still there and began slipping and dancing her way down the boulder slope. The noise of water echoed from ahead. Soon, she was a little black figure in the distance, scattering stones everywhere ahead of her. Sorry mumbled to himself and wearily headed after her.

Urgh took off his pack and loosened the straps before checking that the axe was at the top. He went after his companions, nervously.

The way was steep, and the boulders seemed to work against him, trying to trip him or tease him into believing all was solid. Many of the more cunning boulders—though huge—swayed and buckled as he put his weight on them, some slid downwards quickly, almost causing him to fall. His mind was not concentrating on balance and again and again he stumbled and bruised or scraped his shins. Eventually, Urgh reached his companions who were sat on a great grey stone. They smiled at him and began heading down through low grasses and bog. The bog proved damper than it looked, and, several times, Sorry or Urgh put a foot in a nasty grey-green patch of mud, often sinking up to their knees. The Wise Wench somehow seemed to pick her way across the mire without even getting mud on her clogs. The grim land was bare and unfriendly, and ravens and hooded crows were its only inhabitants. The Wise Wench, however, seemed in good spirits as she rounded a hilltop where a stunted elder was trying to grow against the harshness of the land.

The elder, thought Urgh. *The elder shall be the last tree before she falls.* He reached into his pack and pulled out the axe. Taking care to conceal it from his companions, he held it behind his back and carried nervously on. Beyond the hill, the land fell into a green meadow, where a broad stream gurgled through rocks and long grass. The edge of the forest lay ahead, and the Wise Wench seemed to pick up her pace.

Urgh ran after her, gripping the axe.

She bounded on over hummocks and stones, with Sorry at her side. Sorry jumped as they disturbed a hare, hiding from an earlier flight from a fox. It shot into the green embrace of a patch of giant hogweed and out over the grass by the stream. Urgh was struggling to keep up and gripped the axe harder. He could feel the shaft bruising his fingers as he held it, determined to catch the Wise Wench.

The river was close now, and Sorry had leapt ahead laughing. The Wise Wench came to the edge just as Sorry was jumping a great green boulder in the center of a waterfall. The stream's waters caressed the stone and then went on their way, heading for the freedom of the oceans. The Wise Wench glanced forward at Sorry and smiled, then, suddenly, her ankle turned and she fell into the tall grass. The dew was wet on her face and she wiped herself before beginning to chuckle. She hadn't seen the fall coming and thought it one final joke of the gods. She looked up from the grass.

Urgh was above her, he had an axe in his hand. 'I'm so sorry,' he said and brought the blade down.

CHAPTER 22

The giants sat around the dead campfire eating raw mutton. Ate Eyes was deep in thought. The chief was deep in manure—he'd found a pile at the back of a nearby farm, carted it back, and sat in it, along with its owner, who he was also sat on. It was nice and warm. And smelly. His sons sat either side of the pile scratching behind a dog's ears. It rolled on its back playfully. Several other important giants sat in the circle. The chief's dead head was in a huge bandage; his other heads kept looking at it, worriedly.

'THE WAY I SEE IT,' said Ate Eyes, 'THE SCOUTS SAID THAT THE GIANT CREATURE WAS MADE OF IRON, HAD BIG FLAPPY WINGS, AND WAS TERRIBLE. RIGHT?'

'RIGHT!' said everyone.

'SO, WHAT WE HAVE TO DO IS FACE THIS GIANT CREATURE, AND IT'S EVEN MORE GIANT MOTHER, RIGHT?'

Everyone began to look hopefully at him. 'RIGHT,' they agreed in chorus.

'NOT GOING TO BE EASY,' he said.

Everyone looked deflated.

The chief stood up and growled. The dog rolled over, sat up, and growled. 'I AM NOT GOING TO BE TALKED AT BY A PIP-SQUEAK!'

'QUITE RIGHT,' said everyone but Ate Eyes.

'I HAVE A PLAN,' said the chief, very loudly. 'I SAY WE MARCH INTO THAT VILLAGE AND KILL EVERYONE IN IT, INCLUDING THIS HUGE IRON MONSTROUS MOTHER! MNARRRRRR!'

Everyone looked at the floor.

'WELL?' growled the chief.

'SIR,' said Ate Eyes, 'EVERYONE'S AFRAID OF THE MOTHER IRON MONSTER OF TERROR, BUT I ALSO HAVE A PLAN. WE HAVEN'T SEEN THIS MOTHER, RIGHT?'

'RIGHT!' said everyone.

'SO I SAY THAT WE MARCH UP TO THE GATES TOMORROW MORNING AND DEMAND TO SEE IT. THAT WAY, WE'LL KNOW HOW DIFFICULT IT WILL BE TO KILL IT!'

'BRILLIANT!' said the chief, as he rubbed his dead head, tenderly.

At exactly the same moment, not far away, the king was staring upwards. He looked at it again. It was a nasal masterpiece.

Looti looked confused.

The fake nose was colossal; nearly as big as a house.

Whippet smiled broadly as he saw the king's face.

The villagers gathered about and scratched their heads. Or, in the case of the older goblins, their bottoms.

'Whippet, I see now why the gob-wench puts her trust in you. It is, to put it quite simply, almost as good as I could do!' The king moved closer to it and tapped it with a finger.

'Careful, your Density, it is only made of wood. To your exact directions, of course,' said Whippet, who smiled, bashfully.

'What is it?' asked Looti.

'What is it?' said the king. 'Why, this nose is our salvation!' Everyone around clapped politely, sure that their old king had finally snapped under the pressure. The colossal nose stood, colossally, in their midst.

'It's a brilliant idea, whatever it is,' said Looti, encouraging.

'Agreed,' said the king,' and what's more, it was entirely my own idea! I can absolutely vouch for that part as your king.'

In the trees above, a raven gave a little curt caw and glided off.

The king moved conspiratorially over to Durth who was standing nearby picking his own nose. Durth stood to attention. 'Now, Durth,' said the king, 'tonight, I want you and your thugs to do me a little service.'

It was a bit later. The nose just fitted into the cart, and the thugs began to tie it on. Durth stood back proudly and smiled. Whippet appeared with a huge jar of lard, and patted Durth on the back. 'What's that?' asked Durth, officiously, adding, 'and don't ever touch me again. I don't like to be touched,' as he checked that his hair was still in place.

'Chicken grease,' answered Whippet, as he proceeded to rub it on the cartwheels. 'It'll keep the wheels from making so much noise'. Durth wished he was clever. Being clever must be really clever. He thought that thinking that probably showed how stupid he was. Not that anyone would tell him. Not if they didn't want to meet Mr. Corkscrew or Professor Hatpin.

The stars glittered above; candles that lit up the sky every night.[85] The royal party came from the Moot House. The bearers carried the king aloft in his special subterfuge palanquin, with Looti trailing behind. Eventually, after dropping the king a couple of times in the dark, they arrived. The king smiled at everyone present. 'Do the thugs know what to do, Durth?' he whispered.

The thugs nearby suddenly woke up.

'Not yet, sire. Actually, they haven't volunteered yet.'

The thugs looked nervous. Durth smiled and said, 'But they are just about to, Your Nosemakership. That is, if they don't want to suffer the penalty for NOT volunteering.'

The thugs all stepped forward, well aware of what would happen in the event of having a choice and not choosing what Durth wanted them to do, and volunteered. The Head Thug beamed. 'That's my lads!' he said, proudly.

The king cleared his throat noisily. 'Right, lads,' he said, 'you are to take the colossal conk in the direction of the giants' camp. Not too close, mind, but close enough. Then, you will quietly remove it from the cart and come back....with *everything bar the nose*. Do I make myself clear?'

The thugs nodded even though some of them weren't sure.

---

[85] That is, when Prendy the Candlekeeper of the gods could be bothered to do them, and didn't instead put the Eiderdown of the Gods over the forest and curl up under it himself.

'I should add,' said the king, hedging his bets, evilly, 'that the penalty for leaving anything else behind will be imprisonment with the village leopard. Understood?'

They understood and nodded.

'Then fortune smile on you, and may this night go down in history as the Night of the Colossal Conk!'

The group watched as the thugs slowly wheeled the huge nose off out of the gates and towards the giants.

It was not much later but even darker when the thugs got as far as they thought *not too far but far enough* might be. They undid the straps, and, hardly daring to breathe, lay down the monstrous wooden nose on the small grassy bank under the yew. Then the thugs silently shook hands, mouthed giggles, and headed back into the forest with the cart.

The morning brought a steady drizzle on the giant camp. Ate Eyes bowed low. He had a tray of hot, freshly-made, hedgehogs toast. Both heads grinning, he cleared his throat and, in his softest, most feminine, voice, said, 'AHEM, YOUR PREVIOUSLY-TREBLE-HEADED-DIVINITY. HERE IS BREAKFAST. WAKEY, WAKEY, LOVELY CHIEFY.'

The chief grabbed him by the left throat and had a knife, with many blades, drawn at his other throat before Ate Eyes could say, 'YOU DO THIS EVERY MORNING AND ADD 'OH IT'S YOU' STRAIGHT AFTER.'

'OH, IT'S YOU,' said the chief, as he relaxed. Then he stood up, yawned, and checked his head. It was still dead. The chief knocked the tray out of Ate Eyes' hands and shouted, 'I'VE NO TIME FOR FOOD. LET'S GET AND SEE THIS MOTHER!' He marched off towards the village, pausing only to kick some elderly giants in the shins and say several entirely new swear words, as was his custom of a morning.

The other giants eventually caught up and began to walk with him, waving their clubs and moving their shoulders from side to side in a way they had been brought up to believe was tough. Giant mothers were hard, and ruled with an iron hand. And quite often an iron switch-stick. And a toasting fork of immense size and sharpness. And lots of other things for mashing, like child-mangles and stompy-boy-booties.[86]

They picked their way along the foul trail they had made, knocking aside bits of discarded food and other less pleasant items. Then suddenly the chief stopped and shielded his eyes, before pointing ahead and shouting, 'WHAT'S THAT?'

It looked like a big boat turned upside down. Ate Eyes called over some more giants and walked cautiously forward. As they approached it, Ate Eyes thought it looked familiar but couldn't give it a name, so, in the best tradition of servants, he said, 'IT'S SAFE. IT'S JUST SOME SORT OF GOBLIN BOAT, YOUR UP-UNTIL-RECENTLY   HEAD-AHEAD-OF-THE-RESTOFUSNESS!'

The others came forward, and one especially green and yellow giant said, 'SHALL I SMASH IT?' to the chief. The chief smiled and nodded with his remaining heads, and then proceeded to rub his dead head with his fingers. Ate Eyes immediately offered the chief a dead neck massage, digging his fingers deeply into the chief's shoulders.

Then he noticed the chief's long grubby noses.

In the distance, the yellowy green giant was lifting up his club, Ate Eyes could see the chief's nose, very close up and very big, next to the very big thing they had found. They were identical.

He thought.

Then thought harder.

'A NOSE, VERY BIG, VERY CLOSE, AND A VERY BIG THING FAR AWAY THAT LOOKS IDENTICAL,' he said to himself quietly.

It was a tricky one.

Identical. *HMMM.*

'WAIT!' he shouted.

---

[86] Giant mothers aren't very maternal, but every giant ever has been too scared to point it out, and so the sorry cycle of misery goes on unchecked from generation to generation.

The king had sausages for breakfast. He burped and praised Lord Noc.

'I wish you would reconsider!' said Looti, as she blew her nose. 'It's far too dangerous. You can't just go out and meet them, away from the safety of the village!'

The king smiled, wiped the corners of his mouth, and grinned at her in a disconcerted way. Then he reached over and pinched her cheek.

She tried to pretend she didn't hate it.

'All part of the plan, m'dear,' he said, patronizingly.

She folded her arms and began to pretend to cry again. 'And what about the key?'

The king leapt back in terror and checked he had it. It still dangled, regally, from his regal key ring. He pretended to suddenly be very cool about it. 'Oh, the key,' he said, casually, 'yes, I forgot I had it. What about it?'

'Well, I think you're taking a chance. Suppose you drop it and the giants get it?'

'Impossible!' he smiled, and rose to do something unusual. He walked to the village gates and out by himself. As the others tried to follow, Durth held them back with his most wicked gardening instrument. 'The king knows what he's doing,' he added, his chest swollen with pride for his enlightened ruler.

'IT CAN'T BE!' said the chief's left head, as it looked at his other head's nose, then at the colossal thing. They did look very similar. Very, very similar. His brain tried to work.

He sat down.

The other giants began squinting and holding up their noses, comparing them to the colossal nose they had found. Ate Eyes had become more nervous than ever, and posted yet more guards around the group, to look out for the *thing* the nose belonged to. 'IT'S THE ONLY EXPLANATION. IT'S THE MOTHER WINGED THING'S NOSE. IT MUST BE! WHAT ELSE COULD IT BE?'

'BUT HOW BIG MUST SHE BE?' said the chief, still confused and still comparing his own noses with the colossal thing in front of him.

Ate Eyes loved these little problems. He happily got a few straight sticks together and measured a giant with them, then he broke off a bit of the stick and measured his nose. He drew a little outline on the ground and stood back proudly for a moment.

A raven flew over, calling, and for a moment the giants scattered in panic. For one part of one second, Ate Eyes was sure the raven call had said some words. 'They're here,' was what he thought he heard it say, but he dismissed it. Birds couldn't talk, they didn't have lips. When everyone had calmed down, Ate Eyes measured the nose, then began walking off. He was almost out of sight when he stopped and said, 'ABOUT THIS BIG!' The chief looked at how far away Ate Eyes was. He thought for a while but couldn't come up with any numbers big enough. He'd need to be able to make two or even three numbers lie together to be able to work it out. Such calculations were beyond giant lore. His mouth dropped. 'IT MUST BE—'

The giants waited.

'—MUST BE—'

They gaped, waiting for the wisdom to fall out of his mouths.

'—REALLY BIG!'

Some bushes nearby suddenly parted with a crash.

Most of the giants fled, leaving the chief, who had fallen backwards with shock, staring between his legs at the goblin king. He was proffering his hand.

Stunned, the chief took it and was soon stood again.

The air was filled with the sound of fleeing giants.

'Thank goodness I've found you!' said King Stormgrunties, frowning. 'Listen! Look, sorry about what happened yesterday. How's the head? Not good? Oh dear, I'll have him punished. Sorry. I came to warn you, however, something terrible has happened!' He began to move about, agitated, checking behind bushes for imaginary enemies.

The giant chief began to join in, checking the higher branches before saying, 'JUST HOW TERRIBLE?'

'Very terrible.'

'VERY TERRIBLE?' he added, nervously looking about.

'The worst.'

The giant chief's remaining living faces fell.

'*It's* escaped.'

'IT?'

'It.'

The giant looked even more nervous and pointed to the nose. The king suppressed a smile and walked up to it, giving it a nervous prod.

'IT?'

'It! Ah, I see you've found a little bit of it. Its nose, by the looks of it.'

'IS IT—VERY BIG, THEN?'

'That's the nose off its smallest face,' improvised the king, proudly, staring at the giant chief.

The giant's faces dropped.

The king moved up in a conspiratorial manner and put his hand by his mouth. 'That's why I'm here,' he said covertly. 'You see, it's pretty mad about being cooped up. Pretty mad. When I got up this morning, it shouted me from the wood saying it would come back to the village in one-after-ones days' time and eat us all for keeping it locked up in a shed for several winters.' The king stepped onto the giant's boots and beckoned him closer, finally whispering straight into his right, right ear, 'Only, it eats giants too, you know. Prefers them, in fact.'

The giant chief began to shake a tiny bit.

'And if I were you,' he added, 'I'd try not to be around when it gets back. I should go soon. We're all packing now.'

The chief stepped back and nodded. 'GOOD IDEA,' he said, nervously glancing about. 'IN FACT, I'LL GO NOW,' he said, and ran off into the gloom.

The king began to chuckle as he wandered back to the village, congratulating himself on being so clever and not noticing the harrumphs coming from a bird sat high above in the trees.

It was jolly cold. And clammy. The king strode back into the village flanked by Durth and Whippet, who he was telling the tale of the 'nose meeting' to in great mirth, pulling on his own considerable conk to assist in the demonstration of just how amazingly clever he was and how dim the giants were. They were greeted by a cheering mob. He doffed an imaginary hat and waved regally and absentmindedly at the crowd. *King saves the day. Again*, thought the king, modestly. Looti ran forward and embraced him. He hugged her back until he realized that everyone was watching, and reddened quickly. 'Erm, yes, the traditional, not-too-long-after-All-Shark's-Eve-greeting,' he said casually. 'Thank you for reminding me of that, adviser,' he said, very loudly. Whippet called Looti over and they chatted briefly while Durth looked on at the adviser.

In the distance, lace curtains twitched.

'I don't remember Kringe ever doing that with the king in his several-but-not-many summers,' said Dome Eyes to a friend who was covered in lumps. The lumpy goblin scratched one of her lumps and smiled before elbowing Dome Eyes in the ribs and laughingly saying, 'Well, you wouldn't let Kringe kiss you if you were king, would you?' They both began to laugh. The movement caused one of the lumpy goblin's boils to pop very loudly. Bits of it hit Dome Eyes. He decided he'd save them for later.

The king cleared the crowd about him and, clearing his throat, shouted 'Friends!'

Cheers.

'By my own cunning, skill, bravery, assertiveness, fortitude, strength, fitness, firmness, vitality, goblinliness, regality, cleverness, resourcefulness, determination, effectuality, brawn, steadfastness, inviolability, and guts, I have today, single-handedly, saved the village. Nay, the whole forest!'

345

Huge cheers, mumbles amongst some of the more stupid goblins[87] about what *inviolability* meant, and whether it was edible.

The king raised a calming hand. The crowd stilled. 'But this is just an everyday duty for a king. I want you to know that I am happy, at all times, to put myself in situations where death is a certainty, just for you.' He bowed. 'I expect,' he said, greedily, 'nothing in return, though death stalks my every waking moment just to keep all you worthless, dismal wretches alive.' He smiled at his adviser before continuing loudly. 'However, nothing is ever without cost. So, this evening, to show your appreciation, I announce a '*We're so rubbish and you're so great and Kingly*' gift-giving, where, in my honor, you may give me whatever tokens you feel pay suitable homage to the way I have single-handedly ended our battle with the giants! I should add, that as tradition dictates, should I find myself *displeased* with your tokens, I may have each of you—or, possibly, all of you—fed to the village crocodile. Adviser, go and fetch Petal from the pond and lead her crocodilianness here for later. Dismissed!'

The crowd began to disperse. 'I knew it would all end up costing us something,' muttered several goblins at once.

'That's leaders for you,' added Dome Eyes, with some general accuracy.

The king watched as Looti issued instructions to the royal crocodile-keeper to fetch Petal. The pair then entered the Moot House. Within, all was still save for the drooling and sobbing of Tongue, who remained suspended nearby. The king looked at him, suspiciously.

'Whippet tells me the Hamster is being sent back to the Kettle Hall for repairs, Your Greedyness,' said Looti.

The king stared at her deep eyes. 'Who?' he said.

'Whippet, Your Bouncyness. One of your loyal subjects.'

'Never heard of him. And why is he doing that, pray?' said the king while admiring himself in the mirror.

---

[87] That is, most of the goblins.

She smiled. 'One of the wings fell off!' They both laughed and began pointing at Tongue, who joined in with the laughter, hoping it might lead to him being let down.

'One thing is worrying me, Your Correctness,' said Looti.

'Oh?'

'Yes. Now, please don't take this the wrong way, Your Neverwrongness, but didn't the Wise Wench say the giants would be back on Thodsday *once-more-than-once* now?'

'Irrelevant,' said the king closing the subject and changing it with admirable self-importance. 'You!' he said, pointing again at Tongue. 'What are you doing in the Royal Moot House? Come on, speak up, peasant.'

'You ordered it, Your Justiceforallitude,' said Tongue. The king smiled and closed another subject in as many moments.

'But—' interrupted Looti.

'—no buts. The battle is over, and we won.' Outside, he could hear the sound of someone being eaten. 'Ah, and here, unless I'm very much mistaken, which I'm not,' he said, shooting his adviser a curt glance, 'is Petal come to get ready for the day's festivities. Adviser, bring my monocle, fez, and the ultramarine paint. *Some* things, I'm glad to say, are never questioned and *tradition* is one of them.'

* * *

Ate Eyes ran on through the forest, his breathing hard and deep. One head looked ahead for danger, while the other looked backwards for more danger. His spectacles were beginning to steam and, after a while, reluctantly, he stopped, leaning against a tall pine. He listened as he wiped his glasses, sure that every startled bird and every distant call was *it*.

He was scared of *it*, there was no doubt about that, but the curious side of him wanted to snatch a quick look, especially if it was going to eat all the goblins. He wondered if it'd be able to eat them in one bite, perhaps even the whole forest in one mouthful, so he'd lingered, but then, in his lingering, became lost and he wandered

347

about terrified that he'd bump into it. He put his spectacles back on and suddenly jumped back. Before him, a long swathe had been cut through the forest. The fallen trees lay like dead bodies at the side. There was something strange through the middle of the clearing: long, straight, metal lines. And then he heard it; the *something* he had been dreading.

A strange noise.

A grinding and wheezing and flapping. Terrified, he looked around for cover, and spied a great laurel hedge nearby. He plunged into it and prayed to the gods that he would not be discovered. 'LORD SQUASH, PROTECT AND WATCH OVER ME THIS DAY,' he whispered in terror.

Then he saw it, the iron-skinned beast, slowly coming towards him. He watched as it came into view, hardly daring to breathe. A hand pinched his right nose, another pinched his left. It came closer, closer, closer. And then he saw it more clearly.

The beast from the village, the baby beast.

Its wing was tied onto its back, it had fallen off.

As it moved closer, he held his breath, waiting in horror. Slowly, slowly he saw the whole of it.

It had wheels, not feet. And between the wheels were lots of other little feet—little goblin feet—pushing from inside. The wheels rolled on the iron rails.

And it breathed smoke, but on its back sat a little goblin. In fact, a pair of little goblins.

Durth patted Whippet on the back. Whippet had hold of the great lever which made the Hamster run and was whistling. He pushed it further forward and, inside, lots of pointy sticks pricked the pushers who squeaked a little and pushed faster. 'We sure fooled those stupid giants!' shouted Durth, in an unfortunately clear, loud voice. 'They're so dim, they couldn't light up a doll's house!' He began to laugh so much he choked.

Whippet patted him on the back. 'I wish I'd been there when they found the nose. Imagine a false nose causing the giants to flee. Even though the Wise Wench said they'd be back, I'm not sure she's right! Fancy a bit of iron and wood fooling the idiots. You'd think with that many heads they'd have a brain between them!' He laughed and began to sing, 'They have one-more-than-one heads but have no brain, those giants from the bog! If I were them I'd swap my chief with the dog! Burn, burn, burn it, oh!'

Whippet pulled the lever and the hamster halted. 'I still think we should fix it, though. You know, the Wise Wench said it should be ready for Thodsday.'

'But the king said the battle was over, remember?' said Durth, snarling lightly.

'Calm down, old chum,' answered Whippet, calmly. 'I know the king is never wrong, but, then again, neither is the Wise Wench. It's a tricky one.'

Durth nodded in agreement, suddenly feeling hot.

'I'll tell you what, master Durth. Let's fix it now and bring it back anyway, as a sort of memento. Then the king can be paraded about in it when the Wise Wench returns the day-after-the-day-after-tomorrow bearing the milk of the Fire-breathing Heifers from the Atrocious Meadows of the Awful Conflagration. Tell you what: we could fix up a big long nose on it!' The goblins patted each other on the back and laughed so much they didn't notice that the other wing had fallen off and was lying on the tracks. As the thing creaked away, a few of the goblins inside started 'mnarr'ing and laughing.

Ate Eyes stared at the fallen wing. He waited until the beast was well out of sight before moving to it. He picked it up easily and could see marks along the side where it had been fixed to the body.

Iron. Like a smithy's work. Made.

'THE CHIEF HAS BEEN TRICKED,' said Ate Eyes to his other head, 'I CAN'T WAIT TO SEE HIS FACES WHEN I TELL HIM.' He began to laugh, then suddenly stopped and added, 'OR CAN I?' He dashed off into the forest repeating the phrase, 'IS HE GOING TO BE CROSS! OH DEAR, SOOO CROSS!'

When they returned this way some time later, Durth and Whippet noticed the wing had gone. Quite naturally, however, they assumed a group of magpies had ganged up and stolen it.

Ate Eyes finally caught up with the chief quite some time later. By that time, he was already half-way back to his dreadful, draughty tower. It had then taken about half the night for the truth to sink in, and, when it did, the chief went on a frenzy of killing anything that wasn't a giant within a large radius. By that time, the chief had calmed down enough to know what he wanted to do: rush straight back to the goblin village, kill everyone in it, break everything in it apart, burn it to the ground, till the soil, plant it with a crop of some sort (Ate Eyes recommended barley), wait a summer to reap the crop, build it into an effigy of the goblin king, burn it, and then stamp on the ashes until even they were crushed to nothingness.

Everyone agreed it was a reasonable plan, in light of what had happened.

Then they dashed back towards the village, crosser than any giants had been for many years.[88]

---

[88] Which is *really* cross. Giants get angry about pretty much everything, in the same way, more or less, that goblins get scared by pretty much everything. Giant tales—which aren't really very interesting and generally involve lurid descriptions of very horrible things being done to things that are invariably smaller than giants—tell of properly cross giant chiefs, kings, and princesses going on killing sprees lasting several months. This pretty much sums up the general mood of our giants as they approached the goblin village.

CHAPTER 23

Urgh let the axe fall and began to sob. The heavy tool dropped just behind the Wise Wench with a dull thud.

She realized she was shaking.

'It's not fair!' screamed Urgh to the sky. 'I can't do it! I'm sorry, father,' and, under his breath he said, 'but not as sorry as I am to the forest. It's over! Everything will fail and it's all my fault!' He sank to his knees waiting for the sky to fall.

The Wise Wench leapt up and backed away from him. Her hands were trembling so much she could hardly make a fist. She had been taken by surprise. Sorry had stopped in mid-stream when he saw the axe. He stared at it incredulously until he forgot he was standing on a slippery rock and plunged backwards into the water. The splash and screams for help brought Urgh and the Wise Wench to their senses. They leapt along the bank and, stretching over a rock and holding hands to keep balance, Urgh reached down and grabbed Sorry and the churn as he slid past. He pulled him out of the stream and led him to the bank. Sorry gasped for breath. Tears still stung Urgh's eyes but he had stopped sobbing. The Wise Wench put an arm around his shoulders and said, quietly, 'I think you'd better tell me what happened.' The Wise Wench sat back, and from nowhere produced a lit clay pipe, blackened at the bowl. She lay against the rock and listened.

Urgh stared at the ground as he spoke. 'It was when I was in the giants' keep. I had a dream, or at least I thought it was a dream, but it wasn't. It was real.' He stopped and looked confused. The Wise Wench blew a smoke ring at him. He coughed. 'I saw a very old goblin with a long, wispy beard and an even longer, wispy nose. He seemed very familiar.'

'And who was he?' asked the Wise Wench.

'He said he was my father. I never knew my father, you see, and mummy never liked to talk about him. She was always so busy disemboweling someone or something to cook, or slaughtering some small furry animal, or hurting things. She never liked to talk about it. Whenever I raised the question, she got quite cross.'

'Quite cross?'

'Well, very cross. She did mention once when she'd had a bit too much elderberry wine that he'd been a handsome prince astride a war-pig, but I never knew if it was truth or elderberry. Usually, she just said she'd found me in a cowpat. Anyway, this old goblin, I *knew*, I just *knew* it was him.'

'What did he ask you to do?'

'Kill you. He said, if I didn't, a terrible boring would fall across the whole forest. Everything would wither and die—even fire—and...'

'And?'

'He said you would do it—accidentally—but that it would happen, would begin to happen, unless I took the one chance I'd have, which was just now.' Urgh looked troubled and confused. 'I knew I would never be able to do it.'

The Wise Wench brooded on his story. After a time she looked up and patted Urgh on the shoulder before saying, 'I do not blame you, young Born with an Upside-down Face. If this goblin is indeed your father, then I fear for you, for I believe he is none other than a consort of she who should not be named.'

'What, Queen Quench?' said Sorry.

The Wise Wench gave him a sharp clip around the ear. 'She hears all things, and knows when her name is spoken. Name her not or she may appear.'

Sorry ran away just in case she did.

Urgh tried to take it all in.

'This could explain,' she added, 'why you are so ug—why you are *so different* to the rest of us. We must talk to your mother when we return. Possibly. But for now, young Urgh, I think you may have saved the forest from an eternity of darkness and boredom by your actions. Someone very powerful wanted us to fail, and, with Queen Quench personally involved, I should have been more on my guard for the unexpected. You are well named, hero, and now you have mingled with one of the gods themselves! You must be terribly, terribly important somehow.'

Urgh puffed his chest out. *Mingled with gods. Gosh,* he thought.

'But don't do it again, eh,' added the Wise Wench, admonishingly. He nodded.

They soon moved on, leaving the axe behind. The Wise Wench kept along the edges of the forest and river tributaries. Deep, ancient groves of oak and sycamore surrounded them and the goblins breathed a sigh of relief.[89] They moved easier in the forest, despite Sorry's protestations that his back was on fire and that his knees were ablaze with pain. They made good progress, and, within an hour or so, were in fine spirits, having covered quite a few miles. They passed a couple more painted arrows, and, eventually, heard the great river roaring in the distance. As they approached, they saw the Wise Wench talking to the Great Mole. They couldn't hear over the roar of the river ahead.

'Thank you for saving me from the false one, oh Wise Wench,' said the Great Mole, using the Wise Wench's mouth to form mortal words.

'You're welcome, Great Mole, but tell me: are you badly injured?' she inquired, implausibly, of the glove puppet.

'Just a surface wound. 'Tis nothing, but I wonder how the great king is faring back at the village?'

'Don't worry, Great Mole, your wise kin, the Substitute Great Mole, has been passing on his divine, but slightly below-par, wisdom.'

'Then all is well,' he said, and bowed, his paws sticking out feebly at right angles to his body.

The group arrived at a high bank above the roaring torrent, where they stood, deep in awe. The river ahead was wider than the village, turning and dancing endlessly through a great valley beneath a canopy of huge and ancient trees. Here, many willows wept for the

---

[89] The thing is, forests of any kind are great to hide in, which makes them so great for goblins. The problem is, most forests are full of juicy trees that just demand to be cut and burned. It's a tricky dilemma for a goblin, but, luckily, they don't think too deeply about such things and aren't organised enough to do irreparable damage to forests, unlike some more organized tribes of creatures.

passing waters, perhaps anxious to join the freedom of the torrents jig. 'Welcome again to the River Runny!' shouted the Wise Wench. 'And welcome, too, to the home of Chinnery.' She pointed a little way upstream.

A rubbishy timber lodge lay at the river's edge; a dying hovel of hewn logs with a grey stone chimney emerging. A jetty of crooked timbers lay by the side of the house and a boat was drawn there. Smoke drifted out of the chimney. 'Ah, well, isn't that lucky,' said the Wise Wench. 'He appears to be home.' She grabbed a hand of each of her companions and led them along a stone footpath down the bank and along the wooden jetty, passing the fragile-looking punt on the way.

Oars, they both thought at exactly the same moment.

Once again, in the Great Oak of the Gods, Hoggy-Uncannythoughts smiled and rubbed a phrase from his blackboard. Below, countless-many-and-more phrases were laid out for the day. He was going to be busy.

They reached the cabin's great dirty door and it was opened by a quite revolting-looking creature; someone with so many chins, he looked like he had no chest or neck. He was dressed in a wax coat and carried a meat cleaver. He bowed to the Wise Wench and stood back. 'Thank you, Master Chinnery!' she said, and hurled Urgh and Sorry in.

'One-one-and-one of you, oh Wise Wench?' asked Chinnery in broken Goblin. 'I thought you said there'd be just you and one?' The stranger smelt very much of fish.

'Change of plan, old friend. Is the stew ready? We must rush; we have very little time to get back.'

'Of course it's ready, as per your instructions.'

'*Request*,' she corrected him with a smile. 'I would never dare demand anything off a bogie. You are far too mighty and impressive in bearing to do so.'

Chinnery smiled and smelt, indicating for the goblins to sit on his hairy sofa while he waddled off into what must be, by the smell of it, the kitchen. 'What are bogies?' whispered Urgh.

'They are cousins to the goblins,' said the Wise Wench, 'but are bigger and much more ug– have much nicer personalities than goblins,'[90] she said as their host came in with a bucket of stew and a group of bowls which he set down.

'Oh, but one more thing,' she added to her companions.

As she spoke, Chinnery burst apart–fleshy sacks heaving out across the room, mouths popping out, and then being swallowed by long scraggy necks of flesh.

'They're shapeshifters,' she said, but Urgh and Sorry had already left the building.

Chinnery smiled back. His body a heaving mass of swollen flesh that loosely resembled a many-headed pig sat upon by a grinning milk maid. 'I think you may have got a couple mixed up, old friend,' said the Wise Wench.

The creature burped and became something a little less bizarre.

A short while later, after she'd caught them, the companions were sat on the verandah, finishing the last of their stew with some hard black bread their host had brought them. He was nowhere to be seen at that moment, but there were the most peculiar gurgling and fluting noises coming from the house.

'That boat's only big enough for one-more-than-one goblins, and that's at a push,' croaked Sorry, still keeping a wary eye out for their host.

'I know,' said the Wise Wench.

'So, I think it's only fair if I– what do you mean 'I know?''

'You're absolutely right, dear Sorry.'

Dear, oh dear, I don't like the sound of that.

'This is why I've decided you should stay and keep young Chinnery here company. He won't bite.'

---

[90] Which is not hard.

'Me? Here? With him?' said Sorry, laughing. 'Oh, I don't think so.' He crossed his arms and turned his back on them.

The Wise Wench gathered up the churn and a few other belongings, giving Urgh a gentle tug while saying, 'I'm afraid so, and we must be going right now.'

There was a strange swallowing sound from around the corner and Chinnery reappeared in his old form.[91]

'I've just been speaking with my companions here,' said the Wise Wench to their host, 'and young Sorry has decided to stay and keep you company. He's decided that rather than risk the coming battle with the giants, a battle I cannot in any way guarantee his safety in, he'll stay here in the warm with you and your very full larder. He doesn't want to risk being pulled apart or have his arms and legs bitten off by giants, nor face the terrible risk of drowning he may have in the coming river journey. Furthermore,' she added sternly to the back of his head, 'he's going to be your friend and is very much looking forward to it, aren't you Sorry?'

Sorry turned his head, a huge false smile riven across it.

A small tear formed in Chinnery's eye.

'And so, regrettably, old friend, we must take your boat and go as agreed, and we must do so now, I'm afraid.' She moved over and shook his hand while Urgh loaded up the boat and got out the oars from the Wise Wench's sack. A few moments later, they were both in the boat. The Wise Wench pulled a pair of inflated pig bladders from her sack and, stuffing one up Urgh's tunic, put one below her bodice. Then she smiled and shouted, 'I'm sorry this has to be a dashing visit, Master Chinnery, but as I told you when I came last winter, the village is in dire need. Even now, the giants have found out that the hamster is fake, and one of them is running around the forest gathering his clan members on his way to our village. They will attack very soon now, and we must be there to unexpectedly save the day. Oh, I almost forgot. I have a present for you.' She hefted him the vice she'd been saving for him. 'That'll help you keep timber still

---

[91] More or less.

while you saw it up and fix your house when the roof springs a leak next week,' she added, cheerily.

Chinnery nodded. He was a bogie of few words.

I carried that flippin heavy thing all the way here so he can fix his roof with it, and it isn't even broken yet, sulked Sorry, silently.

'But, Master Chinnery, you have done an excellent job, and one for which you shall be regally rewarded when the king gets to hear the whole story. I shall return.'

Chinnery smiled and put his arm around Sorry. 'It gets very lonely here by the river,' he said. Sorry smiled back as Chinnery squeezed him.

Urgh waved to Sorry. 'Well, dearest friend, may we meet again soon. I'll never forget your kindness, our adventures in the giants' keep, and all your help. You saved my life and I know we'll meet again soon. I'm going to miss you. You're a true friend,' he blubbered, just a little.

'Yeh, whatever,' said Sorry, fighting a little for breath.

With a sniff, Urgh cast off and the goblins bobbed away into the torrid waters beyond.

Chinnery and Sorry continued to wave long after the boat had disappeared from sight. When finally they stopped, the bogie gave Sorry a little squeeze and said, 'I'm going to take very, very good care of you, little pal' and led him, rather forcefully, back into the log cabin.

Sorry smiled deviously. 'Yes, I'll ease your loneliness, alright matey. We're going to have lots of fun!' He fumbled with the marbles in his pockets as he followed him in, grinning from ear to ear.

From inside the house came the sound of stretching skin, retching, and strange, fleshy, pipe music.

The waters crashed into the side of the boat, conceded, succumbed, and re-joined the torrent. Urgh was rowing with the oars as fast as he could.[92] He quite liked the water. He had won many races in his youth and had less fear of it owing to his unique head arrangement; he was the only goblin who could look through it and still breathe. Rowing, however, was a little beyond him.

The Wise Wench smiled thinly. 'No matter, young Urgh,' she said, 'we shan't be in the boat too long—'

'—before we sink,' added Urgh, knowledgeably and patting his pig bladder.

The broad river had short, steep sides of mossy limestone which had aged with the river's passing. Its strange shapes echoed the anger of the mighty river as the stone was slowly devoured. On either bank were great trees, often willows, whose canopies occasionally met above and plunged the boat into shadow.

After a few hours, Urgh had got the hang of the oars and was able, in a fashion, to steer the boat from one bank to the next. All day, they were drawn downstream, with the Wise Wench keeping a careful eye in her bodice for figurines of obstacles ahead; her knitted warning signs helped them avoid a pair of dangerously narrow clefts, a fallen tree, and a waterfall. Urgh thought she looked odd with her pig bladder stuffed under her black dress, giving her the appearance of a gob-wench in gob. The irony was not lost on her, either, and she occasionally patted it. 'There, there, little baby,' she said, before pulling a face and pretending to be sick over the side of the boat.

Night came, and they pushed on under a high cliff. The Wise Wench brought a lantern from her sack and lit it, fastening it to the front of the boat. A raven shot by, disturbed by light, and called a greeting to the Wise Wench. Ravens were the masters of the cliff above, which they called the Grey Capitol, for here was the home of one of their chiefs, the great Chief Grawk, the sire of countless eggs. The ravens took flight at the sight of the goblins and swooped above them for a time before being sure that they were not raiders sent by their enemy, the dreaded Taupe Magpie Club.

---

[92] Goblins have a general dislike of water for very good reasons: it wipes off all the interesting smells you collect over the years, and, you can drown in it.

'I'm afraid I have nothing to eat,' said the Wise Wench with unusual candor. 'I only bargained for us, but we were one-one-and-one for so long the food is finished.' Urgh smiled and seemed rather glad of the fact. Sorry had his faults. In fact, he had a whole moot house full of faults, crammed from floor to ceiling and filling up all the cupboards in a fault frenzy, but Urgh had known him a long time. He laughed lightly to himself. 'When do we sink?' he shouted to his companion.

The Wise Wench smiled back and shrugged her shoulders. 'Soon. I'll shout a warning, but don't worry. Where we sink I put a rope down to the river last winter, when I was on my way to Chinnery. We crash into a huge rock shaped like a duck. There is a little sandy shore under the cliffs there with no way out. That's where we'll end up sinking.

'And will we be on time to save the village?'

The Wise Wench nodded, and then put a finger in her mouth. 'Well, I hope so, but, with you around, who can tell? Perhaps even the great Very Wise Wench of old could not foresee. Maybe your movements are beyond all Wise Wenches, and I am as much use as the Not in the Slightest Bit Wise Wench over at Scummy.' She sighed and gazed at Urgh for a long time.

A quiet fell over the forest, and even the river seemed to fall into a slumber.

Urgh suddenly awoke in panic. The Wise Wench steered with an oar and smiled as he blinked at her. Dawn brought a thick mist which obscured all but the fierce sounds of the river. The day was only moments old when there was a colossal roar ahead. Urgh began to struggle manfully with the other oar in an attempt to move the little boat from side to side. However, he stopped when the Wise Wench held out a figurine of wool. It was of one-more-than-one goblins—clearly them—swimming in water beneath a rock shaped like a vast duck. He gulped when he saw the next figure—a massive giant with one-more-than-one heads and another bandaged head between squashing goblins. Urgh smiled and let go of the oar, resignedly. The

Wise Wench smiled back and did the same. Within moments the oars vanished in the boiling waters.

Soon, the rapids had hold of the boat, and they began to crash from rock to rock, all the time whooping and cheering, safe in the knowledge that they were about to capsize. They turned a corner and shot into a narrow valley, the noise deafening and the spray showering them. The Wise Wench made sure of the knot on the rope tying her to the churn, while Urgh made sure his tunic was tightly-buttoned over the pig's bladder and his magic sack.

Then, with a crash, they turned and came face-to-face with a huge rock, a towering sentinel of limestone which leant from the valley side. From here, in the churning, boiling waters, it looked like a duck.

Urgh began to laugh. 'This is it! We're going to sink,' he said. But the Wise Wench only saw him mouth words she already knew.

The boat hit the edge of a sharp stone and split. Water began to pour in, but, before it could sink them, they hit another, wider rock at great speed and the little vessel simply fell in half. Urgh saw the Wise Wench turning as she held onto the churn, and uttered a silent oath to Lord Noc as he was pulled under. He swam, as hard as he could, towards the shore while looking for the Wise Wench. The current was strong but, luckily, they were both pushed into and under the great stone. Soon, the waters calmed about them and Urgh was able to easily swim to the little sandy shore. He looked up and saw a rope, dangling above.

The Wise Wench spluttered and dragged herself from the water, the churn still in her arms.

They both fell down and began to laugh.

CHAPTER 24

Everyone looked nervously at Petal, who stared hungrily at the gathered villagers. A pathetic assortment of tat, rubbish, and flotsam was being gripped, held, worn, or ridden by the locals, some of whom had gone to the trouble of wrapping it. The crocodile wriggled in her leather and metal collar tied to a stump of a tree. Nearby, wearing his ceremonial executioner's hood and balloon, was her keeper.

The king emerged from the Moot House astride Gherkin, his own false crocodile, his bearers grunting below as he gave them a quick swish with his riding crop. His Majesty was in a playful mood, and rode his crocodile jauntily around the village brown and along the battlements before finally arriving at a small stage immediately above, but at a safe distance from, Petal. 'Right, let's get on with it!' shouted the king. 'Who's first?'

The crowd muttered and then, at some prearranged signal, everyone pushed an old goblin called Maester Raggedy forward. The old goblin held up something wrapped in straw, twigs, and twine. The king took it disdainfully but unwrapped it, greedily.

There was nothing inside. 'Well,' he scowled, 'what is supposed to be in it?' His monocle dropped from his wrinkled eye into his mug of malted milk.

'No, no, Your Burpitude,' said Maester Raggedy nervously. 'That *was* the present Your Looks-Could-Curdle-Milkitude. It was a representation of yourself in straw and twigs.'

Everybody winced.

Some time had passed, somewhat painfully. All seemed quiet in the village now, save for a noisy crocodile, with an enormous stomach, which was wriggling about happily as it was led out of the village by its keeper towards a distant mire. Everyone else was hiding. The king had been generous and only got cross a few times with a few subjects; the rest had run off after delivering their own feeble gifts.

The king had his brunch on the battlements with Looti at his side and a collection of rubbish scattered at his feet. A rag wolverine with smiling face glowered up at him from the feeble gathering of gifts. Huge slug crumpets as big as hats were piled high on a plate and the pair tucked into them greedily. The king picked up his goblet of wine and indicated for Looti to do the same. He smiled broadly, and, for the first time, she noticed that he always picked his nose before drinking. 'A toast,' he said, picking his nose, 'to the Wise Wench! She says a thing, and it is true—mostly!' They drank heartily and began to laugh.

'Tell me, Your Inventiveness, what are we going to do now, exactly?' said Looti, batting her eyelashes.

'Well, the Wise Wench is coming back the day after tomorrow. The giants will appear shortly after and then we shall use the kettle on them. Its dreadful kettleular wrath shall defeat them, and we'll be finished by tea time. At least, that's what the Wise Wench told me,' he smiled and chuckled to himself. 'Except, of course, that she is *wrong*. Wrong, wrong, wrong. I've already driven the giants off with my cunning, so I think we'll do a spot of actor-hunting. According to the ancient rites, open season on actors, thespians, and mummers begins today.' He toasted himself and they emptied their goblets.

Suddenly, at the edge of the clearing around the village, a countless number of giants appeared. They all looked really, really cross. The chief's dead head was beginning to ooze a bit, and smell. Even from where he was, the king thought he caught a whiff.

'Oh bugger,' muttered the king into his crumpet.

'WHERE IS *THE TRICKSTER*?' shouted the giant chief, impatiently. 'I CAN COUNT TO THREE!' he yelled, more as a statement of threat than a boast. Everyone clapped. He paused and signaled for his best tosser[93] to come forward. A giant came forward holding a massive boulder which had an oil-soaked cloth tied around it. The tosser, on a signal from the chief, lit it.

---

[93] That is, a tosser of rocks.

'What's 'three'?' muttered the king. 'Is that one-more-than-one or is it a few? Damn these giants with their complicated language.'

'ONE...'

'TWO...'

In the village, the king gaped at the giant horde. Looti, seeing the tosser, grabbed the king and dived behind the timber battlements.

'ERM.'

'THREE!' whispered Ate Eyes.

'THREE!'

The chief waved at the tosser and he hurled the rock. The stone took a high arc over the walls and landed on one of the far houses in the village. There was a dull plop. Moments later, doors opened throughout the village and goblins began to understand what was happening. 'Ah, one-one-and-one, I thought so,' said the king to himself from behind cover.

The chief puffed his chest out and laughed before shouting, 'WE SHALL TRY AGAIN! ONE—' The giants were all laughing now, and began to taunt the village. The giants' dogs, held by collars that were far too tight, began to bark when they were tugged.

'—TWO—'

The king stood up on the battlements. 'Wait!' he shouted.

The giant chief took an exaggerated step forward and picked up the metal hamster wing before winking at Ate Eyes with both his remaining heads. The third was still oozing something and was itching considerably. He cleared his throats before calling in a clear, unnecessarily gruff, voice, 'DO YOU KNOW WHAT THIS IS?'

The giants began to laugh even louder.

The king peered into the gloom. 'Is it a harpsichord?' he shouted, smiling to himself on how clever he was when faced with doom.

'A WHAT?' shouted the chief.

'Harpsichord. You know, the musical instrument. My lad has a penchant for destroying them,' added the king, helpfully. 'Well, that's what it looks like. Mind you, it is very dark. I'll tell you what, why not come back *tomorrow* when it's a bit lighter, or, ideally, the day after tomorrow. In fact, why not come back late in summer when the quality of light is rea—'

'—A WING!' interrupted the reddening chief.

The king shuffled about. 'Oh, not quite right, then,' he shouted. Looti stayed in cover signaling frantically that he should do the same. Nearby, Durth was bullying his bullies into position. The king winked at him, nervously.

The giant chief signaled to his tosser and grinned. The giant hefted up a really massive rock and lit another oily rag about it. The chief held up what was left of Mister Smellpipe and shouted, 'AND DO YOU KNOW WHAT THIS IS?'

The king squinted into the gloom and, for no apparent reason, shielded his eyes. He could see nothing, 'I really can't see any—'

'—WRONG! TIME'S UP! MNARRRRRR!' shouted the chief, and winked at the tosser. The next massive rock flew, straighter and lower this time, just over the king's head and into Dome Eyes' cottage. There was a resounding final whump.

'BECAUSE I LIKE YOU, I'LL GIVE YOU ONE MORE GUESS BEFORE I EAT YOU!' he shouted and signaled to the giant rock thrower again.

The king frowned, stared, and said, 'Well, that's very decent o—'

'—WRONG!' roared the laughing chief. Another lighter rock sped over and, just missing the Moot House, hit the cottage of Old Mother Crunty. It began to glow. The other goblins began dashing about, but soon met groups of thugs, who herded them into groups and began handing out weapons, which the other goblins weren't at all happy about. The king signaled to Durth, pointed at the catapult, and made a baaing noise, before quickly turning. 'Wait!' he shouted. 'You win, chief of the giants. You are the greatest! We surrender to the greatness that is the until-recently one-one-and-one-headed giant chief.' Everyone save Durth turned to the king and their faces fell in terror.

The chief laughed and did a little jig on the spot before saying, lightly, 'WELL, THAT'S BETTER NOW. WE MAY ACCEPT YOUR SURRENDER, BUT FIRST WE HAVE A FEW

DEMANDS. FIRST, YOU WILL CRAWL OVER HERE AND I WILL EAT YOU, VERY SLOWLY.' He turned and winked to his giants, adding, 'I'M FEELING LIGHTLY PECKISH, BUT IT WILL TAKE ME SOME TIME TO NIBBLE ALL OF YOU UP.'

Roars of giant laughter and back-slapping greeted his unexpected turn of humor.

'We accept!' shouted the king. Nearby, he could hear baaing as baskets of sheep were loaded onto the catapult by an eager Durth, overseen by Master Whippet.

Ate Eyes leant over and whispered to the chief, who grinned before saying, 'AND ANOTHER TAX. EVERY VILLAGER SHALL GIVE HIS RIGHT ARM TO COME AND WORK FOR ME IN THE TOWER. QUITE LITERALLY. YAR-HAR!' The giants all howled with amusement.

'We accept!' shouted the king, anxiously looking at Durth. He could see little, but he could hear the baaing growing.

'AND!' shouted the chief, 'EACH GOBLIN WILL GIVE ME, FREE OF CHARGE, THEIR HEADS, ARMS, AND LEGS!'

'We accept!' shouted the king. He smiled as he heard the rope being strung taught.

Ate Eyes whispered to the chief and he peered, suspiciously at the village. There was a pause, then someone in the village shouted 'Miffed!' and a hail of sheep fell from the sky on the giants. The giants, startled by the projectiles, backed away, but as the sheep fell they realized they were wrapped in vests with spikes sticking out of them. A few giants fell dead and others, momentarily, backed away.

A further cry of 'Miffed!' was followed by a hail of smells and stones, some very large, which fell amongst the giants. More giants fell under the barrage and did not get up. The king's voice sounded in the distance as he shouted to the giants. 'Oh, did I say I surrender? I'm sorry, I was lying!'

Nervous cheers came from the goblins. Durth and Whippet dashed over to the king. They stared at the giants, who seemed to be readying weapons for an immediate attack. The catapult kept them at bay momentarily as newly-appointed thugs filled it and fired. This time they used burning things.

Whippet cleared his throat. 'The way I see it, Your Doomeditude,' he said, hastily, 'the giants will soon rush us, en masse. We probably have only moments to form a plan.'

Everyone nodded or said, 'hmmmm,' in agreement under their breath. Or both.

'And which way will they come, do you think?' said the king, who suddenly noted Whippet's considerable eyebrows for the first time. They seemed to have a life of their own, rising and lowering on a whim. The king made a mental note that, if he didn't die as seemed beyond certainty, he would have Whippet's eyebrows for his own. The giants were shouting something and forming a group.

Whippet coughed and looked at Durth, who was wearing his finest battle-pants—pants with a pathetic stick figure supposed to be Moaris Miffed chalked on them. Whippet and Durth both pointed at the gate. 'Giants are pretty stupid, Your Potentry. They are likely to head straight for the gate. Probably.'

There was a cough, and a pair of thugs moved to the foot of the battlement holding a papier-mâché goblin making a very rude gesture. His Majesty smiled and clapped. 'Excellent. Put it on the top of the pit.' The thugs smiled and nodded, before staggering off with the mannequin.

Rocks began to fly and the giants began to slowly walk forwards.

'If we can bunch the giants up there, we may kill a few before—'

The king nodded solemnly and said, '—before we die.'

Everyone nodded. A silent air of acceptance fell on them.[94] 'I can't understand,' said Whippet, looking out towards the distant fiery hills. 'What has happened to the Wise Wench?'

'Alas, I have to be honest with you,' said the king. 'She's lost her touch. She said she'd be back in time for the battle which she

---

[94] Possibly the first time this many goblins had been in one place without any noise being generated.

366

said was Thodsday, and, as you know, that's not for one-more-than-one-days. In fact, all those predictions, they were all mine. It was me that asked for the hamster to be built, and got all those dates right.'

'So why did she—sorry you—ask me to build a dragon kettle?' asked Whippet, suspiciously.

'Yes, it was actually me that told her to ask you,' said the king, solemnly. 'Yes, I'm sorry. I've been covering for her for some time.'

'Then why did you—' asked Whippet, but stopped when Durth grabbed his mouth under the king's silent instruction.

'Enough now, Master Wipple,' said the king, waving a hand dismissively. 'Now is not the time for recriminations, or for who and why and wherefore, or whose badger is the biggest. Now is the time for heroism.' He pointed for Durth to release Whippet and wagged a regal finger, regally, towards the frail-looking gate that was surrounded by pointed sticks and still adorned with cut-out figures and monstrosities in silhouette form. 'So, what can we do to hold them there?' asked the king, eyeing the approaching, laughing, giants and dodging a huge boulder.

'The way I see it,' said Whippet, 'we should pretend that we are weak there. Lull them. Then, when they're through, they'll get a surprise. There was a sound of creaking branches, a crash, and a pair of goblin screams. Everyone looked at the pit and tutted. Whippet produced a pipe, and proceeded to give an animated description of his plan. 'This pipe,' he said, 'is the catapult,' and placed it on the table. 'And this darning needle is Durth.'

Durth pricked his finger on the needle, started to bleed, and smiled while nodding. A rock flew over and wafted his hair upwards. He slapped it back down with finality.

'This huge walnut is you, Your Nuttynness, while this mushroom is the adviser. These acorns are thugs, and these slices of dried apple are the giants.'

The king began to look incredulous. 'We'd be all right if the giants turned out to be massive squirrels! Get to the point!' Everyone tittered except Durth, who looked around nervously.

'Now, the acorns are arranged, in a line, behind and to either side of the gate, while the dried apples move up, en masse, to the gates thus. Now, observe this slice of angel cake, which is the hamster.

'But they know the hamster isn't real!' interrupted the king.

'Ah, but wait, Your Wobblyness. The hamster, specially changed, and instead of having me and Durth on board, it has barrels of pitch and oil. Now, what's so special about the gate?'

Everyone looked at each other. There was an embarrassed pause.

Everyone looked at the gate, below them, at the edge of the village.

The pause continued, embarrassingly, while the giants readied weapons as they continued their steady approach.

'It's at the bottom of a slope?' said Durth, hopefully.

'Exactly!' said Whippet. Everyone patted Durth on the back and smiled.

Whippet cleared his throat noisily and continued. 'So, the angel cake is up here, laden with pitch and oil. The dried apples come in through here, smashing down the gate. The acorns move back and above them, so they can fire arrows at them, while the angel cake is set alight and, pushed, rushes straight at the apples, burning them and blocking that entrance, thus buying us time. In the meantime, the pipe is used liberally upon the giants.'

The king looked confused. 'What are the apples? Us or them?'

'Them!' everyone said.

'Buying us time for what?' asked Durth, incisively.

Looti shushed him. He misinterpreted her and turned bright red.

'So, what we need is a short delay to stop them rushing in, and so we can load up the hamster with flammables, and then for someone heroic and regal to draw them to him at the gate, Your Obvious-Volunteerness,' said Whippet.

The king nodded, his mind on udders.

'Ahem,' ahemed Whippet.

'What? Yes, yes I know, you need a foolhardy, futile, and ridiculous act to give your plan any chance to succeed. Well, let me tell you something, common-person,' smiled the king, regally, 'that there is no one more foolhardy and ridiculous than me. All I ask is that when you are ready, sound me a horn and I will know. When something stupid and suicidal needs doing, turn to your king! So fetch me my quickest, sprinting pig and a giant chicken costume, and fetch them right now!'

Looti thought he'd never looked more regal.

The giants were now barely a field's length from the bottom of the slope the village sat on. They seemed to be enjoying walking slowly to the village.

'Great giant chief!' shouted the king above them through his megaphone. 'We can see that we are truly beaten. In truth, we dare not fight you. We are but little goblins that you could squash in the blink of an eye. Wait there. I'm coming out as you commanded, but, if it pleases you, I shall bring the most priceless gift from my royal treasury and wear my surrendering costume. I think it will amuse you, mightiest of giants. I'll just fetch it. One moment, great chief of the giants.'

The giants paused. 'THE MOMENT HE CRAWLS TO ME, I'LL EAT HIM, THEN WE RUSH UP INTO THE VILLAGE,' said the giant chief, cleverly. All the other giants nodded, except Ate Eyes, who scowled through narrowing eyes up towards the goblin village.

Looti ran after the king as he dashed into the Moot House gripping the key. He paused as he moved a couple of boxes and shelves. There was a crash and a squeal as Tongue hit the ground. Behind one box was a circular door with a keyhole in the center. 'Stay here,' he said to Looti as he turned the key in the lock and entered a dark space beyond. She could hear some sort of strange snuffling. A minute or so later, he emerged gripping a large, clinking sack, and, above him, floated a large, black balloon. He shut the door and locked it behind himself, putting the boxes back to hide it. The king glanced at his sack, sighed, and kissed Looti, pressing something into her hands.

The key.

'Take care of the treasury, and may Todger smile on all your doings. You were well chosen, adviser, and never was one more well named. May you serve my son as well as you have served me.' He kissed her again, before adding, after a thought: 'The treasury is cunningly hidden. If a chance emerges, whisk the rest of the Royal Treasury—including the arcane whisks—into a hiding place. There is some powerful magic amongst it. Perhaps, one day, my son will be able to teach the giants a lesson with it.' He strode out. The sound of impatient oinking echoed nearby.

The king leapt onto the battlements once more as he was handed the chicken costume. 'Just coming,' he shouted, and hefted up the sack, adding, 'with magic presents!'

'OOH, PRESENTS,' whispered the more trusting and less fierce of the giants gathered below.

Behind, in the village, the hamster had been pushed up and was being loaded with every flammable thing left in the village. The thugs stood ready behind the gates below. Further back, up in the village, the females were all holdings sticks, pitchforks, hedgehogs, stones—anything that could be thrown and would hurt. Further back still were the rest of the males, anxiously seeking an escape route beyond the under-thugs, who now moved them forwards.

Below, the giants prepared. They were now barely a legendary piglet throw away from the base of the village. Weapons were gripped and shields held ready. Spit went into hands and onto hafts. Clubs whooshed in arcs, spears jabbed at the air. Meat-mincer wheels turned in a frenzy.

The costume associates and dressers got the king into the costume in moments and helped him mount Dash, his favorite sprint pig.[95] He hefted up the sack and turned to his admiring, quaking crowd. 'Have no fear!' he shouted. 'We of royal goblin blood cannot die. I am indestructible!' He turned and trotted down to the gate, which was opened by bowing guards. As he passed them, the king paused. 'Remember, lads,' he whispered, 'keep it open until the last moment. You'll have the most crucial job of all!'

---

[95] That is, a pig bred for sprinting. Obviously.

370

'Don't worry, Your Swinemountedness, you can rely on us,' lied the larger one of them.

Whippet surveyed the slope to the gate and sucked his teeth. He then got them out and gave them a polish before popping them back in and saying, 'I'm not sure it'll run straight without rails,' he said, glaring at the steep drop between hidden hamster and gate.

'Don't worry. Noc will protect us,' said Durth with admirable over-confidence.

The king slowly moved towards the vast line of giants that were scowling and grinding their teeth and spinning their meat-mincers with fury. When they saw him, they began to laugh and point and make clucking noises. The king played up to the crowd, riding in circuits and pecking at his mount's head, always keeping a watchful eye back towards the village. He galloped and then cantered and then trotted in wide circles, sometimes crowing, sometimes clucking, sometimes tugging the balloon which was tied to his head, making pretend thunder noises. His display went on for some time.

The giants laughed and clapped as he got closer and closer to them. Finally, he dismounted, and crawled the final few feet to the giant chief, proffering the sack at his huge, smelly feet. The smell from the chief's dead head was really strong and the king had to struggle to stop gagging.

'WHAT'S IN THE BAG?' grumbled the giant chief, suspiciously.

'I'm glad you asked that, oh great and wise one-more-than-one-headed ruler, for it is the sort of clever question only a ruler would ask. This bag contains treasure—magic treasure—which I give to you. It is very powerful magic indeed, and, if you will allow me to, I'll explain how it all works and what it is.'

'NOPE, I THINK I'LL EAT YOU NOW,' said the chief, picking the king up in one calloused hand and opening his jaw wide. His breath smelt of pickled cabbage and walnuts.

'ONE MOMENT, MIGHTY ONE!' interjected Ate Eyes. 'PERHAPS THIS REPULSIVE, POINTLESS CREATURE MAY TELL US SOMETHING USEFUL. DON'T FORGET, THAT THOUGH THESE VILE LITTLE GRUBS ARE OUR SLAVES

NOW, WE STILL HAVE OTHER BATTLES TO COME. DO WE NOT STILL NEED TO OVERCOME THE MAGENTA HABETROT OF SPONGE, THE TERRIBLE YELLOW HAG OF MUGGY MIRE, AND DO WE NOT YET HAVE TO FACE DOWN THE APPALLING SPRIGHTLY SLANGE?'

The chief paused in mid-bite and nodded, saying, 'TELL ME, TIFFIN, ARE ANY OF THESE MAGICS WEAPONS?'

The king bobbed vigorously. 'Oh yes, very mighty weapons, indeed. If I may be allowed to tell you before you devour me...?'

The chief put him down and the goblin king reached into his sack. 'This desiccated kipper, for example,' he said earnestly, 'is none other than Xerces the Slayer, Bane of The Terrible Goose of Moggly Farm!'

The giants looked impressed.

'If I might tell you the tale of how we came by it and what great, magic qualities of terror it has?'

The giants nodded and sat down to listen.

In the village, goblins were furiously packing the iron hamster with wood, cloth, wool, and anything else that might burn. A few goblins that had been pushed in it by relatives managed to escape. Durth keenly oversaw the work, occasionally barking an order at a goblin, something that made at least one of them pass out in sheer terror. He found Whippet. 'Do you think we should stuff the Dragon Kettle, too?' he said. 'It's not far away.'

Whippet stared out at the forest and mountains beyond. 'No, let's keep it in reserve, just in case.' He wandered off in the direction of where it was being stored, tweaking the ears of half a dozen goblins as he did. 'Come this way, lads, I have a little job for you,' he said.

Nearby in the Moot House, Looti had moved the boxes and pushed the key into the lock.

'You shouldn't do that,' whimpered Tongue.

'Slice, slice, slice!' went the great kipper, cutting and slicing and slaying as she turned. Her edge was death and her eye was doom.

372

Sirs, great chief: she is yours. But she is but a minor item compared to these other great things within my sack. Would you care to hear more, or shall I rub a little salt upon my royal head and prepare to be devoured?'

'YOU MAY CONTINUE,' muttered the giant chief, holding the kipper between his thumb and forefinger dubiously.

The king pulled out a huge ear-trumpet with a trio of preserved toads at its edge and shouted, 'Behold! The Listener at the End of Days! With this object, great chief, you can hear the gods themselves speak!' The king handed the object to the giant chief with great reverence. As he did, he heard the sounding of a horn and suppressed a smile. He glanced over his shoulder to check Dash was close by and indicated for the giant chief to put the trumpet end into his ear, while he reached into his belt and pulled a knitting needle out. 'Can you hear them, great chief? They are honoring you. Listen. Listen closer.' The king tugged the wider end of the trumpet down to his mouth, the other end still stuck in the chief's ear. 'Can you hear them, great chief? They have a message for you. Listen closely, the gods are speaking to you. They are saying something.

The giant chief put the trumpet to his ear.

The king sucked in a massive breath, and shouted 'STORMGRUNTIES!' into the ear trumpet. The giant chief fell over, holding his ear. When he looked up, his faces were livid.

As he growled, the king poked his knitting needle into the balloon, which burst, surrounding the area with soot. When it had cleared, the king was gone, riding off on his steed for all he was worth; so fast, in fact, that his shorts slipped down slightly exposing his royal posterior. He gave it a royal smack in the direction of the giants and dashed for the open gates.

The giants gave chase immediately.

'LOOSE THE DOGS! EAT THEM! EAT THEM ALL! CHARGE!' shouted the giant chief. The dogs began to yelp and chase, and the giants picked up rocks and charged towards the village, chasing the king who had reached the gates...

...which slammed shut in his face, the terrified gate guards beyond looking both relieved and almost guilty.

'Bugger,' said the king.

Ate Eyes suddenly grabbed his chief and pulled him over. The chief picked up his spiked club and readied it to swing, 'WAIT, CHIEF, PLEASE,' whimpered Ate Eyes, and whispered something in his ear. The chief nodded and the pair slunk off in another direction.

In the village, a torch was lit. The goblins braced themselves. Steps back were taken. Durth pushed his thugs forward, mumbling. 'Steady, lads,' he said under his breath.

The giants rushed forward, waving weapons and screaming insults, closing on the king. The king turned his steed, raced back, and then cantered straight at the gate. He gave a cry as his steed leapt, cleared its pointy top, landed on the fleeing guards on the far side, and galloped up to the battlements. He pulled level with his warriors and the hamster at the village. 'To battle,' he cried as he drew out his other knitting needle. The thugs gasped, recognizing them as Yulty, the Slayers, War Knitting Needles of Woe.

The goblins' spirits raised, and they cheered.

At a signal, bearers came out of a timber building nearby. They were clad in jerkins and held aloft the king's siege grater.

The troops cheered again.

Below, the giants had reached the gate and had begun smashing it while their dogs barked hungrily. Beyond it, the little path picked its way narrowly upwards to where the goblins were amassed. Along with the hamster.

Durth leapt onto the hamster and stood before them, proudly. He grinned and shouted above the roar from outside and in. 'Now, lads, this is it. We have a few ugly giants to sort out before lunch, and I want you to be kind to our guests—give them something. I've got something I'm especially looking forward to giving them!' He paused, and, from behind his back, produced his huge corkscrew before waving it in the air. He tore his shirt open and stood with his legs very, very far apart. 'For the king!' he shouted, at the top of his voice. His hair flopped onto one side and swung over one ear. He was so cross, he didn't care.

The goblins nearby waited for Whippet's signal to push.

374

Crash! The feeble gates, remarkably, held again.

I must promote the carpenter, thought the king.

Crash! The gate gave way.

'Now!' yelled Whippet.

'Ahem!' said the king. 'I give the orders around here, lowly common person.' The king paused and smiled, taking in the charging mass of giants as they staggered through the gates and raced their dogs up towards the goblins.

'Sorry, great king,' said Whippet and he stood back.

The king stared downwards again, looked at his goblins. 'Now,' he said calmly, while frowning at Whippet.

A very round goblin lit the flames, happily. The hamster burst into a ball of fire as it was pushed forward. It teetered on the edge of the hill and then began to gather speed. There was a pause below as the giants saw the goblins looking down and pulling rude faces. Then they saw the burning hamster. It hurtled towards them, a vast ball of iron and fire.

They began to make a tactical withdrawal but simply succeeded in falling over each other and their dogs. Some tried to scramble away but it was too late.

The false hamster crashed into them, crushing heads, burning bits and searing hides. The stench of burning and the screams of falling giant filled the air.

'Now!' yelled Durth.

A hail of stones and sticks, spears, hedgehogs and pitchforks flew into the conflagration. The rain didn't stop for over a minute.

Looti slunk into the treasury.

In the cramped chamber beyond, she saw a lantern and flint, and eagerly lit it. Slowly, the flame guttered and coughed out black smoke. The room began to brighten. Things began glinting; precious things in abundance, precious things everywhere—in recesses, on shelves, in open boxes, in bags.

She fell down with joy, her face split by a greedy smile.

Then she heard a snuffling behind her.

Turning round she saw piles of chests at the distant edge of the room. But something else was taking her attention. A foul, hairy abhorrence, with claws, and tusks, and teeth. Lots of teeth. It bared them and began to snuffle incomprehensibly. From the side of the chests, more appeared.

Flames and smoke, the twitching of legs and screaming. The goblins peered into the murk. A few giants stood, but lots stayed on the ground.

Then the outer wall of a house burst apart in the village itself and, there, Ate Eyes stood, his eyes ablaze, almost lighting up the village. Behind him was his chief. He shouted 'I TOLD YOU THEY'D TRY TO MAKE US GO THERE. I TOLD YOU MY PLAN WOULD WORK!' Ate Eyes faces grimaced in fury and joy.

The chief whispered his answer, 'YOU ARE SMART, AND NO MISTAKE. TOO SMART!' as he plunged his spiked club into his back.

Ate Eyes dropped, dead.

The chief moved on, looking for his foe.

The villagers could see the remaining giants rushing up the path through the smoldering iron hamster with their dogs. There were still too many. Durth and the king ran to face them, but their troops were backing off, afraid. The villagers began to scatter and panic. The giants reached the top of the path and joined their chief.

Only Durth and the king stood before the giants now; the sweaty horrible creatures just a few feet away. The other goblins had cowered back, afraid. The giant chief laughed and stepped forward to tower above King Stormgrunties and Durth. 'SO WE MEET AGAIN!' he shouted. 'ME WITH MY GREAT CLUB VANSKOR, WHICH HAS FLATTENED AND PIERCED AND STABBED A THOUSAND UGLY LITTLE FACES, AND YOU WITH YOUR KNITTING NEEDLES. YAR-HAR!'

The king stepped forward and, momentarily, the giant chief seemed to back away before raising his club, ready for the kill. Stormgrunties cleared his throat. 'I'm afraid—' he said.

The giants began to laugh.

The remaining villagers and thugs all sagged, beaten.

'—yes, I'm afraid. I'm afraid that, if I'm hacked limb from limb, squashed into a pulp, danced on, stomped and turned inside out, I'm afraid I'd still be prettier than you!' The king leapt with his needles, and plunged them straight into the chief's right knee.

The chief roared in pain and surprise as he collapsed, only to be swiftly dragged back by his followers as more giants stepped forward in his place.

The goblins shouted oaths and leapt at the giants, seized with unexpected loyalty to their king.

They fought heroically, but were soon beaten back by the huge giants, many goblins fell in the first attack, but at least some giants were struck and did not rise, as well as one-more-than-one of their great dogs. It was soon obvious, however, that they were losing, and the king called in a clear voice. 'To me, goblins!' before dashing back to the Moot House.

Durth and the king rallied the few remaining brave goblins outside the Great Mouth of the royal seat of royalness, but at least half the village goblins already lay dead. Durth had a huge gash on his head, and the king had a deep cut in his shoulder. He smiled at his gob-boys and gob-wenches and patted Durth fondly on the shoulder. 'A last stand, gob-boys and gob-girls! Remember, you die for the honor of the village of Bliss! We'll feast in the boughs of the Great Oak tonight!'

Seeing no chance of escape, the goblins agreed and got ready for the final combat. The giants slowly encircled the Moot House. They advanced, savoring the moment. The chief bellowed in anger and hate as he limped over the iron rail that ran through the village and beyond, his right leg smeared with blood.

A noise behind him bellowed in answer.

Everyone turned.

'MNARRRRRRRR!' A gout of flame, bigger than a great pine, shot from the moving Dragon Kettle as it hit a group of giants at the back.

They screamed and fell dead.

Urgh leant out of the Great Dragon Kettle with a megaphone and shook his fist. 'Stormgrunties!' he yelled. Another gout of flame shot across, just missing Durth, who grabbed a pair of shears. 'Careful Wise Wench,' Urgh shouted down to the control platform, where the Wise Wench was busy pulling levers and twiddling knobs. She looked happy. Below them, the pushers were pushing the Great Dragon Kettle as fast as they could along its iron rails.

The giants began to panic.

Another gout of exploding flame shot out from the Dragon Kettle, the biggest yet. Several goblins put down their weapons and clapped. A line of hounds fell dead, their burning leashes held by dead giants.

The goblins looked at each other.

The king smiled. 'Charge!' he shouted.

The goblins charged.

The giants began to rout, heading for the broken gate as the goblins chopped at the backs of their legs or tripped them and plunged blades into them. The king wielded the knitting needles as well as anyone had wielded knitting needles as weapons in the history of goblins, and their points dripped with giant blood. Durth had only one quarry, however: the chief had been the first to flee, but now he was closing on him. The giant approached the gate, wheezing, his living heads sweating profusely as he headed for freedom. 'Oy, ugly!' yelled Durth.

Instinctively, the chief turned. He stared at the little figure of Durth and angrily shook his great club. He then swung it in a huge arc, getting ready to throw it at the goblin. Suddenly, a young bird flew across his path and startled him. The club fell between goblin and giant. Durth had been improbably saved by the bird's passing.

The Wise Wench pulled the next to last figurine from her knitted ensemble—a young bird hatching from an egg and startling a giant—and smiled.

Durth hurled his spears with all his might; they flew straighter and truer than any he had hurled before. He somewhat hypocritically blessed the countless starlings he had practiced on over the years. Durth's hair fell from his bald pate and he smiled.

378

A spear hit each head.

The giant chief didn't even have time to say anything before dropping to the floor, dead. Durth strode over and grinned. 'That's for Moaris!' he roared, before turning to the heavens and yelling, 'Miffed!' at the top of his voice. He pulled his shirt open and stretched his legs so far apart that he fell over and ruptured something. Above him, the sky growled.

The giants were scattering now. Those that lived clambered over the burning bodies of the others as the great Dragon Kettle breathed again and again. The dogs, terrified by the noise and fire, were dashing about the village yelping in terror. The thugs fell on them one by one, beating them with sticks, or hurling ladles laden with hot battle-sprouts at them. Soon, all the dogs were dead.

What few giants escaped would tell of a terrible dragon that breathed fire and befriended goblins; it would be a long time before they returned.

The battle was over; the goblins had won.

'Well done, you ugly scum!' shouted the king, warmly, to no one in particular. Durth was still hobbling about the village yelling 'Miffed!' and 'Stormgrunties!' at the top of his voice, but, by now, there were no giants alive to shout it at, so he began shouting it at the older goblin ladies instead.

The Wise Wench pulled a huge lever on the kettle and it wheezed fitfully, closing its vast iron maw before becoming still. Below, the gob-boys and gob-girls that had pushed it wheezed too and collapsed; it was damnably heavy. The Wise Wench, like her creation, was blackened, and her bonnet was singed, but she was in good spirits as she clambered out of the kettle. Urgh, taking her hand, followed her. She glanced at the king. 'Well?' she said.

The king stared at the floor.

'Well?' she said, again.

'How dare you fill my head with false hopes and misrepresentations, keeping the future a dark secret,' he said.

'Isn't that what it is?' she said, with a glint in her eye. 'Anything else to add, great king?' she added, patting Urgh and the kettle.

'Nope!' he said, sulkily.

She eyed him curiously and smiled.

'Well, alright. You were right. Well done, even if you lied about timings,' whispered the king, under his breath.

'Female prerogative,' she said, and winked. 'And?' she added, looking at Urgh and pushing him forwards.

'And this ugly thing here was right, as well,' admitted the king. 'We, erm, well, we—that is, to say, everyone except me—owes our village to you...a bit...but also *a lot* to my heroism.' The king frowned as the Wise Wench looked on expectantly. 'That's it. I'm not saying anything else; I'm king,' added the king. 'Is someone going to pick me up or what?' he shouted. 'Honestly, I've had to sully my boots just to save you lot. Now, where are my bearers and where is my hedgehog? And you—build me a harpsicord!' he shouted at no one in particular.

Urgh smiled and embraced the Wise Wench. 'So, that's it then? The giants are finished?' he asked, grinning broadly.

'Not quite,' replied the Wise Wench. 'As one story ends, another begins. Speaking of which...' she said, checking the last figure on her battered daisy chain of figures.

Suddenly, the Moot House door flew open and Looti ran out screaming, with several hideous hairy creatures in close pursuit.

'There, *now* it's finished,' said the Wise Wench, and she threw the knitting onto a burning dog.

AFTERWARDS

It took a long time to clear the mess up. Indeed, a special post of Master of the Battle-Crap was set up, with Bertram Bobblestrange being the first and, hopefully, last occupier of the post.

The summer blossomed and so, in time, the special midsummer feast arrived, the so-called Festival of Saint the Badger, when the villagers gave thanks for the summer, and for the fact that badgers couldn't work out how to make goblin-traps or use bows.

The whole village gathered around a little stage where the king, the Wise Wench, and Urgh, were watched by Durth Dimbits, Toughest Thug Ever, along with newly-appointed Thinker (First Class), the Master Very Clever, Whippet. Fires illuminated the scene. The king was resplendent in his blue and white octagonal festival shorts, and his magnificent, striped violet and orange shirt, depicting, as it did, the Dreaded Day of Badger Retribution, when badgers finally work out what they've been missing.

He stood.

Cheers.

'Friends!' he shouted.

More cheers, together with a totally uncalled for exposure of scabs and boils by the older gob-wenches.

'You may recall, we had a minor spot of bother earlier this year!'

Laughter.

'A few giants came along and told us what we could do in our own Kingdom.'

Boos.

'But I didn't listen, did we?'

Roars of 'NO!'

'And I sent them packing, didn't we?'

Cheers and lots of goblins pretending to run away, childishly.

'And, besides me, you all have one-and-one folk you are especially grateful to. I refer to none other than our dear Wise

Wench and the, frankly, very ugly village hero, Upside Down Face, who, between them, made sure that my elaborate plan succeeded!'

The Wise Wench groaned, but then winked to someone in the crowd, giving a little signal. Lady Carline flapped onto her shoulder. Urgh and the Wise Wench whispered to each other and then stared at the king, knowingly, as he continued to address the crowd.

'They may have thought that that was the end of their adventures, but no! I have another task for them! They shall have other duties to perform for me, and I shall not release them from their toils. Tomorrow, I wish them to go—'

A figure pushed through the crowd, moved before the king, and bowed. It was dressed in bright orange.

The king grimaced.

'Youw Majestwy!' it said. 'We, the mummers of the village, have pwepared an epic song about owr hewoes'. He bowed, and a huge group of mummers moved to the edge of the stage, each carrying a flaming pig symbol. Some were stood on each other's shoulders and dressed as giants.

The king wished the giants were back. Just for a little while.

The Wise Wench began to chuckle. 'It was the Great Mole's idea,' she said, truthfully. From her pocket came a giggle.

They all coughed, hummed, and began to sing very loudly.

'Young Urgh and his friend, called Sorry, did set out with a message,
As bid by our Wise Wench after she had eaten porridge,
While Moaris Miffed showed which way to go,
Burn, burn, burn it, oh!'

The Wise Wench noticed that Urgh was staring at the stars, and leant closer to him. 'We'll find out who *he* was one day,' she said, and smiled. The sky lit up, as a shooting star leapt across the heavens. 'Looks like Moaris is throwing his weight about. What a surprise,' she said, and winked.

Urgh looked like he was about to ask a question, then stopped.

The singing grew in vigor, and the sounds of the king grinding his teeth echoed past them. Durth stood smiling at the crowd, quietly picking out his next set of bullies, while Whippet was drawing a plan for a huge, iron, battle haddock on the back of his hand.

Urgh grinned at her. 'So what happens next?' he asked.

'Who knows,' the Wise Wench answered, as she drew out a long, new set of knitted figures from her pocket and winked. 'I hope we won't any more giants, or the former adviser. Thanks to her exposure to the very thing she had planned to steal for ages, she tried to do so hastily—with painful consequences—and failed.' At the top of her new figures were lots of very fat goblins with crowns mounted on palanquins designed like ducks, pigs, hedgehogs, and other improbable animals. Behind each whispered an elderly gob-wench dressed in black. Above them was a thunderclap and a huge scary gob-wench that looked like the Wise Wench. 'However, there are other things coming, young Urgh,' she added and grinned at him. 'At least, I think so. But, then again, who can tell what tomorrow will bring for you?' She grinned and put her list away in the folds of her shawl. Urgh also saw a beatific pig, a one-more-than-one-headed cockerel, and a vast tree on the daisy chain of figures.

'I was just thinking about Zephyr. If only she was here,' he said.

'Ah, well, young hero. Our Zephyr is the cause of the next spot of bother. Her looks are getting her into all sorts of trouble.'

'She's still alive? That's great news! Hadn't we better get moving to rescue her? How does our next story begin?'

In the distance, the king was shouting the phrase, 'it's far too *callithumpian*,' over and over again, with regal self-importance.

The Wise Wench smiled. 'We'll have to see, young Urgh,' she said. 'We'll just have to see. That, as they say, is another tale.'

Urgh smiled, shook his head and reached for his ale.

ACKNOWLEDGEMENTS

I've found with this book, as in life, that when you need help, many, many people are glad to give it. I can't begin to count the number of times people have offered help here; former strangers who gave up time to read sections, people who helped in deciding what language to use and gave advice, friends who have stepped up and offered support, sometimes giving up lots of time just to help, people who've read and liked my blog, and those who offered jokes about poultry. You know who you are, and I'm so grateful to all of you. Thank you. I hope you enjoyed reading Goblins!

I'm particularly indebted to Al for his hard work on editing the book and for his honesty, particularly on matters of taste and British humor, a big huzzah and thank you Al for all your hard work, you are, sir, a top man. Thank you Jeremy Zerfoss for coming up with such a fabulous cover and for being, as always, ridiculously positive and creative and wonderfully mad.

A particular thank you to Adam Daigle and James Sutter (the latter formerly) at Paizo Publications for the feedback. You are both splendid men and I'm grateful for your time and the pleasure of dealing with you over this, and many other joyful tasks.

Huzzah!